MARGARET WEIS and TRACY
HICKMAN both live in Wisconsin.
They have co-authored seven previous
books, including the bestselling
Dragonlance Legends. They are currently
polishing up *Triumph of the Darksword*,
Volume III of the *Darksword Trilogy*, and
beginning work on their new fantasy
series, *Rose of the Prophet*, which
Bantam will also publish.

THE DARKSWORD TRILOGY

VOLUME TWO

Doom Of The Darksword

MARGARET WEIS & TRACY HICKMAN

BANTAM BOOKS
TORONTO · NEW YORK · LONDON · SYDNEY · AUCKLAND

DOOM OF THE DARKSWORD
A BANTAM BOOK 0 553 17535 1

First publication in Great Britain

PRINTING HISTORY
Bantam edition published 1989

Chapter art by Valerie A. Valusek
Front matter map by Stephen D. Sullivan
Cover art copyright © 1988 by Larry Elmore
Copyright © 1988 by Margaret Weis and Tracy Hickman

Bantam Books are published by Transworld Publishers
Ltd., 61–63 Uxbridge Road, Ealing, London W5 5SA, in
Australia by Transworld Publishers (Australia) Pty. Ltd.,
15–23 Helles Avenue, Moorebank, NSW 2170, and in New
Zealand by Transworld Publishers (N.Z.) Ltd., Cnr. Moselle
and Waipareira Avenues, Henderson, Auckland.

Printed and bound in Great Britain by
Cox & Wyman Ltd., Reading, Berks.

Doom
Of The
Darksword

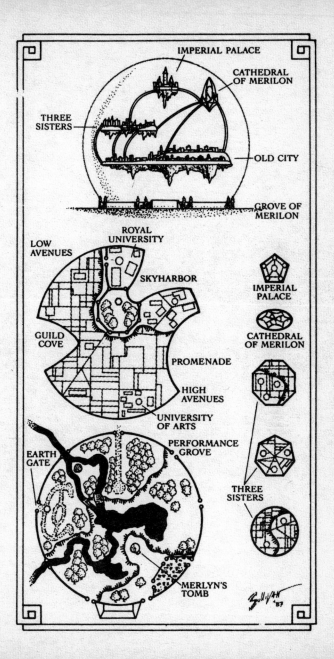

Reprise

There was no dinner party at Bishop Vanya's this night.

"His Holiness is indisposed," was the message the Ariels carried to those who had been invited. This included the Emperor's brother-in-law, Prince Xavier, whose number of invitations to dine at the Font were increasing proportionately with the declining health of his sister. Everyone had been most gracious and extremely concerned about the Bishop's welfare. The Emperor had even offered his own personal *Theldara* to the Bishop, but this was respectfully declined.

Vanya dined alone, and so preoccupied was the Bishop that he might have been eating sausages along with his Field Catalysts instead of the delicacies of peacock's tongue and lizard's tail which he barely tasted and never noticed were underdone.

Having finished and sent away the tray, he sipped a brandy and composed himself to wait until the tiny moon in the timeglass upon his desk had risen to its zenith. The waiting was difficult, but Vanya's mind was so occupied that he found the time sliding past more rapidly than he had expected. The pudgy fingers crawled increasingly along the arms of the chair, touching this strand of mental web and that, seeing if any needed strengthening or repair, throwing out new filaments where necessary.

The Empress — a fly that would soon be dead.

Her brother — heir to throne. A different type of fly, he demanded special consideration.

The Emperor — his sanity at the best of times precarious, the death of his beloved wife and the loss of his position might well topple a mind weak to begin with.

Sharakan — the other empires in Thimhallan were watching this rebellious state with too much interest. It must be crushed, the people taught a lesson. And with them, the Sorcerers of the Ninth Art wiped out completely. That was shaping up nicely . . . or had been.

Vanya fidgeted uncomfortably and glanced at the timeglass. The tiny moon was just now appearing over the horizon. With a growl, the Bishop poured himself another brandy.

The boy. — Damn the boy. And damn that blasted catalyst, too. Darkstone. Vanya closed his eyes, shuddering. He was in peril, deadly peril. If anyone ever discovered the incredible blunder he had made . . .

Vanya saw the greedy eyes watching him, waiting for his downfall. The eyes of the Lord Cardinal of Merilon, who had — so rumor told — already drawn up plans for redecorating the Bishop's chambers in the Font. The eyes of his own Cardinal, a slow-thinking man, to be sure, but one who had risen through the ranks by plodding along slowly and surely, trampling over anything or anyone who got in his way. And there were others. Watching, waiting, hungry . . .

If they got so much as a sniff of his failure, they'd be on him like griffins, rending his flesh with their talons.

But no! Vanya clenched the pudgy hand, then forced himself to relax. All was well. He had planned for every contingency, even the unlikely ones.

With this thought in mind and noticing that the moon was finally nearing the top of the timeglass, the Bishop heaved his bulk out of the chair and made his way, walking at a slow, measured pace, to the Chamber of Discretion.

The darkness was empty and silent. No sign of mental disturbance. Perhaps that was a good sign, Vanya told himself as he sat down in the center of the round room. But a tremor of fear shivered through the web as he sent forth his summons to his minion.

He waited, spider fingers twitching.

The darkness was still, cold, unspeaking.

Vanya called again, the fingers curling in upon themselves.

I may or may not respond, the voice had told him. Yes, that would be like him, the arrogant —

Vanya swore, his hands gripping the chair, sweat pouring down his head. He *had* to know! It was too important! He would —

Yes. . . .

The hands relaxed. Vanya considered, turning the idea over in his mind. He had planned for every contingency, even the unlikely ones. And this one he had planned for without even knowing it. Such are the ways of genius.

Sitting back in the chair, Bishop Vanya's mind touched another strand on the web, sending an urgent summons to one who would, he knew, be little prepared to receive it.

BOOK ONE

The Summons

"**S**aryon. . . ."
The catalyst floated between unconsciousness and the waking nightmare of his life.

"Holiness, forgive me!" he muttered feverishly. "Take me back to our sanctuary! Free me of this terrible burden. I cannot bear it!" Tossing on his crude bed, Saryon put his hands over his closed eyes as though he could blot out the dreadful visions that sleep only intensified and made more frightening. "Murder!" he cried. "I have done murder! Not once! Oh, no, Holiness! Twice. Two men have died because of me!"

"Saryon!" The voice repeated the catalyst's name, and there was a hint of irritation in it.

The catalyst cringed, digging the palms of his hands into his eyes. "Let me confess to you, Holiness!" he cried. "Punish me as you will. I deserve it, desire it! Then I will be free of their faces, their eyes . . . haunting me!"

Saryon sat up on his bed, half-asleep. He had not slept in days; exhaustion and excitement had temporarily overthrown his mind. He had no conscious thought of where he was or why this voice—that he knew to be hundreds of miles away—should be speaking to him so clearly. "The first, a young man of our

Order," the catalyst continued brokenly. "The warlock used my Life-giving force to murder him. The wretched catalyst never had a chance. And now the warlock, too, is dead! He lay before me helpless, drained of his magic by *my arts*! Joram—" The catalyst's voice sank to a hushed whisper. "Joram. . . ."

"Saryon!" The voice was stern, urgent and commanding, and it finally roused the catalyst from his confused exhaustion.

"What?" Shivering in his wet robes, Saryon looked around. He was not in the sanctuary of the Font. He was in a chill prison cell. Death surrounded him. Brick walls—stone made by the hands of man, not shaped by magic. The wood-beam ceiling above bore the gouges of tools. Cold metal bars forged by the hand of the Dark Arts seemed a barrier against Life itself. "Joram?" Saryon called softly through teeth clenched against the cold.

But a glance told him the young man was not in the prison cell, his bed had not been slept in.

"Of course not," Saryon said to himself, shuddering. Joram was in the wilderness, disposing of the body. . . . But then, whose had been the voice he heard so clearly?

The catalyst's head sank into his shaking hands. "Take my life, Almin!" he prayed fervently. "If you truly do exist, take my life and end this torment, this misery. For now I am going mad—"

"Saryon! You cannot avoid me, if such is your intent! You *will* listen to me! You have no choice!"

The catalyst raised his head, his eyes wide and staring, his body convulsing with a chill that was colder than the breath of the bitterest winter wind. "Holiness?" he called through trembling lips. Rising stiffly to his feet, the catalyst looked around the small cell. "Holiness? Where are you? I can't see you, yet I hear— I don't understand . . ."

"I am present in your mind, Saryon," the voice said. "I speak to you from the Font. How I am able to accomplish this need be of little importance to you, Father. My powers are very great. Are you alone?"

"Y-yes, Holiness, for the moment. But I—"

"Organize your thoughts, Saryon!" The voice sounded impatient again. "They are such a jumble I cannot read them! You need not speak. *Think* the words you say and I will hear them. I will give you a moment to calm yourself with prayer, then I expect you to be ready to attend me."

The voice fell silent. Saryon was still conscious of its presence inside his head, buzzing like an insect in his mind. Hurriedly he sought to compose himself, but it was not with prayer. Though he had begged only moments before that the Almin take his life — and though he had sincerely meant that despairing plea — Saryon felt a primal urge for self-survival well up inside him. The very fact that Bishop Vanya was able to invade his mind like this appalled him and filled him with anger — though he knew that the anger was wrong. As a humble catalyst, he should be proud, he supposed, that the great Bishop would spare time to investigate his unworthy thoughts. But deep within, from that same dark place whence had come his night-dreams, a voice asked coldly, *How much does he know? Is there any way I can hide from him?*

"Holiness," said Saryon hesitantly, turning around in the center of the dark room, staring fearfully about him as though the Bishop might at any moment step out of the brick wall, "I . . . find it difficult to compose my . . . thoughts. My inquisitive mind —"

"The same inquisitive mind that has led you to walk dark paths?" the Bishop asked in displeasure.

"Yes, Holiness," Saryon replied humbly. "I admit this is my weakness, but it prevents me attending to your words without knowing how and by what means we are communicating. I —"

"Your thoughts are in turmoil! We can accomplish nothing useful this way. Very well." Bishop Vanya's voice, echoing in Saryon's mind, sounded angry, if resigned. "It is necessary, Father, that as spiritual leader of our people, I keep in contact with the far-flung reaches of this world. As you know, there are those out there who seek to reduce our Order to little more than what we were in the ancient days — familiars who served our masters in the form of animals. Because of this threat, it is necessary that many of my communications with others — both of our Order and those who are helping to preserve it — must be on a confidential basis."

"Yes, Holiness," Saryon murmured nervously. The dark night beyond the cell's barred window was thinning into gray dawn. He could hear a few footsteps in the streets — those who began their workday the same time as the sun began his. But otherwise the village slept. Where was Joram? Had he been caught, the body discovered? The catalyst clasped his hands together and attempted to concentrate on the Bishop's voice.

"Through magical means, Saryon, a chamber was devised for the Bishop of the Realm whereby he can minister in private to his followers in need of support. Known as the Chamber of Discretion, it is particularly useful for communicating with those performing certain delicate tasks that must be kept secret for the good of the people —"

A network of spies! Saryon thought before he could stop himself. The Church, the Order to which he had devoted his life, was in reality nothing more than a giant spider, sitting in the midst of a vast web, attuned to every movement of those caught within its sticky grasp! It was a dreadful thought, and Saryon tried instantly to banish it.

He began to sweat again, even as his body shivered. Cringing, he waited for the Bishop to read his mind and reprimand him. But Vanya continued on as though he had not heard, expounding upon the Chamber of Discretion and how it worked, allowing one mind to speak to another through magical means.

So tense that his jaw muscles ached from the strain of clenching his teeth, Saryon pondered. "The Bishop did not notice my random thoughts!" he said to himself. "Perhaps, as he said, I have to concentrate to make myself heard. If so — and if I can control my mind — I might be able to cope with this mental invasion."

As Saryon realized this, it occurred to him that he was hearing only those thoughts Vanya wanted him to hear. He wasn't able to penetrate beyond whatever barriers the Bishop himself had established. Slowly, Saryon began to relax. He waited until his superior had reached an end.

"I understand, Holiness," the catalyst thought, concentrating all his effort on his words.

"Excellent, Father." Vanya appeared pleased. There was a pause; the Bishop was carefully considering and concentrating on *his* next words. But when he spoke — or when his thoughts took form in Saryon's mind — they were rapid and concise, as though being repeated by rote. "I sent you on a dangerous task, Saryon — that of attempting to apprehend the young man called Joram. Because of the danger, I grew concerned about your welfare when I did not hear from you. Therefore, I deemed it best to contact a trusted associate of mine concerning you —"

"Simkin!" Saryon thought before he could stop himself. So intense was the image of the young man in his mind that it must have translated to the Bishop.

"What?" Thrown off in the middle of his speech, Vanya appeared confused.

"Nothing," Saryon muttered hastily. "I apologize, Holiness. My thoughts were disturbed by . . . by something occurring outside. . . ."

"I suggest you remove yourself from the window, Father," the Bishop said ascerbically.

"Yes, Holiness," Saryon replied, digging his nails into the flesh of his palms, using the stimulus of pain to help him concentrate.

There was a second's pause again — Vanya attempting to remember where he was? Why didn't he just write it down? Saryon wondered irritably, sensing the Bishop's thoughts turned from him. Then the voice was back. This time, it was filled with concern.

"I have been, as I said, worried about you, Father. And now this associate, who was assigned to keep an eye on you, has not been in contact with me for the last forty-eight hours. My fears grew. I hope nothing is wrong, Saryon?"

What could Saryon answer? That his world had turned upside down? That he was clinging to sanity with his fingertips? That a moment before, he had been praying for death? The catalyst hesitated. He could confess everything, tell the Bishop he knew the truth about Joram, beg His Worship's mercy, and arrange to deliver the boy as he had been ordered. All would be over in moments. Saryon's tormented soul would be at peace.

Outside the prison, the wind — a last remnant of last night's storm — struck the walls, beating against them in a futile effort to break in. Saryon heard words in the wind. He had heard them seventeen years ago — Bishop Vanya sentencing a child to death.

"Father!" Vanya's voice, taut and cold, was an echo of the memory. "You are wandering again!"

"I — I assure you I am fine, Holiness," Saryon stammered. "You have no need to be concerned about me."

"I thank the Almin for that, Father," Vanya said in the same tone he used to thank the Almin for his morning egg and bread. Again he paused. Saryon sensed some inner turmoil, a mental struggle. The next words were reluctant. "The time has come, Father, for you and your . . . um . . . guardian — my associate — to make contact. I know about the creation of the Darksword —"

Saryon gasped.

"—and now we can delay no longer. Our danger from this young man is too great." Vanya's voice grew cold. "You must bring Joram to the Font as soon as possible, and you will need my associate's assistance. Go to Blachloch. Inform him that I—"

"Blachloch!" Saryon sank down on the cot, his heart beating in his ears with the din of Joram's hammer. "Your associate?" The catalyst put his shaking hands to his head. "Holiness, you can't mean Blachloch! . . ."

"I assure you, Father—"

"He's a renegade, an outcast of the *Duuk-tsarith*! He—"

"Outcast? He is no more an outcast warlock than you are an outcast priest, Saryon! He *is one of the Duuk-tsarith*, a high-ranking member of their organization, hand-picked for this delicate assignment, just as you were."

Saryon pressed his hands against his head as though he might actually keep his scattered thoughts from tumbling about his brain. Blachloch, the cruel, mudererous warlock, was *Duuk-tsarith*, a member of the secret society whose duty it was to enforce the laws in Thimhallan. He was an agent for the Church! And he was also responsible for cold-blooded murder, for raiding a village and stealing its provisions, for leaving its people to starve in the winter. . . .

"Holiness"—Saryon licked his dry, cracked lips—"this warlock was . . . an evil man! A wicked man! He—I saw him kill a young Deacon of our Order in the village of—"

The Bishop interrupted. "Have you not heard the old saying, 'Night's shadows are deepest to those who walk in the light'? Let us not be too hasty in our judgment of ordinary mortals, Father. If you reflect back calmly upon the incident of which you speak, I am certain you will find the killing was motivated by necessity, or perhaps it was accidental."

Saryon saw the warlock call upon the wind, he saw the gale-force blast pick up the defenseless Deacon as though he were a leaf and toss him against the side of a dwelling. He saw the young body crumple lifelessly to the ground.

"Holiness," ventured Saryon, shuddering.

"Enough, Father!" the Bishop said sternly. "I do not have time for your sanctimonious whinings. Blachloch does what is necessary to maintain his disguise as a renegade warlock. He plays a dangerous game among those Sorcerers of the Dark Arts who surround you, Saryon. What is one life, after all, compared to the lives of thousands or the souls of millions! And that is what he holds in his hand."

"I don't understand —"

"Then give me a chance to explain! I tell you this in the strictest confidence, Father. I told you before you left of the trouble we are having in the northern kingdom of Sharakan. It worsens daily. The catalysts who have abandoned the laws of our Order are growing in popularity and in numbers. They are giving freely of their power of Life to anyone who asks. Because of this, the king of Sharakan believes he can treat us with impunity. He has impounded Church funds and put them into his treasury. He has sent the Cardinal into exile, and replaced him with one of these renegade catalysts. He plans to invade and conquer Merilon, and he is in league with the Sorcerers of Technology among whom you live to provide him with their demonic weapons. . . ."

"Yes, Holiness," Saryon murmured, only half listening, trying desperately to think what to do.

"The king of Sharakan plans to use the Sorcerers' weapons to help him in his conquest. Although Blachloch appears to be furthering the ambitions of Sharakan and helping the Sorcerers, he is — in reality — preparing to lead them into a deadly trap. Thus we will be able to defeat Sharakan and crush the Sorcerers utterly, finally banishing them from this world. Blachloch has everything under control, or at least he had until the young man — this Joram — discovered darkstone."

As Vanya grew angrier, his thoughts became gradually more rambling and incoherent. Saryon could no longer follow them. Sensing this, there was a moment of seething silence as Vanya attempted to regain control, then his communication continued, somewhat calmer.

"The discovery of darkstone is catastrophic, Father! Surely you see that? It can give Sharakan the power to win! That is why it is imperative that you and Blachloch bring the young man and the dreadful force he has brought back into this world to the Font at once, before Sharakan discovers it."

Saryon's head began to ache with the strain. Fortunately, his own thoughts were in such turmoil that he must have transmitted only confused and scattered fragments: Blachloch a double agent . . . the darkstone a threat to the world . . . the Sorcerers walking into a trap. . . .

Joram . . . Joram . . . Joram. . . .

Saryon grew calmer. He knew now what he must do. None of the rest of it was important. Wars between kingdoms. The lives of thousands. It was too enormous to comprehend. But the life of one?

How can I take him back, knowing the fate he faces? And I *do* know it now, Saryon admitted to himself. I was blind to it before, but only because I deliberately shut my eyes.

The catalyst lifted his head, staring intently into the darkness. "Holiness," he said out loud, interrupting the Bishop's tirade. "I know who Joram is."

Vanya stopped cold. Saryon sensed doubt, caution, fear. But these were gone almost immediately. Nearly eighty years old, the Bishop of the Realm of Thimhallan had held his position for over forty of those years. He was highly skilled at his job.

"What do you mean"—the Bishop's thoughts came across as genuinely confused—"you know who he is? He is Joram, son of a mad woman named Anja. . . ."

Saryon felt himself gaining strength. At last, he was able to confront the truth.

"He is Joram," the catalyst said in low tones, "son of the Emperor of Merilon."

2

A State of Grace

There was silence within the silence of the cell. So deep was it that, for a moment, Saryon thought—hoped—that Vanya had broken contact.

Then the words reverberated in his head once more. "How did you come by this supposed knowledge, Father Saryon?" The catalyst could feel the Bishop treading carefully on the soft, unknown ground. "Did Blachloch—"

"By the Almin, did he know?" Saryon spoke aloud again in his amazement. "No," he continued in some confusion, "no one told me. No one had to. I just . . . knew. How?" He shrugged helplessly. "How do I know how much magic to draw from the world and give to a shaper of wood so that he may mold a chair? It is a matter of calculation, of adding all factors together—the man's weight and height, his ability, his age, the degree of difficulty in his project. . . . Do I think of these things consciously? No! I have done it so often, the answer comes to me without thinking about how I have obtained it.

"And so, Holiness, this was how I came to know Joram's true identity." Saryon shook his head, closing his eyes. "My god, I held him in my arms! That baby, born Dead, doomed to die! I was the last person to hold him!" Tears crept beneath his eyelids.

"I took him to the nursery that terrible day and I sat beside his crib and rocked him in my arms for hours. I knew that once I laid him down, no other person would be permitted to touch him until you took him to . . . to the Font." Saryon's emotion lifted him from his cot to pace the small cell. "Maybe it is my fancy, but I have come to believe this created a bond between us. The first time I saw Joram, my soul recognized him if my eyes did not. It was when I began to listen to my soul that I knew the truth."

"You are so certain it is the truth?" The words were strained.

"Do you deny it?" Saryon cried grimly. Halting in his pacing, he stared up into the rafters of the prison cell as though his Bishop hovered among them. "Do you deny that you sent me here purposefully, hoping that I would find out?"

There was a long moment's hesitation; Saryon had a mental image of a man looking over a hand of tarok cards, wondering which to play.

"Have you told Joram?"

There was very real fear in this question, a fear that was palpable to Saryon, a fear he thought he understood.

"No, of course not," the catalyst replied. "How could I tell him such a fantastic tale? He would not believe me, not without proof. And I have none to give."

"Yet you mentioned adding *all* factors?" Vanya persisted.

Saryon shook his head impatiently. He began to pace again, but stopped short at the cell window. Day had dawned completely now. Light streamed into the cold prison house, and the village of the Sorcerers was beginning to waken. Smoke curled upward, blown raggedly in the whipping wind. A few early risers were up and trudging to work already, or were inspecting their dwellings for damage from last night's storm. Off in the distance, he saw one of Blachloch's guards hurrying between the buildings at a run.

Where was Joram? Why hasn't he returned? Saryon wondered. Immediately he shoved the thought from his mind and began pacing again, hoping the activity would help him concentrate and warm him at the same time.

"All factors?" he repeated thoughtfully. "Yes, there are . . . other factors. The young man looks like his mother, the Empress. Oh, not a striking resemblance. His face is hardened by the difficult life he has led. His brows are thick and brooding, he rarely smiles. But he has her hair, beautiful black hair that curls down around his shoulders. I am told his mother—that is, the woman who raised him—refused to let it be cut. And there is an expression in his eyes sometimes—regal, haughty. . . ." Saryon sighed. His mouth was dry. The tears in his throat tasted like blood. "Then, of course, he is Dead, Holiness—"

· "There are many Dead who walk this world."

The Bishop is trying to find out how much I know, Saryon realized suddenly. Or maybe looking for proof. His legs weak, the catalyst sank down at the small, plain table standing near the firepit. Lifting the hand-fashioned clay pitcher, he started to pour himself a drink, only to discover that the water inside was covered with a layer of ice. Casting a bitter glance at the cold ashes of the firepit, Saryon set the pitcher back upon the table with a thud.

"I know that there are many Dead, Holiness," the catalyst said heavily, still speaking aloud. "I myself found enough of them in Merilon, if you remember. To be declared Dead, a baby had to fail two of the three tests for magic. But you and I both know, Holiness, that these Dead still possess some magic, even if it is very little." He swallowed painfully, his parched throat aching. "I never saw a baby—except one—who failed all three tests. Failed them utterly. And that baby was the Prince of Merilon. And I have never met a person, not even among the so-called Dead who live in our settlement, who has no magic—except one. Joram. He is Dead, Holiness. Truly Dead. No Life stirs within him at all."

"Is this a matter of common knowledge among the Sorcerers there?" The interrogation continued relentlessly. Saryon's head began to throb. He longed for quiet, longed to rid himself of the probing voice. But he couldn't think how to do it, short of dashing his head against the brick wall. Biting his lip, he answered the question.

"No. Joram has learned to hide his deficiency superbly. He is skilled in illusion and sleight of hand. Apparently that woman who passed herself off as his mother—Anja—taught him. Joram knows what would happen to him if anyone found out. Even among the Dead and the outcasts here, he would be banished at the best, murdered at worst." The catalyst grew impatient. "But surely Blachloch reported all this—"

"Blachloch knows what it is necessary for him to know," Vanya answered. "I had my suspicions, I admit, and he did what was necessary to either confirm or refute them. I did not see the need to discuss the matter with him."

The catalyst shifted restlessly in his chair. "But there is a need to discuss it with me," he muttered.

"Yes, Father." The Bishop's voice was now cold and firm. "I sense in you an attachment to this young man, a growing affection for him. It is acting as a deadly poison in your soul, Brother Saryon, and you must purge yourself of it. Yes, perhaps I did send you in hope that you would confirm what I had long suspected. Now you know the secret, Saryon, and it is a terrible one! The knowledge that the true Prince lives would leave us at the mercy of our enemies. The danger is so vast that it is almost unthinkable! What if it were known, Saryon, that the true Prince was Dead? Rebellion would be the least of our worries! The ruling family would be cast out, reviled. Merilon would be in chaos, fall easy victim to Sharakan! Surely you see this, Saryon!"

"Yes, Holiness." Once more Saryon attempted to moisten his mouth, but his tongue felt as if it were made of wool. "I see it."

"And so you understand why it is imperative that Joram be brought to us—"

"Why wasn't it imperative before?" Saryon demanded, cold and exhaustion giving him unwonted courage. "You had Joram here, you had Blachloch. The man was a warlock, *Duuk-tsarith*! He could have handed Joram to you in pieces if you'd ordered it! Or why bother to bring Joram to the Font at all? If he's that dangerous, just be rid of him! It would have been easy to kill him, especially for Blachloch!" Saryon was bitter. "Why involve me—"

"You were necessary to provide the truth," Vanya answered, severing Saryon's thoughts with one swift stroke. "Until now, I could only surmise that this Joram was the Prince. Your 'factors' add together well, as I thought they might. As for assassinating him, the Church does not commit murder, Father."

Saryon hung his head. The rebuke was well deserved. Though he had lost his faith in both his church and his god, he could not find it in his heart to believe that the Bishop of Thimhallan would order a man's death. Even the babies—the ones judged Dead—were not put to death but were taken to the Chambers of Waiting, where they were allowed to slip quietly out of a world in which they had no place. As for the murder of the young Deacon, that had been Blachloch's doing. Saryon could well believe that the warlock had been difficult for the Bishop to control. The *Duuk-tsarith* lived by their own laws.

"I am going to confess something to you, Father." Vanya's thoughts came to Saryon laden with pain. The catalyst winced, feeling the same pain inside himself. "I tell you this, in order that you will understand more clearly. If it were not for this wretched young man's discovery of the darkstone, I would have been content to let him live out his life, hidden among the Sorcerers — at least until such time as we were ready to move against all of them. Don't you see, Saryon? It would have been so easy to lose Joram among them, to eliminate all these dangers to the world at one blow, without upsetting the people. Chastise Sharakan, punish the rebellious catalysts, eliminate the Sorcerers of the Dark Arts, rid ourselves of a Dead Prince. It was all to have been so simple, Saryon."

Once again, that silence within the silence. Saryon sighed, letting his head sink into his hands. The voice resumed, speaking so softly it was a whispering in his mind.

"It can still be simple, Father. You hold the fate of Merilon in your hands, if not the fate of the world."

Saryon, appalled, looked up, protesting. "No, Holiness! I don't want —"

"You don't want the responsibility?" Vanya was grim. "I am afraid you have little choice. You made a mistake, Father, and now you must pay for it. I know something of darkstone, you see. And I know that Joram could not have learned to use it without the help of a catalyst."

"Holiness, I didn't understand —" Saryon began in misery.

"Didn't you, Saryon? Your head may have condoned your actions, but your soul knew you sinned! I sense your guilt, my son, a guilt that has destroyed your faith. And you will not be absolved of it until you do your duty. By bringing the young man to me, by turning him over to the Church, you will ease your tortured conscience and find the peace that you once knew."

"What — what will happen to Joram?" Saryon asked hesitantly.

"That should not be your concern, Father." Vanya was stern. "The young man has twice broken our most sacred laws — he committed murder and he has brought back into the world a dread, demonic power. Consider your own black soul, Saryon, and seeks its redemption!"

If I only could, Saryon thought wearily.

"Father Saryon"—Vanya was clearly angry now—"I sense doubt and turmoil where there should be only contrition and humility!"

"Forgive me, Holiness!" Saryon pressed his hands to his temples. "This has all been so sudden! I can't understand—I must have time to think and . . . and consider what is best to be done—" A sudden suspicion crossed his mind. "Holiness, how is it that Joram came to live? How did Anja—"

"What is that, Father? More questions?" Bishop Vanya interrupted severely. There was a pause, heavy, waiting.

Saryon swallowed, though there was nothing in his mouth but the taste of blood. He tried to clear his mind, but the questions were there—persistent, nagging. The Bishop may have sensed this, for the thoughts that came to Saryon next were as warm as a blanket.

"Perhaps you are right, Father," Vanya said gently. "You need time. I am impatient, I admit. The matter is so critical to me, our danger so real, that I have been unfeeling. A day more cannot make any difference. I will contact you this evening to make the final arrangements. The Chamber of Discretion gives me the ability to find you any time, any place. You are always in my thoughts, as the old saying goes."

Saryon shivered. This was not a comforting idea. "I am honored, Holiness," he mumbled. .

"May the Almin walk with you and guide your stumbling steps."

"Thank you, Holiness."

The silence was back, and this time Saryon knew that the Bishop was gone. Creeping from his chair, the catalyst crossed the cell and lay down once more upon his cot. He pulled the thin, meager blanket up around his shoulders and lay there, shaking with cold and fear. The early morning sun shown through the barred window, shedding such a pale, wan light that, if anything, it intensified the chill atmosphere rather than warmed it. Saryon stared bleakly at the shadows wavering in the mocking brightness and tried to understand what had happened to him.

But he was consumed with such horror and loathing that he could barely concentrate. Angrily he struggled with such rebellious feelings.

"I should be filled with humble gratitude to think the Bishop cares about his people so much that he devised this means of watching over them. If my soul were cleansed, as he says, then I would not resent this invasion," Saryon told himself bitterly. "It is my own sins that make me shudder in fear at the thought that he has the power to finger through my mind like a thief! My life belongs to the Church, after all. I should have nothing to hide."

He rolled over on his back, watching the moving darkness in the rafters.

"Oh, to find peace again! Perhaps what the Bishop said was true. Perhaps I have lost my faith because of my own guilt, a guilt I refuse to admit? By confessing my sins and accepting my punishment, I would be free! Free of these tormenting doubts! Free of this inner turmoil!"

The catalyst felt an instant's peace wash over him as he considered this. It was warm and soothing and it filled up the terrible, black, cold emptiness inside him. If Vanya had been present, Saryon would have flung himself at the Bishop's feet then and there.

But . . . Joram. . . .

Yes, what about Joram? The memory of the young man pricked the bubble of peace. The warmth began to ooze away. No! Saryon fought to hang onto it.

"Admit it," he argued with himself. "Joram frightens you! Vanya is right. The young man is a very real danger. It would be a relief to be rid of him and the responsibility of that weapon of evil, especially now that I am certain of the truth. After all, what was it the ancients said—'The truth shall make you free'?"

Very well, countered Saryon's black, cynical soul, but what *is* the truth? Did Vanya answer your questions? What truly happened seventeen years ago? If Joram is the Prince, how and why is he still alive?

The catalyst's eyes closed, trying to block out sun and shadows alike. Once again, he held that small baby in his arms, rocking it gently, his tears falling upon the unconscious head. Once again, he felt Joram's touch—the young man's hand resting upon his shoulder as it had done in those dreadful moments last night in the forge. He saw the look of starved longing in the black, cold eyes—the longing for love Joram's soul had so long denied itself. Joram saw that love in Saryon. The bond was there! Yes. If Saryon had believed in the Almin, he might almost have said it was there by the god's will. Could he break it, betray it?

What will happen to Joram? His words to the Bishop echoed in his mind. And he knew the answer. Bishop Vanya had taken the baby away to die. He could do no less with the man.

Saryon opened his eyes, facing the gray dawn in which there was no warmth but in which there was truth — cold though it might be.

If I take Joram back, I take him back to death.

The false peace seeped out of the catalyst, leaving behind the same bleak, dark void. There were too many unanswered questions, too many lies. Bishop Vanya had lied to the Emperor and Empress, who believed their baby dead. He'd lied to Saryon when he sent him out after Joram. And he would have continued to lie if Saryon had not caught him. Of that, the catalyst felt certain. He could not trust Vanya. He could trust no one. The only truth Saryon had to cling to was within himself. He sighed heavily. He would follow that truth, and hoped it would guide him through the morass surrounding him.

And where was Joram, anyway? He should have been back by now. Something must have gone wrong. . . .

The sunlight was blotted out by two dark shapes materializing within the center of the room like the ghosts of Saryon's conscience. Fearfully, the catalyst stared at them, his heart in his throat, until one spoke.

"I say," remarked a voice, as bright and mocking as the sun, "look here, Joram. You and I are out there, braving the peril of the wilds, and here lies the Priest of Bald Pates, sleeping like the dead as the Baron of Dunstable Manor was wont to do before they buried him by mistake."

3

Stain Removal

"Joram?" Saryon said hesitantly.

Sitting upright, the catalyst stared at the two young men standing in the center of the cell. They had come so suddenly, appearing out of nowhere, that Saryon wondered if they were real or were a manifestation of his thoughts.

But the voice that answered was real enough, as was the irritation. "Who the hell else would it be?" snapped Joram, further proving his reality by walking over to the table and grabbing the water pitcher. Upon discovering the ice inside, he set it back down with a bitter curse.

"Hush!" Saryon warned, but it was too late.

At the noise, a guard's face suddenly peered in the barred window, causing the other young man accompanying Joram to shout in alarm.

"Egad! Run for your lives! A loathsome beast is upon us — Oh, beg your pardon" — as the guard's face twisted into a scowl — " 'tisn't a loathsome beast. Just one of Blachloch's men. My mistake. Must have been the smell that confused me." The guard disappeared with a snarl, and Simkin, sniffing, covered his nose with his hand.

Saryon hurried across the small room. "Are you all right?" he asked Joram, looking at him in concern.

The young man raised dark eyes that were shadowed with fatigue; his stern face was haggard. His clothes were torn and stained with dirt and a substance Saryon realized with sick horror was blood. There were traces of blood upon his hands as well.

"I'm fine," Joram responded tiredly, sinking down in a chair.

"But . . ." Saryon laid a hand upon the slumped shoulder. "You look dreadful—"

"I said I'm fine!" Joram snarled, jerking away from Saryon's sympathetic touch. He glanced at the catalyst through a tangle of glossy, black hair. "We've all seen better days, if it comes to that. . . ."

"I resent that remark!" Simkin said, drawing a bit of orange silk from the air with a flourish and dabbing at his nose. "Please don't lump me in amongst you rabble."

Indeed, Simkin appeared to have just come from an evening with the Emperor. The only change noticeable in the foppish young man was the somewhat startling fact that his usually colorful clothes were now completely black—even to the lace that covered his wrists.

Sighing, Saryon drew away from Joram. Rubbing his cold hands, he wrapped them in the sleeves of his shabby robe in a futile endeavor to warm them.

"Did you have any trouble getting back here last night?" Joram asked the catalyst.

"No. The guards knew I was with . . . Blachloch." Saryon coughed, choking over the name. "I told them he had finished with me and . . . sent me back. They shut me up in here without question. But you?" The catalyst stared at Joram, then Simkin, in wonder. "How did you get here? And where have you been? Did anyone see you?" He glanced involuntarily out the window at the house across the street where Blachloch's guards lived, keeping watch on the prisoners.

"See us! Gad, how insulting!" Simkin sniffed. "As if I would appear in public in this garb!" He raised a black sleeve contemptuously. "I'm wearing this now only because it seems suited to the occasion."

"But how did you get here?" Saryon persisted.

"The Corridors, of course." Simkin shrugged.

"But . . . that's impossible!" Saryon gasped, almost incoherent in his amazement. "The *Thon-Li*, the Corridor Masters!

They would have stopped— You had no catalyst to grant you sufficient Life or . . . or open them—"

"Technicalities." Simkin waved a black lace-covered hand. He took a turn about the room, admiring his black shoes and continuing to talk. "I was speaking of something when we came in, and between you and the appearance of that loutish face in the window, which has, by the way, completely taken away my appetite for breakfast, it's been quite driven from my mind. What was it?"

"Joram," Saryon began, trying to ignore Simkin. "Where were—"

"Oh, yes. I recall." Simkin frowned, hand to his head. "Burying the baron by mistake. He took it all quite well. Thought it a capital joke, in fact. He did have a small problem crawling out from beneath the marble slab and then there were a few tense moments when we mistook him for a vampire and attempted to drive a stake through his heart. Discovered he was flesh and blood, however, and sent for the *Theldara* at once. Patched up the hole in his chest. Never better. Understandable mistake. But the grieving widow, a different story." Simkin heaved a sigh. "Never forgave him for ruining the funeral."

"Joram! Where have you been? What happened?" Saryon asked insistently when Simkin paused for breath.

"Where's the Darksword?" Joram demanded abruptly.

"Where you keep it hidden. I brought it back, as I promised. It is safe," Saryon added, seeing Joram's dark eyes rest on him with sudden suspicion. "As you said, I could not destroy what I had helped create."

Joram stood up. "Simkin, watch the window," he ordered.

"Must I? If that lout looms up at me, I'll vomit. I swear—"

"Just watch the window!" Joram said grimly.

Placing the orange silk firmly over his mouth and nose, Simkin moved obligingly to the window, peering outside. "The lout in question has gone to speak to his fellow louts across the street," he reported. "They all seem fearfully excited. I wonder what's going on?"

"They've probably discovered that Blachloch's missing," Joram said, walking over to the bed. Kneeling down beside it, he placed his hands beneath the filthy mattress and drew forth a cloth-covered bundle. Hastily unwrapping it, he glanced at the sword inside and, nodding in satisfaction, looked back at

Saryon. The pale sunlight cast a gray glow upon the face of the older man, who was regarding him with a solemn, grave expression.

"Thank you," Joram said grudgingly.

"Don't thank me. I would to the Almin that it were at the bottom of the river!" Saryon said fervently. "Especially after this night's business!" He raised his hands pleadingly. "Reconsider, Joram! Destroy this weapon of evil before it destroys you!"

"No!" Avoiding the catalyst's sorrow-filled eyes, Joram angrily shoved the bundle back beneath the bed. "You saw the power it gave me *during* tonight's business. Do you truly believe I'd give that up? It's my concern, not yours, old man!"

"It *is* my concern," Saryon said softly. "I was there! I helped you commit mur—" The catalyst bit off his words, glancing at Simkin.

"It's all right," Joram said, standing up. "Simkin knows."

Of course, Saryon said to himself bitterly. Simkin knows everything, somehow. The catalyst had the feeling that truth—his guide through the morass—had just left him floundering in a bog.

"In fact," Joram continued, sinking down on the bed, "you should thank him, Catalyst. I would never have been able to complete 'last night's business,' as you call it, without him."

"Yes," said Simkin cheerfully, turning from the window. "He was going to dump the body just any old place and, of course, that wouldn't do at all. I mean, you want this to look like centaurs killed dear old Blachloch, don't you? 'Pon my honor. The warlock's—pardon: late, unlamented warlock's—henchmen are stupid, but, I ask you, are they that stupid?

"Suppose that they find their erstwhile master at the foot of some tree with a great, bloody hole in his gut and not a track or weapon in sight. Is it likely, I wonder, that they'd remark casually, 'Zounds! Looks like old Blachloch's got himself done in by a maple!' Not on your Aunt Minnie! They'd hurry back here, line everyone up in the square, and ask nasty, insulting questions like 'Where were you between the hours of ten and twelve?' and 'What was the dog doing in the nighttime?' So, to avoid that, we arranged the body—quite tastefully, I assure you—in a picturesque attitude in the center of a small glade, complete with embellishing touches."

Saryon felt suddenly sick. He saw Joram leaving the forge, the warlock's corpse slung over his shoulders, Blachloch's limp arms dangling down behind. The catalyst's knees gave way. Sinking down into a chair, he couldn't help staring in horror at Joram, at the bloodstained shirt.

Joram followed the catalyst's gaze, glancing down at himself. His mouth twisted. "This make you squeamish, old man?"

"You should get rid of it," said Saryon quietly. "Before the guards see it."

Joram stared at him a moment, then, shrugging, he tugged at the shirt. "Simkin," he ordered, "start a fire —"

"My dear fellow!" Simkin protested. "Waste of a perfectly good shirt. Toss it here. Remove the stain in an instant. The Duchess D'Longeville showed me — You remember hearing of her, the one with all the husbands who kept dying mysteriously. An expert on stains, too. 'Nothing easier to take out than dried blood, Simkin, my dear,' she said to me. 'Most people make such a fuss over it.' All you do is —" Catching the shirt as Joram threw it, Simkin shook it out, then rubbed the stain vigorously with the bit of orange silk. At its touch, the blood vanished. "There, what'd I tell you? Pure and white as the driven snow. Well, not counting that grime around the collar." Simkin regarded the shirt with a disdainful smile.

"What about the body?" Saryon interrupted hoarsely. "What 'touches'?"

"Centaur tracks!" Simkin smiled proudly. "My idea."

"Tracks? How?"

"Why, turned myself into a centaur, of course," Simkin replied, leaning back against the wall. "Jolly fun. Do it on occasion to relax. I stomped about, tore up the turf, made it appear as though there'd been the most savage fight. Considered seriously killing myself and leaving my body beside Blachloch's. Would have been the ultimate in realism. But" — he sighed — "one can give only so much to one's art."

"Don't worry, Catalyst," Joram snapped irritably. "No one will suspect a thing." Taking his shirt back from Simkin, he started to put it on, hesitated, then tossed it on the mattress. Yanking a worn leather pack from beneath his bed, Joram took out another shirt. "Where's Mosiah?" he asked, looking about with a frown.

"I — I don't know," Saryon answered, realizing suddenly that he had not seen the young man. "He was asleep when we left. The guards must have taken him somewhere!" He half-rose in alarm, walking toward the window.

"He probably escaped," Simkin said nonchalantly. "Those louts couldn't keep a chick from breaking out of its shell, and you know Mosiah was talking of heading out into the wilds on his own." Simkin gave a jaw-cracking yawn. "I say, Saryon, old boy, you don't mind if I use your cot, do you? I'm frightfully sleepy. Witnessing murders, hiding bodies — been a full day. Thanks." Without waiting for Saryon's reply, Simkin crossed the small room, and stretched himself luxuriously on the cot. "Nightclothes," he said, and was immediately garbed in a long, white, linen, lace-decorated nightshirt. Winking at Saryon, the young man smoothed his beard, brushed up his mustache; then, closing his eyes, he was fast asleep in an instant, and within three was snoring blissfully.

Joram's face darkened. "You don't think he did, do you?" he asked Saryon.

"What? Leave, go off by himself?" The catalyst rubbed his aching eyes. "Why not? Mosiah certainly thinks he has no friends here." He glanced bitterly at Joram. "Would it matter to you?"

"I hope he did," Joram said flatly, tucking his shirt into his breeches. "The less he knows about this, the better. For him . . . and for us."

He started to lay back down, thought better of it, and walked over to the table. Lifting the pitcher, he broke the ice inside and poured the water into a slop bowl. Then, grimacing, he plunged his face into the chill water. After washing away the black soot of the forge, he dried himself with his shirtsleeve and brushed back his tangled, wet hair with his fingers. Then, shivering in the dank cell, he began to resolutely scrub his hands, using chunks of ice to scrape the dried blood from his fingers.

"You're going out somewhere, aren't you?" Saryon asked suddenly.

"To the forge, to work," Joram answered. Wiping his hands upon his breeches, he then began to separate his thick, tangled hair into three parts, to braid it as he did every day, wincing as he tugged impatiently at the glossy black mass in his hands.

"But you're falling asleep on your feet," Saryon protested. "Besides, they won't let you out. You're right, something's going on." He motioned to the window. "Look there. The guards are nervous. . . ."

Joram glanced out the window, twisting his hair with skilled hands. "All the more reason for us to act as if nothing has happened. While I'm gone, see what you can discover about Mosiah." Slinging a cloak over his shoulders, Joram walked over to the window and began to bang impatiently on the bars. The knot of guards in the street turned suddenly, and one — after a moment's conference with the others — came over to the cell, unlocked the door, and yanked it open.

"What do you want?" the guard growled.

"I'm supposed to be at work," Joram said sullenly. "Blachloch's orders."

"Blachloch's orders?" The guard frowned. "We haven't had any orders from —" he began, then stopped, biting off his words and swallowing them with a gulp. "Just get back in the cell!"

"Sure." Joram shrugged. "Only you tell the warlock why I wasn't at the forge when they're working overtime to turn out weapons for Sharakan."

"What's going on?" Another guard came up. All the guards, Saryon noticed, appeared nervous and ill at ease. Their eyes shifted constantly among each other, people in the street, and Blachloch's house upon the hill.

"Says he's supposed to go to the forge. Orders." The guard jerked his thumb at the house.

"Then take him," said the other guard.

"But yesterday we was told to keep 'em locked up. And Blachloch's not —"

"I said take him," the guard growled with a meaningful look at his fellow.

"Come on, then," the man said to Joram, giving him a vicious shove.

Saryon watched as Joram and the guard made their way through the streets. The guards' nervousness had spread to the populace. The catalyst saw men passing by on their way to work cast dark glances at Blachloch's henchmen, who glared at them with equal enmity. Women who should have been going to market or taking laundry to the stream stared out the windows of their houses. Children starting to go out to play were yanked back indoors. Did the Sorcerers know about Blachloch's disappearance or were they simply reacting to the nervous state of the warlock's henchmen? Saryon couldn't guess and he dared not ask.

His brain numb with exhaustion and fear, the catalyst sank down in a rickety chair and leaned his head in his hand. A loud voice made him start, but it was only Simkin muttering about cards, apparently playing a game of tarok in his sleep.

"Last trick falls to the King of Swords. . . ."

4

Waiting

Never had a morning passed more slowly for Saryon, who tracked it by the counts of his heartbeat, the drawing of his breath, the blinking of his gummed eyes. There had been a flurry of activity in the house across the street shortly after Joram left, and the catalyst guessed that a contingent of Blachloch's henchmen had decided to go off in search of their missing leader. Now, every second that dragged past, Saryon expected to hear the commotion that would tell him the warlock's body had been discovered.

The catalyst could do nothing but wait. He actually envied Joram his work at the iron forge, where mind and body — tired though they might be — could find refuge in numbing labor. The sight of Simkin, sprawled luxuriously on his cot, made every muscle in the catalyst's middle-aged body ache for rest, and he tried to seek refuge in sleep. Saryon lay down on Joram's bed, tired enough that he hoped he would sink into oblivion swiftly. But the moment he began to slip over the edge of consciousness, he imagined he heard Vanya's voice calling him, and he started awake, sweating and trembling.

"Vanya is going to contact me again tonight!" In his excitement over Joram's return, Saryon had shoved that threat from his mind. Now he remembered, and the minutes that had been creeping past on leaden feet suddenly sprouted wings and took off.

Locked in the prison cell, light-headed from lack of food and sleep, Saryon's thoughts centered on this forthcoming confrontation with the Bishop, going round and round, caught like a stick in a whirlpool.

"I will not surrender Joram!" he said to himself feverishly. That much was certain. As the catalyst envisioned this meeting with Vanya, however, he began to realize helplessly that he might have little choice in the matter. Unless Vanya had ways of talking with the dead as the ancient Necromancers were said to have possessed, the Bishop's attempt to contact Blachloch this day must fail. Vanya would demand of Saryon where the warlock was, and Saryon knew he would not have the strength to hide the truth.

"Joram killed the warlock, murdered him with a weapon created of darkness, a weapon created with my help!" Saryon heard himself confess.

How is that possible? Bishop Vanya would question in disbelief. A seventeen-year-old youth and a middle-aged catalyst destroying one of the *Duuk-tsarith*? A powerful warlock who could drag the winds from the skies to crush a man like a dried, autumn leaf? A warlock who could inject a fiery poison into a man's body, setting ablaze every nerve, reducing the victim to little more than a convulsing, writhing blob of flesh? This was the man you destroyed?

Sitting on the edge of the Joram's cot, the catalyst nervously clasped and unclasped his hands. "He was going to kill Joram, Holiness!" Saryon murmured to himself, rehearsing. "You said the Church did not condone murder. Blachloch called upon me to grant him Life, to draw the magic from the world and feed it into his body to do this foul deed! But I could not, Holiness! Blachloch was evil, don't you see that? I saw it. I had seen him kill before. I could not let him kill again! I began to drain the Life from him! I took away his magic. Was that wrong? Was it, Holiness? To try to save another's life? I never meant for the warlock himself to die!" Saryon shook his head, staring down at his worn shoes. "I only wanted to . . . render him harmless. Please believe me, Holiness! I never meant for any of this to happen. . . ."

"Who holds the Fool card?" Simkin asked sternly, the unexpected voice causing the catalyst's heart to leap into his throat. Shaking, Saryon glared at the young man angrily.

Simkin appeared to be sound asleep. Rolling over on his stomach, he clutched the hard pillow to his chest and rested his cheek against the mattress. "Do you hold the Fool card, Catalyst?" he asked dreamily. "If not, your King must fall. . . ."

The King must fall. Yes, there was no doubt about that. Once Vanya knew his agent was dead, nothing his catalyst could do or say would prevent the Bishop from sending the *Duuktsarith* immediately to bring Joram to the Font.

"What am I doing?" Saryon gripped the edge of the mattress, digging his fingers through the worn fabric. "What am I thinking? Joram is Dead! They will not be able to locate him! That is why Vanya must have me or Blachloch. He cannot find the boy on his own. The *Duuk-tsarith* track us by the Life, the magic within our bodies! They will find me, but they cannot track the Dead. Or maybe they won't find me. Maybe they won't find Joram."

An idea struck Saryon a blow that was physical in its intensity. Trembling in excitement, he stood up and began to pace the small cell. His mind went over the calculations swiftly in search of a flaw. There were none. It would work. He was as certain of it as he was certain of the very first mathematical formula he had learned at his mother's knee.

For every action, there is an opposite and equal reaction. So the ancients taught. In a world that exudes magic, there is a force that absorbs it as well — the darkstone. Known to the Sorcerers at the time of the Iron Wars, they had used it to forge weapons of tremendous power. When the Sorcerers were defeated, their Technology was labeled a Dark Art. Their kind was persecuted, banished from the land or forced into hiding, as were those in this small colony where Saryon now lived. The knowledge of darkstone had sunk under the turbulent harshness of their lives and their fight for survival. It had sunk beyond memory, becoming only meaningless words in a ritual chant, unreadable words in old, half-forgotten books.

Unreadable except to Joram. He had found the ore, learned its secrets, forged a sword. . . .

Slowly, Saryon reached beneath Joram's mattress. He touched the cold metal of the sword, wrapped in torn cloth, and he cringed away from its evil feel. His hands kept searching, however, and found what they sought — a small leather bag. Pulling it out from its hiding place, Saryon held it in his hand, pondering. It would work, but did he have the strength, the courage?

Did he have a choice?

Slowly, he tugged open the leather string that held the bag shut. Inside were three pieces of rock. Plain and unlovely, they looked very much like iron ore.

Saryon hesitated, holding the bag in his hand, staring inside in rapt fascination.

Darkstone — this would protect him from Vanya! This was the card he could play that would keep the Bishop from winning the game! Reaching inside the bag, Saryon drew forth one of the rocks. It felt heavy and strangely warm in his palm. Thoughtfully, he closed his hand over it and, with an unconscious movement, pressed it against his heart. Bishop Vanya contacted him through the magic. The darkstone would absorb that magic, act as a shield. He would be — to Vanya — as one of the Dead.

"And I might as well be one of the Dead," Saryon murmured, clutching the stone close to his body, "for this act will put me outside the laws, both of my faith and of the land. By doing this, I repudiate everything I have been brought up to believe. I repudiate my life. All I have lived for up until this time will crumble and slip through my fingers as so much dust. I will have to learn the world all over again. A new world, a cold world, a frightening world. A world without faith, a world without comforting answers, a world of Death. . . ."

Drawing the leather thong tight, Saryon shut the bag and slipped it back once more into its hiding place. He kept one rock fast in his hand, however, holding it tightly. His decision made, he moved rapidly now, plans and thoughts falling into place in his mind with the logic and clarity of the skilled mathematician.

"I must go to the forge. I must talk to Joram, convince him of our danger. We'll escape, travel into the Outland. By the time the *Duuk-tsarith* arrive, we will be far away."

Still clutching the rock in his hand, Saryon splashed water on his face and, grabbing up his cloak, flung it — all tangled and awry — around his shoulders. With a backward glance at the slumbering Simkin, he tapped on the barred window of the prison house and beckoned to one of the guards.

"What do you want, Catalyst?"

"Weren't you given orders this morning regarding me?" Saryon asked, assuming a smile he hoped would be taken for bland innocence but which felt more like the frozen grin of a dead possum.

"No," the guard said with a frightful scowl.

"I — um — am needed at the forge this day." Saryon gulped. "The smith is undertaking a difficult project and has asked to be infused with Life."

"I don't know." The guard hesitated. "Our orders were to keep you inside."

"But surely those orders were for last night," Saryon said. "Haven't you . . . er . . . received new orders today?"

"Maybe we have and maybe we haven't," the guard mumbled, with an uneasy glance at the house on the hill. Following the guard's gaze, Saryon saw a group of Blachloch's henchmen gathering in a small, dark knot outside the door. He wished desperately he knew what was going on.

"I guess you can go," the guard said finally. "But I'll have to take you."

"Of course." Saryon checked a relieved sigh.

"Is the twit still in there?" The guard jerked his head toward the prison house.

"Who? Oh, Simkin." The catalyst nodded.

Peering through the barred window, the guard saw the young man stretched out on the bed, his mouth wide open. His snores could be heard clearly in the street and, at that moment, he was seized with a particularly violent one that practically lifted him from the bed.

"Pity he don't choke." The guard opened the door, let the catalyst out, then shut it with a vicious snap. "Come on, Priest," the guard said, and the two began their walk.

As they passed through the village streets with their rows of brick houses — houses that Saryon could still not look upon without a shudder, houses that had been made by the tools and hands of man instead of molded from the elements by magic — the catalyst noticed the restlessness growing among the people. Many men had given up all pretense of working and now stood around in small groups, talking in low tones, glaring at the guard as he passed with grim defiance.

"Aye, just wait," the guard muttered, glaring back at them. "We'll take care of you shortly." But Saryon noticed that

Blachloch's henchman said this beneath his breath. Clearly, he was nervous and worried.

The catalyst did not blame him. Five years ago, the man called Blachloch had appeared in the Sorcerers' village. Claiming to be a renegade from the ranks of the powerful *Duuk-tsarith*, the warlock had easily wrested control from Andon — the gentle, old man who was the leader of the Coven. Bringing in his henchmen — thieves and murderers sent expressly by the *Duuk-tsarith* for this purpose — the warlock tightened his grip upon the Sorcerers, ruling through both fear and the promise that it was now time for the Sorcerers to rise up and take back their proper place in the world. But there were those — Andon among them — who had openly defied the warlock and his guards. Now that the powerful warlock was missing, his men were understandably concerned.

"So, what project are they working on today, Priest?"

Saryon started. He had the vague awareness that this was the second time the guard had asked the question, but he had been so lost in his thoughts he had not noticed.

"Uh, a special weapon . . . for the . . . the kingdom of Sharakan, I believe," Saryon stammered, flushing uncomfortably. The guard nodded and lapsed into his uneasy silence again, darting swift, suspicious glances from the corners of his eyes at the townspeople they met as they continued toward the forge.

Saryon knew he was safe in mentioning Sharakan. A large kingdom lying well to the north of the Outland, Sharakan was preparing for war and had incurred the wrath, and fear, of the catalysts by daring to seek out the Sorcerers of the Dark Art and engage their help. Thus, for the past year, the Sorcerers had been working day and night, forging iron arrow-points, spearpoints and daggers. Enhanced by the powerful magic of Sharakan's own warlocks, these weapons could make them an extremely formidable enemy. And, right now, the iron dagger of Sharakan was pointed directly at the ancient and beautiful throat of the kingdom of Merilon.

No wonder Bishop Vanya was frightened. In this, Saryon did not blame him, and, as he thought about it, his heart almost misgave him. The Order of catalysts had kept the peace among the various kingdoms of Thimhallan for centuries. Now it was unraveling, the frail fabric being ripped apart. Sharakan made no secret of its plans for conquest and, though the Church was doing its best to keep this from the rest of the world lest it start a panic, rumors were spreading and fear was growing daily.

But surely, Saryon thought, now that Blachloch is dead, that will all end! Andon, the wise, elderly leader, was opposed to this talk of war among the Sorcerers. With Blachloch no longer around to foment the idea, the old man could bring his people back to their senses.

I will warn him of their danger before we leave, Saryon thought. I will tell him that Blachloch was leading them into a trap. I —

"Here we are," announced the guard, catching hold of the catalyst, who had, in his dark musings, nearly stumbled head-long into the forge. Once again cognizant of his surroundings, Saryon heard the pounding of the hammers and the harsh breathing of the bellows, like the heart and lungs of some great beast, its eyes gleaming fiery red from the darkness of the lair in which it crouched. The beast's master, the smith, stood within the doorway. A giant of a man, skilled in both magic and tech-nology, the smith led the faction of Sorcerers who favored war. He favored it, however, without interference from Blachloch. No one would be more pleased to hear of the warlock's death than the smith. And there was no doubt that the henchmen had much to fear from this big man and the large number of Sor-cerers who supported him.

The smith was talking with several young men now. Seeing the guard, they broke off their conversation. The young men drew back into the shadows of the cave where the forge was housed, and the smith returned to his work, though not before he cast the guard a glance of cool defiance.

"Father . . ." There came a touch on his arm.

Saryon looked around behind him, startled.

"Mosiah!" he cried, reaching out to clutch the young man thankfully. "How did you esca—" Glancing at the guard, he broke off. "That is, we were worried—"

"Father," said Mosiah, interrupting gently, "I must speak to you. In private. It is a . . . spiritual matter," he said, looking at the guard. "It will not take long."

"All right," the guard said grudgingly, conscious of the smith watching him closely. "But don't get out of my sight, either of you."

Mosiah drew Saryon into the shadows of a stable where they kept the horses for shoeing. "Father," the young man whis-pered, "where are you going?"

"To—to talk with Joram. I have something . . . we need to discuss . . ." Saryon stammered.

"Is it about this rumor?"

"What rumor?" the catalyst asked uneasily.

"Blachloch. . . . He's missing." Mosiah regarded Saryon intently. "Hadn't you heard?"

"No." Saryon averted his eyes and drew further back into the shadows.

"They've sent a search party into the wilderness."

"How—how do you know?"

"I was at Blachloch's house when Simkin came to tell the warlock's men the news."

"Simkin?" Saryon stared at Mosiah. "When? What did he say?"

"Early this morning. You see, Father," Mosiah continued hurriedly, his eyes on the guard, "last night, after you and Joram left, the guards came and took me away. Blachloch wanted to question me, or something like that, they said. When we arrived at the house, he wasn't there. Someone said he'd gone with you to the forge. We waited, but he never came back. Some of his men went to the forge looking for him and couldn't find him. Then, near morning, Simkin turned up with a story about how Blachloch had gone into the woods to settle an old score with centaurs—"

Saryon groaned.

Mosiah looked at the catalyst intently.

"This isn't news to you, Father, is it? I didn't think it would be. What's going on?"

"I can't tell you now!" Saryon said in a low voice. "How did you get away?"

"Just walked off in the confusion. I came to warn Andon. Blachloch's men are gathering up there, making plans to take over the village and crush any rebellion before it starts. They've got weapons—clubs and knives and bows—"

"Hey, come along! I ain't got all day," the guard shouted, obviously eager to escape the smith's wrathful gaze.

"I've got to go," Saryon said, starting for the forge.

"I'm coming with you," Mosiah said firmly.

"No! Go back to the cell! Keep an eye on Simkin!" Saryon ordered desperately. "The Almin knows what he'll say or do next!"

"Yes," Mosiah said, after an instant's consideration, "that's probably a good idea. You'll be coming back?"

"Yes, yes!" Saryon answered hastily. He saw the guard glance at the young man uncertainly, as though thinking it odd that Mosiah was free to walk the streets. But if the guard had any intentions of stopping Mosiah, another glance at the frowning smith caused him to reconsider.

"The priest here says he's come to help you with some special project," the guard said to the smith, each eyeing the other darkly.

"You know . . . the special project, for Sharakan," Saryon added, licking his dry lips. The sound of hammering from the back ceased. The catalyst saw Joram looking at him, his black eyes gleaming as red as the coals in the pit. "The project the young man Joran is working on . . ." Saryon's voice gave out, his well of lies run dry.

A smile twitched on the smith's lips, but he only shrugged and said, "Aye, that project." He made a gesture with a blackened hand. "Go on back, Father. Not you!" he ordered in a stern voice, glaring at the guard. The guard's face flushed, but the smith lifted his gigantic hammer, holding it easily in one huge fist. With a muttered curse, the guard backed off. Turning on his heel, he headed up the street toward the house on the hill.

"Better hurry, Father," the smith said coolly. "There's going to be trouble and you don't want to be caught in the middle, I'll wager."

The smith struck a horseshoe he was holding in his tongs a ringing blow with his hammer. Saryon, glancing at it, saw that the horseshoe was stone cold, already shaped and finished, in fact. The crowd of young men had reappeared, converging in front of the cavern entrance. Their numbers appeared to be growing.

"Yes, thank you," the catalyst said. "I — I'll be quick."

Hardly able to hear himself think over the hammering, Saryon made his way through the clutter of the forge. Memories of last night assailed him. His gaze went involuntarily to the place on the floor where the warlock's bleeding body had rested —

"Almin's blood! What are you doing here?" Joram swore through clenched teeth. A red-hot, glowing spear-point lay on the anvil before him. He started to lift it with the tongs, to plunge it into a bucket of water. But Saryon stopped him with a hand on his arm.

"I must talk to you, Joram!" he yelled over the sound of the smith's hammer blows. "We are in danger!"

"What? Have they discovered the body?"

"No. Another danger. A more deadly one. I— You know that I was sent by . . . Bishop Vanya to . . . bring you back. I told you that, when I first came."

"Yes," returned Joram, his heavy black brows coming together to form a thick black line across his face. "You told me— after Simkin had told me, but you told me."

Saryon flushed. "I know you don't trust me, but . . . listen! Bishop Vanya has contacted me again. Don't ask how, the means are magical." The catalyst's hand went to a pocket in his robes where he had secreted the darkstone. Taking hold of it, he clasped it reassuringly. "He demands that Blachloch and I bring you to the Font, you and the Darksword."

"Vanya knows about the Darksword?" Joram hissed. "You told—"

"Not I!" Saryon gasped. "Blachloch! The wizard is—was— the Bishop's agent—*Duuk-tsarith*. I don't have time to explain everything now, Joram. The Bishop will soon find out that Blachloch is dead and that you killed him, using the darkstone. He will send the *Duuk-tsarith* here to apprehend you. He must, he fears the power of the Darksword—"

"He *wants* the power of the Darksword," Joram amended grimly.

Saryon blinked; that was something he had not considered. "Perhaps," he said, swallowing, his throat raw from the need to shout to be heard. "But we must leave, Joram! Every moment that passes, our danger grows!"

"*Our* danger!" Joram smiled the half-smile that was nearer a twisted, bitter grimace. "*You* are in no danger, Catalyst! Why don't you just hand me over to your Bishop?" He turned his head away from the catalyst's intense gaze, thrusting the cooling spear-point back into the coals. "You're afraid of me, after all. You're afraid of the darkstone. It was my hand that killed Blachloch. You're innocent of that." Bringing the spear-point back out with his tongs, Joram rested it upon the anvil. For long moments, he stared at it, unseeing. "We'll be going into the Outland," he said, his voice so soft that Saryon had to lean close to hear above the pounding behind him. "You know the danger, the risks we'll face. Especially since neither of us is powerful in magic. Why? Why do you want to go with me?"

Joram returned to his work, keeping his face averted.

Why indeed? Saryon asked himself, staring at the bent head; the strong shoulders, naked in the heat of the forge; the crisp, black hair that had fought loose of its braid and hung down in shining tendrils around the cold, stern young face. There was something in the voice. . . . Thick with fatigue, it was thick with fear. And something else — hope?

Joram is afraid, Saryon realized. He plans to leave the village and he's been trying to get up the courage to go into those strange, savage lands by himself.

Who do I want to go with you, Joram? A burning lump formed in the catalyst's throat, as though he had swallowed one of the hot coals. I could tell you that I held you once in my arms. I could tell you that you rested your small head upon my shoulder, that I rocked you to sleep. I could tell you that you are the Prince of Merilon, heir to the throne, and that I can prove it!

But no, I cannot tell you that now. I don't think I can ever tell you. With this dangerous knowledge and the bitter anger inside you, Joram, you would bring tragedy down upon all of us — your parents, the innocent people of Merilon . . .

Saryon shuddered. No, he repeated. At least I will not be guilty of *that* sin! I will carry the secret to my death. Yet what other reason can I give to this young man? I want to go with you, Joram, because I care about you, what happens to you? How he would sneer at this . . .

"I am going with you," answered Saryon finally, "because I seek to regain my own faith. The Church once stood, for me, as strong as the mountain fastness of the Font. Now I see it crumbling, falling in deceit and greed. I told you that I could not go back to it. I meant that."

Joram turned from his work to face the catalyst. The dark eyes were cool and dispassionate, but Saryon saw a brief flicker of disappointment, a tiny flame of longing to hear something else that was quickly and coldly quenched. The look startled the catalyst, and he wished he'd said the words that had been in his heart. But the moment passed.

"Very well, Catalyst," Joram said coolly. "I think it's a good idea you come with me anyway. I don't trust you out of my sight.

You know too much about the darkstone. Now go back to the cell. Leave me alone. I've got to get this finished."

Saryon sighed. Yes, he'd said the right thing. But how empty it felt. Reaching into his pocket, he drew out the small piece of darkstone. "One thing more. Can you set this in a mounting for me?" the catalyst asked Joram. "And fasten it to a chain so that I can wear it?"

Surprised, Joram took the stone, looking from it to Saryon. The dark eyes were suddenly suspicious. "Why?"

"I believe it will enable me to escape the Bishop's attempt to contact me. It will absorb the magic."

Shrugging, Joram took it. "I'll bring it to you when I return this afternoon."

"It must be soon!" Saryon said nervously. "Before this evening—"

"Do not worry, Catalyst," Joram interrupted. "By this evening, we will be long gone from this place. By the way," he added casually, once again turning to his work, "did you find Mosiah?"

"Yes, he is waiting at the prison, with Simkin."

"So, he didn't leave. . . ." Joram murmured to himself.

"What?"

"We'll take him with us. And Simkin. Go tell them and start making ready."

"No! Not Simkin!" Saryon protested. "Mosiah, perhaps, but not—"

"We'll need magic-users like Simkin and Mosiah, Catalyst," Joram interrupted coldly. "With you to give them Life, and my power with the Darksword, we might live through this yet." He glanced up, dark eyes cold. "I hope that doesn't disappoint you."

Without a word, Saryon turned from Joram and walked back to the front of the forge, carefully avoiding as he did so the place on the floor where the warlock had died. Was that blood there? He fancied he could see a pool of it beneath a bucket, and quickly looked away.

He would not be sorry to leave this place. Though he had come to like the people and understand their way of life, he could never overcome in his soul the repugnance he felt for the Dark Arts of Technology, the repugnance that had been bred in him over a lifetime. He knew of the perils of the Outland—or assumed he did—and thought naively that life among nature would be preferable to a life where man engineered nature.

Where will we go? He didn't know. Sharakan, perhaps—although they might be walking into the midst of a war. It didn't matter. Anywhere would do—as long as it wasn't Merilon.

Yes, he would be glad to go, willing to face the perils of the Outland. But blessed Almin, Saryon thought glumly as he walked back to the prison house.

Why Simkin?

5

Lying in a Manger

"**I** was there. I saw the whole thing, and sink me," said Simkin in hushed, awful tones, "if our Dark and Gloomy Friend didn't plunge his shining sword straight into the warlock's writhing body."

"Good for Joram," Mosiah said grimly.

"Well, actually not 'shining sword,'" Simkin amended, producing an ornate, silver-framed looking glass from the air with a gesture of his hand. Holding it up, he examined his face, meticulously smoothing his soft brown beard with his fingers and deftly twirling the ends of his mustache. "Actually, that sword's the ugliest thing I've seen, not counting the Marchioness of Blackborough's fourth child. Of course, the Marchioness herself is no prize. Everyone who knows her knows that the nose she wears at night is *not* the same nose that she starts out with in the morning."

"What—"

"It's never the same nose twice, you see. She's not very skilled in magic. It's been rumored that she's Dead, but that could never be proved, and then her husband is such a *frightfully* good friend of the Emperor's. And if she would just take a bit of time, who knows? She might get the nose right.

"Simkin, I —"

"Still, I don't understand why she persists in having children, particularly ugly children. 'There ought to be a law against it,' I suggested to the Empress, who quite agreed with me."

"What does the sword look like?" Mosiah managed to insert the sentence as Simkin paused for breath.

"Sword?" Simkin looked at him vaguely. "Oh, yes. Joram's sword, the 'Darksword,' as he calls it. Quite aptly, too, I might add. What does it look like?" The young man pondered, first sending the looking glass away with a snap of his fingers. "Let me think. By the way, do you like my ensemble? I prefer it to the black. I call it *Blood and Gore* in honor of the dear departed."

Mosiah glanced at the blood-red breeches, purple coat, and red satin vest in disgust and nodded.

Adjusting the lace at his wrist — lace that was splotched with red spots, for "that splatter effect" — Simkin sat down upon the cot in the prison house, crossing his well-shaped legs to show off his purple hose to their best advantage.

"The sword," he continued, "looks like a man."

"No!" Mosiah scoffed.

"Yes, Almin's truth," Simkin averred, offended. "A man of iron. A skinny man of iron, mind you, but a man nonetheless. Like so . . ." Rising to his feet, Simkin stood stiffly upright, his ankles together, his arms thrown straight out to either side. "My neck is the handle," he said, stretching his scrawny throat to its utmost. "It has a knob on top for a head."

"You're the one with a knob for a head!" Mosiah snorted.

"Take a look at it, if you don't believe me," Simkin said, collapsing suddenly upon the cot. He yawned. "It's under the mattress, wrapped like a babe in swaddling clothes."

Mosiah's gaze went to the bed, his hands twitched. "No, I couldn't," he said after a moment.

"Suit yourself." Simkin shrugged. "I wonder if they've discovered the body yet. And do you think this is too gaudy for the funeral?"

"What powers did you say the Darksword had?" Mosiah asked, his eyes fixed in fascination upon the bed. Slowly he rose to his feet, crossed the room, and came to stand beside the cot, though he did not venture to touch the mattress. "What did it do to Blachloch?"

"Let me recall," Simkin said languidly, lying down on the cot and putting his arms underneath his head. Staring at his shoes, he frowned and experimentally changed their color from red to purple. "You must realize it was a bit difficult for me to see, situated as I was, hanging from the wall by one wretched nail. I thought about becoming a bucket, they have such better vision than tongs, you know. When I'm tongs, one eye generally gets located on each side. It gives a wide range, but I can't see a thing in the middle. Buckets, on the other hand—"

"Oh, just get on with it!" Mosiah snapped impatiently.

Simkin sniffed and changed his shoes back to red again. "Our Hated and Ruthless Leader was casting a Green Venom spell upon our friend— Ever see that spell in action, by the way?" Simkin asked casually. "Does nasty things to your nervous system. Paralyzes, causes excruciating pain—"

"Poor Joram," said Mosiah softly.

"Yes, poor Joram," Simkin repeated slowly. "He was about done for, Mosiah." The bantering voice was suddenly serious. "I really thought it was all over. Then I noticed the strangest thing. The green venomous light that the spell casts over one's body glowed around Joram everywhere except his hands, where he was holding the Darksword. And, slowly, the glow began to fade from his arms, and was fading from the rest of his body, as well, when our jolly old friend, the catalyst, stepped in and sucked the Life from the warlock. Good thing, too. Most timely. Even though the Darksword was having some sort of reversing effect on Blachloch's spell, it obviously wasn't going to act fast enough to save Joram from being turned into a quivering mass of green pudding."

"So it somehow nullifies the magic," Mosiah said wonderingly. He stared at the bed in longing, irresolute. Glancing out the barred window, he shivered in the chill air. Though it was midafternoon, it had grown no warmer. The weak sun had disappeared completely beneath sullen, gray clouds. It looked and felt as if the clouds had dropped down and were lying on top of the town, slowly smothering the life from it. The streets were empty. There were no guards, no townspeople. Even the noise of the forge had ceased.

Making up his mind, the young man walked swiftly to the cot. Kneeling beside it, he inserted his hands beneath the mattress. Gently, almost reverently, he pulled out the bundle of rags.

Leaning back upon his heels, Mosiah unwrapped the sword and stared at it. The young man's face—the open, honest face of a Field Magus—twisted in repugnance.

"What did I tell you?" Simkin said, rolling over on the cot and propping himself up on one elbow so that he could see. "Beastly looking piece of work, isn't it? I personally wouldn't be caught dead carrying it, though I don't suppose that bothers Joram. Get it," he persisted playfully when Mosiah did not laugh. "Caught Dead?"

Mosiah ignored him. Both fascinated and repulsed, he stared at the sword, unable to withdraw his gaze. It was, in truth, a crude and ugly weapon. Once, long ago, the Sorcerers had made swords of shining beauty and graceful design, with flashing steel blades and gold and silver hilts. Magical swords, they were endowed as well with various properties laid on them by rune and spell. But all swords had been banished in Thimhallan following the Iron Wars. Weapons of evil, they were called by the catalysts, demonic creations of the Dark Art of Technology. The making of steel swords passed out of knowledge. The only swords Joram had seen were pictured in the books he found. And although the young man had some skill in metal work, he was not skilled enough, nor did he have the time or the patience, to craft a weapon such as men of ancient days had carried with pride.

The Darksword that Mosiah held in his hands was made of darkstone, an ore that is black and unlovely. Given life in the fires of the forge, and granted magical Life by the reluctant catalyst Saryon, the Darksword was nothing more than a shaft of metal beaten and pounded and clumsily sharpened by Joram's inexperienced hand. He had no knowledge of how to craft hilt and blade and then join the two together. The sword was made out of one piece of metal and — as Simkin said — it did resemble a human being. The hilt was separated from the blade by a crosspiece that looked like two arms outstretched. Joram had added the bulbous-shaped head at the hilt in an attempt to weight it, causing it to look very much like the body of man turned to stone. Mosiah was about to slide the ugly and unnerving object back beneath the mattress when the door slammed open.

"Put that down!" came a harsh voice.

Startled, Mosiah nearly dropped the weapon.

"Joram!" he said guiltily, turning around. "I was just looking—"

"I said put it down," Joram said gruffly, kicking the door shut behind him. Crossing the cell in a bound, he snatched the sword from Mosiah's unresisting hands. "Don't ever touch it again," he said, glaring at his friend.

"Don't worry," muttered Mosiah, standing up and wiping his hands on his leather breeches as if to wipe off the touch of the metal, "I won't. Ever!" he added feelingly. Giving Joram a dark glance, Mosiah turned from him and went to stare moodily out the window.

The silence of the streets flowed into the cell, settling over them all like an unseen fog. Joram thrust the weapon into a leather sling he had fashioned in a crude imitation of the sword sheaths he had seen in the books. Casting a sideways glance at Mosiah, Joram started to say something, then checked it. He pulled a bag from beneath his bed and began to fill it with his few clothes and what little food there was in the cell. Mosiah heard him but did not look around. Even Simkin was quiet. Contemplating his shoes, he was in the act of changing one to red and the other to purple when there came a soft knock and the door opened.

Saryon stepped inside. No one spoke. The catalyst looked from the flushed, angry face of Joram to the pale face of Mosiah, sighed, and carefully shut the door behind him.

"They've found the body," he reported in low tones.

"Smashing!" cried Simkin, sitting up and swinging his multi-colored feet over the side of the bed. "I must go watch—"

"No," said Joram abruptly. "Stay here. We've got plans to make. We have to get out! Tonight!"

"The devil you say!" Simkin wailed in dismay. "And miss the funeral? After I took such pains—"

"I'm afraid so," Joram said dryly. "Here, Catalyst." He handed Saryon a crude chain from which dangled a piece of dark rock. "Your 'good luck' charm."

Saryon accepted the chain with a grave expression. He held it for a moment, staring down at it, his face growing increasingly pale.

"Father?" asked Mosiah. "What's wrong?"

"Too much," the catalyst replied softly, and, with the same solemn look upon his face, he hung the darkstone around his neck, being careful to tuck the rock beneath the collar of his robes. "Blachloch's men have sealed off the town. No one is to go in or out."

Joram swore a bitter oath.

"Dash it all!" Simkin burst out. "The very devil! It'll be such a wonderful funeral, too. Highlight of the year around here. And the best part," he continued gloomily, "is that the townspeople will undoubtedly take the opportunity to whack a few of Blachloch's henchmen. I was quite looking forward to a nice round of lout-whacking."

"We have to get out of here!" Joram said grimly. Tying his cloak around his neck, he arranged the folds so that the fabric covered the sword, hiding it from sight.

"But why should we leave?" Mosiah protested. "From what Simkin's told me, everyone will believe Blachloch was killed by centaurs. Even his henchmen. And they won't be hanging around long to ask questions. Simkin's right. I've seen how the townspeople are looking at that scum. That's why Blachloch's men have sealed off the town. They're scared! And with good cause! We'll fight them! Drive them out, and then there won't be anything to fear from anyone—"

"Yes, there will," Saryon said, his hand lingering on the amulet. "I have been contacted by Bishop Vanya."

"I bet *he* gets to go to the funeral," sulked Simkin.

"Shut up, fool," Mosiah growled. "What do you mean, 'contacted', Father? How could he?"

Speaking hurriedly, with frequent glances out the window, Saryon told the young men of his conversation with the Bishop, leaving out only what he knew about Joram's true identity.

"We must be gone by nightfall," Saryon concluded. "When Bishop Vanya cannot reach either me or Blachloch, he will know something dire has happened. By nightfall, the *Duuk-tsarith* could be here."

"See? Everyone who's anyone will be at that funeral," said Simkin moodily.

"The *Duuk-tsarith*, here!" Mosiah paled. "We must warn Andon—"

"I have just come from Andon," Saryon interrupted with a sigh. "I tried to make him understand, but I'm not certain I succeeded. Frankly, he's not worried half as much about the *Duuk-tsarith* as he is over the people getting into a fight with Blachloch's men. I don't think the *Duuk-tsarith* will bother the Sorcerers if they do come," Saryon added, seeing Mosiah's concern. "We can assume now that the Order was in constant touch with Blachloch. Had they wanted to destroy the village, they could have done so at a moment's notice. They will be searching for Joram and the darkstone. When they discover he is gone, they will follow his trail. They will follow us. . . ."

"But these people are my friends, like my family," Mosiah persisted. "I can't leave them!" He stared worriedly out the window.

"They're my friends, too," Joram said abruptly. "It's not like we're running out. The best thing we can do for them is to leave."

"Believe me, there's nothing we could do if we stayed, except perhaps bring greater harm to them," Saryon said gently, resting his hand on Mosiah's shoulder. "Bishop Vanya told me once that he wanted to avoid attacking the Sorcerers, if possible. It would be a bitter battle and, no matter how quiet the Church kept it, word would get out and throw the people into a panic. That was why Blachloch was here—to lead the Sorcerers to their own destruction along with Sharakan. Vanya still hopes to carry out his plan. There's not much else he can do."

"But surely Andon won't let them now that he knows—"

"It's not our problem anymore!" Joram interrupted tersely. "It doesn't matter to us. At least, not to me." He cinched the bundle together tightly and slung it over his back. "You and Simkin can stay here if you want."

"And let you and the bald-headed wonder go traipsing off into the wilds alone?" said Simkin indignantly. "I couldn't sleep nights, thinking of it." With a wave of his hand, he shifted his attire. His red clothes changed to an ugly greenish brown. A long gray traveling cloak settled over his shoulders, hip-high leather boots crawled slowly up his legs. A cocked hat with a long, drooping pheasant feather appeared on his head. "Back to *Muck and Mud*," he said gloomily.

"You're not going with us!" Mosiah said.

"Us?" Joram repeated. "I didn't know *we* were going anywhere?"

"You know I'll go," Mosiah retorted.

"I'm glad," Joram said quietly.

Mosiah flushed in pleasure at the unexpected warmth in his friend's voice, but his pleasure didn't last long.

"Of course, *I'm* going," Simkin struck in loftily. "Who else do you have to guide you? I've come and gone safely through the Outland for years. How about you? Do you know the way?"

"Perhaps not," Mosiah said, eyeing Simkin darkly. "But I'd a damn sight rather be lost in the Outland than guided to wherever it is *you've* got in mind. *I* don't want to end up the husband of the Faerie Queen!" he added, with a glance at the catalyst.

Saryon appeared so alarmed at this reminder of a near disastrous adventure he'd had with Simkin as guide, that Joram cut in. "Simkin goes," he said firmly. "Perhaps we could make it through the Outland without him, but he's the only one who can get us in to where we want to go."

The catalyst regarded Joram with concern, having a sudden chilled feeling he knew the young man's destination. But before he could say a word, Joram continued, "Besides, Simkin's magic can help us get past Blachloch's men."

"That's nothing to worry about!" Simkin scoffed. "There's always the Corridors, after all."

"No!" Saryon cried, his voice hoarse with fear. "Would you walk into the arms of the *Duuk-tsarith*?"

"Well, then, I could change us all into rabbits," Simkin offered after a moment's profound thought. "Get away in a hop, skip, and—"

"Father?" called a quavering voice from outside the prison window. "Father Saryon? Are you in there?"

"Andon!" cried the catalyst, flinging open the door. "Name of the Almin, what's the matter?"

The old Sorcerer appeared ready to drop on the spot. His hands trembled, the usually mild eyes were wild, his clothes disordered. "Joram, bring a chair," Saryon ordered, but Andon shook his head.

"No time!" He was gasping for breath, and they realized he had been running. "You must come, Father." The old man clutched at Saryon. "You must talk them out of it! After all these years! They must not fight!"

"Andon," said Saryon firmly, "please, be calm. You will only make yourself ill. That's it. Breathe deeply. Now, tell me what's going on!"

"The smith!" Andon said, his thin chest rising and falling more slowly. "He's planning to attack Blachloch's men!" The old man wrung his hands. "He and his band of young hotheads may already be on their way to the warlock's house! I am thankful to see"—the old man looked at Joram and Mosiah bleakly—"that you are not among them."

"I don't think there's anything I can do, my friend," Saryon started to reply sadly, but Joram caught hold of the catalyst's arm.

"We'll come with you, Andon," he said, giving Saryon a meaningful glance. "You will think of something, I am certain, Catalyst," he continued, nudging Saryon. "The perfect time for one of your sermons." Moving closer, he whispered fiercely, "This is our chance!"

Saryon shook his head. "I don't see—"

"In the confusion, we'll escape!" Joram hissed, exasperated. He glanced quickly at Mosiah and Simkin, both of whom appeared to comprehend his plan at once. At that moment, screams and shouts could be heard, coming from the direction of the forge. Somewhere a child wailed. Window shutters slammed shut, doors were being bolted.

"It's started!" Andon cried in a panic. Hastening out the door, he broke into a tottering run. Joram and Mosiah dashed after him. There was nothing for the catalyst to do but gather up his robes and follow, running as fast as he could to catch up.

"Ah, ha," reflected Simkin, flitting along merrily behind. "Maybe I'll attend a funeral after all."

6

Ambushed!

"**H**ere's the catalyst! I told you the old man would fetch him!"

Saryon heard the words and caught an indistinct impression of movement out of the corner of his eye. He heard Mosiah cry out, then Simkin shriek, "Let loose of me, you great, hairy beast!" Then everything was a confusion of panic, futile struggle, and grunting voices.

"Do as you're told and you won't get hurt."

A hand caught hold of Saryon's wrist, wrenching his arm behind his back. Pain seared like flame from his elbow to his shoulder, and Saryon gasped. But he was astonished to find himself more angry than afraid. Perhaps it was because he sensed the fear of his captors. He could hear it in the harsh, heavy breathing and the husky voices. He could smell it, a rank odor mingled with sweat and the fumes of the false courage Blachloch's men had been gulping down from a wineskin.

The attack was swift and sudden. The warlock's henchmen may not have been smart in many respects, but they were skilled and knowledgeable at their trade. Having been sent to fetch the catalyst, they had seen Andon enter the prison and guessed that the old man would inadvertently deliver Saryon into their hands. Ducking back into an alley, the former henchmen of the late warlock had waited for the group to pass by, and the fight was over practically before it had begun.

Pinned in the grip of one brawny thug, Joram could not reach his sword. Mosiah lay facedown in the street, blood streaming from a cut on his head, a booted foot planted firmly on the back of his neck. The guards flung Andon to one side; the old man lay like a discarded doll in the street, blinking dazedly up at the sky. One man held Saryon, twisting the catalyst's arm painfully behind his back. As for Simkin, he had completely disappeared. The guard who had jumped the gayly clad figure now stood staring at his empty hands in disbelief.

One of the thugs, obviously the leader, glanced around the field of battle to make certain the quarry had been run to the ground. Then, satisfied, he came to stand before Saryon. "Catalyst, grant me Life!" he demanded, making some attempt to imitate the cool, intimidating manner of the late Blachloch.

But these were common criminals, not disciplined *Duuk-tsarith*. Saryon saw the leader's eyes shift nervously from him to the empty street, glancing in the direction of the forge. Sounds of shouts and cries indicated something was going on up there. The Sorcerers were going to war. Saryon shook his head, and the thug lost control.

"Damn it, Catalyst, now!" he shouted, his voice cracking. "Break his arm!" he ordered the man who held Saryon.

"Almin's blood, Catalyst, don't be a fool!" Joram said. "Do as he says. Grant *him* Life."

The man holding Saryon gave his arm another expert twist. Biting his lips to keep from crying out in pain, the catalyst glanced at Joram in astonishment, only to see the young man's dark eyes flick quickly and meaningfully to Mosiah.

"Yes, Father," Mosiah mumbled, his cheek pressed down into the mud and filth of the street by the foot of the guard. Though it was impossible that he could have seen Joram, he had picked up on the subtle emphasis in the voice. "Do as they say. *Grant Life!*"

"Very well," said the catalyst, bowing his head in apparent defeat. The look of relief on the leader's face was almost pathetic.

Trying desperately to concentrate through the pain, Saryon began to repeat the prayer that drew the magic from the world and focused it within his body. Fortunately it was a prayer he had learned as a child, so he did not have to think about it. There was no time to determine the amount of Life he could safely extend to the young man, even if his disordered faculties had been able to make the mathematical calculations. He would have to open the conduit completely, let Life flow unstinted into Mosiah. This would drain the catalyst of energy, but they had no choice. They had one chance, and one chance only. *If this fails,* the catalyst thought with a coolness that amazed him, *it won't matter anyway. Blachloch's men will kill us out of rage and panic.*

In response to his prayer, the magic flowed into the catalyst. There had been a time when this holy feeling of oneness with the world gave Saryon an almost sublime feeling of pleasure. Blachloch had ended that. In granting Life to the warlock — Life that Blachloch had subverted to death — Saryon had come to hate the tingling of the blood, the thrill that went through every nerve. Now he was too tense, too eager to strike back at these murderers, to notice. But he was, once again, enjoying the experience of possessing the magic within him, even though he must soon release it. Suffused with Life, Saryon opened a conduit to Mosiah.

The magic leaped from the catalyst to the young man in a flash of blue light, an occurrence that happens only when the catalyst gives of himself completely to his wizard. The magic crackled in the air. The thug holding Saryon started, slightly loosening his grip. But in that moment, the leader realized he'd been betrayed. The blade of a knife flashed in the late afternoon sun.

Involuntarily raising his arm in a feeble attempt to fend off the attack, Saryon heard a ferocious growl. The thug holding Saryon shouted a warning, and the leader whirled around, his knife raised. He faced Mosiah, but the apparently harmless young man had changed. Fur covered his body, his teeth were fangs, his hands paws, his nails claws. The leaping werewolf crashed into the man, driving him to the ground. The knife flew from his nerveless hand as scream after scream rent the air, then ended suddenly in a horrible gurgling sound.

Turning from its victim, the werewolf's fiery red eyes stared straight at Saryon and the catalyst could not help falling backward, feeling his soul shrivel in primal terror. Blood and saliva dripped from the creature's jaws; a rumbling growl shook its massive chest. But the eyes were not on Saryon, they were on the guard crouching behind the catalyst, pitifully attempting to use the catalyst's body as a shield. Hands shoved Saryon from behind, propelling him forward into the teeth of the animal. But the werewolf leaped nimbly to one side. The catalyst fell heavily on his hands and knees. The werewolf sprang past him, and Saryon heard the thug's high-pitched wail of terror and a savage growl of triumph.

Dazed and hurting, drained of all energy, Saryon watched the battle raging around him in a dreamlike state, unable to react. He saw Joram kick a dagger from the hand of the man who had been holding him, and round upon the thug with a clumsy swing. The flailing fist missed its mark and the thug landed a blow to the young man's jaw. Joram stumbled backward, fumbling for his sword. The guard pressed his advantage, jumping on him, when a broom appeared out of nowhere and began to pummel the guard viciously.

"Take that, you lout!" the broom shrieked grimly, coming at the astounded man from every conceivable angle, striking him on the head and whacking him across the backside. Thrusting itself in between the thug's legs, it tripped him, sending him sprawling. Lying in the street, the thug covered his head with his hands, but the broom kept at him, crying "lout!" with every blow.

The catalyst had the vague impression that their attackers were fleeing. He tried to stand, but there came a roaring in his ears; he felt sick and faint. Hands that were strong yet surprisingly gentle helped him to his feet. Though the words were cold as always, he felt more than heard an underlying warmth of concern that startled him.

"Are you all right?"

Weak and dizzy, the catalyst looked into Joram's face. What he expected to see — from the tone — he wasn't certain. Flesh and blood, perhaps. Instead he saw stone.

"Are you all right, Catalyst?" the young man repeated coldly. "Can you walk, or must we carry you?"

Saryon sighed. "No, I can walk," he said, pushing himself away from the young man with quiet dignity.

"Good," Joram remarked. "Go see to the old man."

He gestured at Andon, who was on his feet staring around him in sorrow. Three of the thugs lay in the street; the others had run off, leaving their fallen comrades behind. Two of the guards were dead, their bodies mauled, their necks broken by the snapping jaws of the werewolf. Saryon was surprised that he felt no regret, only a grim kind of satisfaction that shocked him.

A third man lay some distance away, alive and groaning, his face and head covered with red welts. Broomstraws stuck out of his clothing like scrawny feathers. Simkin stood over him.

"Lout," he muttered, administering a swift kick.

The henchman moaned, and covered his head with his arms. Sniffing, Simkin pulled the orange silk from the air and mopped his brow. "Dreadful melee," he remarked. "I'm perspiring."

"You!" Mosiah — back to his own form — sat on a doorstop, panting in the manner of the werewolf he had been. The cut on his head bled freely, his face was covered with dirt and grime and sweat, his clothes were torn. Leaning back wearily against the door, he tried to catch his breath. "I've never . . . experienced any magic . . . like that before!" he admitted, sucking in air. Shutting his eyes, he put his hand to his head. "I'm so . . . dizzy . . ."

"The feeling will pass soon," said Saryon gently. "I had no idea you were such a powerful magus," the catalyst added as he went to offer what empty words of comfort he could to the distraught Andon.

"Neither did I," Mosiah remarked in a kind of awe. "I . . . I don't remember even thinking about it. It's just — Simkin said something about a great, hairy beast and the image was in my mind and then the magic filled me! It was like the Life of everything around me was pouring into me, surging through me. I felt a hundred times more alive! And I —"

"Oh, who cares!" Joram broke in impatiently. "Just shut up about it! We've got to get out of this damned place!"

Mosiah fell silent abruptly, swallowing his words. He rose to his feet without a word, his eyes flashing in anger. Andon stared at Joram in wonder. Simkin — embarrassed — began to hum a little tune. Only Saryon understood. He, too, felt the sharp tooth of envy gnaw at him. He, too, knew what it was to be jealous of those blessed with the gift of Life.

No one spoke, but stared at each other uneasily, nobody seeming to quite know what to do. It was all unreal, dreamlike. The sun, setting in a fiery blaze, cast long fingers of red through the streets. Flame flared from the windowpanes of the ugly brick dwellings. It flashed off the glazed eyes of the dead. At the forge, it glistened brightly on the metal of knife and spear-point, arrow-tip and dagger. Farther off, in the center of the village, they could hear the shouts growing louder.

"Joram's right," Saryon said finally, trying to shake off the disquieting feeling of both standing in this place and being somewhere else at the same time. "The sun is setting and we must be gone before evening."

"Gone?" Andon came back to reality, staring at the catalyst in bewilderment. "But you can't go, Father! Listen!" The wrinkled, gentle face twisted in fear. "Our peaceful life is ended! They're—"

At that moment, the sound of a gong rang out, booming, angry.

"The Scianc!" Andon cried, grief contorting his face.

Nine times the gong dinned, its vibrations jarring body and mind. Saryon felt the shock come up from through his feet, and wondered if the earth itself shivered in rage.

"It's war," Joram said grimly. "Which way, Simkin?"

"This way, down the alley," Simkin said, pointing, his usually flighty manner disappearing into the air with the orange silk. He was off at a run.

"C'mon! We better keep up!" Joram urged. "We'll lose sight of him."

"Only if we're lucky," Mosiah growled. Hurriedly, he shook hands with the old man. "Good-bye, Andon. Thank you for everything."

"Yes, thank you," Joram said briefly, his dark-eyed gaze going toward the forge. The sounds of battle were louder, coming closer. After a last look Joram started down the alley with Mosiah. The figure of Simkin could bearly be seen in the twilight, the feather in his cap fluttering in the air like a banner. He half-turned. "Hurry up, Saryon!"

"Yes, go along. I'll catch up," the catalyst said, reluctant to leave, afraid to stay. Andon seemed to know something of what he was feeling.

The old man smiled wanly. "I know why you are leaving, and I suppose I should be grateful that you are taking the darkstone away from us. At least we will be spared that temptation." He sighed. "But I am sorry to see you go. The Almin walk with you, Father," he said softly.

Saryon attempted to return the blessing, but the words would not come to his lips. It was said that in the ancient world, those who had sold their souls to the powers of darkness were physically unable to speak the name of God.

"Catalyst!" came Joram's irritated shout.

Saryon turned and left the old man without a word. Looking back from the shadows of the alley as twilight closed over them, he saw Andon standing in the street beside the bodies of the dead henchmen, his head bowed, shoulders slumped. The old Sorcerer's hands covered his eyes, and the catalyst knew that he wept.

7

The Outland

Leaving the Sorcerers' village, Simkin led his charges north through a ravine filled with thick brush, canopied by broad-leafed trees. Twilight deepened to night swiftly among the trees and it was "as dark as the inside of a demon's eyelids," as Simkin put it. Walking through the dense tangle of vegetation became difficult, and, on occasion, almost impossible. Though Joram argued against it, the others insisted upon light.

"Blachloch's men have other things to worry about, from the sounds of it," Mosiah said grimly, pulling thorns from his legs where he'd crashed headlong into a gorse bush in the darkness. "One of us could break an ankle or maybe even tumble into a hole and vanish completely in this godforsaken place! I'd rather take my chances on torchlight."

"Torchlight!" Simkin snorted. "How primitive you think, dear boy!"

Huge moths with green-glowing wings appeared in the air. Fluttering above them, the gleaming moths shed a warm, soft light that extended outward in a surprisingly wide radius.

Unfortunately, after one look into the wild- and forbidding-looking forest through which they traveled, Saryon was considerably more frightened than he had been stumbling about it in the dark.

They continued walking down the gully until its sharp-thorned bushes opened out suddenly into a swamp. Giant trees rose from the mists of a thick fog; their roots — exposed by the water — looked like claws in the eerie light cast by the glowing moths. At the sight of this, Simkin called a halt.

"Keep to the high ground on your left," he said, from his position in the lead. He waved a hand vaguely. "Don't fall in. Nasty sort of mud in that beastly pool. Grabs hold and won't let go."

"We better not try that 'til daylight," Joram said wearily, and it suddenly occurred to Saryon that the young man must be near dropping over from exhaustion. The catalyst was bone tired, but at least he'd been able to rest some during the day.

"Certainly," said Simkin with a shrug. "I don't *think* anything's liable to munch on us during the night," he added ominously.

"I'm too tired to care one way or the other," Joram muttered.

They made their way back down into the gully and found a relatively dry place to spend the night. Taking off the Darksword, Joram laid it on the frozen ground, then made his bed beside it. Lying down, sighing in weariness, he rested his hand upon his sword and closed his eyes.

"Simkin, where are we headed, anyway?" Mosiah asked in a whisper.

Rousing himself, Joram looked up at them. "Merilon," he said, and the next moment was fast asleep.

Mosiah glanced at Saryon, who shook his head.

"I feared as much. He must be persuaded from this course. Joram must *not* go to Merilon!" The catalyst repeated this several times, his hands rubbing back and forth on the worn cloth of his robe.

Mosiah shifted uneasily, but said nothing.

Saryon sighed. He could expect no help from this ally, he could see that now — and this was his *only* ally.

The catalyst knew that Mosiah agreed with him in his head, but it was the young man's heart that kept his tongue silent in the matter. Mosiah, too, longed to see Merilon the Beautiful — the fabled, enchanted city of dreams.

Saryon sighed again, and saw Mosiah's face grow tense; evidently fearing that the catalyst would take up the matter once more.

Saryon didn't bring up his arguments, however. He kept silent, glancing about nervously, all his fears and terrors of the wilderness returning to him.

"Goodnight, Father," Mosiah said awkwardly, resting his hand on Saryon's shoulder. "I'll help you argue with Joram in the morning, though I don't think it will do much good."

He went over to lie down upon the cold ground, huddling near Joram for warmth. Within moments, he, too, was asleep— sleeping the sleep of youthful innocence. The catalyst stared at him in gloomy jealousy. Then Simkin sent the moths away, and the night returned. The darkness seemed to crawl out from the clawed trees, obliterating everything from sight. Saryon shivered in the chill air.

"I'll keep watch," Simkin offered. "I slept all day, and whacking that lout quite stirred up my blood. Put your bald head to bed, Father."

Saryon was tired, so tired that he hoped sleep might overwhelm him, shutting down the waterwheel of thoughts that cranked over and over in his mind. But the terrors of the wilderness and the sound of Joram's voice saying "Merilon" flowed through the catalyst's brain and kept the wheels turning.

The bitter-cold winds of approaching evening rustled the few dead leaves still clinging stubbornly to the trees. Clutching his robes close about him, Saryon tried to shake off the growing feelings of gloom and despair. He told himself they were due to his fatigue and the horror over the death of the warlock that was only gradually beginning to fade from his mind.

But he wasn't succeeding, and now this announced decision of Joram's made matters worse.

Saryon shifted restlessly, shivering with cold and fear. The slightest noise made him cringe in terror. Were those eyes, staring at him from the shadows? He sat up in alarm, looking wildly around for Simkin. The young man was sitting peacefully on a tree stump. Saryon fancied he could see Simkin's eyes shining in the darkness like an animal's, and they appeared to be watching him with amusement. The catalyst huddled back down in his robes, shut his own eyes against the night, and tried to take his mind off his fear and cold by going over and over what he intended to say to Joram tomorrow.

Eventually, the wheel bogged down and ceased to turn. The catalyst drifted into a dream-haunted, restless sleep. His hand went reassuringly to the darkstone that hung around his neck, and he realized, sleepily, that the ore's power had apparently worked.

Bishop Vanya had not contacted him.

Saryon woke next morning, aching and stiff. Though he was not hungry, he forced himself to eat. "Joram," he said reluctantly, mechanically chewing and swallowing stale bread, "we must talk."

"Brace yourself, my friend," said Simkin cheerfully, "Father Spoilsport intends to talk you out of going to Merilon."

Joram's face darkened, his expression grew stern, and Saryon cast an irritated glance at the mischievous Simkin, who simply grinned innocently and sat back upon his stump, legs crossed, to enjoy the fun.

"Bishop Vanya will expect you to go to Merilon, Joram!" Saryon argued. "He knows about Anja and her promise that you would find fame and fortune there. He'll be waiting, and so will the *Duuk-tsarith*!"

Joram listened in silence, then he shrugged. "The *Duuk-tsarith* are everywhere," he said coolly. "It seems that I am in danger no matter where I go. Isn't that true?"

Saryon could not deny it.

"Then, I will go to Merilon," Joram said calmly. "My birthright is in that city, according to my mother, and I intend to claim it!"

Oh, if only you knew what you truly meant! Saryon thought bitterly. You are not the illegitimate son of some poor, deluded girl and her hapless lover. You do not need to go back a beggar, returning to lay claim on a family who spurned their daughter and turned her from their door seventeen years before.

No. You could go back a prince. To be wept over by your Empress mother, to be embraced in the arms of your Emperor father. . . .

To be condemned to death, dragged by the *Duuk-tsarith* to the Borders of Thimhallan, to the magic-guarded, mistenshrouded edges of the world, and there cast out.

"The soul of this unfortunate is Dead." Saryon imagined Bishop Vanya's voice echoing through the chill, dank fog. "Let now the physical body join the soul and provide this wretched being with his only chance for salvation."

I must tell Joram the truth, Saryon thought desperately. Surely that will dissuade him from going!

"Joram," he said, his heart pounding so he could barely talk. "Joram, there is something I have to—"

But the catalyst's logical mind stepped in.

Go ahead, his brain told him. Tell Joram he is the son of the Emperor. Tell him he can walk in and claim the title Prince of Merilon. Is that going to *stop* him from going there? Where would be the first place *you'd* go if you heard that news?

"Well, what now, Catalyst?" Joram said impatiently. "If you have anything to say, say it and quit muttering to yourself. Although, I warn you, you are wasting your breath. My mind is made up. I am going to Merilon, and no words of yours will change that!"

Yes, he is right, Saryon realized. Biting back his words, he swallowed them like bitter medicine.

And they continued on toward Merilon.

As far as Saryon could recall, the next five days were the most miserable of his life. The swamp took three days to traverse. The smell of the place made the stomach turn and left an oily taste in the mouth that completely killed the appetite. Although there was no lack of pure water—even children can work that simple magic—the putrid smell of the swamp made the water taste bitter and tainted. Their thirst never seemed quenched, no matter how much they drank. And not even magic could start a fire that would burn the wet wood. They never saw the sun, were never warm. Tendrils of perpetual fog coiled about them, haunting the imagination. Nothing materialized out of that fog, but they had the feeling they were being watched. This was made worse by Simkin's frightful hints.

"What's all that sniffing you're doing?" Mosiah asked grumpily, plunging through the marshy grass behind Simkin. "Don't tell me you're determining the direction we're heading by smell!"

"Not the direction. The path," corrected Simkin.

"Oh, come on! How can you tell the path by smell? And how can you smell anything besides rot in this awful place, anyhow?" Mosiah stopped to wait for the weary catalyst to catch up with them.

"It's not the path I smell so much as *what's* making the path up ahead of us," Simkin said. "You see, I don't believe It is likely to misstep and lose Itself in the swamp, having been brought up around here. But then, I always say it is better to be safe than sorry."

"It? What It? Why are we following an It?" Mosiah started to ask in alarm, but Simkin clapped his hand over his friend's mouth.

"There, there. Mustn't worry. Generally, It sleeps through the day quite soundly. Exhausts Itself during the night—all that ripping and tearing with Its fangs and those great, ugly claws. Don't mention It to the bald party," he murmured into Mosiah's ear. "Nervous enough. Never get anywhere."

And as if these terrifying hints weren't bad enough, there were occasional alarms from their "guide" as well.

"Look! Ahead of us!" Simkin cried, grabbing Mosiah and clinging to him, trembling in every limb of his body.

"What?" Mosiah's heart leaped into his throat, the expression "great, ugly claws" having left an indelible impression on his mind.

"There! Don't you see It?"

"No—"

"Look! Those eyes! All six of 'em! Ah, gone now." Simkin heaved a sigh of relief. Dragging forth the orange silk, he mopped his brow. "Lucky thing, too. We must have been up-wind of It. Fortunately It doesn't have a very keen sense of smell. Or was that hearing? I always get those mixed up. . . ."

Either It knew where It was going or their "guide" did, because they reached the end of the swamp safely at last, coming out at the bottom of a box canyon. So thankful were they to be out of the horrid place and away from the stench that the prospect of a steep climb up into the rocky cliffs towering above them appeared an inviting one. The path was clearly marked— Mosiah wisely refrained from asking Simkin who or what had marked it—and in the beginning it wasn't difficult to follow. Breathing crisp, cold air and feeling the sunlight upon their faces again gave them added energy. Even the catalyst cheered up and kept pace with them.

But the trail grew more indistinct the farther they went, and the way grew steeper.

After two days of clambering over rockfalls, backtracking to find the trail, and sleeping out on windswept, exposed ledges, Saryon was so exhausted that he walked in a somnambulic state half the time, starting to wakefulness when he stumbled off the path or felt Mosiah's guiding hand upon his arm. He managed to keep going only by setting his mind to walking — putting one foot in front of the other — and shutting it off to the cold and the pain of both body and mind. In this state, he often staggered on when the others had stopped to rest, and when they had caught him and brought him back, he slumped down on the ground, his head on his knees, and dreamed he was walking still.

Eventually, however, the exercise and the fresh air gave the catalyst what he had long been needing — nights of sleep so deep that not even the memory of the dying warlock or the aching of his sore muscles could penetrate it. One morning, on the fifth day of their journey, he woke to find his head clear and, other than stiffness in his joints and sharp pain in his back from lying on the ground, he felt unusually refreshed.

It was then he noticed that they were traveling in the wrong direction.

8

The Glade

They were on top of the cliffs now, looking down into thick, rolling woodland. The morning sun, which should have been shining directly in their eyes as they walked, was rising to its zenith from their right.

We're heading almost due north, toward Sharakan, Saryon realized. Merilon, if that was still their goal, lay much farther to the east. Should I say something? he wondered uneasily. Perhaps Joram has come to his senses, changed his mind and decided not to go to Merilon after all. Perhaps he's too proud to admit to the rest of us he might have been wrong. Or perhaps he made the decision, discussed it with the others, and I was just simply too exhausted to pay it any heed. Saryon tried to remember if he had heard the young men talking about a change in direction, but so thick had been his fatigue that all memories of the last few days were hazy and distorted.

Rather than appear foolish, the catalyst decided not to mention the matter, hoping something would happen to explain it. Simkin led them down the cliffs, into the forest below. At first, all of them were thankful to see that it wasn't swamp but thick woods. They felt less cheerful about the forest on entering it, however. Although it was winter, the trees unaccountably retained their leaves. A sickly brown color, the foliage smelled of decay. The trail they were following was overrun with a broad-leafed vine that twined among the trunks of the tall trees, blocking their way.

"There's something about this plant . . . Can't remember what, though," Simkin mused, staring at it. "I think maybe it's edible. . . ."

Mosiah stepped gingerly in among the tangle of the vines. Instantly the leaves wrapped around his ankles, tripped him, and pulled him headfirst into it.

"Help me!" he shouted wildly. Long thorns emerged, digging into his flesh, and Mosiah began to scream in pain. Drawing the Darksword, Joram waded into the plant, slashing at it with the blade. At the sword's touch, the vine's leaves blackened and curled up. The vine — with seeming reluctance — loosed its victim. They dragged Mosiah out, bleeding, but otherwise unharmed.

"It was sucking my blood!" he said, shuddering and staring at the plant in horror.

"Ah, I forgot," said Simkin. "A Kij vine. It considers *us* edible. Well, I knew it had something to do with food," he added defensively, as Mosiah glared at him.

They trudged on, Joram going ahead to clear the path with the Darksword.

Saryon watched the young men closely, hoping to catch some hint of their plans. Joram and Mosiah seemed content to follow Simkin's lead, and, strolling unconcernedly in his *Dirt and Dung* or *Mud and Muck* attire, Simkin led them confidently wherever it was they were going. He never hesitated, never appeared lost. The paths he found among the winding labyrinth of Kij vines were easy to follow — too easy. Mosiah pointed out more than once where bones had been stacked in a deliberate manner to mark the trail. Centaur tracks could be seen in the frozen mud. Once they came to a place where all the vines had been smashed flat and several tall trees snapped off like twigs.

"A giant," said Simkin. "Good thing we weren't around when he came through. They're not very bright, you know, and — while not dangerous — they *are* fond of playing with humans. Unfortunately, they have a nasty habit of breaking their toys."

Every time they came to a break in the trees, and the sun was visible, Saryon saw that they were still heading due north. And no one said a word.

Perhaps Joram and Mosiah have no idea where Merilon is, the catalyst thought. Both were raised in a Field Shaper village on the borders of the Outland. Joram can read, having been taught the skill by Anja. But has he ever seen a map of the world? Does he trust Simkin implicitly?

That was hard to believe — Joram didn't trust anyone. But the more Saryon listened and watched, the more the catalyst began to think this was the case. Their talk almost always centered around Merilon.

Mosiah told childhood stories about the crystal city floating upon planes of magic. Simkin regaled them with more incredible tales about life in court. On rare occasions when a talkative mood was on him, Joram contributed stories of his own, tales he had heard from Anja.

Having lived in Merilon many years, Saryon was most touched by these stories of Anja's. There was a sadness and a poignancy in them — the memories of an exile — that brought visions of the city to the catalyst's eyes. In them, he saw a Merilon he recognized, certainly different from Mosiah's faerie tale and Simkin's imagination.

But if Joram hadn't changed his mind, why was Simkin guiding them the wrong way?

Not for the first time, the catalyst studied Simkin as they trudged after him through the forest, trying to guess his game. And, as before, Saryon had to admit utter defeat. Not only was it impossible to figure from the young man's play what cards he held, the catalyst had seen with his own eyes that Simkin could literally pull tricks out of the air.

Older than the other two, probably in his early twenties (though he could easily pass for anything from seventy to fourteen if he chose), Simkin was a mystery. A man who shifted stories of his past as often as he shifted his clothes, a man in whom the magic of the world sparkled through his veins like wine, a man of disarming charm, outlandish lies, and an irreverent attitude toward everything in life including death, Simkin was liked by all and trusted by none.

"No one takes him seriously," said Saryon to himself. "And I have a feeling that more than one person has lived to regret it — if he was lucky, that is." The disturbing thought helped the catalyst make up his mind.

"I am thankful you have reconsidered journeying to Merilon, Joram," Saryon said quietly one day when they had stopped to rest for lunch.

"I haven't reconsidered," Joram said, his gaze focusing on the catalyst with immediate suspicion.

"Then, we are traveling the wrong direction," Saryon said gravely. "We're heading north, toward Sharakan. Merilon lies almost due east. If we turned we would—"

"—run smack into the realm of the Faerie Queen," Simkin interrupted. "Perhaps our celibate friend has dreams of returning to her perfumed bower—"

"I do not!" Saryon snapped, his face—and, it must be admitted, his blood—burning at the memories of the wild, beautiful, half-naked Elspeth.

"We can turn east, if you like, O Frigid Father," Simkin continued, staring nonchalantly into the tops of the trees. "There is a path, not far from here, that will take you back into the swamp you enjoyed so much. It will lead you, eventually, to the ring of mushrooms and, on the way, takes you deep into the heart of the centaur country for a fascinating look at these savage creatures—a very brief look before they rip your eyes out of your skull, of course. If you survive that, there are interesting and entertaining side trips into dragons' lairs, chimeras' caves, griffins' nests, wyverns' lodgings, *and* giant's hovels, not to forget the fauns, satyrs, and other beasties . . ."

"You mean you are taking us this way because it's safer," said Mosiah impatiently.

"Egad, of course," replied Simkin, looking hurt. "I'm not so fond of walking *or* your company that I'd prolong this journey, dear boy. By avoiding the river, where most of the nasties lurk, we save in skin what we expend in boot leather. When we reach the northern border of the Outland, we'll veer east."

It sounded plausible, even Mosiah admitted that, and Saryon made no further objection. But still he wondered. He wondered, too, if Joram had been aware of this or if he had been blindly following Simkin.

Characteristically, the taciturn young man said nothing, his silence implying that he had planned this out with Simkin long beforehand. But Saryon had detected a brief flicker of alarm in the dark eyes when the catalyst first questioned Simkin, and he guessed that Joram had been sleeping with his eyes open, as the saying went. And a certain grim tightening of Joram's mouth when Simkin next spoke indicated to Saryon that this wouldn't happen again.

They journeyed deeper into the forest and, by the seventh day in the Outland, the spirits of all of them began to darken. The sun abandoned them, as though it found this land too dark and dismal to bother brightening. Day after day of traveling beneath slate-gray skies that darkened sullenly into pitch-black night cast a pall over the group.

There seemed no end to the trees, and the murderous Kij vines were everywhere. There were no animal sounds; undoubtedly nothing could live long among the carnivorous plants. But each man had the distinct feeling he was being watched and continually looked over a shoulder or whirled around to confront something that was never there.

There were no more stories of Merilon. No one talked at all, except out of necessity. Joram was sullen and morose, Simkin insufferable, Saryon frightened and unhappy, and Mosiah angry at Simkin. Everyone was tired, footsore, and nervous. They kept watch by night in pairs, staring fearfully into the darkness that seemed to be staring right back.

Day after weary day dragged past. The woods went on and on; the Kij vines never lost an opportunity to pierce flesh and drink blood. Saryon was trudging along the path, head down, not bothering to look where he was going, not caring since it was bound to look just the same as where he'd been, when suddenly Mosiah — ahead of him — came to a stop.

"Father!" he said in a low voice, clutching Saryon's arm as the catalyst drew near him.

"What is it?" Saryon's head snapped up, fear tingled in his veins.

"There!" Mosiah pointed. "Ahead of us. Doesn't that look like . . . sunshine?"

Saryon stared. Joram, coming up beside him, looked ahead as well.

Around them stood the tall trees. Below them crawled the Kij vines. Above them, the sky was dull, dreary gray. But ahead of them, not far off — perhaps half a mile — they could see what appeared to be warm, yellow light filtering through the trunks of the trees.

"I think you're right," Saryon said softly, as though speaking aloud might cause it to vanish. He hadn't realized, until this moment, how much he longed to see sunshine, to feel its warmth ease the chill from his bones. He looked for Simkin. "What is that?" he asked, gesturing ahead. "Have we reached the end of this wretched forest?"

"Uh," said Simkin, appearing ill at ease, "I'm not quite certain. Better let me check." And before anyone could stop him, he had disappeared, cloak, boots, hat, feather, and all.

"I knew it!" Mosiah said grimly. "He's gotten us lost and he won't admit it! Well, it doesn't matter. I'm not going to wait here in this horrible forest one moment longer."

He and Joram plunged forward, hacking grimly at Kij vines with renewed effort. Saryon hurried after them.

The light grew brighter the closer they came. It was about midday, the sun would be at its zenith, and the catalyst thought longingly of warmth and light and an end to the oppressive trees and the blood-sucking plants. As they drew nearer, he heard a welcome sound—the sound of fresh water, splashing over rocks. Where there was fresh water, there might be fresh food: fruits and nuts—no more clumsily conjured, tasteless bread, no more water that tasted like Kij vine.

Throwing caution to the wind, the group hurried forward, no longer caring if anything or anyone was watching them. Saryon believed he might well give his life for the warmth of sunlight on his face one last time.

Bursting through the trees, the men came to a stop, staring in awe.

Sunlight from a cloudless sky beamed down through a break in the forest canopy. The sun sparkled upon a cascade of blue water falling from a high cliff, danced in the ripples of a shallow stream. It formed rainbows in steam that drifted above a bubbling pool. It shone down upon a glade filled with tall grass and sweet flowers.

"Thank the Almin," breathed the catalyst.

"No, wait!" Simkin appeared suddenly, out of nowhere. "Don't go in. This isn't supposed to be here."

"So this is not supposed to be here!" Mosiah muttered lazily.

Three of them, Mosiah, Joram, and Saryon, lay in the tall grass, reveling in its warm, fragrant sweetness, sated with the luscious fruit they had found growing on bushes lining the hot springs.

"If anything, this place is more real than he is!"

Although Simkin protested even entering the glade — "I tell you, it wasn't here the last time I was" — the other three were determined to camp here for the night.

"We'll keep low," Joram told him impatiently when Simkin's vague hints became too ridiculous to tolerate. "It's actually safer in this grass. We'll see and hear anything that enters this glade long before it gets to us!"

Simkin fell into a sulking silence. Trailing after the rest as they entered the sunlit glade, he moodily ripped off the heads of flowers. The others drank their fill of the cool water from the falls, bathed in the warm spring, and hungrily devoured the fruit. Then they spread their blankets beneath a giant tree at the glade's edge, resting in the tall grass, a feeling of comradeship enveloping them in its warmth.

But Simkin spent the time prowling about restlessly. He fidgeted in the grass, kept starting up to peer into the woods, and changed his clothes from one garish color to another.

"Ignore him," Mosiah said, as he saw Saryon watching the young man, a worried expression on the catalyst's face.

"He's acting strangely," Saryon said.

"Since when is that anything new!" Mosiah retorted. "Tell us about Merilon, Father. You're the one who's lived there and you've never said a word. I know you don't exactly approve of us going. . . ."

"I know. I've been sulking as badly as Simkin." Saryon smiled. Feeling comfortably weary, he began to talk at length about the Merilon he remembered — telling of the beauty of the crystal Cathedral and the wonders of the city. He described the fanciful carriages drawn by huge squirrels or peacocks or swans that flew in the air upon the wings of magic, carrying their noble passengers up into the clouds to make their daily appearances in the crystal palace of the Emperor. He told about the Grove where stood the Tomb of Merlyn, the great wizard who had led his people to this world. He spoke of the enchanted sunsets, the weather that was always spring or summer, the days when it rained rose petals to sweeten the air.

Mosiah listened open-mouthed, propped up against a tree. Joram, lying prone, turned his face toward the sun, an unusually relaxed expression softening the sharp, angular lines. He listened with apparent enjoyment, a dreamy look in the dark eyes, perhaps seeing himself riding in one of those carriages.

Suddenly Simkin popped out from behind a tree, interrupting the catalyst, staring into the glade with an intense frown.

"Lie down, you're driving us crazy," Mosiah said irritably.

"If I did lie down, I'd never get up," Simkin responded in ill humor. "You'd find me bored stiff by nightfall, just as we found the Duke d'Grundie after one of the Emperor's speeches. Had to soak him in a vat of wine to limber him up."

"Go ahead, Father," Mosiah said. "Tell us more about Merilon. Ignore this fool."

"No need," said Simkin loftily. "I'm leaving. I tell you again I don't like this place!"

With a toss of his head — which now sported a green pointed hat with a long pheasant feather dangling down his green-cloaked back — Simkin left the campsite, disappearing into the wilderness.

"He's in an odd mood," the catalyst remarked thoughtfully. Noticing that he had spread his blanket down over a protruding tree root that was poking him uncomfortably in the back, Saryon stood up and shifted his blanket to another location. "Perhaps we shouldn't have let him go. . . ."

"How do you propose to stop him?" Joram asked lazily, tossing bits of bread from his pack to a raven. The bird had been perched in the branches of the tree under which they lay, and now fluttered down to the ground to accept the food with a condescending air. So comfortable were they that no one thought to wonder why this bird was here, when they had seen no animal for days.

"Oh, Simkin's all right," said Mosiah, watching the bird's dignified strutting with a smile. "He's just mad because he's lost and won't admit it. Go on about Merilon, Father. Tell about the floating platforms of stone and the Guild Houses —"

"If he's lost, so are we!" Saryon's peaceful mood was broken. The sunlight in the glade was suddenly too hot, too bright. It was giving him a headache.

"Don't start on Simkin again, Catalyst!" said Joram, scowling and accidentally hitting the bird with a hunk of bread. Squawking indignantly, the raven flew up into the tree again, where it sat moodily pruning its ruffled feathers. "I'm sick and tired of you two —"

"Hush!"

Seemingly coming out of the empty air, the voice startled all of them. Mosiah cast a wild glance at the bird, but before he could react, Simkin materialized in the center of the glade, his hat askew, his thin, sharp face pale beneath the soft beard.

"What is it?" Joram was on his feet, his hand reaching instinctively for the Darksword.

"Down! Hide!" Simkin gasped, pulling him back into the tall grass.

The rest followed, flopping down flat on their stomachs, hardly daring to breath.

"Centaurs?" Mosiah asked in a choked whisper.

"Worse!" Simkin hissed. *"Duuk-tsarith!"*

9

Caught!

"**D**uuk-tsarith!" Mosiah gasped.
"But that's impossible!"
Saryon whispered. "They could never have tracked us; the Darksword shields us! Are you certain?"

"Almin's blood, Hairless One," sputtered Simkin, staring at them wild-eyed from among the tall grass. "Of course, I'm certain! Granted, it's a bit hard to see in the dark woods, of course, especially if the parties you are observing are all wearing *black robes*. But if you'd like, I can return and ask them —"

At that moment, the raven gave a loud caw that sounded exactly like raucous laughter and flew from the trees. "Or better yet, ask him," Simkin said with grim irony. "How long has that bird been here?"

Shaking his head, Saryon sighed. Sprawled flat, he still felt little protection from the tall grass, and hugged the ground as though he could crawl into it. The forest was more than a hundred feet away. They might make a run for it.

"Name of the Almin, what do we do now?" Mosiah asked urgently.

"Leave!" said the catalyst urgently. "Get out of here quickly —"

"That won't do any good!" Simkin retorted. "They know we're here, and they're not far away — in the woods on the other side of the waterfall. There's two of them, at least. They've obviously been watching us through the eyes of their little feathered friend. Where can we go that he can't spot us — unless we use the Corridors —"

"No!" Saryon said hastily, his face pale. "That would be throwing ourselves into their hands."

"This time I agree with the Priest," Joram said abruptly. "You forget that I am Dead. Once in the Corridors, they would have me trapped."

"Then, what do we do?" Mosiah asked, his voice too shrill. "We can't run, we can't hide. . . ."

"Shush. We attack," Joram replied.

The dark eyes were cool; a half smile touched the full lips. His face, seen from its hiding place among the grass, looked almost bestial.

"No!" Saryon said emphatically, shuddering.

"Excellent idea, really," whispered Simkin in excitement. "The raven will tell them that we're alerted to their presence. They'll expect us to run and probably have their plans laid for that. What they *won't* expect us to do is circle around and attack them!"

"It's *Duuk-tsarith* we're talking about!" Saryon reminded them bitterly.

"We have surprise and we have the Darksword!" returned Joram.

"Blachloch nearly destroyed you!" Saryon cried softly, clenching his fist.

"I've learned from that! Besides, what choice do we have?"

"I don't know!" Saryon murmured brokenly. "I just don't want any more killing. . . ."

"It's them or us, Father." Bringing his hands together, Mosiah spoke a few words. There was a shimmer of air as a bow and quiver of arrows materialized in his grasp. "Look at this," he said proudly. "I've been studying war spells. We all were, back in the village. And I know how to use it. With you to grant me Life, and Joram and the Darksword —"

"We better hurry," urged Simkin, "before they lay any spells of entrapment or enchantment on the glade itself."

"If you don't want to come, Father," said Mosiah, "just grant me Life here. You can stay —"

"No, Joram's right," Saryon said in low tones. "If you insist on this madness, I'm coming. You might need me for . . . for other things. I can do more than grant Life," he said with a meaningful glance at Joram. "I can take it away, as well."

"Follow me, then!" whispered Simkin. Rising to a half crouch, he began to creep slowly through the tall grass toward the waterfall.

"Where will *you* be?" Mosiah asked Simkin, who was changing his attire as he moved.

"In the thick of the battle, you may rest assured," Simkin replied in a deep, grating voice. He was now clad in snakeskin, highly suitable for crawling through the grass. Unfortunately, the overall effect was rather marred by a metal helm complete with visor that covered his face, obscured his vision, and looked vaguely like an overturned bucket.

"They're *Duuk-tsarith*, all right," whispered Saryon.

It was late afternoon. The sun was just beginning its downward slide to night. Crouched in the grass at the border between meadow and forest, the catalyst could see the two men and their long black robes clearly. Saryon sighed in despair. He had been hoping that this was another of Simkin's "monsters" which would unaccountably disappear the moment anyone looked for it.

But these were, indeed, warlocks—members of the deadly Order of *Duuk-tsarith*. They stood motionless, as though listening intently. Their hands were clasped in front of them as was proper, their faces hidden in the shadows of their black pointed hoods. If there was any further doubt, it was dispelled by the sight of the raven, sitting on a tree limb near the two, its eyes gleaming red in the sunlight filtering through the leaves. Saryon watched the black-robed men. His mind went back to the Font, when the two *Duuk-tsarith* had discovered him reading the forbidden books. . . .

"That must be their catalyst," he whispered, hurriedly banishing those fearful memories. Moving cautiously, afraid that they might hear the sound of his hand raising, he pointed out a third individual dressed in a long traveling cloak. Although the cloak concealed his robes, the man's tonsured head marked him a priest. He and a fourth man stood apart from the warlocks. Close together, they were obviously involved in conversation and every so often the hand of the fourth man moved as if to emphasize a point. It was this fourth man who drew the catalyst's attention. Taller than the rest, his cloak was made of costly fabric. When the man gestured, Saryon caught the glint of jewels upon his fingers.

The catalyst pointed him out. "I'm not certain about that fourth man. He isn't *Duuk-tsarith*. He's not dressed in the black —"

"Is he a warlock of any type?" Joram asked. Shifting the Darksword restlessly in his hand in order to get a better grip on the heavy weapon, he nearly dropped it, and irritably wiped his sweaty palms on his shirt.

"No," the catalyst answered, puzzled. "It's odd, but by his clothes I'd take him for a —"

"It doesn't matter, as long as he's not *Duuk-tsarith*," interrupted Joram impatiently. "There's only two of them we have to worry about now. I'll take one. You and Mosiah deal with the other. Where's Simkin?"

"Here," said a sepulchral voice from beneath the helm. "Got dark awfully quick, didn't it."

"Raise the visor, fool. You take care of the fourth man."

"What visor?" came the pathetic response, the helm turning this way and that. "What fourth man?"

"The man standing by — Oh, never mind!" Joram snarled. "Just keep out of the way. Come on. Mosiah, go left. I'll go right. You stay between us, Catalyst." He crept forward through the brush. Mosiah headed the opposite direction while Saryon, his face haggard and drawn, followed behind.

"'Tisn't my fault," Simkin muttered gloomily from beneath the helmet. "Wretched invention, this. I'm completely in the dark. Knights of old and all that. Bloody nonsense. No wonder Arthur had a round table. He couldn't see the damn thing! Probably kept bumping into it and knocking off the corners. I —"

But Simkin was talking to himself.

Mosiah fit an arrow to the bow, his hands shaking so with fear and excitement that he had to try several times before he succeeded. "Grant me Life, Father," he whispered.

His throat dry from fear, the catalyst repeated in a cracked voice the words that absorbed the magic of the world into his body. He had not been trained in the art of supporting fighting warlocks; that required certain specialized skills that he did not possess. He could enhance Mosiah's already strong magical powers, enabling the young man to cast spells that otherwise would have been beyond his strength, such as they had done in the fight in the village. But that had been using magic against unthinking brutes. This was far different. They were fighting experienced warlocks. Neither of them had ever been in a battle like this, neither truly knew what he was doing.

This is insane! Saryon's mind repeated to him over and over urgently. Insane! Stop it before it goes too far!

"But it's already gone too far," Saryon told himself. "We have no choice now!"

"Father!" Mosiah whispered urgently.

Head bowed, Saryon laid his hand upon the boy's quivering arm and chanted the words that opened the conduit to him. The magic flowed from the catalyst into Mosiah like sparkling wine.

Watching Mosiah's face in the sunlight, the catalyst saw the young man's lips part, the eyes glow. He looked like a child tasting his first sweets.

Saryon's heart misgave him. "No, Mosiah, wait . . . You can't —"

But he was too late. Whispering words the young man had learned from the Sorcerers, Mosiah let fly his arrow in the direction of the man in black robes nearest him. His aim was hurried, but it was not important. As the arrow flew, the young magus cast a spell upon it, causing the arrow to seek out and kill any warm-blooded, living object. Used by the Sorcerers of old, the spell permitted even untrained troops to be highly effective in battle.

But not this battle.

What drew the warlock's attention? Perhaps it was the rustle of Mosiah's clothes brushing against the grass. Perhaps it was the twang of the arrow leaving the string or the whisper of the feathers on the shaft as it flew through the air. Or perhaps it was the warning caw of the raven, although that came late.

Swifter than the arrow flying toward his heart, the man in the black robes spoke and pointed. There was a flash of flame and the arrow was nothing more deadly than a streak of ashes that vanished upon the winds.

The second *Duuk-tsarith* acted as quickly as his partner. Raising his hands to heaven, he shouted a command and darkness fell upon them with a swiftness of a thunderbolt. Brilliant, sunlit day became blinding, stifling night. Saryon could see nothing, and crouched helplessly in the brush, afraid to move. Then, just as his eyes were beginning to adjust to the darkness, strange silver moonlight filled the forest. Though it lit up everything in the woods, it caused human flesh to glow brightly, with an eerie purplish-white radiance. The catalyst — blinking — could see clearly the astonished faces of the fourth man and the priest as they turned in their direction.

More by accident than by design, Saryon was crouched down among the brush. Even though the moonlight made his flesh gleam, he knew he must be difficult to see. But Mosiah had risen out of the grass to fire his arrow. Struggling to adjust his vision to the sudden darkness, he was bathed in the silver pool of moonlight, plainly visible to the two black-robed men. With a cry, he raised his bow.

The *Duuk-tsarith* spoke.

Dropping the bow, Mosiah clutched his throat.

"I — I —" He tried to speak, but the magical paralysis cast upon him by the warlock cut off his words, as it was cutting off his ability to breathe. His eyes rolled upward until the whites showed, the young man fought desperately to draw air into his lungs, but it was a futile struggle.

Saryon half rose, thinking to plead for surrender, when a dark shape hurtled past the catalyst, nearly knocking him to the ground. Mosiah's eyes were bulging, his face was slowly darkening. Leaping in front of his friend, Joram raised the Darksword. The strange moonlight did not touch the metal, the weapon was a streak of night in his hand.

The moment the sword came between the *Duuk-tsarith* and Mosiah, the warlock's spell shattered. Gasping for breath, the young man collapsed. Saryon caught hold of Mosiah and eased him to the ground as Joram stood above them protectively, holding the crude sword in his strong hands.

Saryon waited grimly for the blast of icy wind that would freeze their blood in seconds or the shattering crack as the ground opened and swallowed them — not even the power of the Darksword would stop such spells as those, he imagined. But nothing happened.

Peering out from the tall grass, Saryon saw the fourth man walking toward them. Perhaps he had spoken; the catalyst could not hear over the splashing of the waterfall some distance behind him. But both of the *Duuk-tsarith* had turned their hooded heads toward the tall man. He made a motion with his hand, telling them to back off, and the warlocks bowed in obedience.

Saryon's wonder increased, as did his fear. Who was this man the powerful *Duuk-tsarith* obeyed without question?

Whoever he was, he approached Joram coolly, without fear, his eyes studying the young man intently as he drew near.

"Be careful, Garald," called the man in the long traveling cloak whom Saryon had taken — and rightly so — for a catalyst. "I sense something strange about the weapon!"

"Strange?" The man referred to as Garald laughed, mellow, cultivated laughter that seemed to be made of the same rich material as the fabric of his cloak. "Thank you for the warning, Cardinal," he continued, "but I see only one strange thing about this sword — it is the ugliest of its kind my eyes have ever beheld!"

"It is that, Your Grace —"

Cardinal! Saryon, staring in bewilderment, could see the color of the catalyst's holy robes beneath his cloak and knew him for what he was — a Cardinal of the Realm! And this Garald; that name seemed familiar, but Saryon was too nervous to be able to think clearly. The costly clothes, the man referred to as Your Grace. . . .

The Cardinal continued speaking. "— but it is this ugly sword, Your Grace, that has disrupted the spell of your guards."

"The sword did that? Fascinating."

The richly dressed man was close enough that Saryon could see him clearly in the magical moonlight. The beauty of the voice matched the features of the face, delicately crafted without being weak. The eyes were large and intelligent. The mouth was firm, the lines about it indicative of smiling and laughter. The chin was strong without arrogance, the cheekbones high and pronounced. Brown hair, with a slight reddish cast in the bright moonlight, was worn short in military fashion. One lock dipped down over the man's forehead in a graceful, careless wave.

Taking a step nearer Joram, the man called Garald held out a hand gloved in fine lambskin. "Surrender your sword, boy," he said in a voice that was neither threatening nor demanding, yet obviously accustomed to being obeyed.

"Take it from me," Joram said defiantly.

"'Take it from me,' *Your Grace*," the Cardinal amended, shocked.

"Thank you, Cardinal," Garald said, and a smile played about his lips, "but I do not think this is the time for coaching thieves in court etiquette. Come now, boy. Surrender your sword peacefully and nothing will happen to you."

"No! Your Grace," Joram said with a sneer.

"Joram, please!" whispered Saryon in despair, but the young man ignored him.

"Who is this Garald guy?" Mosiah whispered. He started to sit up, but he froze almost immediately. The elegant man had warned the *Duuk-tsarith* away from Joram, but he had apparently left Mosiah in their care. Mosiah saw the glittering eyes of the warlocks fixed on him, he saw the hands clasped before the black robes make a slight movement, and he held quite still, hardly daring to breathe.

Saryon shook his head, keeping his eyes on Joram and this Garald, who drew several steps closer. Joram shifted in his position, raising the sword.

"Very well," the elegant man said, shrugging, "I accept your challenge."

Tossing his cloak over one shoulder, Garald drew a sword from its scabbard and stepped expertly into a fighting stance. Saryon's throat tightened. The sword, of ancient design and make, was as delicate and beautiful and strong as the man who wielded it. The moonlight burned in it with a cold, silver flame, dancing off the sharp edge and flashing from the carved, hawk-winged hilt.

The hawk. Something stirred in Saryon's mind, but he could not relax his attention on Joram long enough to attend to it. The boy was a shabby, almost pathetic figure compared to the tall, noble man in his rich clothes. Yet there was a pride in Joram, a fearlessness and courage in his dark eyes that rivaled his opponent's and spoke to Saryon of the noble blood that flowed in the boy's veins as well as in the man's.

Moving awkwardly, Joram imitated his enemy's fighting stance, knowing little about it except what he had been able to pick up from the books he'd read. His clumsiness appeared to amuse Garald, although the Cardinal—his eyes still on the Darksword—shook his head and murmured once more, "Your Grace, I think perhaps—"

Garald motioned the Cardinal to silence even as Joram, confident in the power of his sword and angry at the arrogant demeanor of his opponent, leaped forward.

Heedless of the watching *Duuk-tsarith*, Saryon sprang to his feet. He could not allow Joram to harm this man!

"Stop—" the catalyst cried, but the words died on his lips.

There was a clash of steel, a yelp of pain, and Joram stood, wringing an injured hand and staring stupidly at the Darksword as it flew through the air to land at the feet of the Cardinal.

"Seize him and the other one," Garald said coolly to the waiting *Duuk-tsarith*, who did not hesitate to use their magic now that they were permitted.

With a word, they cast the Nullmagic spells that robbed their victims of all the magical energy upon which every person in the world depends. Mosiah fell over with a cry. But Joram remained standing, staring at the *Duuk-tsarith* with grim defiance, rubbing the swordhand that still tingled from the jarring blow.

"I beg your pardon, Your Grace," said one of the *Duuk-tsarith*, "but the boy there does not respond to our spell. He is Dead."

"Is he, indeed?" Garald regarded Joram with a look of cool pity more wounding to Joram than any sword thrust. The young man's face flushed deeply, his mouth twisted in fierce anger. "Use something stronger," the elegant man said, watching Joram. "Be careful not to injure him, however. I want to learn more about this strange sword."

"And what about the catalyst, Your Grace?" asked the warlock, bowing.

Glancing about, Garald's gaze fixed on Saryon, and the man's eyes widened.

"Almin's blood, Cardinal," Garald said in astonishment. "Here is one of your Order! Let me assist you, Father," he added courteously, extending his hand to the confused catalyst.

Though spoken in the utmost respect, the words were not an invitation so much as a command, and Saryon had no choice but to obey. Garald took hold of Saryon's arm, gently assisting the catalyst to step out of the tangle of thick brush.

Seeing Garald preoccupied, Joram made a move toward retrieving his sword. He came to an abrupt halt as three rings of pure fire descended from the air and hovered about him—one level with his elbows, one dropping to his waist, the other to his knees. The flaming rings did not touch Joram, but they were close enough to his skin that he could feel their flesh-searing heat and he dared not move.

Satisfied that their prey was, for the moment, under control, the *Duuk-tsarith* looked expectantly at their lord, asking in their silent way for further instructions.

"Search the glade," Garald ordered. "There may be others out there, hidden in the grass. Oh, first — get rid of this confounded darkness, will you?"

The *Duuk-tsarith* complied. Night departed and day returned with a suddenness that left everyone blinking in the bright afternoon sunlight. When Saryon could see again, he noted that the warlocks, like darkness embodied, had vanished with it. He was staring around in confusion when he became aware that Garald was speaking to him.

"I trust you are not in league with these young bandits, Father," he said steadily, but with a certain coldness in his voice. "Although I have heard that there are renegade catalysts abroad in the land."

"I am not a renegade catalyst, Your . . . Your Grace," Saryon began, then stopped, flushing, as he remembered. "Well, perhaps I am," he faltered. "But, please listen to my story," he said, turning to the Cardinal who had joined them. "I — We are not thieves, I assure you!"

"Then, what is the meaning of the invasion of our glade and this attack upon us?" Garald asked with increasing coldness and a hint of anger in his voice.

"Please, let me explain, Your Grace," Saryon said desperately. "It was a mistake —"

The two *Duuk-tsarith* appeared suddenly, materializing out of the air to stand in front of Garald.

"Yes?" he said. "What have you found?

"There was nothing in the glade, Your Grace, except this." Extending his hand, one of the black-robed figures held out a large wooden bucket.

"A curious object in these savage lands, but not particularly worthy of your attention, I should think," remarked Garald, glancing at it without interest.

"It is a rather remarkable bucket, Your Grace," said the *Duuk-tsarith*.

"No, no," said the bucket hastily. "Just a plain, ordinary bucket. Nothing remarkable about me, I assure you."

"Name of the Almin!" Garald breathed, while the Cardinal took a hasty step backward, muttering a prayer.

"A humble bucket. The old, oaken bucket," continued the bucket in a husky voice. "Allow me, kind sir, to carry your water. Soak your feet in me. Soak your head —"

"I'll be damned!" Garald cried. Springing forward, he grabbed the bucket from the hands of the warlock. "Simkin!" he said, shaking the bucket. "Simkin, you rattle-brained fool! Don't you recognize me?"

Two eyes appeared suddenly on the bucket's rim, and studied the tall man intently. The eyes widened, then, with a laugh, the bucket transformed itself into the figure of the bearded young man, clad in his favorite *Muck and Mud* outfit.

"Garald!" he cried, flinging his arms around the elegant man.

"Simkin!" Garald clapped him on the back.

The Cardinal appeared to be less pleased at the sight of Simkin himself than he had been at the talking bucket. Glancing heavenward, the priest folded his hands in the sleeves of his robes and shook his head.

"I didn't recognize you," said Simkin, standing back and regarding the nobleman with a delighted gaze. "What *are* you doing in these beastly parts? Oh, wait," he said, appearing to remember something. "I must introduce you to my friends."

"Joram, Mosiah" — Simkin turned to the two, one lying spellbound on the ground, the other imprisoned by rings of flame — "may I present His Royal Highness, Garald, Prince of Sharakan."

10

His Grace

"**S**o these are friends of yours, are they, Simkin?" The Prince's gaze flickered over Mosiah to rest more intently on Joram. Imprisoned by the fiery rings, the young man dared not move or risk being severely burned. But there was no fear on the stern face; only pride, anger, and humiliation at his ignominious defeat.

"Closer to me than brothers," averred Simkin. "You recall how I lost my brother? Dear little Nat? It was in the year—"

"Uh, yes," interrupted the Prince hastily. He turned to the *Duuk-tsarith*. "You may release them."

The warlocks bowed and, at a gesture and a word, they lifted the Nullmagic from Mosiah, who gasped and rolled over on his back, breathing heavily. The rings disappeared from around Joram, but still the young man did not move. Folding his strong arms across his chest, Joram stared off into the sunlit forest. He looked at nothing in particular, but was simply making it clear that he had chosen to stand in that spot of his own free will and would continue standing there until he dropped over dead.

Garald's mouth twitched. Putting his hand on his lips to hide his smile, he turned again to Simkin. "What about the catalyst?"

"The bald party is a friend of mine, too," remarked the young man, glancing about vaguely. "Where are you, Father? Oh, yes. Prince Garald, Father Saryon. Father Saryon, Prince Garald."

The Prince bowed gracefully, hand over his heart as was the custom in the north. Saryon returned the bow more clumsily, his mind in such a state of confusion that he barely knew what he did.

"Father Saryon," said the Prince, "may I present His Eminence, Cardinal Radisovik, friend and adviser to my father."

Walking forward, Saryon knelt humbly to kiss the fingers of the white-robed Cardinal. But the Priest took him by the hand and raised him to his feet.

"We have dispensed with those degrading obeisances in the north," said the Cardinal. "It is a pleasure to meet you, Father Saryon. You appear exhausted. Will you return with me to our glade? The springs warm the air most pleasantly there, don't you agree?"

Suddenly aware that he was bitterly cold, Saryon realized that it *was* as if he had stepped from spring to winter again by entering these woods. Simkin's words came back to him. *This glade isn't supposed to be here.* Undoubtedly it wasn't! The Prince had conjured up a pleasant place for his campsite and they had stumbled into it! What incredible, naive fools. . . .

"I sense a tale of great adventure about you, Father," Radisovik continued, walking toward the glade. "I would be interested in hearing how a man of the cloth comes to be in such"—the Cardinal appeared momentarily at a loss—"um . . . interesting company."

Nothing could have been more polite than the Cardinal's words, but Saryon had seen the exchange of swift glances between the Prince and Radisovik just prior to the Cardinal's formal welcome of the catalyst. Now Radisovik was leading Saryon back to the glade, and the Prince and Simkin were walking over to assist Mosiah.

Saryon understood. We are to be interviewed separately. Then the Prince and the Cardinal will compare notes. It had all been settled between them gracefully, without a word spoken. Court manners, court intrigue. Remembering his dread secret, Saryon felt a pang of fear. He had never been at all good at this sort of thing.

Following the Cardinal, half listening to his polite conversation, it suddenly occurred to Saryon that Radisovik must be a renegade as well; the man of whom Vanya had spoken, the priest who had forced the Church's true minister into exile.

How strange that they should meet! Was this encounter an answer to prayers Saryon had not prayed? Or merely another indication that the universe was a cold, empty, and unfeeling void?

Only time would tell. Saryon wondered how much of that they had left.

"How are you feeling, sir?" the Prince asked Mosiah.

"Much . . . much better . . . Your . . . Grace," stammered Mosiah, flushing in embarrassment. Seeing the Prince prepared to kneel to assist him, he hurriedly attempted to stand on his feet. "Please . . . don't trouble yourself . . . mi-milord. I'm all right now, really."

"You will forgive us for this treatment, I hope," Garald said with concern in his cool voice. "You can understand that we have been unusually wary in these uncivilized lands."

"Yes, Your Grace." Mosiah, helped to his feet by Simkin, was so red in the face that he appeared feverish. "We . . . we mistook you for . . . someone else, too. . . ."

"Indeed?" Garald lifted his soft eyebrows in surprise.

"Pardon, Your Grace," said the *Duuk-tsarith*. "But night is falling. We should return to the safety of the glade."

"Ah, yes. Thank you for reminding me." The Prince made a graceful gesture with his hand. "Would one of you be so kind as to assist this young man to the glade where he may rest?"

One of the *Duuk-tsarith* glided over to Mosiah, the black robes barely skimming the ground. He did not touch the young man; he merely stood beside him, his hands folded in front of him. Mosiah recognized, however — as had Saryon — that this was an order, not an invitation, and he would disobey it at his peril. He moved off toward the glade, the warlock drifting along behind him, dark and silent as the young man's shadow. Joram remained in his place some distance from them, watching yet not watching. The second *Duuk-tsarith* had not taken his eyes from the stern young man.

Looking at Joram, Garald turned to Simkin, speaking in a low voice. "This other friend of yours, the one with the sword, fascinates me. What do you know of him?"

"Claims noble birth. Wrong side of sheets. Mother disgraced. Ran away. Son grew up a Field Magus. Rebellious sort. Killed overseer. Fled Outland. Something odd, though. Bald party sent to bring him to Bishop Vanya. Didn't do it. Deep trouble. Dark Arts now, both of them," Simkin rattled off glibly, quite pleased with his summation.

"Mmmm," Garald mused, his gaze fixed on Joram. "And the sword?"

"Darkstone."

Garald drew in a deep breath.

"Darkstone? Are you certain?" he whispered, drawing Simkin close.

Simkin nodded.

The Prince let his breath out in a sigh. "Praise be to the Almin," he said reverently. "Come with me. I want to talk to this young man and I'll need your help. So, you are from the Sorcerers' village?" he remarked aloud to Simkin, as the two walked over to Joram.

"Yes, O High and Mighty One," Simkin said gaily. "And I must admit, I am quite relieved to be away from there." The orange silk fluttered from the sky to his hand. Catching the sunlight, it looked like a bit of dancing flame. "The smell, milord"— Simkin put the silk to his nose —"quite intolerable, I assure you. Hot coals, sulfurous fumes. To say nothing of infernal hammering, day and night."

The two came to stand before Joram, who stared past them, refusing to acknowledge their existence.

"Your name is Joram, sir?" Garald inquired politely.

Lips compressed, Joram's gaze shifted to the Prince. "Return my sword," he said, his voice thick and husky.

"'Return my sword,' *Your Grace*," Simkin corrected, mimicking the Cardinal.

Joram cast him an angry glance. Garald coughed, covering his laughter, and made a show of clearing his throat. As he did so, he took the opportunity to study Joram intently, having the advantage of seeing the young man's face in the afternoon sunlight.

"Yes," he murmured to himself, "I can believe his claim to high birth. There is noble blood there, if not noble manners. I know that face, in fact!" Garald frowned in thought. "And the hair . . . magnificent! The eyes . . . proud, sensitive, intelligent. Too intelligent. A dangerous young man. I can believe he discovered darkstone. Now what does he intend to do with it? Does he know, even, what dread power he has brought back to the world? Does anyone know, for that matter?"

"My sword!" Joram repeated stubbornly, his face growing dark under the Prince's scrutiny.

"Please forgive me. Slight tickle in my throat. The wind-flowers . . ." Garald bowed slightly. "The sword is yours, sir." He glanced over to it where it lay on the ground. "And please accept my apology for our actions. You took us by surprise, and we reacted in haste." The Prince straightened, regarding the young man with a grave smile.

Completely taken aback, Joram looked from the Prince to the sword to the Prince again. His face flushed, the brows came together. But it was no longer in anger. His rage was deserting him and taking its strength with it, leaving behind nothing but humiliation and shame. For the first time in his life, Joram was acutely conscious of his shabby clothes, his tangled hair. He looked at the Prince's hand, smooth and supple, and he saw his own hand, calloused and dirty by comparison. He tried to fan the coals of rage, but they only glimmered to life then died, leaving his soul cold.

Keeping his eyes on Garald, suspecting some trick, Joram walked slowly over to where the sword lay — an object of darkness — in the sunlit grass. The Prince did not move. Neither did the watching *Duuk-tsarith*. Bending down, Joram lifted his weapon. He thrust it into the crude sheath hurriedly, flushing as the Prince's eyes glanced at it in — he thought — scorn.

"Am I free to go?" Joram asked harshly.

"You are free to go, though you are, I suppose, still our prisoners," the Prince answered smoothly. "But I would much prefer it if you would remain with us tonight as our guests. Let us make amends for attacking you —"

"Stop mocking us!" Joram sneered. "Your Grace." He could taste the bitterness in his voice. "You had every right to attack us — kill us, even. As for the sword, it's crude enough. Worthless, compared to yours" — Joram could not help himself, his eyes went longingly to the beautiful sword the Prince wore at his side in its magically tooled leather scabbard — "but I made it myself." His voice softened, he sounded like a wistful child. "And I had never seen a real sword like that before."

"Not worthless, I think," Garald said. "Not a sword of darkstone that absorbs magic. . . ."

Joram looked sharply at Simkin, who smiled innocently.

"Come with me to the glade," Garald continued. "It is much warmer there and, as my guards remind me, it is dangerous in the Outland at night." Walking over to the young man, Garald rested his hand lightly on Joram's shoulder.

It was an affectionate gesture, as a man might make to a friend. Or as a man might calm a restive animal. Joram flinched at Garald's touch. He saw the pity in the man's eyes and he barely resisted the temptation to strike the hand aside. Why did he resist? Why did he bother? How Joram knew it, he could not have told, but he understood that while Garald would respect a refusal to be pitied, he would never forgive a blow. And it had suddenly become important to Joram to gain this man's respect.

"Where are you from, Joram?" Garald asked.

"What has that got to do with anything?" Joram demanded sullenly.

"Where does your *family* come from, I meant to say," the Prince amended.

Once again, Joram glanced darkly at Simkin, flitting along beside them, and Garald smiled. "Yes, he's told me something about you. I confess to being quite curious. I understand from Simkin's brief description that your life has been . . . difficult"— he phrased it delicately—"and you may consider this an improper question between gentlemen. If so, I hope you forgive me. But I have traveled extensively and have a knowledge of most of the noble families in this part of the realm, and I confess that you look extremely familiar to me. Do you know your family name?"

The shame that burned in Joram's face was answer enough for the Prince, but the young man tossed his head proudly. "No." It was all he meant to say, but the grave interest on Garald's face drew him into speaking more than he had intended. "All I know is that my mother's name was Anja, and that she came from Merilon. My father was . . . was a . . . catalyst." His lip twisted as he spoke; his eyes went to the glade where Saryon could be seen, standing among the flowers and tall grass, talking to the Cardinal.

"Life's blood!" The Prince's gaze followed. "You don't mean—"

"Of course not!" Joram snapped, realizing Garald's mistake. "Not *him*!" The bitterness returned. "My creation was my father's crime. He was sentenced to the Turning, and now he stands, a living statue, upon the Border."

"My god," the Prince murmured, and there was no longer pity in his voice but sympathy. "So you come from Merilon by birth." Once again, he studied Joram in the sunlight. "Yes, that fits somehow. Yet . . . I cannot place . . ."

Irritably, he shook his head, trying to remember. But his thoughts were interrupted by Simkin, who gave a great, gaping yawn. "Hate to break up this frightfully fascinating little party, don't you know. And I am most awfully tickled to see you again, Garald, old bean. But I should like a brief nap before dinner." Another yawn. "It isn't easy being a bucket. To say nothing of the fact that those black-robed guards of yours are, in reality, two great oafs who tripped over me in the grass. Gave me a turn, so to speak, from which I may doubtless never recover." Sniffing indignantly, he dabbed his nose with the orange silk.

"By all means, go rest in the glade, my friend." Garald smiled. "You do seem a bit pale."

"Ouch!" Simkin winced. "A pun that was quite unworthy of you, my prince. Sweet dreams. You, too, O Dark and Gloomy One." Waving negligently at Joram, the bearded young man drifted forward, riding on the warm currents of spring air that could be felt as they drew nearer the magical campsite.

"How do you know Simkin?" Joram asked involuntarily, watching as the green cape and the green hat with the pheasant feather fluttered away.

"Know Simkin?" Glancing at Joram, the Prince raised one eyebrow in amusement. "I wasn't aware anyone ever did."

"Well, Radisovik, what have you found out?"

Night — real night, not magical — had come to the glade. A campfire burned in the center of a cleared area. It had been used for cooking a brace of rabbit the Prince had snared earlier in the day, and now it cast a pleasant, warm light throughout the peaceful glade. With the magic of himself and his guards at his command, Prince Garald could have dispensed with the need for fire and snares. The rabbits could conceivably have cooked themselves. But Garald liked to keep in training. A man never knew, particularly in these unsettled times, when he might be forced to live without the magic.

Tonight the Prince and his Cardinal walked slowly among the trees, keeping within sight of the camp, both under the watchful, protective eyes of the black-hooded *Duuk-tsarith*. Some distance from where they walked, the catalyst sat, nodding by the fire, drinking a cup of hot tea. Mosiah lay near him, asleep, wrapped in soft blankets that the Prince had conjured up for them with his own hands. Joram lay near his friend, but he was wide awake. His eyes followed the Prince and the Cardinal; his sword lay by his side, within easy reach. Garald wondered if the young man intended trying to remain awake all night, watching. Grinning to himself, he shook his head. He had been seventeen once himself. Not that long ago either. He was twenty-eight now. And he could remember.

Their other guest, Simkin, had spread his blanket in a flower bed some distance from his companions. Attired in a frilled lace nightshirt, complete with tasseled hat, he snored loudly, but whether truly asleep or shamming was anyone's guess. Certainly Garald had no idea. He knew enough about Simkin, however, to know that it *was* a guess.

"Your Grace?"

"Oh, I beg your pardon, Cardinal. My thoughts wandered. Please continue."

"This is most important, Your Grace." The Cardinal's voice held a hint of rebuke.

"You have my complete attention," the Prince said gravely.

"The catalyst, Saryon, has been in direct contact with Bishop Vanya."

"How?" Garald looked immediately concerned.

"The Chamber of Discretion, undoubtedly, milord, although the poor man has no idea what that is. I recognize the description, however. According to him, Bishop Vanya is actively working for our destruction. . . ."

"Hardly news," Garald murmured, frowning.

"No, milord. What *is* news is the fact that Blachloch was acting as a double agent. Yes, Highness"—in answer to a look of astonishment from the Prince—"the man was Vanya's tool, sent to the Sorcerers' village to lure us into war. Once we were dependent upon the Sorcerers and their weapons of the Dark Arts, Blachloch was to turn upon us *and* upon them. We would have fallen, defeated at the hands of our enemies, and the Sorcerers would have been destroyed."

"Clever bastard, Blachloch," Garald said grimly. "But I note you speak of him in the past tense."

"He is dead, Your Grace. The young man"—Radisovik glanced at Joram—"killed him."

"A *Duuk-tsarith*?" Garald appeared dubious.

"With the sword, milord, and help from the catalyst."

"Ah, the sword of the darkstone." Garald's brow cleared. Then he frowned again, his eyes on Joram. "Truly a dangerous young man," he remarked, then fell silent, lost in his thoughts. The Cardinal, walking beside him, kept quiet as well.

"Do you trust this catalyst?" Garald asked suddenly.

"Yes, milord, to an extent," Radisovik answered.

"What do you mean, 'to an extent'?"

"Saryon is a scholar at heart, Your Grace, a genius in mathematics. Thus was he lured to the study of the Dark Arts of Technology. He is a simple man. One who longs to be sheltered within the safe walls of the Font, spending his life in his books. But something has happened to him, something that casts a shadow over his life."

"Something tied to the young man?"

"Yes, Your Grace."

"Simkin said as much—talk of Vanya sending this catalyst after Joram to bring him back to the Font." Garald shrugged. "But . . . that is Simkin. I disbelieved most of it."

"The catalyst corroborates his story, Your Grace. According to him, he was sent by Bishop Vanya to bring Joram to justice."

"And you think—"

"He is telling us the truth, milord, but not all of the truth. In fact, Your Grace, that is why I believe he is being so free with his information. Saryon appeared pathetically eager to tell me as much or more than I wanted to know about Blachloch. The poor man is transparent. He is obviously fluttering this broken wing to keep me away from whatever it is he has hidden in his nest."

"What reason does he give for Vanya wanting to apprehend the young man?"

"Only the obvious reason that Joram is Dead, milord, and a murderer was well. The young man killed an overseer. According to the catalyst, Joram had just provocation. The overseer killed the young man's mother."

"Bah!" Garald's frown deepened. "Bishop Vanya would not concern himself with such a petty crime. He would turn that over to the *Duuk-tsarith*. The catalyst holds with this wild story?"

"And will hold with it, Your Grace, to his death. I note one other thing of interest about the catalyst, milord."

"And that is?"

"He has lost his faith," said Radisovik softly. "He is a man wandering alone in the darkness of his soul, without the guidance of his god. Such a man—who has a secret as does this one—will cling to that secret all the more tenaciously since it is the only thing he has left to him." The Cardinal shrugged, shivering slightly in the chill of the forest. "I don't know for certain, however. Perhaps the warlocks with their special means could get it from him—"

"No!" Garald said firmly, his gaze going involuntarily to the black-robed figures standing in disciplined silence near the fire. "We will leave that type of thing to Vanya and his puppet Emperor of Merilon. If it is the Almin's will that this man's secret become known to us, then we will discover it. If not, then we are not meant to know it."

"Amen," murmured the Cardinal, appearing relieved.

"After all, the Almin willed it that we discovered Blachloch's treachery in time," Garald continued with a smile.

"All praise to our Creator," responded the Cardinal. "And now, knowing this, milord, do we proceed with our journey to the Sorcerers?"

"Yes, of course. If you agree, I mean," Garald added hastily. Accustomed to acting quickly and decisively, the young Prince occasionally forgot to seek the advice of the older, more experienced Cardinal. It was one reason his father, the King, had sent the two of them together on this mission.

"I think it would be wise, Your Grace. Particularly now," Radisovik said, it being his turn to conceal his smile. "The Sorcerers will be in confusion following the death of their leader. The catalyst tells me that there is one faction who wants peace, but another, stronger faction that favors pursuing this war. It should be easy to step in, take control, and work with them in earnest now that the warlock is gone."

"Yes, that is how I see it." Garald smiled. "In the meantime, I suppose there is no hurry?"

The Cardinal appeared surprised. "Well, no, I shouldn't think so, Your Grace. We must arrive in the village before the people have had a chance to establish a firm leadership figure—"

"A week would make no difference more or less, do you think?"

"N-no, milord," said the Cardinal, mystified. "I should think not."

"And what are the intentions of our guests? Where are they bound?"

"To Merilon, Your Grace," said the Cardinal.

"Yes, that makes sense," Garald said, speaking more to himself than to his companion. "Joram seeks his name and his fortune. This could work out quite nicely. . . ."

"Your Grace?"

"Nothing, just talking to myself. I believe we will camp here for a week, if you do not object, Radisovik."

"And what do you intend to do here, milord?" asked the Cardinal.

"Turn fencing instructor. Good night, Eminence."

Bowing, Garald walked back toward the fire.

"Good night, Your Grace," murmured Radisovik, staring after the Prince in astonishment.

Joram

Garald returned to the fire, his head bent in thought. The Cardinal continued on across the glade, entering a silken tent that had appeared near the hot springs by the command of one of the *Duuk-tsarith*. The Prince noted, as he walked, that both he and Cardinal were under the catalyst's careful scrutiny, and that Saryon's gaze went from them to Joram. The young man had finally fallen asleep, his hand still resting on his sword.

The catalyst loves him, that much is certain, the Prince thought, watching Saryon from beneath lowered lids as he drew near. And what a difficult love it must be. It is apparently not returned. Radisovik is right. There's some deep secret here. He won't give it up, that's obvious. But, in talking about the young man, he might say more than he realizes. And I will find out something about Joram.

"No, please don't rise, Father," the Prince said aloud, coming to stand beside the catalyst. "If you have no objection, I would like to sit with you for a while, unless you plan to retire, that is."

"Thank you, Your Grace," replied the catalyst, sinking back down into the soft, fragrant grass that had been magically transformed into a carpet as thick and luxurious as any in court. "I would be glad of your company. I—I find that I suffer from insomnia on occasion." The catalyst smiled wearily. "It seems that this is one of those nights."

"I, too, am often wakeful," the Prince said, seating himself gracefully beside the catalyst. "My *Theldara* prescribes a glass of wine before bed." A crystal goblet appeared in the Prince's hand, filled with a ruby-red liquid that gleamed warmly in the firelight. He handed it to the catalyst.

"I am obliged, Your Grace," Saryon said, flushing at the attention. "To your health." He sipped at the wine. It was delicious, and brought memories of court life and Merilon back to him.

"I would like to speak to you of Joram, Father," Garald said, settling himself onto the grassy carpet. Leaning on one elbow, he looked directly into the catalyst's face while keeping his own turned from the firelight.

"You are direct and to the point, milord." said Saryon, smiling faintly.

"A failing of mine, sometimes," said Garald with a rueful grin, plucking at the grass beneath his hand. "Or at least so my father tells me. He says that I scare people, pouncing on them like a cat when I should creep up on them from behind."

"I will tell you gladly what I know of the young man, milord," Saryon said, his gaze going to the sleeping form that lay near the fire. "The story of his early life I heard from other people, but I have no reason to doubt the facts."

The catalyst continued to speak, telling of Joram's bleak, strange upbringing. The Prince listened, silent, absorbed, fascinated.

"There is no doubt Anja was mad, Your Grace," said Saryon with a soft sigh. "Her ordeal had been a terrible one. She had seen the man she loved—"

"Joram's father, the catalyst," clarified the Prince.

"Um . . . yes, milord." Saryon coughed and was forced to clear his throat before he could resume. Garald noted that the man did not look at him as he talked. "The catalyst. She had seen him sentenced to the Turning. Have you ever watched that punishment, Highness?" Now the catalyst turned his gaze to the Prince.

"No," Garald replied, shaking his head. "As the Almin is my witness, may I be spared that."

"You do well to pray so, milord," Saryon replied, his gaze going once again to the dancing flames of the fire. "I saw it. In fact, I saw the edict carried out on Joram's father, though, of course, I didn't know it at the time. How strange is fate. . . ." He was silent for so long that Prince Garald touched him on the arm.

"Father?"

"What?" Saryon started. "Oh, yes." Shivering, he drew his robes close around him. "It is a dreadful punishment. In the ancient world, so we are told, men were sentenced to die for their crimes. We consider that barbarism, and I suppose it is. Yet sometimes I think death must be easy compared to our more civilized ways."

"I have seen a man sent Beyond," said the Prince in a low voice. "No, wait. It was a woman. Yes, a woman. I was only a boy. My father took me. It was the first time I had traveled the Corridors. I remember being so excited about the journey that I scarcely knew its intent, although I am certain my father must have tried to prepare me for it. If so, he did not succeed."

Restlessly, the Prince shifted. Sitting up from his comfortable lounging position he, too, stared into the flames. Memory shadowed his handsome face and clear brown eyes.

"What was her crime, milord?"

"I was trying to remember." Garald shook his head. "It must have been a heinous one; probably something to do with adultery, because I remember my father being rather confused and vague about the details. She was a wizardess, I remember that. *Albanara* — a high-ranking member of the court. There was something about casting spells of enchantment, enticing a man against his will." Garald shrugged. "At least I suppose that was *his* story.

"Boy that I was," he continued, "I thought it was going to be a game. I was terribly excited. All the members of the royal courts were there, dressed in their lovely clothes, specially colored in varying shades of blood red for the occasion. I was quite proud of my outfit and wanted to keep it, but Father forbade me. We stood there, on the Border, at the feet of the great living guardians . . ."

He paused. "I didn't know then that these men and women of stone were alive. My father never told me. I was in awe of them, towering thirty feet into the air, staring eternally with unblinking eyes into the shadowed mists of Beyond. A man came forward, dressed in gray robes. *Duuk-tsarith*, I suppose, though I recall that there was something different about his manner of dress —"

"The Executioner, milord," Saryon said in a tight voice. "He resides in the Font and serves the catalysts. His robes are gray — the neutrality of justice — and they are marked with the symbols of the Nine Mysteries, to show that justice knows no distinction."

"I don't recall. He was impressive. That's all I remember. A tall man, he towered over the woman he held bound at his side as the stone statues towered over the rest of us. The Bishop — it must have been Vanya, he's been Bishop for as long as I can remember — made a speech, going over the woman's crimes. I didn't listen, I am afraid." The Prince smiled sadly. "I was bored. I wanted something to happen.

"Anyway, Vanya came to an end. He called upon the Almin to have mercy upon the poor woman's soul. She had been standing quite still the entire time, listening to the charges with a defiant air. She had fiery red hair and wore it loose, tumbling down her back past her waist. Her robes were blood red, and I remember thinking how alive her hair seemed, glistening in the sun, and how dead her clothes appeared in contrast. But when the Bishop called down the blessing of the Almin, she threw back her head and fell to her knees with a wail that shattered my boyish innocence.

"My father felt me trembling, and understood. He put his arm around me, holding me close against his body. The Executioner grabbed hold of the woman and dragged her to her feet. He motioned, with his robed arm, that she was to walk forward. . . . My god!" The Prince closed his eyes. "Walk forward into that dreadful fog! The woman took a step toward the swirling mists, then fell to her knees again. Her screams tore the air. She begged and pleaded. Groveling in the sand, she began to crawl back toward us! Crawling on her hands and knees!"

Garald fell silent, staring into the fire, his mouth a grim, straight line.

"In the end," he resumed, "the Executioner carried her, kicking and struggling, to the very edges of the Border. The mists curled up about his robes, obscuring both of them from our sight. We heard a last, terrible wail . . . and then silence.

The Executioner returned . . . alone. And we went back to the palace at Merilon. And I was sick."

Saryon said nothing. Garald, glancing at him, was alarmed to see that the catalyst had gone deathly white.

"It is nothing, Your Grace," Saryon said, in response to the Prince's concerned query. "Only that . . . I have seen several Banishments myself. The memories haunt me. And it is always the same, as you say. Some walk by themselves, of course. Proud, defiant, heads held high. The Executioner accompanies them to the Border and they step into the mist as though merely walking from one room to another. Yet"—Saryon swallowed—"there is always that last cry, coming from the swirling fog—a cry of horror and despair that is wrenched from even the bravest. I wonder what it is they see—"

"Enough of this!" Garald said, wiping the chill sweat from his face. "We will both have night terrors if we keep on. Return to Joram."

"Yes, milord. Gladly. Although"—the catalyst shook his head—"his story itself is not conducive to a night's restful sleep. I will not tell you the details of the Turning to Stone. Suffice it to say that the Executioner plays his part and that—if I had my choice of punishments—I would choose that last moment of terror in the mists over a life of living death."

"Yes," murmured Garald. "You were speaking of the young man's mother."

"Thank you for reminding me, Your Grace. Anja was forced to watch her lover transformed from living man to living rock, and then she was taken back to the Font, where she gave birth to . . . to their child."

"Go on," the Prince prodded, seeing the catalyst's face pale, his eyes averted.

"Their child . . ." Saryon repeated in some confusion. "She . . . took the . . . baby and fled the Font, traveling to the outlying districts where she found work as a Field Shaper. In that village, she raised her chil— she raised Joram."

"This Anja, she came of a noble family? You know that for certain? Joram *is* of noble blood?"

"Noble blood? Oh, yes, Your Grace! At least, that is what Bishop Vanya has told me," Saryon faltered.

"Father, you appear to be growing increasingly unwell," Garald said in concern, noting the catalyst's ashen lips and the beads of sweat upon the man's tonsured head. "We will continue this some other time . . ."

"No, no, Your Grace," Saryon said hastily. "I am . . . glad you are taking . . . an interest in Joram. And . . . I need to talk about this! It's been . . . a great burden on my mind. . . ."

"Very well, Father," said the Prince, his cool gaze on the catalyst. "Please continue. The boy was raised as a Field Magus."

"Yes. But Anja told him he was of noble birth, and she never allowed him to forget it. She kept him isolated from the other children. According to the catalyst in the village, Joram wasn't allowed out of the shack in which they lived except in his mother's company, and then the boy wasn't permitted to speak to anyone. He stayed in the house, alone, all day, while she worked in the fields. Anja was *Albanara*. Her magic was strong, and she cast spells of protection around the shack to keep the child in and others out. Not that anyone would have tried to get inside anyway," Saryon added. "No one liked Anja. She was cold and aloof, always telling the boy that he was above the others."

"She knew he was Dead?"

"She never admitted it, not to him, not to herself. But I imagine that is another reason she kept him isolated. When he was nine, however, she knew he would have to go into the fields—all children do—to earn his keep. That was when she taught him to cover for his lack of magic by using illusion and sleight of hand. She learned this herself in court, no doubt, where it is a game played for amusement. She also taught him to read and to write, using books she undoubtedly stole from her home. And"—Saryon sighed again—"she took him to see his father."

Garald stared at the catalyst incredulously.

"Yes. Joram never speaks of it, but the village catalyst told me. It was he who opened the Corridors to her. What happened there, we can only guess, but the catalyst said that when the boy returned, he was white as a corpse; his eyes were the eyes of one who has looked into the mist of Beyond and seen the realm of death. From that day when he saw the stone statue of his father, Joram became as stone himself. Cold, aloof, unfeeling. Few have seen him smile. No one has ever seen him cry."

The Prince's eyes went to the young man, lying beside the fire. Even in slumber, the stern face did not relax, the brows remained drawn over it in a brooding, heavy line.

"Continue," the Prince said quietly.

"Joram was good at illusion and he was able to conceal the fact that he was Dead for many years. I know, for he has told me, that he kept hoping the magic would come to him. He believed Anja when she said he was late in developing, as were many of the *Albanara*. He believed because he wanted to believe, of course. Just as he still believes all her stories about the beautiful city of Merilon. He worked in the fields with the others and no one questioned him. It was easy to fool the Field Magi," the catalyst said. "Boys his age are not given Life, for obvious reasons."

"Thus the overseer maintains control over them," the Prince said grimly.

"Yes, Your Grace," Saryon said, flushing slightly. "The young men do mostly hard physical labor, such as clearing the land. This type of labor does not require the use of magic. Joram was lucky for a while. When he was growing up, the village had a good overseer. He tolerated Joram's sullen ways and black humors. He understood. After all, he'd seen how the boy was raised. Anja's madness was, by this time, obvious to everyone—even Joram, I am certain. But he had shut himself away from the others. Except Mosiah, that is."

"Ah, I wondered about that," the Prince remarked, his gaze going to the other young man, who lay sleeping near Joram.

"An odd friendship, milord. It was certainly never encouraged by Joram, from what I've heard. But he has grown close to Mosiah, as you can see by the fact that he was willing to fight you to protect his friend. And Mosiah is close to him, though I am sure he often wonders why he bothers. But, to go on . . ." Saryon rubbed his eyes. "The day came—as it must have sooner or later—when Joram found out he was Dead. The old overseer had died. The new one, who took his place, took personal offense at Joram's sullen withdrawal. He saw it as rebellion and he was determined to break the boy's spirit.

"One morning, the overseer ordered the catalyst to give Joram Life so that he could fly over the fields and aid in the planting like the other Field Magi. The catalyst gave the boy Life, but he might as well have given it to a rock. Joram could no more fly than a corpse can breathe. The catalyst—not a very bright member of our Order, I am afraid," Saryon added, shaking his head, "cried out that the young man was Dead. The overseer was well-pleased, no doubt, and began talking of sending for the *Duuk-tsarith*.

"At this point, Anja completely lost whatever tenuous hold she had on sanity. Changing her form into that of a were-tiger, she leaped for the throat of the overseer. He reacted instinctively, shielding himself with his magic. The shield was too powerful. Fiery bolts of energy struck Anja, and she fell dead at his feet. Her son watched, helpless."

"Name of the Almin," whispered the Prince reverently.

"Joram picked up a heavy stone," Saryon continued, speaking steadily, "and threw it at the overseer. The man never saw it coming. It smashed his skull. So now Joram was twice damned—first he was one of the walking Dead, now he had committed murder.

"He fled into the Outlands. There he was attacked and left for dead by centaurs. Blachloch's men, who were always on the watch for those who enter the Outlands, and particularly for one they knew might be persuaded to join their foul cause, discovered the young man and brought him back to the village. The Sorcerers nursed him back to health and set him to work in the forge. He did not join Blachloch, however. I don't know why, except that he resents any figure of authority, as you have seen."

"The forge . . . Was that where he learned the secret of the darkstone?"

"No, Your Grace." Saryon swallowed again. "That is a secret not even the Sorcerers themselves know. It has been lost to them through the centuries—"

"So we had been led to believe."

"But Joram found books—ancient texts—that the Sorcerers had brought with them when they fled into exile. They have lost the ability to read over the years. Poor people. Theirs is a daily struggle just to survive. But Joram could read the books, of course, and it was in one that he discovered the formula for extracting the metal from the darkstone ore. With this knowledge, he forged the sword."

The catalyst fell silent. He was aware of Garald's intense gaze turned now upon him and, his head bowed, Saryon nervously smoothed the folds of his shabby robe.

"You are leaving something unsaid, Father," the Prince remarked coolly.

"I am leaving a great deal unsaid, Your Grace," said the catalyst simply, lifting his head and looking directly at the Prince. "I am a poor liar, I know. Yet the secret I carry in my heart is not my own and would prove dangerous knowledge to those involved. Better that I bear it alone."

There was a quiet dignity about the middle-aged man, dressed in the humble, worn robes of his calling, that impressed Garald. There was a sorrow about him, too, as if this burden was almost too heavy to bear, yet bear it he would until he dropped. *The man has lost his faith*, the Cardinal had said. This secret is all he has . . . .

That, and his pity and love for Joram.

"Tell me about darkstone," said the Prince, letting the catalyst know that he would not press him further. Saryon smiled in gentle thanks, relieved.

"I know very little, Your Grace," he answered. "Just what I was able to read in the texts, which were very incomplete. The writers assumed that rudimentary knowledge of the ore was well-known, and so they spoke only of advanced techniques for forging it and so forth. Its existence is based on a physical law in nature that for every action there is an equal and opposite reaction. Thus, in a world that exudes magic, there must also be a force that absorbs magic."

"Darkstone."

"Yes, milord. It is an ore, similar in appearance and properties to iron, and is ideal for use as a weapon. The sword, in particular, was the favored weapon of the ancient Sorcerers. The wielder uses the sword to protect himself against any magical spells cast upon him. He then uses it to penetrate the magical defenses of his enemy, and finally has the weapon itself to end his enemy's life."

"So, knowing this, Joram forged the Darksword,"

"Yes, Your Grace. He forged it . . . with my help. A catalyst must be present, to give the ore Life."

Garald's eyes widened.

"I, too, am damned, you see," Saryon said quietly. "I have broken the holy laws of our Order and given Life to . . . a . . . thing of darkness. Yet what could I do? Blachloch knew about the darkstone. He was planning to use it for his own terrible purposes. At least, that is what we believed. Too late I found out he was working for the Church. . . ."

"It would have made no difference," Garald said. "I have no doubt that when he came to realize the darkstone's power, he would have broken faith with the Church and used it himself."

"Undoubtedly you are right." Saryon lowered his head. "Still, how can I forgive myself? Joram murdered him, you see. The warlock lay helpless at his feet. I had drained the Life from him, the Darksword had absorbed his magic. We . . . were going to turn the warlock over to . . . the *Duuk-tsarith*. Set him in the Corridor for them to find. There was a yell—"

Saryon could not continue, his voice broke. Garald laid his hand on the man's shoulder.

"When I looked around"—the catalyst spoke in a horror-filled whisper—"I saw Joram standing over the body, the Darksword wet with blood. He thought I planned to betray him, to turn *him* over to the *Duuk-tsarith* as well. I told him I did not . . ." Saryon sighed. "But Joram trusts no one.

"He hid the body, and that morning I was contacted by Bishop Vanya, who demanded I bring Joram and the Darksword to the Font." Saryon raised his haunted eyes. "How can I, Your Grace?" he cried, wringing his hands. "How can I take him back to be sent . . . into Beyond! To hear that frightful yell and know that it is his! The last place he should go is to Merilon! Yet I cannot stop him! You can, Your Grace," Saryon cried suddenly, feverishly. "Persuade him to come to Sharakan with you. He might listen . . ."

"And what do I tell him?" Garald demanded. "Come to Sharakan and be nobody? When he can go to Merilon and discover his name, his title, his birthright? It is a risk any man would take, and rightly so. I will not dissuade him."

"His birthright . . ." Saryon repeated softly, in agony.

"What?"

"Nothing, milord." The catalyst rubbed his eyes again. "I suppose you are right."

But Saryon appeared so upset and distraught that Garald added more kindly, "I tell you what, Father. I will do what I can to help the young man at least have a chance of succeeding in his goal. I will teach how to protect himself if he should get into trouble. That much, at least, I owe him. He saved us from Blachloch's double-dealings, after all. We are in his debt."

"Thank you, Your Grace." Saryon seemed somewhat eased in his mind. "Now, if you will forgive me, milord, I believe that I can sleep now. . . ."

"Certainly, Father." The Prince was on his feet, helping the catalyst to rise. "I apologize for having kept you up, but the subject is a fascinating one. To make amends, I have had a bed prepared. The finest silken sheets and blankets. But perhaps you would prefer a tent? I can conjure—"

"No, a bed by the fire is fine. Much better than what I am accustomed to, in fact, Your Grace." Saryon bowed wearily. "Besides, I am suddenly so tired that I will probably never know whether I am lying on swan's down or pine needles."

"Very well, Father. I bid you good-night. And, Father"— Garald rested his hand on the older man's arm—"erase your conscience of the guilt of Blachloch's death. The man was evil. Had you allowed him to live, he would have killed Joram and taken the darkstone. It was by the Almin's will that Joram acted, the Almin's justice that Joram meted out."

"Perhaps." Saryon smiled wanly. "To my mind, it was still murder. Killing has become easy for Joram—too easy. He sees it as his way to gain the power he lacks in magic. I bid you good-night, Your Grace."

"Good night, Father," said Garald, considering his words thoughtfully, "May the Almin watch over you."

"May He indeed," Saryon murmured, turning away.

The Prince of Sharakan did not retire to his own tent until far into the starlit hours of early morning. Back and forth he walked over the grass in the cold night air, cloaked in furs that he caused to appear without thinking about it. His thoughts were occupied by the strange, dark tale of madness and murder, of Life and Death, of magic and its destroyer. At last, when he knew himself to be tired enough that he could banish the tale into the realm of sleep, he stood looking down at the slumbering group fate had cast into his path.

Or was it fate?

"This isn't the way to Merilon," he said to himself, the fact suddenly occurring to him. "Why are they traveling this route? There are others to the east far shorter and safer. . . .

"And who has been their guide? Let me guess. Three who have never traveled in the world. One who has been every-where." His eyes went to the figure in the white nightshirt. No babe in his mother's arms slumbered more sweetly than Simkin, though the tassel of the nightcap had fallen down over his mouth and there was every likelihood that he would inhale it and swal-low it before the night was ended.

"What game are you playing now, old friend?" muttered Garald. "Certainly not tarok. Of all the shadows I see falling across this young man, why is yours, somehow, the darkest?"

Musing on this, the Prince retired to his tent, leaving the unmoving, watchful *Duuk-tsarith* to rule the night.

But Garald's sleep was not unbroken as he had hoped. More than once, he found himself waking with a start, thinking he heard the gleeful laughter of a bucket.

12

The Fencing Master

"**G**et up!"

The toe of a boot struck Joram in the ribs, not gently. Startled, half-asleep, his heart pounding, the young man sat up from his blankets and shoved the tangled black hair back from his eyes. "What—"

"I said, get up," repeated a cool voice.

Prince Garald stood above Joram, regarding him with a pleasant smile.

Joram rubbed his eyes and glanced about. It was just before dawn, he supposed, although the only indication was a faint brightening of the sky above the treetops to the east. Otherwise, it was still dark. The fire had burned low; his companions lay asleep around it. Two silken tents, barely visible in the prelight, stood at the edge of the clearing, flags fluttering from their pointed tops. These had not been there the day before and were, presumably, where the Prince and Cardinal Radisovik spent the night.

In the center of the clearing, near the dying fire, stood one of the black-robed *Duuk-tsarith* in what Joram could swear was the same position he had seen him standing in last night. The warlock's hands were folded before him, his face lost in shadow. But the hooded head was turned toward Joram. So, too, were the unseen eyes.

"What is it? What do you want?" Joram asked. His hand crept to the sword beneath his blanket.

"'What do you want, *Your Grace*,'" corrected the Prince with a grin. "That does stick in your craw, doesn't it, young man. Yes, bring the weapon," he added, though Joram had supposed he was making his move unobserved.

Chagrined, Joram drew the Darksword from beneath the blanket, but he did not stand up.

"I asked what you wanted . . . Your Grace," he said coldly, his lip curling.

"If you are going to use that weapon"—the Prince glanced at the sword in amused distaste—"then you had better learn how to use it properly. I could have skewered you like a chicken yesterday instead of merely disarming you. Whatever powers that sword possesses"—Garald regarded it more intently—"won't do you much good if it is lying on the ground ten feet away from you. Come on. I know a place in the woods where we can practice without disturbing the others."

Joram hesitated, studying the Prince with his dark eyes, searching for the man's motive behind this show of interest.

Undoubtedly he wants to learn more about the sword, Joram thought. Perhaps even take if from me. What a charmer he is—almost as good as Simkin. I was duped by him last night. I won't be today. I'll go along with this, if I can truly learn something. If not, I'll leave. And if he tries to take the sword, I'll kill him.

Anticipating the chill air, Joram reached for his cloak, but the Prince stepped on it with his foot. "No, no, my friend," Garald said, "you'll be warm enough soon. Very warm indeed."

An hour later, laying flat on his back on the frozen ground, the breath knocked from his body and blood trickling from the corner of his mouth, Joram thought no more of his cloak.

The steel blade of the Prince's sword slammed into the ground near him, so close that he flinched.

"Right through the throat," Garald remarked. "And you never saw it coming. . . ."

"It wasn't a fair fight," Joram muttered. Accepting the Prince's hand, he heaved himself to his feet, swallowing a groan. "You tripped me!"

"My dear young man," said Garald impatiently, "when you draw that sword in earnest, it is—or should be—a matter of life and death. Your life and your opponent's death. Honor is a very fine thing, but the dead have little use for it."

"A pretty speech, coming from you," mumbled Joram, massaging his aching jaw and spitting out blood.

"I can afford honor," Garald said with a shrug. "I am a skilled swordsman. I have trained in the art for years. You, on the other hand, cannot. There is no way, in the short time we have together, that I can teach you even a part of the intricate techniques of sword fighting. What I can teach you is how to survive against a skilled opponent long enough to permit you to call upon the sword's . . . um . . . powers to defeat him.

"Now"—more briskly—"you try it. Look, your attention was concentrated on the sword in my hands. Thus I was able to bring my foot around, catch you behind the heel, drag you off balance, and clout you in the face with the hilt like this—" Garald demonstrated, stopping just short of Joram's bruised cheek. "Now you try it. Good! Good!" the Prince cried, tumbling down. "You're quick and strong. Use that to your advantage." He rose to his feet, taking no note of the mud on his fine clothes.

Stepping into a fighting stance, he raised his sword and grinned at Joram.

"Shall we have a go at it again?"

Hours passed. The sun rose in the sky and, though the day was far from warm, both men soon stripped off their shirts. Their labored breathing misted the air about them; the ground soon looked as though a small army had fought over it. The forest rang with the sound of blade against blade. Finally, when both were so exhausted they could do nothing but lean upon their weapons and gasp for breath, the Prince called a halt.

Sinking down on a boulder warmed by the sun, he motioned for Joram to sit beside him. The young man did so, panting and wiping his face. Blood seeped from numerous cuts and scratches on his arms and legs. His jaw was swollen and aching, several teeth had been knocked loose, and he was so tired that even breathing seemed an effort. But it was a good kind of tiredness. He'd held his own against the Prince in their last few passes and had, once, even knocked the sword from Garald's hand.

"Water," the Prince muttered, glancing about. A waterskin lay near their shirts—far across the clearing. With a weary gesture, Garald motioned for the waterskin to come to them. It obeyed, but the Prince was so tired that he had little energy to expend in magic. Consequently, the waterskin dragged itself across the ground, rather than flying swiftly through the air.

"It looks like I feel!" Garald said, panting.

Catching hold of the skin as it came near, he lifted it and drank a few sips, then passed it to Joram. "Not much," he cautioned. "Cramps the belly."

Joram drank and passed it back. Garald poured some in his hand and splashed it on his face and chest, his skin shivering in the biting air.

"You're doing . . . well, young man . . ." Garald said, drawing deep breaths. "Very . . . well. If . . . we're not both dead . . . at the end of the week . . . you should be . . . ready. . . ."

"Week? . . . Ready?" Joram saw the trees blur before his eyes. Talking coherently at the moment lay beyond his capacity. "I . . . leave . . . Merilon. . . ."

"Not for a week." Garald shook his head, and took another pull at the waterskin. "Don't forget . . ." he said with a grin, resting his arms on his knees and hanging his head down to breathe more easily, "you are my prisoner. Or do you think . . . you could fight me . . . and the *Duuk-tsarith*?"

Joram closed his eyes. His throat ached, his lungs burned, his muscles twitched, his cuts stung. He hurt all over. "I couldn't . . . fight . . . the catalyst . . . right now. . . ." he admitted with almost a smile.

The two sat upon the boulder, resting. Neither spoke, neither felt the need for speech. As he grew more rested, Joram relaxed, a warm and pleasant feeling of peace stole over him. He took note of the surroundings — a small clearing in the center of the forest, a clearing that might have been formed magically, it was so perfect. In fact, Joram realized, it probably *had* been carved from the woods by magic — the Prince's magic.

Joram and the Prince were alone, something else Joram wondered about. They had been making noise enough for a regiment, and the young man expected at any moment to see the snooping catalyst come to find out what was going on, or at least Mosiah and the ever-curious Simkin. But Garald had spoken to the *Duuk-tsarith* before they left, and Joram assumed now that he must have told them to keep everyone away.

"I don't mind," Joram decided. He liked it here — peaceful, quiet, the sun warm upon the rock where he was sitting. He couldn't remember, in fact, ever having felt this content. His restless mind slowed its frenetic pace and glided easily among the treetops, listening to the steady breathing of his companion, the pumping of his own heart.

"Joram," said Garald, "what do you plan to do when you get to Merilon?"

Joram shrugged, wishing the man had not spoken, willing him to be quiet and not break the spell.

"No, we need to discuss this," Garald said, seeing the expressive face grow shadowed. "Perhaps I'm wrong, but I have the feeling 'going to Merilon' is like some child's tale with you. Once you get there, you expect your life to be 'all better' just because you stand in the shadows of its floating platforms. Believe me, Joram"—the Prince shook his head—"it won't happen. I've been to Merilon. Not recently, of course." He smiled sardonically. "But in the days when we were at peace. And I can tell you that—right now—you won't get within sight of the city gates. You are a savage from the Outland. The *Duuk-tsarith* will have you"—he snapped his fingers—"like that!"

The sun disappeared, shrouded by clouds. A wind came up, whistling mournfully among the trees. Shivering, Joram stood up and started to walk across the clearing to where his shirt lay on the grass.

"No, stay. I'll get it," Garald said, putting a restraining hand on Joram's arm. With a gesture, he caused both shirts to take wing, flitting through the air toward them like fabric birds. "I'm sorry. I keep forgetting you are Dead. We have so few Dead in Sharakan, I've never met anyone like you."

Joram scowled, feeling the swift, sharp pain he always experienced whenever reminded of the difference between himself and everyone else in this world. He glared at the Prince angrily, certain the man was mocking him. But Garald wasn't watching, he had his head in his shirt. "I have always envied Simkin his ability to change his clothes at a whim. Not to mention," the Prince grunted, pulling the fine cambric shirt down over his shoulders, "changing himself at a whim. Bucket!"

His head emerging from the collar, Garald smoothed his hair, grinning over the remembrance. Then, growing more serious, he continued on his original topic of thought. "There are many Dead born in Merilon, or so we've heard," he said, his casual acceptance of the fact slowly smothering Joram's fiery anger. "Particularly among the nobility. But they try to get rid of them, putting the babies to death or smuggling them into the

Outland. They are rotting inside"—his clear eyes grew shadowed, darkening with his own anger—"and they would spread their disease to the entire world if they had their way. Well"—he drew a deep breath, shaking it off—"they won't have it."

"We were talking about Merilon," Joram said harshly. Sitting back down, he grabbed a handful of gravel from the ground, and began tossing rocks at a distant tree trunk.

"Yes, I'm sorry," Garald said. "Now, as to getting inside the city—"

"Look," Joram interrupted impatiently, "don't worry about it! We'll have fancy clothes, if that's all it takes. The castoffs from Simkin's wardrobe alone could last us for years. . . ."

"Then what?"

"Then—then. . . ." Joram shrugged impatiently. "What does it matter to you anyway . . . Your Grace?" he said, his lip curling in contempt. Glancing around, he saw Garald regarding him with a calm and serious expression, the clear eyes delving deep into dark, murky parts of Joram's soul that Joram himself had never dared explore. Instantly the young man reinforced the stone wall around himself.

"Why are you doing this?" he demanded angrily, gesturing at the Darksword that lay on the ground near him. "What do you care whether I live or die? What's in it for you?"

Garald regarded Joram silently, then he smiled slowly; a smile of sadness and regret. "That's all there is for you, isn't there, Joram?" he said. "'What's in it for me?' It doesn't matter to you that I've heard your story from the catalyst, that I pity you . . . Ah, yes, that makes you furious, but it's true. I pity you . . . and I admire you."

Joram turned away from the Prince, turned away from the intense gaze of those clear, clear eyes, his own dark eyes staring into the tangled boughs of the bare, dead trees.

"I admire you," the Prince continued steadily, "I admire the intelligence and perseverance you showed in discovering what has been lost to the world for centuries. I know the courage it took to face Blachloch, and I admire you for standing up to him. If nothing else, I owe you something for saving us—if inadvertently—from the double-dealings of the warlock. But, I see that doesn't satisfy you. You want my 'ulterior motive.'"

"Don't tell me you haven't got one," muttered Joram bitterly.

"Very well, my friend, I'll tell you 'what's in it for me.' You take your sword, your Darksword as you call it, and you go to Merilon. And with it or without it" — Garald shrugged — "you win back your inheritance. You conceal the fact that you are Dead — as you are well capable of doing so long as you have the catalyst to cover for you. Never thought about that, did you? Good idea, consider it. Up until now, it hasn't mattered whether or not you called upon a catalyst to give you Life. There weren't any catalysts in the Sorcerers' village to call. But it will be different in Merilon. You will be expected to use your catalyst, to have one with you. With Saryon at your side, you can keep up your pretense of having Life.

"But now, where was I? Oh, yes. You find your mother's people and you convince them that they should accept you into the bosom of their family. Who knows, they may be grieving still over the misguided daughter who ran away before they could show her how much they cared and were willing to forgive. Or perhaps the family has died out, perhaps you can prove your claim and gain their lands and title.

"No matter," Garald continued archly. "Let us suppose that all this has a happy ending and you are a nobleman, Joram; a nobleman of Merilon, complete with title and land and wealth. What do I want from you, noble gentleman? Look at me, Joram."

The young man could not help but turn at the compelling sound of the voice. There was no lightness, no archness in it now. "I want you to come to Sharakan," the Prince said. "I want you to bring your Darksword and to fight with us."

Joram stared at him incredulously. "What makes you think I'll do that? Once I *have* gained my rightful holdings, I'll do nothing but —"

"— watch the world go by?" Garald smiled. "No, I don't think you will, Joram. You couldn't do that among the Sorcerers. Fear for yourself didn't prompt you to fight the warlock. Oh, I don't know the details, but — if that had been the case — you could have always fled on your own, leaving someone else to face him. No, you did it because there is something deep inside you that feels the need to protect and defend those weaker than yourself. *That* is your birthright; you were born *Albanara*. And because of that I believe you will see Merilon with eyes that are not blinded by the pretty clouds among which its people dwell.

"You have been a Field Magus. By the Almin!" Garald continued more passionately as Joram, shaking his head, turned away again. "You have lived under the tyranny of Merilon, Joram! Its rigid traditions and beliefs caused your mother to be cast out, your father to be sentenced to living death! You will see a city of beauty, certainly, but it is beauty covering decay! It is even said that the Empress—" Garald stopped abruptly. "Never mind." He spoke in a low voice, clasping his hands together. "I can't believe *that* is true, not even of them."

The Prince paused, drawing a deep breath. "Don't you see, Joram?" he continued more calmly. "You—a noble of Merilon—come to us, prepared to fight to restore your city's ancient honor. My people would be impressed. And, most importantly, you would help influence the Sorcerers, whom you have lived among. We hope to ally with them, but I am certain they would follow my father's guidance much more readily if he could point to you and say, 'Look, here is one you know and trust, fighting on our side as well!' The Sorcerers do know and like you, I suppose?" the Prince asked offhandedly.

Had Joram been knowledgeable about such things as verbal parry and thrust, he would have recognized that the Prince was maneuvering him into position.

"They know me, at least," Joram said briefly, not giving the matter much thought. He was considering the Prince's words. He could see himself riding into Sharakan, resplendent with the trappings of his rank, to be welcomed by the King and his son. That would be a fine thing. But going to war with them? Bah! What did he care. . . .

"Ah!" Garald said casually. "'They know me, at least,' you say. Which means, I suppose, that they know you but don't particularly like you. And, of course, you don't give a damn about that, do you?"

Joram raised his dark eyes, on his guard at once. It was too late.

"You will fail in Merilon, Joram. You will fail anywhere you go."

"And why is that . . . Your Grace?" Sneering, Joram never felt the point of the verbal blade pressed against his heart.

"Because you want to be a noble, and perhaps by rights you *are* a noble. But unfortunately, Joram, there isn't one ounce of nobility within you," answered Garald coolly.

The words struck home. Torn and bleeding inside, Joram made a clumsy attempt to return the blow. "Forgive me, Your Grace!" he whined in mockery. "I don't have fine clothes, like you. I don't bathe in rose petals, or perfume my hair! People don't call me 'milord' and beg to kiss my ass! Not yet they don't! But they will!" His voice shook in anger. He sprang to his feet, facing Garald, his fists clenched. "By the Almin, they will! And so will you, damn you!"

Garald rose to face the enraged young man. "Yes, I should have guessed that is your idea of a nobleman, Joram. And this is precisely why you will never be one. I'm beginning to think that I mistook you, that you belong in Merilon, because this is exactly what many of them think!" The Prince glanced eastward, in the direction of the faraway city. "They will soon learn they are wrong," he said earnestly, "but they will pay dearly for their lesson. And so will you." He focused his attention on the quivering, angry young man standing before him. "The Almin teaches us that a man is noble, not by some accident of birth, but by how he treats his fellow man. Strip away the fine clothes and the perfume and the gilt, Joram, and your body is no different from that of your friend, the Field Magus. Naked, we are all the same — nothing more than food for the worms.

"The dead have little use for honor, as I said before. They have little use for anything else, either. What are title, wealth, breeding to them? We may walk different paths through this life, Joram, but they all lead the same place — to the grave. It is our duty — no, it is our privilege, as fellow travelers who have been blessed more than others — to make the way as smooth and pleasant for as many as we can."

"Fine words!" Joram retorted furiously. "But you're quick enough to lap up 'Your Grace' and 'Your Highness'! I don't see *you* dressed in the coarse robes of the peasants. I don't see you rising at dawn and spending your days grubbing in the fields until your very soul starts to shrivel like the weeds you touch!" He pointed at the Prince. "You're a wonderful talker! You and your fancy clothes and bright swords, silk tents and bodyguards! That's what I think of your words!" Joram made an obscene gesture, laughed, and began to walk away.

Reaching out, Garald caught hold of him by the shoulder and spun him around. Joram shook free. His face distorted by rage, he struck at the man, swinging his fist wildly. The Prince countered the blow easily, catching it on his forearm. With practiced skill, he grabbed Joram's wrist, gave it a twist, and forced the young man to his knees. Gagging in pain, Joram struggled to stand up.

"Stop it! Fighting me is useless. With one word of magic I could tear your arm from its socket!" Garald said coldly, holding the young man fast.

"Damn you, you —!" Joram swore at him, spitting filth. "You and your magic! If I had my sword, I'd—" He looked around for it, feverishly.

"I'll give you your cursed sword," the Prince said grimly. "Then you can do what you want. But first, you will listen to me. In order to do my work in this life, I must dress and act in a manner befitting my station. Yes, I wear fancy clothes and bathe and comb my hair, and I'm going to see to it that you do these things, too, before you go to Merilon. Why? Because it shows you care what people think of you. As for my title, people call me 'milord' and 'Your Grace' as a mark of respect for my station. But I hope it is a mark of respect for me as a person as well. Why do you think I don't force you to do it? Because the words are empty for you. You don't respect anybody, Joram. You don't care for anybody. Least of all yourself!"

"You're wrong!" Joram whispered huskily, looking for the sword. But it was hard to see, a green-tinged, blood-red pool of rage blinded him. "You're wrong! I care—"

"Then, show it!" Garald cried. Grabbing hold of the long black hair, the Prince jerked Joram's head back, forcing the young man to look up at him. Joram did so, he had no choice. But the pain-filled, defiant eyes glared at the Prince in bitter hatred.

"You were willing to give your life for Mosiah last night, weren't you?" Garald continued relentlessly. "Yet, you treat him as if he were some mongrel slouching at your heels. And the catalyst—a man learned and gentle, who should be spending his middle years in peace, pursuing the study that he loves. He fought the warlock with you, and now he follows you through the wilderness, weary and aching, when he could have turned you over to the Church. For what reason, do you suppose? Ah yes, of course, I forgot. His 'ulterior motive.' He *wants* something from you! What? Insults, gibes, sneers?"

"Bah!" Garald sent Joram sprawling facedown on the frozen ground. Lifting his head, Joram saw the Darksword lying right in front of him. Lunging forward, he grasped the hilt.

He scrambled to his feet, twisting around to face his enemy. Garald stood staring at him coldly, a smile of amused contempt on his lips.

"Fight! Damn you!" Joram shouted, leaping at the man.

The Prince spoke a word of command, and his own sword rose from the grass where it lay and flew into his hand, the blade shining silver in the gray light of sunless sky.

"Use your magic against me!" Joram challenged. He could barely speak; froth covered his lips. "I'm Dead, after all! Only this sword makes me Alive! And I'm going to see you die!"

Joram intended to kill. He wanted to kill. He could feel the satisfying impact of the sword striking flesh, see the blood flow, the proud figure crumble at his feet, the dying eyes gazing up at him . . .

Garald regarded him calmly a moment, then slid his own bright sword back in its leather scabbard. "You *are* Dead, Joram," he said softly. "You stink of death! And you have made a sword of darkness, a thing as dead as you are. Go ahead, kill me. Death is your solution!"

Joram willed himself forward. But he couldn't see. A film coated his eyes and he blinked, trying to clear them.

"Come to *life*, Joram," Garald said earnestly. The Prince's voice sounded far away, drifting to Joram out of the blood-red mist that surrounded him. "Come to life and wield your sword in the cause of life, the cause of the living! Otherwise you might as well turn that sword upon yourself, and spill every drop of that noble blood right here on the ground. At least it will give life to the grass."

The last words were spoken in disgust. Turning his back on Joram, the Prince walked calmly from the clearing.

Sword in hand, Joram lunged after him, determined to slay the arrogant man. But he was completely blind in his fury. Stumbling, Joram fell flat on his face. With a wild, ragged cry of anger, he struggled to stand, but his rage had drained him, left him weak and helpless as a baby. Desperate, he tried using the Darksword as a crutch to pull himself to his feet. But the blade sank deep in the churned-up dirt and Joram sagged to his knees.

His hands clenching around the hilt of the sword that stood before him, buried in the mud, Joram slumped over it. Tears crept from beneath his eyelids. Anger and frustration welled up inside him until he thought his heart would burst. A racking sob tore open his chest, easing the pressure. His head bowed, Joram cried the tears that neither pain nor suffering had wrung from him since he was a small child.

13

Winter Night

"**W**here is Joram?" asked Saryon as the Prince returned to the glade. The catalyst's eyes widened in alarm at the sight of Garald's pale face, his muddy clothes, and the spots of blood upon the white shirt where one of his cuts had come open in his struggles with Joram.

"Rest easy, Father," Garald said wearily. "He is back in the woods. We . . . had a little talk. . . ." The Prince smiled ruefully, looking down at his torn clothing. "He needs time to think. At least, I hope he thinks."

"Should he be out there? By himself?" Saryon persisted, his eyes going to the forest. Above the trees, gray clouds skittered across the sky. To the northwest, darker, heavier masses of clouds could be seen forming. The wind had switched direction, blowing warmer. But the air itself was heavy, laden with moisture—rain almost assuredly, snow by nightfall.

"He'll be all right," Garald said, running his hand through his damp hair. "We've seen no signs of centaurs in these woods. Besides, he isn't by himself. Not really." The Prince glanced around the camp.

Following his gaze, Saryon understood at once. Only one of the *Duuk-tsarith* was present. Instead of being comforted, the catalyst only appeared more worried. "Forgive me, Your Grace," Saryon said hesitantly, "but Joram is . . . is a criminal. I know that they have heard us talking." He gestured toward the black-robed, silent figure. "Nothing escapes their attention. What—"

"What prevents them from disobeying me and taking Joram back to Merilon? Nothing." Garald shrugged. "I certainly couldn't stop them. But, you see, Father, as my personal guard, they are sworn to be loyal to me unto death. If they betrayed me, and took the boy against my command, they would not face a hero's welcome. Far to the contrary. For breaking their sworn oath, they would receive the most severe form of punishment their Order metes out. And what that might be, among their strict kind"—the Prince shuddered—"I dare not venture to guess. No," he said with a smile and shrug, "Joram is not worth that to them."

Joram isn't—but the Prince of Merilon certainly would be, Saryon thought. He would have to guard his secret that much more closely.

The Prince retired to his tent, and Saryon returned to sit by the warm pools of the spring, noticing that Radisovik, at a gesture from Garald, followed the Prince. The remaining *Duuk-tsarith* stood silently, staring at nothing and everything from beneath his black hood. Lounging on the grass beside the steaming waters, Simkin was teasing the raven, trying to make it talk in exchange for a piece of sausage.

"Come on, you wretched bird," Simkin said. "Repeat after me: 'The Prince is a fool. The Prince is a fool.' Say that for Simkin, and Simkin will give you this nice bit of meat."

The bird regarded Simkin gravely, its head cocked to one side, but refused to utter a croak.

"Hush, you idiot!" Mosiah whispered, referring to Simkin, not the bird. He motioned toward the silken tent. "Aren't we in enough trouble?"

"What? Oh, Garald? Bah!" Simkin grinned, smoothing his beard. "He'll think it loads of fun. Quite the joker himself. He once brought a live bear to a costume ball at court. Introduced him as Captain Noseblower, of the Royal Navy of Zith-el. You should have seen the King, keeping up polite conversation with the supposed captain and endeavoring to look perfectly unconscious of the fact that the bear was munching on his cravat. Bear lost the prize for best costume, though. Now, you red-eyed fiend from hell"—Simkin fixed the raven with a stern gaze—"say,

'The Prince is a fool! The Prince is a fool!'" He spoke in a high-pitched, birdlike squawk.

The bird raised a yellow foot and scratched its beak in what might have been taken for a rude gesture.

"Stupid bird!" Simkin remarked testily.

"Simkin's a fool! Simkin's a fool!" cried the raven. With a flutter of wings, it bounced up from the ground, snatched the meat from the young man's hand, and carried off the prize to a nearby tree.

Simkin laughed heartily, but Mosiah's worried expression only grew deeper. Moving near Saryon, he glanced apprehensively at the *Duuk-tsarith*, then said quietly, "What do you think is going to happen? What does the Prince intend to do with us?"

"I don't know," Saryon answered gravely. "A lot depends on Joram."

"Gad! We'll all hang then," Simkin interjected cheerfully, scooting across the ground to sit next to the catalyst. "The two of them got into a frightful row this morning. The Prince stripped the flesh from our poor friend's bones and hung him out to dry, while the ever-tactful Joram called His Royal Highness an —" Simkin didn't say the word, but pointed to the part of the body to which it referred.

"Name of the Almin!" gasped Mosiah, turning pale.

"Pray all you like, but I doubt it will help," said Simkin languidly. He dabbled his hand in the hot water. "We should just count ourselves fortunate that he merely called His Grace an — you know — and didn't turn him into one, as happened to the unfortunate Count d'Chambray. It occurred during a quarrel with Baron Roethke. The Count shouted, 'You're an —!' The Baron cried, 'You're another!' Grabbed his catalyst, cast a spell, and there the Count was, turned into one, right in front of the ladies and everything. Repulsive sight."

"Do you suppose that's true?" Mosiah asked worriedly.

"I swear it on my mother's grave!" vowed Simkin with a yawn.

"No, I don't mean the Count," Mosiah snapped. "I mean about Joram."

The catalyst's gaze went to the woods. "I wouldn't doubt it," he said glumly.

"Hanging isn't a bad way to die," remarked Simkin, lying full length upon the grass, his eyes on the massing clouds above. "Of course, are there good ways? That's the question."

"They don't hang people anymore," Mosiah said irritably.

"Ah, but they might make an exception in our case," Simkin replied.

"Simkin's a fool! Simkin's a fool!" croaked the raven from the branches above, hopping nearer in hopes of more sausage.

Is he a fool? Saryon asked himself. No, the catalyst decided uneasily. If what he said was correct and Joram had insulted the Prince, then — for once in his life and probably without knowing it — Simkin may have spoken the truth.

The storm broke at midafternoon, rain pouring from clouds hanging so low in the sky it seemed they might have been punctured by the tall, prong-branched trees. With the Cardinal granting him Life, the Prince used his magic to create an invisible shield over the glade, protecting them from the deluge. In order to have energy enough to perform this magic, however, it was necessary for Garald to remove the warm springs. Saryon saw the steaming pool go with regret. The shield kept them dry, but it was not particularly warm. And it gave the catalyst an odd feeling to look up and see the rain slashing down at them without touching them; watery spears that were suddenly deflected and turned aside by the unseen shield.

"I miss the warmth of the springs, but this is much better than being cooped up in a stuffy tent all day, wouldn't you agree, Father?" Garald said conversationally. "Under the shield, we can at least move about in the open air. Come nearer the fire, if you are chilled, Father."

Saryon was in no mood to talk, however, although he did walk over to sit by the fire, and even managed to mumble a polite rejoinder. His gaze continually strayed through the curtain of steaming water into the forest. Hours had passed and Joram had not returned.

The Cardinal also attempted conversation with Saryon, but soon gave it up, seeing the catalyst's worried preoccupation. Radisovik, with a meaningful glance at the Prince, retired to his tent to study and meditate.

Gathering near the fire, Garald, Mosiah, and Simkin played at tarok. The game got off to a slow start; Mosiah was so overawed at playing cards with a Prince that he fumbled his cards — dropping them twice — misdealt a hand, and made such glaring errors in play that Simkin suggested the bird take his place. But Garald, without losing any of his dignity or the quiet, regal air that surrounded him, soon made Mosiah so relaxed and at ease that the young man actually dared laugh in the Prince's presence and once made a feeble, blushing attempt at a joke.

Saryon noted uneasily, however, that Garald managed to lead the conversation more than once to Joram, urging Mosiah — during breaks in the game — to tell him stories of their childhood. Having never truly conquered his homesickness, Mosiah was only too happy to recall his early life in the farm village. Garald listened to all the tales with an air of grave interest very flattering to the young man, sometimes allowing him to range far afield, yet always, with a seemingly offhand question, subtly leading the talk specifically to Joram.

Why this interest in him? Saryon wondered with growing fear. Does he suspect the truth? The catalyst thought back to their first encounter. He recalled the strange, intense way the Prince had looked at Joram, as if trying to remember where he had seen the face before. Garald had been to the court of Merilon often as a child. To Saryon, burdened with his secret, it seemed that Joram's resemblance to his true mother, the Empress, grew daily. There was a way he had of throwing back his head in haughty dignity, a way of tossing the rich, luxuriant, wild black hair that made Saryon want to scream at them — "Can't you see, you fools! Are you blind?"

Perhaps Garald *did* see. Perhaps he *wasn't* blind. Certainly he was intelligent, shrewd, and — for all his disarming charm — he was *Albanara*, born to politics, born to rule. The state and its people came first in his heart. What would he do if he did know or suspect the truth? Saryon couldn't imagine. Perhaps nothing more or less than he was doing now — until time came to leave. The catalyst pondered until his head ached, but got nowhere. Meanwhile, the hours passed. The gray stormy afternoon darkened to gray stormy evening. The rain changed to snow.

And still Joram did not return.

The card game broke up for dinner. The meal consisted of a woodland stew that the Prince had proudly concocted with his own hands, expounding at length upon the various herbs that went into its preparation, boasting that he had gathered these himself upon his journey.

Saryon made a show of eating so as not to offend the Prince, though — in actuality — he managed to smuggle most of his dinner to the raven. The *Duuk-tsarith* who had — presumably —

been watching over Joram returned, and the other left to take his place. At least that is what Saryon assumed; he could not distinguish between the two guards, faceless in their black hoods. The warlock conferred with Garald, and by the glances the Prince cast in the direction of the forest, Saryon knew the subject of their conversation. This was confirmed when the Prince came over to talk to the catalyst immediately afterward.

"Joram is safe and well, Father," Garald reported. "Please do not concern yourself. He has taken shelter in a cleft in the cliff face. He needs time to be alone. The wound I inflicted is deep, I think, but not mortal, and he will be better for the blood-letting."

Saryon was not convinced, and neither was Mosiah.

"You remember those black moods that used to come upon him, Father?" the young man said softly, sitting down beside the catalyst as he toyed with his uneaten food. The raven, perched at the catalyst's left hand, kept a hungry eye on them. "He hasn't had any recently, but in the past I've seen him lie on his bed for days, not eating, not talking. Just staring into nothing."

"I know. And if he's not back by morning, we'll go after him," Saryon said resolutely.

The snow continued to fall, and the Prince was forced to remove the shield, since keeping it in place through the storm was draining both his energy and that of the Cardinal. Simkin and Mosiah moved into the Prince's large tent for the night; Saryon accepted the offer to share Radisovik's.

As for the *Duuk-tsarith*, they had both vanished, though the catalyst knew the warlocks were around somewhere, guarding the Prince's rest. When they themselves found time to sleep, the catalyst couldn't imagine. He had heard rumors that the warlocks had the ability to put mind and body to sleep while maintaining unceasing vigilance. That sounded improbable, however, and he disregarded it as legend.

Grateful for any small problem to keep his mind off his worries, Saryon considered the matter as he lay awake in the darkness, listening for the crunch of footsteps in the snow. Eventually, the catalyst slept. But it was a disturbed sleep. Awakening often in the night, he padded softly to the opening of the tent and gently, so as not to disturb the slumbering Cardinal, parted the flaps to look out.

What he hoped to see, he had no idea, for the snow fell so thickly he could barely make out the dark shape of the Prince's tent that stood next to theirs. He did notice that he wasn't the only one keeping watch. Once he caught a gleam of light from Garald's tent and thought he saw, through the snow, the tall figure of the Prince, peering out into the night.

By morning, the snow ended. Lying on thick cushions, the catalyst watched the light of dawn creep slowly into his tent, picturing it filtering through the tangled boughs of the snow-laden trees, leaving a glistening track across the smooth expanse of white outside.

He started to close his eyes, force himself to try to sleep, then he heard what he had been waiting for — footsteps.

His heart constricting in relief, Saryon hastily rose and threw aside the tent flap. There, he stopped, drawing back out of sight.

Joram stood in the center of the snow-covered glade. He was wrapped in a heavy cloak. Where had that come from? Had the *Duuk-tsarith* taken it to him? Saryon found time to wonder as he waited, breathlessly, to see what Joram would do now.

Moving through snow that was halfway up his tall boots, Joram came to a halt outside the Prince's tent. Reaching beneath the cloak, he drew out the Darksword and held it in his hands.

Saryon crouched back into the shadows of the tent, his relief changing to fear at the sight of the expression on Joram's face.

Saryon wasn't certain what change — if any — he had expected to see in the young man. A meek and contrite Joram, humbly begging everyone's forgiveness and vowing to live a better life? No — Saryon couldn't imagine that.

An angry, defiant Joram, determined to go to the devil in his own way and quite willing to let everyone else do the same? That was far more realistic. It was, in fact, what the catalyst expected. He would have welcomed it, he realized, in comparison to the Joram he saw.

There was no expression on the young man's face at all. Pale and wan, cheeks sunken, eyes dark and shadowed, Joram waited silently, unmoving outside the Prince's tent, his hands clasped about the hilt of the sword.

Having undoubtedly heard the same footsteps that had caught Saryon's ear, Garald stepped outside, coming to a halt before the strange figure standing in front of the tent. The Prince was in no danger. The *Duuk-tsarith* were close-by; their magic would dismember Joram before the boy had even raised the weapon.

It was Joram himself who was in danger, and Garald, knowing this, moved slowly, keeping his hands visible.

"Joram," he said gently, pleasantly.

"Your Grace." The words were coldly spoken, deliberately empty and without meaning. Garald's shoulders slumped in defeat; he sighed softly. Then his patience gave way, it seemed — anger at this arrogant young man finally overtook him.

"What do you want?" Prince Garald asked bitterly.

Joram's lips pressed together. He drew a deep breath and let it out slowly, fixing his dark eyes on a point somewhere above the Prince's shoulder. "We haven't much time," he said, speaking to the distance, to the bare trees, the brightening blue sky, the thin rim of the rising sun. "A week, you said."

The words were so cold, Saryon was somewhat amazed to see the warmth of the breath that spoke them form a mist in the chill air. Joram swallowed. The hands, clasping the hilt of the Darksword, tightened. "I have much to learn," he said.

Garald's face brightened with a smile that seemed to warm the glade more than the steaming spring. He made a move as if to take hold of the young man, clap him on the back, grasp him by the shoulders or do something to indicate his pleasure. But Saryon saw Joram's jaw muscles clench, the entire body stiffen. The Prince saw this, too, and checked his impulsive movement.

"I'll get my sword," he said, and went back into his tent.

Unaware that anyone was watching — for the catalyst had kept carefully silent — Joram relaxed. His gaze shifted, he looked directly at the spot where the Prince had been standing, and it seemed to Saryon that he saw the stern face softened by a look of regret. Joram's lips parted, as though he would speak. But he turned away abruptly, his mouth snapping shut. When the Prince came back out — dressed in a fur cloak, sword in hand — Joram met him with a face as cold and trackless as the snow.

How he reaches out for love, Saryon saw, his heart aching. And yet when a hand starts to grasp his in return, he strikes it away.

The two walked off in silence, the Prince glancing occasionally at Joram, Joram walking steadily, his eyes on his destination. In the distance, at the edge of the trees, the catalyst saw a black shadow detach itself from the trunk of a tree and glide slowly and unobserved behind them.

Realizing he was shivering with cold, Saryon returned to his bed. He knew, as he huddled into his blankets, that he should offer a prayer to the Almin in thanks for the young man's safe return.

But Saryon did not trouble his unhearing, perhaps nonexistent god. Recalling Joram's changed attitude and seeing behind it an even more fixed determination and resolve to achieve his goal, Saryon wasn't certain if he wanted to offer up thanks.

He felt more inclined to beg for mercy.

14

The Parting

With the end of the snow, the wind died and the sky cleared rapidly. A hush settled over the forest, but there was a tension in the air that was far from peaceful, almost as though a giant had sucked up cloud and wind and snow and was now holding its breath in a fit of pique. The tension did not lessen during the days that followed, although the sky remained clear — its color the brittle blue seen only in winter — and there was no sign of returning storms.

But everyone in the glade knew that a storm raged, if only in the soul of one young man. The storm clouds were never clearly visible; since the morning of his return, Joram had remained the same — cool and impassive, silent and reserved. He spoke only when spoken to, and then his answers were brief and careless, as though he had not heard. He was gone from camp much of the time, he and the Prince spending the largest part of each day together. When he came back from these sessions, Joram was even more withdrawn. It seemed to those observing him that his nerves were stretched taut as the strings of a badly tuned instrument.

Saryon could only hope (he did not pray) that some master hand was slowly working to ease the pressure on those strings before they snapped, to find the beautiful music that the catalyst was convinced must be locked within the young man's dark soul. Was Garald's the hand? Saryon began to believe it was, and this hope lightened the burden he bore. He had no idea what they did or talked about when alone together. Joram refused to discuss the meetings at all, and Garald said only that they were practicing Joram's swordwork.

Then, one early morning near the middle of the week, the catalyst was invited to accompany them to what the Prince jokingly referred to as "the arena."

"We need you to help us experiment with the Darksword, Father," Garald explained when he and Joram roused the catalyst from his fitful slumbers. The three stood talking outside the Cardinal's tent, speaking in low tones so as not to wake anyone else.

Seeing Saryon's solemn, disapproving expression, Joram gave an impatient sigh that was checked by a slight movement of Garald's hand.

"I understand your feelings, Father Saryon," the Prince said kindly, "but you would not send Joram into Merilon without knowledge of the sword's powers, would you?"

I would not send Joram into Merilon at all, the catalyst thought but did not say.

Saryon agreed to go along, however. He was forced to admit that the Prince's argument had merit. And the catalyst was, in addition, secretly curious about the Darksword himself. Wrapping himself in a warm cloak provided by the Prince, he accompanied the two into the forest.

"I am sorry to trouble you, Father," Garald apologized as they walked through the frozen woods. "I could have asked Cardinal Radisovik, of course, but Joram and I believe that the fewer people who know the true nature of the Darksword, the better."

Saryon agreed wholeheartedly.

"Then, too"—Garald smiled—"despite the fact that Radisovik is quite progressive and liberal in much of his thinking—far too liberal, according to your Bishop—I fear that the Darksword might stretch his tenets just a bit too far."

"I will try to do what I can to help, Your Grace," Saryon replied, wrapping his chilled hands in the sleeves of his robes.

"Excellent!" said Garald heartily. "And we will do what we can to keep the cold from you; something that never seems to be a problem for Joram and me."

He exchanged glances with the young man, and Saryon was astonished to see a slight smile on the stern lips and a flicker of warmth in Joram's dark eyes. Saryon's own heartache eased at that moment, and he felt warmer already.

The "arena" turned out to be a patch of cleared, frozen ground located in the woods some distance from the glade. Though Saryon knew the watchful *Duuk-tsarith* must be around, he could not see the warlocks, and the three had at least the impression of being alone. Or perhaps the *Duuk-tsarith* weren't there after all. The Prince might have meant what he said about keeping the Darksword's powers secret.

Garald settled the catalyst comfortably in a veritable nest of luxurious cushions he conjured up. He would have added wine and any other delicacies the catalyst might have desired had not Saryon, embarrassed, refused.

Saryon could not help liking the Prince. Garald treated the catalyst with the utmost respect and courtesy, always solicitous of his welfare and comfort, yet never demeaning or patronizing. Nor was the catalyst alone in this. Garald treated everyone this way—from Simkin and Mosiah to the *Duuk-tsarith* and Joram.

How his people must love their Prince, the catalyst thought, watching the graceful, elegant nobleman talk to the awkward, diffident youth—listening to Joram respectfully, treating him as an equal, yet not hesitating to point out when he thought the young man was wrong.

Joram, too, appeared to be studying Garald. Perhaps this was what was causing the turmoil in his soul. Saryon knew that Joram would give anything to be accorded the same respect and love that this man received. Maybe the young man was beginning to realize that it had to be given before it could be gained back in return.

Joram and the Prince took their places in the center of the arena, but they did not immediately assume their fighting stances.

"Hand me your sword a moment," said Garald.

Joram's eyes flashed, the brows came together, and he hesitated. Saryon shook his head. Well, he couldn't expect miracles, he told himself. Garald, his gaze on the sword, appeared not to notice but waited patiently.

Finally Joram handed over the weapon with an ungracious "Here."

Keeping his face carefully expressionless, pretending not to notice the rude comment, Gerald accepted the sword and proceeded to study it intently.

"The last few days, we've practiced with it just for the sake of swordsmanship alone," he said. "Yet, all the time, I can feel it tugging at me, draining my magic so that by the end of the day, I can feel the weakness in my body. But it doesn't have that effect on me when, for example, we are back in camp. I don't notice it at all."

"I think it has to be wielded in order to produce the Life-draining effect," Joram said, forgetting himself in his interest in the sword. "I noticed the same thing when I fought the warlock. When Blachloch first came into the forge, the sword did not react. But when he attacked me, and I raised the sword to defend myself, I could feel the weapon begin to fight on its own."

"I think I understand," Garald murmured thoughtfully. "The weapon must react from some sort of energy it feels from you — anger, fear, the strong emotions generated by battle. Here" — casually he unbuckled the scabbard of his own sword and handed the beautiful weapon to Joram — "take mine. Go ahead. You can use it. The fact that you're Dead won't matter. Its magical properties can be activated by command." The Prince took his fighting stance, raising the Darksword awkwardly. "I wish someone had taught you the art of swordmaking," he muttered. "This will always be a clumsy, unhandy weapon. But, never mind that now. Say the words 'hawk, strike,' and attack me."

His hands wrapping lovingly around the finely crafted hilt of the Prince's sword, Joram faced Garald, weapon raised. "Hawk, strike," he spoke, and pressed forward to the attack. Garald raised the Darksword in defense but, as quick as lightning, his own weapon penetrated his guard, wounding him in the shoulder.

"My god!" Seeing blood stream down the Prince's arm, Joram dropped the sword. "I didn't mean to, I swear! Are you all right?"

Saryon jumped to his feet.

"My own fault," Garald said grimly, pressing his hand over the wound. "It's nothing. Just a scratch, as the actors in the play say right before they drop dead — I'm teasing, Father. It really is a scratch, look." He exhibited the wound and Saryon saw, with relief, that the sword had cut through only the surface layers of skin. He was able to stop the bleeding with a spell of minor healing, and the "lesson" continued.

At least, thought Saryon grimly, this proves the *Duuk-tsarith* aren't around. Joram would be torn to a hundred pieces by now. It also pleased him beyond measure to have heard a note of true caring in Joram's voice, although — from the smooth, cold expression on the young man's face — the catalyst could almost believe he had imagined it.

"It was my own stupidity," Garald said ruefully. "I could have been killed by my own blade!" He glared at the Darksword. "Why didn't you work?" he asked, shaking it.

The answer came to Saryon's mind, but — mathematician that he was — he had to prove it first to his own satisfaction before he revealed it.

"Give the sword back to Joram, milord," Saryon instructed. "You take your sword and attack him, using the same spell."

Garald frowned. "It is a powerful spell, as you've seen. I could kill him."

"You won't," said Joram calmly.

"I agreed, milord," added Saryon. "Please. I think you will be interested in the result."

"Very well," Garald said, though with obvious reluctance. He obediently switched blades, and he and Joram took their positions.

"Hawk, strike," Garald commanded.

Instantly, his silver blade flashed in the sunlight, soaring like the bird it was named for toward its victim. Joram defended himself with the Darksword, his movements unskilled and clumsy compared to those of the Prince's magically enhanced weapon. The silver blade skimmed toward the young man's heart, only to be deflected at the last moment and turned aside as though it had hit an iron shield.

"Aahh!" cried Garald. Lowering his weapon, he rubbed his arm that tingled from the jarring blow. He looked over at Saryon. "I take it that's what you wanted me to see. All right, why does it work for him? Does it know its owner?"

"Not at all, milord," answered the catalyst, pleased at the success of his experiment. "Now I understand a statement I read in one of the ancient texts. It said that the swords made of darkstone were wielded by legions of the dead. I discounted it, thinking this a fanciful legend of ghosts and spirits. But now I

see the Sorcerers of old meant legions of men who—like
Joram—are Dead. It has to be used by someone possessing little or no magic of his own that would work against the energy of
the sword."

"Fascinating," said Garald, regarding the weapon with awe.
"This allows those who might otherwise be worse than useless in
a battle against wizards to become an effective fighting force."

"And it requires a minimum of training, milord," said
Saryon, growing more interested in his subject. His thoughts
raced like quicksilver. "Unlike warlocks—whose training begins
practically from birth—warriors armed with darkstone weapons can be taught to use them in a matter of weeks. Then, too,
they require no catalysts—" Saryon stopped abruptly, realizing
he had said too much.

But Garald was quick to catch his meaning.

"No, you're wrong!" he cried in excitement. "I mean yes,
you are right—to an extent. Darkstone weapons don't *require*
catalysts to work. But you spoke of giving the sword Life when
it was forged, Saryon. What if you gave it Life now? Wouldn't
that enhance its powers?"

"It must!" Joram said eagerly. "Let's try."

"Yes!" agreed Garald, raising his sword again.

"No!" said Saryon.

The two turned, staring at him—Joram angry, Garald dis-
appointed.

"Father, I know this is difficult for you—" he began to argue
tactfully.

"No," Saryon repeated in subdued, hollow tones. "No, Your
Grace. Anything else you ask of me, I would grant you, if I
could. But I will not do that, ever again."

"A vow to your god?" Joram could not help but ask bitterly.

"A vow to myself," Saryon replied in a low voice.

"Oh, for the love of—" Joram began, but Garald cut in
smoothly.

"It was a matter of curiosity, nothing more," the Prince said,
shrugging. He turned to Joram. "Certainly, it should not affect
your use of the sword. You could not count upon a catalyst being
with you when you might be called upon to wield it. Come, let
us try it against more powerful magic. I will cast a spell of
shielding around myself and we will see if you can penetrate it.
Father, if you could grant *me* Life . . ."

Saryon granted the prince Life, feeling a true pleasure in pouring the magic of the world into such a noble vessel. He even had the satisfaction of watching Joram struggle to control his anger and eventually get the best of it. Sitting back down among the cushions, the catalyst was able to watch and enjoy the contest between the two, learning more about the Darksword as he did so. But he knew in his heart that he had dropped a notch in Garald's opinion. A warrior to his core, the Prince could not understand what he must consider the catalyst's squeamish reluctance to grant Life to the sword.

To Garald, it was a tool, nothing more. He did not see it as the object of darkness, the destroyer of life that Saryon beheld when he looked at the ugly weapon.

As for what Joram thought, Saryon believed sadly that nothing he did could further lower him in the young man's opinion.

After several hours of hard practice, Joram, the Prince, and Saryon returned to camp. During the remainder of their stay, Garald was unfailingly kind to the catalyst, but he never asked Saryon to go back to the arena with him and Joram.

The week passed uneventfully. Joram and Garald practiced with the swords. Saryon enjoyed several interesting philosophical and religious discussions with Cardinal Radisovik. Simkin teased the raven (the exasperated bird finally bit a chunk out of the young man's ear, much to everyone's delight). Mosiah spent the days leafing wistfully through books he found in Garald's tent, studying the pictures and puzzling over the mysterious symbols that said so much to Joram but spoke meaningless gibberish to him. Evenings the Prince and his guests came together, playing tarok or discussing ways to enter Merilon and how to survive once they were inside the city.

"Simkin can get you through the Gate," Garald said one night, on the eve of their departure. Mosiah and Joram sat inside the Prince's luxurious tent, resting after a delicious dinner. Their idyllic time was coming to an end. Each of the younger men was thinking with regret that tomorrow night they would be fighting Kij vines and perhaps other, more fearsome monsters in the strange and foreboding wilderness. The splendors of Merilon suddenly seemed dreamlike and far away, and it was hard to take the thought of danger in that distant place seriously.

Seeing something of this reflected in their faces, Garald's tone grew more serious. "Simkin knows everyone in Merilon and they know him — which in some instances may make matters very interesting."

"You mean those . . . those outlandish stories of his are true, milord? Did you really bring a live bear to a costume ball?" Mosiah blurted out before he thought. "I beg pardon, Your Grace," he began, flushing in embarrassment.

But the Prince only shook his head. "Ah, he told you about that, did he? Poor Father." Garald grinned. "To this day he refuses to wear a cravat in the presence of a naval officer *or* anyone in a bear costume. But, to return to more serious subjects . . .

"Saryon is quite right when he cautions against going to Merilon. It *is* dangerous," the Prince said, "and you must never relax your guard. Danger is present not only for Joram, who is one of the living Dead and as such can be sentenced to physical death. There is danger for you, Mosiah. You are considered a rebel. You fled your home, you have lived among the Sorcerers of the Dark Arts. You will be entering Merilon under false pretenses. If you are caught, you will be sentenced to the dungeons of the *Duuk-tsarith,* and few come out of those places unchanged. There is great danger for Saryon himself, who lived in Merilon for a number of years and could easily be recognized —

"No, Joram, I'm not trying to keep you from going," Garald interrupted himself, seeing the young man scowl in anger. "I am telling you to be cautious. Be wary. Above all, be on your guard. Particularly around one person."

"You mean the catalyst?" Joram returned. "I already know that Saryon was sent by Bishop Vanya. . . ."

"I mean Simkin," Garald said gravely, with no trace of a smile.

"There, I told you!" Mosiah muttered to Joram.

Almost as if he knew they were talking of him, Simkin raised his voice, and each of them sitting in the tent turned to look. He and the catalyst stood near the fire, Simkin having volunteered to devise a disguise for the catalyst that would get him into Merilon without being recognized. Now he was working magic with Father Saryon, essentially making the poor man's life miserable.

"I've got it!" Simkin cried shrilly. "Come and go entirely unnoticed, plus you'll be useful in carrying our luggage." He waved his hand and spoke a word. The air shivered around the catalyst. Saryon's form changed. Standing near the fire, in place of the unfortunate catalyst, was a large, gray, despondent-looking donkey.

"That fool!" Mosiah said, jumping to his feet. "Why doesn't he leave that poor man alone. I'll go—"

Garald laid a hand on Mosiah's arm, shaking his head. "I'll handle it," he said.

Reluctantly resuming his seat, Mosiah saw the Prince make a sign with his hand to Cardinal Radisovik, who stood nearby, watching.

"What was that you said, Father?" Simkin asked.

The donkey brayed.

"You're not pleased? After all the trouble I've gone to! Egad, man!" He lifted one of the donkey's gray floppy ears. "You've got marvelous hearing! I'll wager you can hear a bundle of hay fall at fifty paces. To say nothing of the fact that now you can roll one eye forward and one backward at the same time. See where you're going and where you've been simultaneously."

The donkey brayed again, showing its teeth.

"And the children would love you so," said Simkin coaxingly. "You could give the little darlings rides. Well, if you're going to be such an old fuddy-duddy . . . There."

The donkey disappeared and Saryon returned, though in an awkward position, being down on all fours, kneeling on his hands and knees.

"I'll just have to think of something else," Simkin said, sulking. "I have it!" He snapped his fingers. "A goat! We'd never want for milk. . . ."

At this moment, Cardinal Radisovik intervened. Mentioning something about discussing ecclesiastical matters with Saryon, he helped the catalyst to his feet and drew him into his tent. Unfortunately, Simkin followed.

"Plus you'd never worry about finding food," he was heard to say persuasively, his voice trailing off. "You could eat anything . . ."

"You know something about Simkin, don't you, Your Grace?" Mosiah said, turning to the Prince. "You know his game. What he's up to?"

"His game . . ." the Prince repeated thoughtfully, intrigued by the question. "Yes," he said, after a moment, "I think I do know Simkin's game."

"Then, tell us!" Mosiah said eagerly.

"No, I don't believe I will," Garald said, his gaze fixed on Joram. "You wouldn't understand, and it might lessen your watchfulness."

"But you must! I—I mean, you should . . . Your Grace," Mosiah amended lamely, realizing he had just issued an order to a prince. "If Simkin's dangerous—"

"Bah!" Joram frowned in disgust.

"Oh, he's dangerous, all right," Garald said smoothly. "Just remember that." The Prince rose to his feet. "And now, if you will excuse me, I had better go rescue poor Saryon, before our friend has him sprouting horns and nibbling on the Cardinal's tent."

The matter of the catalyst's disguise was soon settled—and without turning him into a goat. At the Prince's suggestion, Father Saryon became Father Dunstable, a minor house catalyst who, according to Simkin, had left Merilon over ten years ago.

"A meek mouse of a man," Simkin recalled. "A man no one remembered five seconds after having been introduced to him, much less ten years later."

"And if anyone does remember him after ten year's absence, they would expect him to have changed some," Garald added soothingly, seeing that Saryon was not at all pleased at this idea. "You won't have to *act* any differently, Father. Your face and body will be different, that's all. Inside, you will be the same."

"But I will have to present myself at the Cathedral, Your Grace," Saryon argued stubbornly, his obvious reluctance at opposing the Prince outweighed by his fear—a fact the Prince noted, wondering, once again, what dread secret this man held locked in his heart. "The comings and goings of catalysts are well-documented—"

"Not necessarily, Father," Radisovik put in mildly. "There are more than a few who slip through the bureaucratic cracks, so to speak. A minor house catalyst of no importance—such as this Father Dunstable—who moves with his family to an outlying district might well lose contact with his church for a number of years."

"But why should I—I mean Father Dunstable—come back to Merilon? Begging your pardon, Eminence," Saryon said humbly but persistently, "but the Prince has emphasized our danger . . ."

"You have an excellent point, Father," Garald said. "There are any number of reasons for your return. The wizard you served took it into his head to join the rebellious scum in Sharakan, for example, and left you to fend for yourself."

"This *is* serious, milord." Radisovik ventured a mild reproach.

"So am I," Garald returned coolly. "But perhaps that would draw too much attention to you, Father. How's this? The wizard dies. His widow returns to Zith-el to live with her parents. There is no room for you in her father's establishment and therefore you, Father Dunstable, are dismissed from their service. With loving thanks and references, of course."

Cardinal Radisovik nodded approvingly. "If they checked your story," he said, seeing Saryon's next argument in his face, "which I doubt they would since there are hundreds of catalysts coming and going from the Cathedral every day, it would take them months to track down Lord Whoever He Is and discover the truth."

"And by that time," concluded the Prince in a tone that indicated the matter was settled, "you will be with us in Sharakan."

Hearing a note of irritation creeping into the noble voice, Saryon bowed in acquiescence, fearing that any more argument might appear suspicious. He had to admit that the Prince and the Cardinal were right. Having spent fifteen years in the Cathedral, Saryon had spent many evenings watching the line of newly arrived catalysts shuffle up the crystal stairs and enter the crystal doors. Under the bored eye of some poor Deacon, each catalyst signed his name in a register that was rarely, if ever, looked at again. After all, if one passed the scrutiny of the *Kanhanar*—the Gatekeepers of Merilon—who was the Church to quibble? The very idea of a catalyst sneaking into the city in a disguise was so remote to their thinking that it must appear ludicrous.

Still, there was one person who might have reason to expect Saryon to return Merilon, the catalyst thought uncomfortably, his hand going to the darkstone around his neck. He wondered fearfully what actions Bishop Vanya would take to find him, and he began to almost regret the donkey. . . .

The next morning, everyone rose early, before the sun. Now that it was time to part, they were all anxious to begin their various journeys. The young men and Saryon prepared to take their leave of the Prince and his entourage, who were also leaving that day to continue their journey to the Sorcerers' village.

"All's well that ends well," Simkin remarked as they finished breakfast, "as was said of the Lady Magda by the Count d'Orleans. He spoke of her posteriorly, of course."

"Simkin's a fool!" croaked the raven, perching upon Simkin's head.

"It is not an end, but a beginning, I trust," said Prince Garald, smiling at Joram.

The young man almost, but not quite, returned the smile.

"And now," continued the Prince, "before the sadness of farewells, I have the pleasant task of giving the Journey Gifts. . . ."

"My lord, that is not necessary," murmured Saryon, his guilt once more assailing him. "You have done enough for us as it is—"

"Don't take this pleasure away from me, Father," Garald interrupted, laying his hand upon the catalyst's. "Giving gifts is one of the best parts about being a King's son."

Walking over to stand before Mosiah, the Prince clapped his hands once, and then held them out to catch a book that materialized in midair.

"You are a powerful wizard, Mosiah. More powerful than many *Albanara* I know. And this is not unusual. In my travels, I have discovered that many of our truly strong magi are being born in the fields and the alleys, not in noble halls. But magic, like all other gifts of the Almin, requires disciplined study to perfect it or it will flow into you and out of you like wine through a drunkard."

The Prince cast a glance at Simkin who was, at that moment, tweaking the raven's tail.

"Study this well, my friend." The Prince laid the book in the young man's trembling hands.

"T-thank you, Your Grace," stammered Mosiah, flushing in what he hoped would appear as embarrassment.

Garald understood it, however, and knew it was shame.

"The journey to Merilon is long," said the Prince softly. "And you have a friend who will be more than happy to teach you to read."

Mosiah followed the Prince's gaze to Joram.

"Is that true? Will you?" he asked.

"Of course! I never knew you wanted to learn!" Joram answered impatiently. "You should have said something."

Taking the book, Mosiah held it fast in his hands. "Thank you, Your Grace," he repeated.

The two exchanged looks and, for an instant, the field magus and the nobleman were in perfect understanding.

Garald turned away. "Now, Simkin, my old friend—"

"Nothing for me, Your Grass. Ha, ha. Your Grass. That's how the Duke of Deere referred to his gardener. I know, it's a stupid joke, but then so was the Duke. No, I mean it. I won't accept a thing. Well . . ." Simkin heaved a sigh, as the Prince started to speak, "if you insist. Perhaps one or two of the more valuable jewels of the realm—"

"For you," said Garald, finally able to insert a word. He handed Simkin a deck of tarok cards.

"How delightful!" said Simkin, attempting to stifle a yawn.

"Each card is hand painted by my own artisans," remarked Garald. "They are done in the ancient style, not by magic. The deck is, therefore, quite valuable."

"Thanks awfully, old chap," said Simkin languidly.

Garald raised his hand. "You note I hold something in my palm. Something that's missing from your deck."

"The Fool card," Simkin said, peering at it intently. "How amusing."

"The Fool card," repeated Garald, toying with it. "Guide them well, Simkin."

"I assure you, Your Highness," said Simkin earnestly. "They couldn't be in better hands."

"Neither could you," replied Garald. He closed his fingers over the card and it disappeared. No one spoke, each staring at the other uncomfortably. Then the Prince laughed. "Just *my* joke," he said, clapping Simkin on the back.

"Ha, ha," Simkin echoed, but his laughter was hollow.

"And now, Father Saryon," said Garald, moving on to stand before the catalyst, who was staring down at his shoes. "I have nothing of material value to give you." Saryon looked up in relief. "I sense that would be unwelcome to you anyway. But I do have a gift of sorts, although the present is more to myself than to you. When you return to Sharakan with Joram"—Saryon noted that the Prince always spoke of this as a settled fact—"I want you to join my household."

A catalyst in a royal household! Saryon glanced involuntarily at Cardinal Radisovik, who smiled at him encouragingly.

"This—" stammered Saryon, clearing his throat, "this is an unexpected honor, Your Grace. Too great an honor for one who has broken the laws of his faith."

"But not too great an honor for one who is loyal, one who is compassionate," Prince Garald finished gently. "As I said, the gift is to myself. I look forward to the day, Father Saryon, when I can once again ask you to grant me Life."

Turning from the catalyst, Garald came, at last, to Joram.

"I know, you don't want anything from me either," the Prince remarked, smiling.

"As the catalyst said, you've given us enough," Joram said evenly.

"'Given us enough, *Your Grace*,'" repeated the Cardinal sternly.

Joram's face darkened.

"Yes, well"—Garald struggled to keep his countenance—"it seems to be your lot in life, Joram, to have to keep accepting things from me."

Once again, the Prince held out his hands. The air above the outspread palms shimmered, then coalesced, taking the shape of a hand-tooled leather scabbard. Runes of power were etched upon it in gold, but, other than that, there was no other symbol. The center of the scabbard was blank.

"I left it this way purposefully, Joram," the Prince said, "so that you could have your family crest drawn upon it at some later date. Now, let me show you how this works.

"I had it designed especially for you," Garald continued proudly, exhibiting the scabbard's features. "These straps attach around your chest like this, so that you can wear your sword on your back, concealed beneath your clothes. The runes carved upon the leather will cause the sword to shrink in size and weight when it is in the scabbard, thus enabling you to wear it at all times.

"That is of the utmost importance, Joram," the Prince said, looking at the young man earnestly. "The Darksword is both your greatest protection and your greatest danger. Wear it always. Mention it to no one. Reveal its existence to no one. Use it only if you are in peril of your life."

He glanced at Mosiah. "Or to protect the lives of others."

The Prince's clear brown eyes came back to Joram and Garald saw, for the first time, the stone facade shatter.

Joram stared at the scabbard, his eyes warm with longing and desire and gratitude. "I . . . I don't know what . . . to say," he faltered.

"How about, 'Thank you, Your Grace,'" said Garald softly, and he placed the scabbard in Joram's hands.

The rich smell of the leather filled Joram's nostrils. His hands ran over the smooth finish, touching the intricate runes, examining the complex leatherwork. Looking up, he saw the man's eyes on him, amused, yet expectant, certain of victory.

Joram smiled.

"Thank you, my friend. Thank you — Garald," he said firmly.

Interlude

Bishop Vanya sat behind his desk in his elegant quarters in the Cathedral of Merilon. Though not as sumptuous as his rooms in the Font, the Bishop's chambers in Merilon were large and comfortable, containing a private bedroom, sitting room, dining room, and an office with an antechamber for the Deacon who served as his secretary. The view from any of his rooms was magnificent, though it was not the broad expanse of plains or the jagged edges of mountains such as he was accustomed to enjoying at the Font. From the Cathedral, with its crystal walls, he could look down upon the city of Merilon. Gazing farther off, he could see beyond the dome, into the countryside around the city. Or, glancing above, he could see — through the crystal spires atop the Cathedral — the Royal Palace, which hovered above the city, its walls of shimmering crystal shining in the heavens like a sedate and civilized sun.

This early evening, the Bishop's gaze was lowered, his eyes on the city of Merilon, if not his thoughts. The citizens were providing a spectacular show in the form of an enhanced sunset — a gift from the *Pron-alban* of the Stone Shapers' Guild, intended to welcome His Holiness to the city. Though winter raged outside the city's magical dome and snow blanketed the land, it was springtime in Merilon — spring being the Empress's current favorite season. The sunset was, therefore, a sunset appropriate to spring, being magically enhanced by the *Sif-Hanar* to glisten in colors of muted pinks with here and there a hint of deeper rose or perhaps (most daring) a slash of purple at the heart.

It was truly a beautiful sunset, and the inhabitants of Merilon's City Above — the nobility and members of the upper middle class — floated about the streets in filmy silks, fluttering lace, and shining satins, admiring the view.

Not so Bishop Vanya. The sun might not have set, for all he knew or cared. The weather outside might have been a howling hurricane. In fact, such would have suited his mood. His pudgy fingers crawled over his desk, pushing this, shoving that, rearranging something else. It was his only outward sign of displeasure or nervousness, for the Bishop's broad face was as cool, his regal manner as composed, as ever. The two black-robed figures standing silently before him, however, noted this papershuffling as they noted everything else that went on around them from the sunset to the uneaten remnants of the Bishop's supper.

The Bishop's crawling hand suddenly slammed, palm down, upon the rosewood desk. "I do not understand" — his voice was even and controlled, a control that was costing him — "why it is that you *Duuk-tsarith* with your highly touted powers cannot find one young man!"

The two black hoods turned slightly toward each other, the glittering eyes exchanged glances. Then the black hoods faced Vanya and the wearer of one of them, her hands folded before her, spoke. Her tone was respectful without being conciliatory. Clearly, she knew herself to be mistress of the situation.

"I repeat, Holiness, that if this young man were normal, we would have no trouble locating him. The fact that he is Dead makes locating him difficult. The fact that he carries darkstone upon his person, however, makes it almost impossible."

"I do not understand!" Vanya exploded. "He exists! He is flesh and blood —"

"Not to us, Holiness," the witch corrected him, her warlock partner supporting her arguments by a slight nodding of his hooded head. "The darkstone shields him, protects him from us. Our senses are attuned to magic, Eminence. We move among the people, throwing out tiny filaments of magic as a spider throws out silken filaments of her web. Whenever any normal being in this world comes within our range, those filaments quiver with Life — with magic. This provides us with vital information about the person: everything from his dreams, to where he was raised, to what he has lately eaten for dinner.

"With the Dead, we must take extra measures. We must readjust our senses to react to the Death within them, the *lack* of magic. But with this young man, protected as he is by the darkstone, our senses — our filaments of magic, so to speak — are absorbed and swallowed up. We feel nothing, hear nothing, see nothing. To us, Holiness, he literally does not exist. This was the tremendous power of the darkstone in ancient days. An army of Dead carrying weapons made of darkstone could come up upon a city and remain completely undetected."

"Bah!" Vanya snorted. "You talk as if he were invisible. Do you mean to say that he could walk into this room right now and you wouldn't see him? That I wouldn't see him?"

The black cloth covering the witch's head shivered slightly, as though the woman checked an irritated gesture or suppressed a sigh of impatience. When she spoke, her voice was extremely cool and carefully modulated — a bad sign to those who knew her, as evidenced by the slight whitening of the knuckles on the hands of her companion.

"Of course you would see him, Holiness. And so would we. Isolated and alone in this room, our attention upon him, we would be able to recognize him for what he was and so deal with him. But there are thousands of people out there!"

The witch made a sudden movement with her hand that caused her companion to cringe involuntarily, uncertain what she might do. Though the *Duuk-tsarith* are trained from childhood in strict discipline, the witch — a high-ranking member of the Order — was known to have a volatile temper. Her companion would not have been overly surprised to see the crystal wall behind the Bishop begin to melt like so much ice on a summer day.

The witch restrained herself, however. Bishop Vanya was not one to anger.

"So, as you said before, the only way to catch him is for someone to bring him to us," Vanya muttered, his fingers crawling over the desk.

"Not the only way, Holiness. That would be easiest. There would be the sword to deal with, of course, but I doubt if he has had time to truly learn how to use it or to understand its full powers."

"It was reported to us, Eminence," added the warlock, "that one of your own catalysts was with the young man. Could we not work through him?"

"The man in question is a weak-minded fool! Had I been able to maintain contact with him, I could have kept him under my control," Vanya said, the blood mounting in his puffy face until it was nearly as red as the fabric of his robes. "But he has discovered some way to avoid being mentally summoned through the Chamber of Discretion—"

"The darkstone," interrupted the witch coolly, her hands clasped before her once again. "It would shield him as effectively from your summons as it shields the boy from our sight."

The witch was silent a moment, then she glided nearer the Bishop, causing him a certain amount of uneasiness. "Holiness"—she spoke in gentle, persuasive tones—"if you would grant us permission to go to the Sorcerers' Coven, we could learn what he looks like, who his companions are—"

"No!" said Vanya emphatically. "We must not alert them to their danger! Even though Blachloch is dead, he has advanced matters sufficiently that the Sorcerers will continue to work with Sharakan and so become involved in the war."

"Undoubtedly the catalyst has warned them . . ."

"Then, would you confirm his story by appearing in person, asking questions that sooner or later must start the dullest of them thinking?"

"An army of the *DKarn-duuk* could move against them—" suggested the warlock deferentially.

"—and start a panic." Bishop Vanya bit the words. "News of their existence would spread like flame through dry grass. Our people believe the Sorcerers were destroyed in the Iron Wars. Let them hear that these practitioners of the Dark Arts not only exist but have discovered darkstone and there would be an uproar. No, we will not move until we are prepared to crush them completely."

"And His Eminence can save his skin at the same time!" The witch exchanged mental notes with her companion.

"You must search for the catalyst," continued Vanya, drawing in air through his nose and exhaling with a snort, scowling at the two before him all the while. "I will provide you with a description of the catalyst and Joram, plus another person with whom Joram once associated—a young Field Magus named Mosiah. Though, undoubtedly, they will be disguised," he added as an afterthought.

"Disguise—unless it is very clever—is generally easy to penetrate, Holiness," said the witch coldly. "People think only of changing their outward appearance, not their chemical structure or thought patterns. It should be relatively easy to find a Field Magus among the nobility of Merilon."

"I trust so," the Bishop said, regarding the *Duuk-t͵arith* sternly.

"How certain are you that the boy—this Joram—will come to Merilon, Holiness?" the warlock asked.

"Merilon is an obsession with him," said Vanya, waving a bejeweled hand. "According to the Field Catalyst who lived in the village where he grew up, the madwoman, Anja, told him more than once that he could find his birthright here. If you were seventeen, had come across a remarkable source of power such as the darkstone, and believed that you were heir to a fortune, where would you go?"

The *Duuk-t͵arith* bowed in silent response.

"Now," said the Bishop briskly, "if you find the catalyst, deliver him to me. If you find this Mosiah—"

"You need not tell us our duties, Eminence," the witch remarked, a dangerous edge in her voice. "If there is nothing further—"

"There is. One thing." Vanya held up a restraining hand as the two appeared ready to depart. "I emphasize! *Nothing* must happen to the young man! He must be taken alive! You both know why."

"Yes, Holiness," they murmured. Bowing, hands folded before them, they stepped backward. The Corridor's magical aperture gaped open, admitted them, and swallowed them up within seconds.

Left alone with the fading sunset and the darkening evening sky, Bishop Vanya was about to ring for the House Magi to lower the silken tapestries and light the lights of the Bishop's sitting room. But Vanya's hand upon the bell was stilled by the sight of the Corridor gaping open once again. A figure stepped out of the void and moved with confident stride to stand before the Bishop's desk.

Recognizing the man in his crimson robes, the Bishop should have risen in respect. He did, eventually, but he remained seated long enough to give the delay meaning. Then he rose to his feet with elaborate slowness, making a great show of smoothing his own robes about him and adjusting the heavy miter upon his bald head.

The visitor smiled to show he fully understood and appreciated the subtle insult. The man's smile was not a pleasant one, under the best of circumstances. Thin-lipped, it never extended to any other part of the face — particularly the eyes that were dark and shadowed by heavy, black brows.

Had Saryon been in the room, he would have seen instantly the family resemblance in the man's thick black eyebrows and the stern expression of the cold and handsome face. But the catalyst would have missed an inner warmth in this man that he saw in the man's nephew — a flicker in Joram's dark eyes, like the reflection of the forge fires. There was no light in this man's eyes, no light in his soul.

"Bishop Vanya," said the man, bowing.

"Prince Xavier," said Bishop Vanya bowing. "I am honored. This unexpected and unannounced" — the words were emphasized — "visit is a surprise to me."

"I have no doubt," Xavier said smoothly and evenly. He invariably spoke smoothly and evenly. There was never a touch of emotion. He never allowed himself to become angry, bored, irritated, or happy.

Born to the Mystery of Fire, he was a high-ranking warlock, a *DKarn-duuk*, one who is trained in the art of waging war. He was also the Empress's younger brother — and most important — because the Empress was childless and the inheritance passed through the female side, Xavier was heir to the throne of Merilon. Thus the title, "Prince," and thus Vanya's grudging show of homage.

"To what do I owe the pleasure of this visit?" Bishop Vanya inquired. Standing up as tall and straight as his rotund figure would allow, he stared with undisguised dislike at the Prince, who was coolly returning the compliment.

Xavier clasped his hands behind the skirts of his long, flowing crimson robes. Because he was in court, Xavier could have worn court dress, like everyone else. Unlike the *Duuk-t∍arith*, the *DKarn-duuk* were not required to wear their crimson robes that were an indication of their order. But Xavier found this style of dress advantageous. It reminded people — particularly his brother-in-law, the Emperor — of the warlock's power.

"I desired to welcome you to Merilon, Holiness," Xavier said.

"Most kind of you, my lord, I am sure," said the Bishop, "And now, though I am highly sensible of the honor you do me and completely unworthy of such attention, I beg that you depart. If there is nothing I can do for you, that is."

"Ah, there *is* something." Prince Xavier drew forth one smooth, supple hand from behind his back and held it up before him. With that hand, he might call down lightning from the skies or raise demons from the ground. The Bishop found it difficult to take his eyes off that hand, and waited somewhat nervously.

"My lord has only to name it," he said, more subdued.

"You can end the charade."

A ripple of consciousness passed across the Bishop's face, making it appear as though someone had shaken a bowl of flabby pudding. The lips twitched, and he laid a pudgy hand on them. "Forgive me, Your Highness, but I have no idea what you are talking about. A charade?" Vanya repeated politely, still not taking his eyes from the warlock's hand.

"You know quite well what I am talking about." Xavier's voice was even and pleasant and remarkably sinister. But he let the hand fall to his side, fingering an ornament of silver that hung from his waist. "You know that my sister is—"

Prince Xavier stopped speaking abruptly. Vanya's eyes, nearly hidden by the puffy folds in the face, had suddenly bulged out, staring at him with shrewd intensity.

"Yes, your sister, the Empress," the Bishop prodded blandly. "You were saying? She is . . . what?"

"What you and everyone else knows, yet what you and my imbecile brother-in-law have made treasonable to say," returned Xavier smoothly. "And it is only through your power and that of your catalysts that he can keep this up. Bring it to an end. Put me on the throne." Xavier smiled, and shrugged slightly. "I am no trained bear as is my brother-in-law. I will not dance at the end of your rope. Still, I can be amenable, easy to work with. You will need me," he continued in a softer tone, "when you go to war."

"A tragic circumstance we pray the Almin to avoid," Bishop Vanya said piously, raising his eyes to heaven. "You are aware, Prince Xavier, that the Emperor is opposed to war. He will turn the other cheek—"

"—and get kicked in the ass," Xavier concluded.

Bishop Vanya flushed, his eyes narrowed in rebuke. "With due regard to your station, Prince Xavier, I cannot allow even you to speak with disrespect of my sovereign lord. I do not know what you want with me. I do not understand your words and I resent your insinuations. I must again ask you to go. It is nearly time for Evening Prayers."

"You are a fool," Xavier said pleasantly. "You would find it much to your advantage to work with me, much to your disadvantage to thwart me. I am a deadly enemy. Oh, you and my brother-in-law are protected now, I admit. The *Duuk-tsarith* are in your pocket. But you can't keep this charade going forever."

Xavier spoke a word and the Corridor opened behind him.

"If you are returning to the Palace, my lord," said Bishop Vanya humbly, "please give my regards to your sister and say that I hope to find her in good health . . ."

The words lingered on the Bishop's lips.

For an instant, Xavier's studious, calm demeanor cracked—a flaw in the ice. The face paled, the dark eyes glittered.

"I will give her your regards, Bishop," Xavier said, stepping into the Corridor. "And I will add that *your* health is good, as well, Bishop. For the time being. . . ."

The Corridor closed its jaws over him, and the last Vanya saw of Prince Xavier was a splash of crimson, flowing like a stream of blood through the air. The image was an alarming one, and it remained with Bishop Vanya long after the Prince had disappeared. With a shaking hand, Vanya rang the bell, demanding that the lights in his chamber be lit immediately. And he ordered up a bottle of sherry as well.

BOOK TWO

1

Gwendolyn

"**W**here are you going today, my treasure?"

The young woman to whom this question was fondly addressed bent over her mother, entwining white arms around the elderly lady's neck and laying her naturally rose-tinted cheek against the cheek that magic kept in full bloom.

"I am going to visit Papa at the Three Sisters and dine with him. He said I might, you know. And then I am going to City Below to spend the afternoon with Lilian and Majorie. Oh, don't be a frowning mama. There, you see, a wrinkle line comes when you frown like that. Look, now watch. See, it's gone." The girl—for she was a girl at heart still, though woman in figure and face—laid her delicate fingers on her mother's lips and turned them upward into a smile.

Midmorning sunshine crept into the room like a thief, sneaking between the folds of the drawn tapestries, crawling across the floor and gleaming out suddenly from unexpected places. It flashed off the shaped glass of crystal vases and glistened in the silken thread of gowns tossed carelessly over chairs. The sun did not touch the feather bed that floated beneath the arched canopy in the corner. It wouldn't dare. Full sunshine was never permitted into the room until noon at least, by which time Lady Rosamund had risen from her bed and she and her catalyst had performed the magic necessary for milady to face the day.

Not that Lady Rosamund required much magic to enhance her appearance. She prided herself on that and kept her touches to a minimum, most of these reflecting whatever was currently in style in Merilon. Lady Rosamund made no attempt to disguise her age. That was undignified, particularly when she had a daughter who, at sixteen, had recently left the nursery and entered into adult society.

Milady was wise and observant; she had heard the women of the noble classes laugh behind their fans at those of her own station who looked younger than the daughters they chaperoned. The family of Lord Samuels and Lady Rosamund was not a member of these noble classes, but so close were they that the only thing needed was one hand outstretched in matrimony to lift them into glittering realms of court. Therefore Lady Rosamund maintained her dignity, dressed well but not above her station, and had the satisfaction of hearing herself pronounced "elegant" and "a sweet thing" by her betters.

Milady looked intently into the ice mirror that stood on the dressing table before her and she smiled at what she saw. Her proud gaze was not on her own face, however, but rested on the youthful repetition of her own features that smiled from behind her.

The family treasure — and treasure is an apt word — was their eldest daughter, Gwendolyn. This child was their investment in the future. It was she who would raise them up from the middle class, carrying them skyward on the wings of her rosy cheeks and her substantial dowry. Gwendolyn was not beautiful in the classic sense currently much admired in Merilon — that is, she did not appear to have been sculpted of marble with the same cold and stony charm to match. She was of medium height with golden hair, large blue eyes that laughed their way into a man's heart, and a gentle, giving nature that kept them there.

Her father, Lord Samuels, was *Pron-alban*, a craftsman, though he no longer performed the menial magic of his trade. He was a Guildmaster now, having risen to that high position among the ranks of the Stone Shapers through intelligence, hard work, and shrewd investments. It was Guildmaster Samuels who had developed the means to repair a crack in one of the gigantic stone platforms upon which City Above was built, thus earning for him a knighthood from the Emperor.

Now able to put "Lord" before his name, the Guildmaster and his family had moved from their old dwelling on the northwest side of City Below to the very edge of the Low Avenue of City Above. Situated on the west side of Mannan Park, the house looked out over the rolling green expanse of carefully manicured grass, shaped and nurtured trees with — here and there — a flower.

It was a well-to-do neighborhood without being *too* well-to-do. Lady Rosamund knew the advantage of having her noble visitors admire "what charming things you have done to this dear little cottage" of twenty rooms or so. And it pleased her no end to hear them remark sympathetically when they left, "So unworthy of you, my dear. When are you moving to something better?"

When indeed? Sometime soon, it was hoped — when her daughter became Countess Gwendolyn or Duchess Gwendolyn or Marchioness Gwendolyn. . . . Lady Rosamund sighed with pleasure as she admired the lovely daughter in the icy face of the frozen reflecting pool.

"Ah, Mama, the mirror is weeping!" Gwendolyn said, reaching out her hand to catch a drop of water before it fell upon her mother's feathered hair adornments.

"So it is," said Lady Rosamund with a sigh. "Marie, do come here. Grant me Life." Milady negligently held out her hand to the catalyst. Clasping it, Marie murmured the ritual chant that transferred the magic from her body to the wizardess. Like her husband, Lady Rosamund was born to the Earth Mystery, and though her skills were more those of a *Quin-alban* — a conjurer — she could perform the tasks needed to run a household with admirable skill. Suffused with Life, Lady Rosamund laid her fingers on the reflecting pool and spoke the words that would keep the water — encased in a golden frame that stood upon her dressing table — frozen solid.

"It's this warm weather," Lady Rosamund said to her daughter. "I would certainly not criticize Her Highness for the world, but I wouldn't mind a change of season. Spring does grow tiresome, don't you think, my poppet?"

"I think winter would be fun, Mama," said Gwendolyn, fussing with her mother's hair. A darker gold than her own, but rich and luxuriant still, it needed no magic to make it shine. "Lilian and Majorie and I have been down to the Gates, watching the people come in from Outside. It is so funny to see them covered head to foot with snow, their cheeks and noses red with cold, stamping their feet to warm them. And then, when the Gate was open, we could look Outside and see the countryside, so lovely and white. Ah, there goes my beautiful mama, frowning again and making herself ugly."

Lady Rosamund could not help but smile, so coaxing was Gwendolyn, though she tried to appear firm. "I don't like you spending so much time with your cousins . . ." she began.

This was an old argument and one Gwen knew how to handle. "But, Mama," she pleaded persuasively, "I'm so good for them. You've said so yourself. Look how much improved they were, over the holidays. Their manners at table and their conversation, so much more refined and genteel. Weren't they, Marie?" calling upon the catalyst for support.

"Yes, my lady," the catalyst replied with a smile. There were two other children in the household — a boy to carry on the family name and a girl to delight her parents in their middle years. And though both were cute, they were young and neither had developed much personality yet. The catalyst, who, in this modest household, doubled as nanny and governess, made no secret of the fact that Gwen was her pet.

"Just think, Mama," Gwen continued, "how fine it would be if my cousins married into one of the families of our friends. Sophia told me that her brother told her that Guildmaster Reynald's son, Alfred, said the next day after our party that Lilian was a 'stunner.' His very words, Mama. I can't help but think that, after praise like that, their engagement cannot be far off."

"My dear child, how silly you are!" Lady Rosamund laughed, but it was fond laughter and she patted her daughter's white hand. "Well, if such an event happens, your cousins will have you to thank for it. I hope they realize that. I suppose it will be all right, today, if you visit them. But after this, I don't believe it proper that you should be seen in City Below more than once a week. You are a young woman now, not a child, and such things are important."

"Yes, Mama," said Gwen, more subdued, for she saw the firm set of the mouth and the arch in the eyebrows that indicated to servants, children, catalyst, and husband that Lady Rosamund had issued a decree and was not to be disobeyed.

But, at sixteen, Gwen could not be unhappy long. Next week was far away. Meanwhile, there was today. Lunch with her dear papa, who was to take her to a new inn near the Guild

Halls; an inn famous for its chocolate. Then the rest of the day with her cousins — a day spent in Gwen's newest, favorite pastime — flirtation.

The Earth Gate of Merilon was a place of bustling activity. The great invisible dome that held within its fragile shell the glories of the city of Merilon soared skyward from the Gladewall. Seven Gates pierced the dome, providing entrance into Merilon from Outside. But six of the Gates were used little, if ever. Most of the time, they remained magically locked. Death Gate and Spirit Gate were never used now that the Necromancers were no longer around to treat with visitors from beyond the grave. Life Gate was reserved for victorious processionals following war, and it had not been used in over a century. The only thing that entered by Druid's Gate was the river; the Druids now used the front gate like everyone else. Wind Gate and Earth Gate were the portals of major commerce between the outer and inner worlds. The *Kan-Hanar* — the Gatekeepers — allowed only the Ariels to fly through Wind Gate. Earth Gate was, therefore, the only true access to the city.

There was always a throng of people around Earth Gate, waiting to greet friends and relatives or seeing them off after a visit. It was currently fashionable among the young people of the city to spend at least part of each day there, socializing, flirting, and observing all who entered.

The first to enter this day was a high-ranking *Albanara* from one of the outlying districts. She had traveled through the Corridors and therefore appeared to materialize out of nothing. The wizardess was greeted by her family from City Above, waiting to meet her in their tortoise-shell carriage drawn by a team of a hundred rabbits, their entire equipage floating two feet above the ground.

The noble lady was followed by a party of catalysts from the Font, gliding in through Earth Gate in their winged carriages. The people bowed in respect for the Priests; the men doffing their hats, the women sinking into pretty curtsies, not sorry for the opportunity to show off white bosoms and smooth necks. Next came a humble tradesman, trudging on foot, half-frozen by the snow. He was met with joy by seven rowdy children, whose antics while waiting for their father had been driving the dignified *Kan-Hanar* on duty to distraction. Finally there came a party of university students, returning after a few days spent frolicking in the winter weather, who kept dashing in and out of the Gate to grab handfuls of snow, tossing it at each other and into the crowd.

The *Kan-Hanar* deal with all who enter in the same manner, be they highborn noble or lowborn tradesman. Everyone who arrives in Merilon is subjected to the same scrutiny, asked the same questions. The *Kan-Hanar* are born to the Mystery of Air, and are thus in charge of most of the transportation of Thimhallan (the exception being the *Thon-Li,* the Corridor Masters). They are catalysts, since the Corridors are controlled and regulated by the Church). The magi and archmagi of the *Kan-Hanar* serve the state; a division of the Emperor's household guard. Among their many tasks are to care for and maintain the Ariels, those magically mutated humans with wings who are the messengers of Thimhallan. And though the catalysts guard and watch over the Corridors, it is the *Kan-Hanar* who expend their magical Life in keeping them operational. But guarding the city gates — not only of Merilon but the gates of all the city states in Thimhallan — is their most important task. It is a position of trust and honor, and only archmagi — those of noble birth who have attained their high rank through years of service and study — can become Gatekeepers.

For it is up to the *Kan-Hanar* to make certain that only those *belonging* in Merilon enter Merilon. Further, it is their duty to separate those who are permitted to enter City Below from those who can, literally, rise higher into City Above. Those so designated are provided with a charm that allows them to penetrate the magical, unseen barrier separating the two cities.

Those travelers who cannot prove that they have reason to be in Merilon are turned from the Gate without regard to their rank or station. The *Kan-Hanar* are adept at this, but, in case of undue trouble, they have support in the form of several black-robed *Duuk-tsarith,* who stand in the shadows; silent, unobtrusive, observant.

This day, the Gates were unusually busy, due in part to the nobility in the outlying areas fleeing the inclement winter weather which the *Sif-Hanar* — those magi who control the winds and clouds — had decreed was necessary for the growth of crops in the spring. Gwendolyn and her cousins, ages seventeen and fifteen, spent a merry afternoon strolling among the many shops and outdoor cafes that surrounded the Gate, watching those who entered, studying their dress and hairstyles with the critical eyes of youth, and breaking the hearts of nearly a dozen young men.

This was a particularly entertaining afternoon for Gwen, since she was not hampered in her flirtations by the presence of Marie, the catalyst. Ordinarily Marie would have accompanied her when she went out in public, as was proper for an unwed young girl. But today either the little brother or the little sister was "fractious," due undoubtedly to teeth, and so Marie was needed at home.

At first there had been a dreadful moment when it seemed Lady Rosamund might have insisted her daughter remain at home as well. But a flood of tears with the cry that "poor Papa will be so distressed, he has planned this for so long" won the day. Lady Rosamund was much attached to her husband. The life of a Guildmaster is a demanding one, and she knew — no one better — how hard he labored to maintain their life-style. He was, in truth, looking forward to this luncheon with his daughter — a rare break in his busy life — and milady had not the heart to deprive either him or Gwen of this time together. There was also the thought that certain members of the aristocracy were permitting their daughters to go about unchaperoned — a mark of a new spirit of freedom much in vogue currently. Lady Rosamund therefore allowed herself to be persuaded — an easy task for her bewitching daughter — and Gwen went off happily, having been given Life enough by Marie to sustain her.

The day had been perfect. The clerks in her father's office had admired her immensely. The chocolate had been worthy of all praise and her papa had teased her agreeably about certain young noblemen, one of whom actually left a party of other young men to come over and pay his respects. Now she and her cousins were at the Gate, reveling in the throngs of people, and playing the latest gambit in the game of sex.

The rules of the game were as follows: Each young woman carried a small bouquet of flowers, gathered from the magnificent tropical gardens located in the heart of City Below. Drifting upon the airy walkways, her small, rouged feet bare — the mark of the gentry, who are rarely obliged to walk and thus need no shoes — the young woman will often, quite by accident, drop her bouquet. The blossoms scattering on the pavement, the bouquet will be rescued by a young man, who will return it after first conjuring up a lovely flower of his own to add to it.

"My lady," said a gallant young nobleman, retrieving Gwen's flowers as they fell through the sweet spring air, "this charming nosegay can only be yours, for I see here the blue of your eyes reflected — though not so brilliantly — in the forget-me-nots, the gold of your hair in the cornblume. But there is something missing which you will please allow me the liberty of adding." A red rose appeared in the young man's hand. "The heart of the bouquet, as warm as the one which beats for you in my breast."

"How kind you are, my lord," murmured Gwen with downcast eyes that showed to perfection the length and thickness of her lashes. Blushing prettily, she accepted the bouquet, and giggled over it with her cousins while the young noble continued on his way, conjuring roses by the dozen this day and giving his heart with every one.

By midafternoon, Gwen's bouquet — though not as large as bouquets carried by other young women — spoke well for itself and for her, and (all that really counts) was larger than those carried by her plainer cousins. The three were floating in the air near Earth Gate, wondering whether or not to stop in one of the cafes for a goblet of sugared ice, when the Gates opened to admit a group entering from Outside.

The opening of the Gate caused a blast of cold air to sweep in, bringing a sharp, breath-catching and thrilling change from the perfumed warmth of the enchanted city. The ladies waiting near the Gate clutched their gowns around them and gave tiny shrieks of horrified delight while the gentlemen swore round oaths and spoke critically of the *Sif-Hanar.* All heads craned to see who was entering — a Princess of somewhere-or-other was expected momentarily. But it wasn't the Princess, just a party of snow-covered young men and a half-frozen old catalyst. Glancing at them without interest, most of the crowd returned to its strolling, visiting in the waiting carriages, and drinking wine in the cafes.

But there were a few, however, who did take an interest in the new arrivals, particularly the young men, who had cast off the hoods of their traveling cloaks. Now they stood inside the Gate, looking around in some confusion, the snow on their shoulders and boots starting to melt in the warm, spring air.

"Poor things," murmured Lilian. "They're soaked through and shivering with cold."

"How handsome they are," whispered Majorie, the fifteen-year-old, who never lost an opportunity to prove to the two older girls that she was just as grown-up as they. "They must be students at the university."

The three young men and the catalyst took their places in the line at Earth Gate and the three young women examined them with interest. There were several other arrivals ahead of them in line. One of them, an elderly dowager with three chins (her magical art had reduced that number from five) was arguing loudly with the *Kan-Hanar* about whether or not she should have access to City Above.

"I tell you, my good sir, that I am the mother of the Marquis of D'umtour! As to why his servants aren't here to greet me upon my arrival, I'm certain I don't know, except it is so difficult to hire quality help these days! He always was a young wastral anyway!" she snapped viciously, shaking her chins. "Wait until I see him . . ."

The *Kan-Hanar* had, of course, heard this all before and were listening patiently, having dispatched a winged Ariel to ascertain if the Marquis had, in truth, "forgotten" to send someone to escort the dowager to City Above.

The other new arrivals behind the dowager glared at her in impatience but there was nothing they could do. All had to wait his or her turn. Some drifted about irritably in the air, others lounged back comfortably in their carriages. The young men, standing on the ground, took off their wet cloaks and continued to look around curiously at the city and its people.

Affecting to be interested in the fluttering, silken wares of a ribbon seller, the girls stopped to admire his goods displayed in a gaudy cart near the Gate. In reality, they were watching and listening to the young men.

"Name of the Almin," breathed one with blond hair and an honest, open face, "this is beautiful, Joram! I never imagined anything so splendid! And, it's spring!" He spread his arms, awe and wonder in his voice and his eyes.

"Don't stare so, Mosiah," his companion said reprovingly. He had long dark hair and dark eyes and, too, was looking around him. But if he were at all impressed by the wonders of the city, there was no indication on the stern, proud face. The third young man, slightly taller than the others, with a short, soft beard, appeared amused at the reactions of his friends. He glanced about in bored fashion — yawning, smoothing his mustache, and lounging back against the wall, his eyes closed. Their catalyst, wet and shivering, huddled in his robes, keeping his hood pulled low over his head.

Looking at them, Gwen scoffed. "University students!" she whispered to her cousins. "With an uncouth accent like that? Look at the one gaping like a yokel. It's obvious this is the first time he's ever been here. Probably the first time he's ever been anywhere civilized, from the way he's dressed."

Lilian's eyes widened in alarm. "Gwen! Suppose they are bandits, trying to sneak into our city! They look it, particularly that dark one."

Gwen examined the dark one for several moments out of the corner of her eye, her hands fingering one of the silken ribbons.

"Pardon me, my lady," said the vendor, "but you're crumpling the merchandise. Those particular shades are difficult to conjure, you know. Are you planning to buy—"

"No, thank you." Flushing, Gwen dropped the ribbon. "Lovely, really, but my mama makes all mine. . . ."

Scowling, the vendor moved off, leaving the girls hovering in the air, their heads together, their eyes on the new arrivals.

"You're right, Lilian," Gwen said decisively. "That's what they are—highwaymen, bold and daring."

"Just like Sir Hugo, the one Marie told us the tale of?" whispered Majorie in excitement. "The bandit who stole the maiden from her father's castle and carried her off on his winged steed to his tent in the desert. Remember, he carried her inside and threw her on the silken pillows and then he . . ." Majorie stopped. "What *did* he do with her when she was lying on the pillows?"

"I don't know." Gwen shrugged her shoulders, a movement that showed them off to their best advantage. "I've wondered myself, but Marie always stops there and goes back to the girl's father, who calls his warlocks to rescue her."

"Did you ever ask her about the pillows?"

"I did, once. But she got very angry and sent me off to bed," Gwen replied. "Quick, they're starting to turn this way. Don't look!" Shifting her gaze to Earth Gate, Gwen studied the huge wooden structure with such intense interest that she might have been one of the Druids who formed it, melding it together from the wood of seven dead oak trees.

"If they are bandits, shouldn't we tell someone?" Lilian whispered, staring dutifully at the Gate.

"Oh, Gwen!" said Majorie, squeezing her hand. "The dark one's staring at you!"

"Hush! Take no notice!" Gwendolyn murmured, flushing and burying her face in her bouquet of flowers. She had risked a quick glimpse at the dark young man and had, quite inadvertently, met his gaze. It wasn't like meeting the eyes of other young men, with their arch, teasing stares. This young man looked at her seriously, intently, the dark eyes penetrating her youthful gaiety to touch something deep within her, something that hurt with a swift, sharp pain, both pleasurable and frightening.

"No, we mustn't tell anyone. We mustn't think about them anymore," Gwen said nervously, her face burning so that she thought she might be feverish. "Let's go. . . ."

"No, wait!" Lilian said, catching hold of her cousin as Gwen was about to walk away. "They're going to talk to the *Kan-Hanar*! Let's stay and find out who they are!"

"I don't care who they are!" Gwen said loftily, firmly resolved *not* to look at the dark young man. But though there were a thousand objects of wonder and beauty and enchantment around her, they all blurred into a swirling mass of confused colors. She kept finding herself drawn back to the dark eyes of the dark young man. When he finally turned away — his attention called to the approaching *Kan-Hanar* by the catalyst — Gwen felt as though she had been released from one of the spells she had heard the *Duuk-tsarith* used to keep prisoners in bondage.

"State your names and your business in the city of Merilon, Father," said the archmagus formally, with a slight — very slight — bow to the sodden catalyst, who returned it humbly. The catalyst was dressed in the red robes of a House Catalyst, but they were untrimmed, which meant he did not serve nobility.

"I am Father Sar — Dun . . . dunstable," stammered the catalyst, the blood rising up from his thin neck until it reached his bald crown. "And we —"

"Sardunstable," interrupted the *Kan-Hanar*, frowning in puzzlement. "That is a name with which I am not familiar, Father. Where are you from?" The *Kan-Hanar*, with their well-trained and phenomenal memories, carry directories of those who live in and visit their cities in their heads.

"I beg your pardon." The catalyst flushed even more deeply. "You misunderstand me. My fault, I am certain. I—I speak with a stammer. The name is Dunstable. Father Dunstable."

"Mmmm," the *Kan-Hanar* said, eyeing the catalyst closely. "There was a Dunstable lived here, but that was ten years ago. He was House Catalyst to the—the Duke of Manchua, I believe?" He glanced for confirmation at his companion, who nodded. The *Kan-Hanar* turned his shrewd stare back to the catalyst. "But the family left, as I said. Moved abroad. Why have you—"

"Egad! This grows boring!" With this statement, the tall young man with the beard left the wall and strolled forward. He waved his hand, there was a sudden flurry of orange silk, and the brown cloak and travel-stained clothes he wore vanished.

Gasps of astonishment from several bystanders caused many more in the crowd to turn and look. The young man was now clad in long, flowing purple silken pantaloons. Gathered tightly about his ankles, they billowed out around his legs, fluttering in the spring breeze. A bright-red sash encircled his slender waist, matched by a bright-red vest trimmed in gold. A purple silk blouse—with long flowing sleeves that completely engulfed his hands when he lowered his arms—matched the pantaloons. All this was topped by a most remarkable hat that resembled a gigantic purple puff pastry, adorned by a red, curling ostrich feather.

Ripples of laughter and murmurs ran through the growing crowd.

"Is it?"

"Why, yes! I'd know him anywhere!"

"That garb! My dear, I'd give anything to wear those trousers to the Emperor's ball next week. Where *does* he find those colors?"

There was a scattering of applause.

"Thank you," said the young man, waving a negligent hand to those who were beginning to gather around him. "Yes, it is me. I have returned." Raising his fingers to his lips, he blew kisses to several wealthy women, sitting in a carriage made of pomegranate, who laughed delightedly and tossed him flowers. "I call this," he continued, referring to his purple clothes, "*Welcome Home, Simkin*. You may dispense with the formalities, my good man," he said, regarding the *Kan-Hanar* with a sniff, and dabbing at his nose with the orange silk in his hand. "Simply tell the authorities that Simkin has returned and that he has brought his troupe of traveling players with him!" He made a flourishing gesture with the orange silk at the two young men and the catalyst (who appeared ready to drop from shame) standing behind him.

The crowd applauded more loudly. Women laughed behind their hands, men shook their heads over his attire, but they glanced down at their own elegant robes or brocade breeches, their faces thoughtful. By noon tomorrow, the flowing silk pantaloons would be seen on half the nobility in Merilon.

"Tell the authorities?" repeated the *Kan-Hanar*, not the least disconcerted by the crowd or the antics of the young man in the pantaloons. "Yes, I'll notify the proper people, you may be certain of that."

Making a gesture to the two black-robed figures who stood watching from the shadows, the *Kan-Hanar* laid his hand upon the young man's shoulder.

"Simkin, in the name of the Emperor, I place you under arrest."

2

Welcome Home, Simkin

Calling for the warlocks, the *Kan-Hanar* held Simkin firmly. The black-robed *Duuk-tsarith* floated toward the young man, the crowd parting at their coming like leaves driven by a storm wind. Amid the rustling murmurs of the people, the gasps of shock that were equal parts horror and delight, Gwen's gaze was drawn from Simkin—who was staring at the *Kan-Hanar* in absolute astoundment—to his friends.

Standing behind Simkin, the catalyst had gone from red to a deathly pallor, his hand reaching out and resting on the shoulder of the dark young man in a manner that was both protective and restraining. The other young man, the blond one, laid his hand on his friend's arm as well, and then it was that Gwen noticed the dark young man reached behind his back, beneath his cloak.

Weapons of any type are not used in Merilon, since they are considered to be the evil machinations of those who practice the Dark Art, the Ninth Mystery—Technology. The young girl watching had never seen a sword, but she knew of them through the nursery stories her governess told her of the ancient days. Gwen knew instinctively that this young man carried one, that he and his friends were undoubtedly bandits, and that he intended to fight.

"No!" she breathed, pressing one hand against her mouth, the other crushing the forgotten flowers.

The dark young man had turned to face the approaching *Duuk-tsarith*, his back was to Gwen. The warm spring wind blew his cloak aside, and she saw his hand clenched around the hilt of his sword, slowly drawing it from a sheath that surrounded the object like the skin of a snake. The weapon was dark and hideous, and Gwen wanted to shut her eyes in horror. But her eyelids were dry and burning. She couldn't close them, she could only stare at the weapon and the young man in a dread fascination, a smothering sensation in her chest.

The *Duuk-tsarith*, now clear of the crowd, stretched out their hands toward Simkin, spell chants on their lips. They did not seem to be paying any attention to the dark young man, who was moving slowly up behind his friend.

"'Pon my honor!" cried Simkin. "Must be some mistake. Call me when you've cleared it up, there's a good fellow."

The air shimmered and the *Kan-Hanar* was left standing in front of Earth Gate, his hand resting firmly on nothing.

Simkin was gone.

"Find him!" the *Kan-Hanar* ordered unnecessarily, for the *Duuk-tsarith* were already responding. "I'll watch his friends."

Gwen's eyes — opened wide at this astonishing development — went instantly to the dark young man. Simkin's disappearance had apparently startled him as well. He hesitated drawing the sword, and Gwen saw the catalyst remonstrating with him, speaking earnestly, his hand once more on the young man's shoulder. Just as the *Kan-Hanar* came near, the young man slid the sword back into its scabbard, hastily covering it with his cloak.

Gwen drew a shivering breath in relief, then realized, too late, that she was betraying far more interest in this young man than was maidenly proper. Hoping her cousins hadn't noticed the burning flush in her cheeks, she buried her face in the bouquet.

"I say, loosen up," yelped a voice. "You're pinching me most awfully."

Gwen gasped, dropping the flowers in her amazement. The voice had come from the heart of her bouquet!

"Almin's blood, child!" one of the flowers said irritably. "I didn't mean for you to loosen up quite that much! I've crumpled a petal."

The blossoms lay scattered in the street. Slowly, cautiously, Gwendolyn drifted down out of the air to kneel beside the bouquet, staring at it incredulously. One flower stood out amid the dainty selection of violets and roses. This was a bright purple tulip, adorned by a red streak around its middle and a dash of orange on the top.

"Well, are you just going to leave me lying in the filth?" the tulip asked in aggrieved tones.

Gulping, Gwen glanced up to see if her cousins were looking at her, but they appeared to be totally absorbed in watching the *Duuk-tsarith*. The warlocks had not moved from the spot. Hands clasped before them, their black hoods pulled low over their faces, they appeared to be doing nothing. But Gwendolyn knew that they were mentally going over everyone in the crowd, throwing out the long, unseen filaments of their magical web, seeking their prey.

Her eyes on the warlocks, Gwen reached out and gently picked up the purple tulip.

"Simkin?" she asked hesitantly. "What—"

"Shush! Shush!" hissed the tulip. "There's been a most frightful mistake. I'm positive of it. Why should they arrest me? Well, there was that one incident with the Countess's jewelry . . . But surely no one remembers that! Stuff was all fake anyway. Well, most of it. . . . If I can just get to the Emperor, you see, I'm certain he'll set everything right! Then, there's my friends." The tulip took on an air of importance. "Can you keep a secret, child?"

"Well, I—" Gwen regarded the tulip in bewilderment.

"Shush! The dark young man. Noble family. Father died. Left the boy a fortune. Wicked uncle. Boy kidnapped. Held prisoner by giants. I rescued him. Now he returns, expose uncle, claim inheritance."

"Really?" Gwen raised her eyes to look at the dark young man over the tulip's petals. "I just knew it," she said.

"That's it!" the tulip cried. "Why didn't it occur to me? Wicked uncle behind this! Heard we were coming back. Should have known. Had me arrested to get me out of the way. Too bad," the tulip said gloomily. "He won't stop with kidnapping now. It'll be murder this time."

"Oh, dear, no!" Gwen whispered in alarm. "There must be something you can do!"

"I'm afraid not, unless you would— But no, I couldn't ask it." The tulip gave a gusty sigh. "I'm destined for life in a bud vase. As for my friend? Bottom of the river. . ."

"Oh, no! I'll help, if you really think I can," Gwen faltered.

"Very well," the tulip responded with seeming reluctance. "Although I hate to involve you. But, you see, sweet child, I was thinking that if you were to drift over there quite casually and appear not to notice that anything was amiss and quite casually grab hold of the dear old catalyst, you could say, quite casually, 'Father Dungstable! I'm terribly sorry I'm late. Papa and Mama are expecting you at home this moment!' Then you, quite casually, lead him off."

"Lead him where?" Gwen asked in confusion.

"Why, home, of course," the tulip said matter-of-factly. "I presume you have room enough for us all. I do prefer private quarters, but if I have to, I'll share, though not with the catalyst. You can't imagine how he snores!"

"You mean— Take you all . . . to my home!"

"Of course! And you must do it quickly. Before that wretched catalyst says somethig to ruin us all! Poor man is none too bright, if you know what I mean."

"But I can't! Not without asking Mama and Papa. What would they say—"

"If you brought Simkin to your house? Simkin, the darling of the court? My dear," the tulip continued in bored tones, "I could stay at the homes of twenty Princes, just like that! To say nothing of the Dukes and Earls and Counts who have literally gone down on their knees to beg me to be their houseguest. The Earl of Essac was devastated when I said no. Threatened to off himself. But really, twenty Pekingese? They yap, you know, to say nothing of nipping at the ankles." The tulip flicked a leaf. "And of course I can introduce you into court, once this little matter is set right."

"Court!" Gwen repeated softly. Visions of the Crystal Palace came to her mind. She saw herself being presented to His Royal Highness, curtsying, her hand on the strong arm of the dark young man.

"I'll do it!" she said in sudden conviction.

"Sweet child!" responded the tulip in heartfelt tones. "Now, carry me with you. Don't mind the *Duuk-tsarith*. They'll never penetrate this disguise. I say, though, it would certainly add to the overall effect if you would just tuck me into your bosom—"

"My . . . where? Oh . . . no!" Gwen murmured, blushing. "I don't think so . . ." Placing the tulip among the other blossoms, she hastily gathered up the remainder of the bouquet from the ground.

"Ah, well," the tulip reflected philosophically, "you can't win them all, as the Baron Baumgarten said when his wife ran off with the croquet master . . . and the Baron so fond of the game."

"I am going to ask you again, what are your names and what are your doing in Merilon?" The *Kan-Hanar* glared at them suspiciously.

"And I am going to tell you again, sir," said Joram, his voice taut with the visible effort it was taking him to control his temper, "he is Father Dunstable, he is Mosiah, and I am Joram. We are illusionists—traveling actors—who met Simkin by chance. We agreed to form a troupe and we are here at the invitation of one of Simkin's patrons . . ."

Saryon bowed his head, ceasing in his despair to listen. This was a story Prince Garald had suggested and it had sounded plausible at the time. Those born to the Mystery of Shadow, known as illusionists, are—by and large—a classless society. They are the artists of Thimhallan, traveling extensively throughout the world to entertain the populace with their skills and talents. Illusionists entered Merilon constantly, their skills being in great demand among the nobility.

But this was the third time Joram had told the *Kan-Hanar* his story and it was obvious to Saryon, at least, that the man wasn't having any part of it.

It's all over, Saryon said to himself bleakly.

The guilty secret he carried had burned such a huge hole in his mind that he was convinced it must be visible to all who looked at him—marked on his forehead, perhaps, like a Guild stamp upon a silver butter dish. When the *Kan-Hanar* arrested Simkin, the catalyst immediately jumped to the conclusion that Vanya had caught them. He prevented Joram from using the Darksword in their defense more out of fear for the young man's life than from fear of discovery. To Saryon, the end had come, and he intended, in just a few seconds, to counsel Joram to tell the *Kan-Hanar* the truth. He was just thinking, with a kind of wistful relief, that his bitter suffering would soon be over, when the catalyst felt a gentle hand upon his arm.

Turning, he found himself confronted by a young woman of sixteen or seventeen perhaps (Saryon was not much in the habit of guessing the ages of young women) who was greeting him like a long-lost uncle.

"Father Dungstable! How good to see you! Please accept my apologies for arriving late. I hope you are not angry, but it was such a lovely day that my cousins and I lingered far too long in the Grove. See the bouquet I gathered? Isn't it lovely. There is one flower, Father, that I picked especially for you."

The girl held out a flower. It was a tulip, Saryon saw, staring at it in bewilderment. Just as he was about to take it into his hand, he noticed that it was a purple tulip — a bright purple tulip . . . with a bright red sash and a dash of orange. . . .

Closing his eyes, Saryon groaned.

"And so you are telling me, Gwendolyn of the House of Samuels, that these . . . gentlemen are invited guests of your father's?" The *Kan-Hanar* glanced at Joram and Mosiah dubiously.

After Gwendolyn told her story to the Gate guards, the *Kan-Hanar* had taken them all to one of the guard towers. Magically shaped to stand next to the Earth Gate, the tower existed primarily for the convenience of the *Kan-Hanar*, giving them a place to rest during times when the Gate wasn't busy, and containing supplies for their official duties. It was rarely used for interrogating those seeking admittance to Merilon — that was generally handled at the Gate itself with quick dispatch. But — due to Simkin's dramatic arrival and even more dramatic disappearance — the *Kan-Hanar* discovered the crowd growing just a bit too interested in the proceedings. Therefore, he had herded everyone into the tower and now they stood, crowded together, in a small hexagonal room that had never been intended to accommodate six people and a tulip.

"Yes, of course," the young woman replied, toying prettily with the flowers she held in her hand.

Putting a blossom near her soft cheek, Gwen regarded the archmagus over its petals in a coquettish manner that the man found quite charming. He didn't take any particular notice of the fact that one of these blossoms happened to be an unusual-looking tulip, or that the young woman's speech contained many pauses and hesitations. On the contrary, he attributed this to a maidenly reserve he considered most proper and becoming in a young girl.

Saryon knew the real reason, however—the young woman was being coached in what to say, and she was being coached by the tulip! The catalyst could only wonder bleakly whether this was going to help matters or simply add to their long list of crimes. There was nothing he could do about it now, except to play his part and trust Simkin and the girl to play theirs.

As for Joram and Mosiah, Saryon had no idea whether they had figured out what was going on or not. The *Kan-Hanar* was watching them all closely, and the catalyst dared not give them any type of sign. He did risk a glance at them, however, and was somewhat startled to find Joram's gaze fixed on the girl with such burning intensity that the catalyst hoped she didn't notice. Such ardent and undisguised admiration might frighten and confuse her.

Seeing Joram's look, Saryon realized that he might have an entirely new set of problems to contemplate. Although losing one's heart wasn't exactly in the same category with losing one's life, the catalyst remembered his own days of tortured, dreaming youth and gave a despairing sigh. As if they didn't have trouble enough. . . .

"You see, sir," Gwendolyn was explaining, the tulip's petals brushing thoughtfully against her bejeweled earlobe, "Simkin and my father, Lord Samuels, the Guildmaster—You know him?"

Yes, the *Kan-Hanar* knew her honored father and indicated so with a bow.

Gwen smiled sweetly. "Simkin and my father have long been friends (this would have been news to Lord Samuels) and so when Simkin and his . . . his"—a pause—"tr-troupe of"—another pause—"young actors made known their intention to . . . to . . . perform in Merilon, my father extended an invitation to stay at our home."

The *Kan-Hanar* still appeared doubtful, but it wasn't over the young woman's story. Simkin was well-known and well-liked in Merilon. He often stayed at the very best homes. Indeed, the wonder of this was that he should consent to reside at the relatively humble dwelling of a mere Guildmaster. Lord Samuels and his family had a most honorable reputation, generations of them having dwelt in Merilon practically since its founding with

not a breath of scandal attached to the name. No, the *Kan-Hanar*
was in truth wondering how to cope with this awkward situation
without upsetting Lord Samuels or his charming daughter.

"The fact of the matter is," the *Kan-Hanar* began reluctantly,
aware of the gaze of innocent blue eyes, "that Simkin is under
arrest—"

"No!" Gwen cried in horror and shock.

"That is," the *Kan-Hanar* amended, "he would be under arrest if he were here. But he escap— That is, he left rather suddenly. . . ."

"I am certain there must be some mistake," the young
woman said with an indignant toss of her golden curls. "Simkin
can undoubtedly explain everything."

"I'm sure he can," muttered the *Kan-Hanar.*

"In the meantime," Gwen continued, moving a step nearer
the *Kan-Hanar* and gently laying her hand upon his arm in a
pleading manner, "Papa is expecting these gentlemen, particularly Father Dungstable—"

"Dunstable," corrected the catalyst faintly.

"—who is an old friend of our family's that we have not seen
in years. Indeed"—Gwendolyn turned to look at the catalyst—
"I was quite a child when you saw me last, wasn't I, Father? I'll
wager you didn't recognize me."

"That—that's quite true," stammered Saryon. "I didn't."

He saw that the young woman was enjoying the daring and
danger of this enterprise, never dreaming how very real the danger was. The girl turned back to the *Kan-Hanar* with a smile.
Saryon, his heart pounding in fear, glanced out the door and saw
the *Duuk-tsarith* conferring together near the Gate, their black
hoods nearly touching.

"The catalyst and these gentlemen," said Gwen, with a
seemingly uninterested glance at both Mosiah and Joram, "are
cold and wet and tired from their journey. Surely there can be
no harm in letting me take them to my home. You will know
where to find them, after all, if need be."

Apparently the *Kan-Hanar* considered this a good idea.
Looking through the door, his gaze went to the *Duuk-tsarith* as
well, then went past the warlocks to the line of people waiting
admittance into the city. It was their busiest time of day, the line
was growing longer, people were getting impatient, and his partner looked harried.

"Very well," the *Kan-Hanar* said abruptly. "I'll give you passes for City Above, but they are restricted. These gentlemen"—he looked grimly at Mosiah and Joram—"are to be allowed outside only in the company of your father."

"Or another member of the family?" Gwen asked sweetly.

"Or another member of the family," the *Kan-Hanar* muttered, hurriedly notating the restrictions on the scrolls of parchment that he was filling out.

The *Kan-Hanar* was busy with his work, the catalyst leaned wearily against a wall, and Gwen's blue eyes turned their gaze to Joram. It was the innocent, flirtatious glance of a young girl playing at being a woman. But it was caught in the snare of serious dark eyes, caught by a man who knew nothing of such games.

Gwen was accustomed to shedding her warmth and charm upon men and having them reflect it back to her. She was startled, therefore, to feel that warmth suddenly sucked into the dark well of a cold and hungry soul.

It was unnerving, even frightening. The dark eyes were absorbing her. She had to break their hold or lose something of herself—although just what that might be she didn't know. She couldn't make herself look away; the feeling was frightening, but thrilling at the same time.

It was obvious that the young man wasn't going to quit staring, however! This was growing intolerable. The only thing Gwendolyn could think of to do was drop the bouquet of flowers. It wasn't meant as a flirtatious advance. She didn't even think about that. Leaning down to pick it up would give her a chance to regain her self-possession and break the disturbing gaze of that bold young man. It was not destined to work out that way, however.

Someone else bent down to pick up the flowers as well, and Gwen only found herself in closer proximity to the young man than before. Each reached for the purple tulip—which was exhibiting most untuliplike behavior, its leaves curling, its petals fluttering in what may have been laughter—at the same time.

"Allow me, my lady," Joram said, his hand brushing hers and lingering there.

"Thank you, sir," Gwen murmured. Snatching her own hand back as though it had been burned, she rose hurriedly back into the air.

Gravely, Joram stood up and handed the flowers to her — all except the tulip.

"With your permission, my lady," he said in a voice that was, to Gwen's fluttered mind, as dark as his eyes, "I will keep this, a memento of our meeting."

Did he know who the tulip was? Gwen could say nothing, but muttered something incoherent about being "flattered" as she watched the young man take the tulip, smooth its petals with his hand (such an extraordinary hand, Gwen caught herself noticing, strong and calloused, yet with long, delicate fingers), and then slip the tulip into a pocket beneath his cloak.

Half convinced that she had heard a strangled squeak of outrage before the tulip was extinguished by the smothering fabric, she found herself wondering what it would be like to be pressed against the breast of the young man. Gwen blushed feverishly and turned away. She remembered the passes to City Above only when the *Kan-Hanar* actually laid them in her hand, and forced herself to concentrate on what the man was saying.

"You will not need a pass, of course, Father Dunstable, since you have dispensation to visit the Cathedral. The restrictions do not apply to you, either. You may go there whenever you like, and you will, I am certain, be desirous of making your presence known to your Order as soon as possible."

A delicate hint for the catalyst to report to the Cathedral at once.

Saryon bowed humbly. "May the Almin give you a good day, Archmagus," he said.

"And you, Father Dunstable," the *Kan-Hanar* replied. His gaze flicked over Joram and Mosiah as if they did not exist and he hurried out of the hexagonal tower room to interview the next in line.

Fortunately for Gwen, she was captured by her cousins the moment she left the guard tower. This helped her put disquieting thoughts of the dark young man firmly out of her mind — though her heart seemed to beat in time with his footsteps that she could hear so clearly behind her.

"If — if you will excuse me, Father Dunstable," Gwen said, turning to the catalyst and ignoring his young companions, "I have to tell — explain . . . all this . . . to my cousins. If you would like to refresh yourselves, the cafe over there is quite nice. I'll only be a moment."

Without stopping to wait for an answer, Gwen hurried away, dragging the excited cousins with her.

"What will your mother say?" gasped Lilian when she had heard as much of Gwen's story as Gwen felt capable of telling.

"My heavens! What *will* Mama say?" Gwen had never considered that. To suddenly float in the door with houseguests! And of such an unusual nature!

Lilian and Majorie were hastily dispatched to City Above with news that the renowned Simkin was going to honor the Samuelses with his presence. Gwen hoped fervently that news of his arrest and subsequent disappearing act had not reached her parent's ears.

Then, in order to give Lady Rosamund time to have the guest rooms opened and aired, the cook informed, and a servant sent to apprise Lord Samuels of the honor in store for him, Gwen returned to the cafe and offered to show her guests the wonders of the city.

Although the catalyst appeared reluctant, the young men agreed with an eagerness Gwendolyn found quite charming. Obviously this was their first trip to Merilon, and Gwen discovered she was looking forward to showing it off. Floating into the air, she waited, expecting them to join her. They did not, however, and — glancing down — she was astonished to see them looking at each other in some confusion. It instantly occurred to her that they had been walking everywhere and she wondered why. Of course! They must be tired from their journey, too tired to expend their energy in magic. . . .

"I'll hire a carriage," she offered before any of them could say a word. Waving a white hand, she motioned to a gilded blue eggshell drawn by a team of robins. It flew over to them, and they each climbed in, Gwen finding — to her embarrassment — that Joram managed to be on hand to assist her in entering.

She ordered the driver of the carriage to take them through the shops and stalls that had sprung up around Earth Gate like a ring of enchanted mushrooms. More than a few people glanced at them as they drove by, many pointing them out as Simkin's companions and laughing heartily. Leaving the area around Earth Gate, they drove past the tropical gardens, admiring the flowers that grew here and nowhere else in Thimhallan. Enchanted trees on the Walk of Crafts were singing in chorus, and raised their limbs as the carriage flew beneath them. A unit of

Imperial Guards mounted on seahorses bobbed through the air in perfect unison.

They could have spent hours in the Grove, but the afternoon sun was nearing the point designated by the *Sif-Hanar* as twilight. It was time to start home and—at Gwen's command—their carriage joined others circling upward to reach the floating rock pedestal of City Above.

Sitting in the carriage across from the young men, Gwendolyn thought how time had flown by all too rapidly. She could have stayed here forever. Seeing Merilon's wonders reflected in the eyes of her guests—particularly the dark eyes of one of the guests—she seemed to see the city for the first time and she couldn't remember having noticed before how beautiful it was.

And what did her guests think? Mosiah was wrapped in a spell of enchantment, pointing and gaping at the splendors with a naïveté and childlike wonder that made him a figure of fun to all observers.

Saryon didn't see the city at all. His thoughts were turned inward. The fabulous sights brought back nothing but bitter memories to the catalyst, and only made the knowledge of his secret more burdensome.

And Joram? At last he was seeing the city whose wonders his mother had described in such vivid detail every night of his childhood. But he wasn't seeing it through Anja's half-mad gaze. Joram's first glimpse of Merilon was seen through eyes of blue innocence and a mist of fine, golden hair. Its beauty made his heart ache.

3

The Guildmaster's Home

"**M**ama," said Gwen, "may I introduce Father Dunstable."

"Father." Lady Rosamund gave the catalyst the very tips of her fingers, curtsying slightly. The catalyst bowed, murmuring words of appreciation for milady's hospitality which milady returned cordially, if somewhat vaguely, her gaze fixed expectantly on the gate beyond him. Lady Rosamund greeted her guests in the front court garden as was customary in Merilon, the garden—of which milady was justly proud—providing a beautiful setting of ferns and rose trees.

"And this is Mosiah and . . . and Joram," continued Gwen, blushing prettily. Hearing a smothered giggle from her cousins in the background, the young girl tried to appear completely unconscious of the fact that his name came to her lips like a song of joy. An astute and doting mother like Lady Rosamund ordinarily would have noted the blush and guessed the truth the moment her daughter introduced the young man. But Lady Rosamund was nervous and somewhat flustered.

"Gentlemen," she said, giving them each her hand and looking around them and above them at the gateway. "But where is Simkin?" she asked after a moment passed and no one else entered.

"Lady Rosamund," said Joram, "we thank you for your hospitality. And we would like you to accept this as a token of our gratitude." So saying, Joram drew the tulip—somewhat crushed and battered—from inside his tunic and handed it to his hostess.

Her eyebrows raised and her lips pursed, as if she suspected she was the brunt of some joke, Lady Rosamund coldly reached out her hand—

—and touched Simkin's flowing, purple silk sleeve.

"Merciful Almin!" she cried, backing up with a start. Then, "I ask forgiveness, Father, for the blasphemy," she murmured, blushing nearly as pink as her daughter.

"An understandable reaction, my lady," Saryon said gravely, glancing at Simkin, who was staggering about the garden, gasping for air and fanning himself with the orange silk.

"Almin's Blood! My dear boy"—he turned to Joram—"a bath is requisite. Egad"—bringing his hand to his forehead, his eyes rolling back in his head—"I feel quite faint."

"You poor thing!" said Lady Rosamund, marshalling servants around her with a look. In a cool and calm voice, milady issued orders and directed troop movements with the skill of a warlock. All the while, she exhibited the most tender concern for Simkin, who looked more wilted in human form than he had in tulip. Calling upon the strongest of house magi, milady ordered them to assist Simkin indoors to the best front parlor. A gesture of her own hand brought a fainting couch hurrying to Simkin's side. He collapsed on it, affecting a tragic pose.

"Marie," Lady Rosamund ordered, "conjure the herbal restoratives. . . ."

"Thank you, my dear," said Simkin weakly, his nose wrinkling at the smell of the tea, "but only brandy can bring me out of this shock. Ah, madam!"—Gazing up piteously at Lady Rosamund—"if you only knew what a terrible ordeal I've been through! Oh, I say!" he called after the servant. "Bring the Year of the Frost Grape, will you, my dear? Duke d'Montaigne's vineyard? What, nothing but domestic? Well, I suppose it will have to do."

The servant reappeared with the brandy decanter. Leaning his head back upon the silken cushions of the couch, Simkin suffered Marie to hold a glass to his lips, and took a sip. "Ah, that helps." Marie removed the glass.

"Just a touch more, my dear . . ."

Taking the glass, Simkin sat up, drained it at a gulp, then fell back, exhausted, among the cushions. "Might I have just one more, my dear?" he asked in a voice that—from its weakness—might have been instructing Marie to draw up his last will and testament.

The catalyst brought another brandy as Lady Rosamund gestured for a chair. At her command, one floated through the air, coming to rest near the couch where the young man lay. "Whatever do you mean, Simkin? What terrible ordeal *have* you been through?"

Simkin grasped hold of her hand. "My dear madam," he said, "today"—dramatic pause—"sink me, but I was arrested!" He cast the orange silk scarf over his face.

"Merciful Al— Heavens," Lady Rosamund stammered in astonishment.

Simkin plucked the silk from his face again. "A most dreadful mistake! I have never been so humiliated. And now I am on the run, a common criminal!" His head lolled back, weak with despair.

"Common criminal?" Lady Rosamund repeated in a voice suddenly grown cool, her gaze going to the plainly dressed Mosiah and Joram and even flicking, for an instant, over the untrimmed robes of the catalyst. "Alfred," she said to one of the servants in the hurried undertone, "go to the Three Sisters and tell Lord Samuels to return home at once. . . ."

"Quite kind of you, madam, I assure you," Simkin said, pushing himself up on unsteady arms, "but I doubt seriously if there is anything His Lordship could do. He is, after all, a mere Guildmaster."

Lady Rosamund's face became exceedingly icelike. "My lord," she began, "is—"

"—going to be of no help to me, I'm afraid, 'm'dear," said Simkin with a sigh. Lying back once more, he folded the orange silk and laid it carefully across his forehead. "No, Lady Rosamund," he continued before she could speak, "if Alfred is going out, please send him to the Emperor. I'm certain this can all be cleared up."

"To . . . to the Emperor!"

"Yes, of course," Simkin said, somewhat irritably. "I suppose Alfred *has* been granted entry into the Royal Palace?"

Lady Rosamund's ice melted in the fever of embarrassment. "Well, to be frank— It's just that we have never— I mean, there was the knighting ceremony, but that was—"

"What? No access to the Palace? Sink me!" Simkin murmured, his eyes closing in the most desperate despair.

During this interchange, Mosiah and Saryon stood in extreme discomfort in a corner, feeling forgotten and very much out of place. Mosiah, in particular, was overawed at what he had seen of the enchanted city and its people, who seemed so far above him in appearance, culture, and education that they might have been heavenly angels. He didn't belong here. He wasn't wanted here. He could see Gwen and her cousins smile every time he spoke. Well-bred as they were, the girls tried to hide their mirth at his uncouth way of talking—they weren't particularly successful.

"You were right, Father," he whispered bitterly to Saryon under the cover of Simkin's grand act. "We were fools to come to Merilon. Let's leave, right now!"

"I'm afraid it isn't that easy, my boy," said Saryon with a sigh, shaking his head. "The *Kan-Hanar* must approve all who leave the city through Earth Gate as well as all who enter. We would never be allowed to go now. We must do what we can to survive this."

"Survive?" Mosiah repeated, thinking Saryon was joking. Then he saw the catalyst's face. "You're serious."

"Prince Garald said it would be dangerous," Saryon answered gravely. "Didn't you believe him?"

"I guess not," Mosiah muttered, his narrow-eyed gaze going to Simkin. "I thought he was, well, overreacting. I never dreamed it would be . . . so . . . different! We're outsiders! Some of us, at least," he added softly, with a glance at Joram. Mosiah shook his head. "How does he do it, Father? He seems a part of all this, as though he belonged here! Even more than Simkin! That fool is just a plaything. He knows it, and laps up the attention. But Joram—" Mosiah gestured helplessly—"he has everything these people have—grace, beauty." His voice trailed off despondently.

Yes, thought Saryon, his gaze going to Joram. He belongs. . . .

The young man stood some distance apart from where Saryon and Mosiah huddled near the wall. The separation was not intentional, but as though he, too, sensed the difference between them. His head thrown back proudly, he watched Simkin with that half smile on his lips as though the two were sharing a private joke on the rest of the world.

He belongs, and he knows it now, Saryon saw with a pang of sorrow. Beauty? I would never have said it of him, not cold, bitter, and withdrawn as he is. Yet, look at him now. Much of it is the young woman's influence, of course. What man does not become beautiful under the spell of first love? Yet it is more than that. He is a man in darkness, stumbling toward the light. And, in Merilon, that light beats down upon him, bringing a radiance and a warmth to his soul.

What will he do, Saryon wondered sadly, if he ever discovers that the brightness of that light covers only a darkness deeper than his own? Shaking his head, he felt Mosiah's warning touch on his arm, and returned to their present predicament.

The household of Lady Rosamund that had been marching forward with such dispatch and efficiency suddenly came to a halt in the middle of the road, so to speak. Simkin lay languidly on the couch, moaning bleakly about "docks and gibbets, stocks and thumbscrews" in a manner not at all calculated to endear him to his hostess. Lady Rosamund hovered in the center of the parlor, clearly at a loss for what to do next. The servants stood about, some with teacups balanced in the air before them, others holding brandy decanters or bed linens, all looking uncertainly at their mistress for orders.

The cousins, Lilian and Majorie, had retreated into a far corner, knowing that they, too, were not wanted and both wishing devoutly they were at home. Gwen stood near Marie, the catalyst, trying very hard not to look at Joram, though her gaze constantly strayed in his direction. The pretty flush had drained from her cheeks at the dreadful turn of events; however, her pallor made her more lovely than ever. The blue eyes were large and lustrous with tears; her lips trembled.

But she's our only hope, Saryon said to himself. Going over his idea once more in his mind, he decided to act on it. Things couldn't get much worse. It was becoming increasingly obvious that Lady Rosamund was going to send for her husband and then, though a "mere" Guildmaster, Lord Samuels would undoubtedly turn them all over to the *Duuk-tsarith*. Saryon may have been dealt a losing hand, but he was suddenly determined to play it out to its final, bitter finish. Besides, he was startled to find within himself a perverse desire to call Simkin's bluff.

The catalyst moved forward silently and unobtrusively to stand beside Gwendolyn. "My child," he said softly, "have you considered the Ariels?"

Gwen blinked—the tears had been just on the verge of falling; she knew her mother's intention as well as the catalyst—and then her face brightened, color came and went in her cheeks. "Of course," she said. "Mama, Father Dunstable has an idea. We can send for the Ariels. They can carry a message to the Emperor!"

"That's true," said Lady Rosamund hesitantly.

Saryon stepped backward, fading into the background as Gwen surged forward to plead with her mother.

"What *have* you done?" Mosiah asked, aghast, as Saryon returned to stand next to him.

"I'm not really certain," the catalyst admitted reluctantly, folding his hands in his robes.

"You don't think the fool actually meant any of that nonsense about the Emperor, do you?"

"I don't know," Saryon snapped, beginning to have misgivings himself. "He knew Prince Garald . . ."

"A Prince close to his own age who admits he loves a bit of partying now and then is a lot different than the Emperor of Merilon," said Mosiah grimly. "Look at him!" He gestured at Simkin.

The young man was greeting the idea with his usual aplomb —"Ariels? Capital idea. Can't imagine why I didn't think of it first. Extend my sincere thanks to the bald party in the corner, will you?"

Simkin appeared pleased but Saryon thought he detected a distinctly hollow ring in the dulcet tones.

"Well, you've made one person happy, at least," Mosiah said sourly.

Joram was looking at the catalyst with undisguised admiration. He even went so far as to nod his head slightly, and there was a flicker of light in the dark eyes, a grudging thanks, that warmed Saryon's heart even as it increased his misgivings.

"What does this do for us, besides further the course of true love?" Mosiah asked bitterly, beneath his breath.

"Buys us time, if nothing else," Saryon returned. "It will be days before the Emperor can possibly be expected to answer."

"I suppose you're right," said Mosiah gloomily. "But Simkin's certain to do something worse in the meantime."

"We have to leave Merilon before then," Saryon said. "I have an idea, but in order to act upon it I must get to the Cathedral, and it's too late now. They will be going to Evening Prayers."

"I'll leave with you, and gladly, Father," Mosiah said earnestly. "I was a fool to come. I don't belong here. But what about him?" Nodding, he turned a serious, concerned gaze on his friend, Joram, who was watching Gwen. Mosiah's voice softened. "How will we get him to leave? He's just found what he has hungered for all his life."

Prince Garald, what have you done? the catalyst said to himself. You taught him to be polite, you taught him to act as a nobleman. But it is an act still — the silken glove concealing the tiger's paw. His claws are sheathed now, but someday, when he is starving or threatened, they will tear apart the fragile fabric. And the silk will be stained with blood. I must get him out! I must!

You will, he reminded himself, growing more calm. Your plan is a good one. You can have everything arranged by tomorrow or the next day. By then, we will probably have been turned out of this fine establishment. As for the Emperor. . . .

Simkin was dictating a letter to Marie.

"'Dear Bunkie —'" Simkin began. "His nickname," he added, seeing Lady Rosamund turn pale.

Saryon smiled grimly. It didn't appear as if the Emperor was going to be much of a problem.

"You realize that if they had a barn, we'd be sleeping in it?" Mosiah said bitterly.

"What can you expect for a man on the run!" Simkin replied tragically, hurling himself upon the bed.

The young men were spending the night in what was obviously meant to be a carriage house when Lord Samuels could afford such luxury. The servants had conjured up beds and clean linens, but the small house — located in back of the main dwelling — was devoid of decoration or any other sort of amenities.

Lord Samuels, as it turned out, had heard the entire story of Simkin's arrest and disappearance during a Guild meeting that afternoon, It was the talk of Merilon, in fact, whose people always enjoyed anything bizarre and out of the ordinary.

Lord Samuels had enjoyed the story himself — until he arrived home and found it developing further in his own living room.

Simkin expounded fully upon the very great honor of having himself as a houseguest.

"My dear sir, a thousand Dukes, to say nothing of several hundred Barons and a Marquis or two, crawled — simply crawled — on their hands and knees and begged me to favor them with my presence whilst in town. I hadn't made up my mind, of course. Then there was that unfortunate incident" — he looked pained and much injured — "from which your sweet child rescued me" — he kissed his hand to Gwen, who sat with lowered eyes — "and how could I refuse her kind offer of sanctuary?"

But it did not appear to be an honor that Lord Samuels appreciated.

Furthermore, the father's guardian eye saw what the doting mother's had not. He saw immediately the danger in Joram's darkly handsome good looks. The smoldering black eyes were enhanced by the shining hair which Prince Garald had persuaded Joram to cut and comb. He wore it loose on his shoulders, the thick curls framing the stern, serious face. The young man's fine physique, his cultured voice and graceful hands accorded oddly with his plain clothing, lending an air of romantic mystery about him that was further enhanced by the nonsensical story of wicked uncles and lost fortunes. As if this weren't enough to turn the head of any girl, there was a sense of a raw animalistic passion about the man that was, to Lord Samuels, particularly disturbing.

Lord Samuels saw his daughter's flushed face and quickened breathing. He saw that she wore her best gown to dinner and that she talked to everyone *but* the young man — sure signs of her being "in love." This in itself did not bother Lord Samuels a great deal. Gwen had, of late, been "in love" with some young man at the rate of about one a month.

What concerned milord — and caused him to send his daughter to her chamber immediately following dinner — was that this young man was so different from the young noblemen Gwen regularly was in raptures over. *They* were boys, as young and flighty and puppyish as his sweet girl. This one was not. Though young in years, he had somehow acquired a man's seriousness of purpose and depth of feeling that Lord Samuels feared must completely overwhelm his vulnerable daughter.

Joram knew his enemy immediately. The two regarded each other coolly over dinner. Joram said little, concentrating, in fact, on maintaining his illusion of being Alive, using his sleight-of-hand techniques to eat the rich food and drink the fine wines with the appearance of magic. In this he succeeded well, due, in part, to the fact that Mosiah, though highly skilled in magic, was a peasant when it came to dining. The bowls that were supposed to float gracefully to his lips dumped soup down his shirt. The meat on its sizzling skewer nearly skewered him. The crystal globes of wine bounced about him like so many balls.

Lilian and Majorie — they had been invited to spend the night — giggled so much at these mishaps that they spent half the meal with their faces hidden behind their napkins. Ashamed and embarrassed, Mosiah could not eat and sat red-faced and silent and sullen.

Lord Samuels retired early and bid his guests — in a glacial tone of voice — to do likewise, saying he was certain they wished to rest before their *eminent departure*. As for Simkin's assurances that the Emperor would doubtless bestow a duchy upon Lord Samuels in return for his kindness toward "one whom the Emperor considered a wit and a *bonhomme* of the first order," milord was not delighted at the prospect, and bid them good-night quite coldly.

The guests went to their beds accordingly, the servants lighting the way to the carriage house. That night, while Saryon and Mosiah discussed plans for leaving Merilon and Simkin prattled away about the dire revenge he intended to ask the Emperor to inflict upon the *Kan-Hanar* at the Gate, Joram was thinking about his enemy, carefully plotting Lord Samuels's overthrow and defeat.

Joram had decided to make Gwendolyn his wife.

4

A Falling Star

The next day was Seventh Day, or Almin's Day, though few in Merilon ever thought of it in those terms. It was a day of rest and meditation for a few, a day of pleasure and relaxation for many. The Guilds were closed, as were all other shops and services. Prayers were held twice in the morning at the Cathedral, with an early mass at sunrise for the ambitious, and what was laughingly known as the Drunkard's Mass at noonday for those who found it difficult to rise after a night of revels.

The family of Lord Samuels, as might be expected, was up with the dawn—which the *Sif-Hanar* always made particularly ethereal in honor of the day—and off to the Cathedral. Lord Samuels stiffly and perfunctorily invited the young men to come with him. Joram might have been inclined to accept, but an alarmed look from Saryon caused him to decline. Mosiah refused summarily, and Simkin announced himself as being unwell and quite incapable of summoning the strength needed to attire himself properly. Besides, he added with a prodigious yawn, he had to wait for the Emperor's response. Saryon might have gone with the family, but he said, quite truthfully, that he had not yet had the opportunity of making his presence officially known to his brethren and added, also quite truthfully, that he preferred to spend this day alone. Lord Samuels, with a smile more chilled than the melon, left them to their breakfast.

It was a silent meal; the servants being present hampered conversation. Joram ate without tasting a thing. From the dreamy look in his eye, he was feasting on rosy lips and white skin. Mosiah ate hungrily, now that he was no longer under the laughing eyes of the cousins. Simkin went back to bed.

Saryon ate little and retired from the table quickly. A servant took him to the family chapel, and the catalyst knelt down before the altar. It was a beautiful chapel, small yet elegantly designed. The morning sun streamed in through brilliantly colored windows of shaped glass. The rosewood altar was an exact replica in miniature of the altar in the Cathedral—carved with the symbols of the Nine Mysteries. There were six pews, enough for the family and servants. Thick tapestries carpeted the floor, absorbing all sound—even the song of the birds outside.

It was a room conducive to worship. But Saryon's thoughts were not on the Almin nor was his mind on the ritual words he was mumblng for the benefit of any servants who might happen past.

How could I have been so blind! he asked himself over and over, clutching the darkstone pendant he wore around his neck, concealed beneath his robes. How could Prince Garald have been so blind? I saw the danger we faced, certainly. But what I saw as a dark crevice that might be leaped has widened into a gaping, bottomless pit! I saw the danger in the large things but not in the small! And it is the small that will entrap us in the end.

Yesterday, for example, when viewing the wonders of the town, Saryon had seen Gwendolyn on the verge of asking him to grant them all Life that they might float upon the wings of magic—something which, of course, was absolutely impossible for Joram to either do or fake. Fortunately she had said nothing, probably assuming they were tired from their journey. Today they had been fortunate as well; catalysts were given the Almin's Day to meditate and study, and so were not expected to provide Life for the family except in great need.

Everyone walked to the Cathedral, therefore—a feat that was quite a novelty for the residents of Merilon, who wore special shoes—known sacrilegiously as Almin Shoes—for the day. These took varying forms—depending on the wearer's wealth and class—from silken slippers to more elaborate shoes of crystal, shoes of gold encrusted with jewels, or shoes molded from jewels themselves. It was quite the fashion, currently, to train animals as shoes, and men and women both could be seen around the city wearing snakes or doves, tortoises or squirrels, wrapped around their feet. Of course, it was generally impossible to walk in such footwear, requiring the nobility to be carried by their servants in chaises also designed for this day alone.

Lord Samuels and family, being only of the upper middle class, wore very fine, but very plain, slippers of silk. They did not fit particularly well — they didn't need to — and Gwen's slipper fell from her foot before leaving the house. Joram retrieved it and was granted the honor by Gwen — following a timid glance at her father — of putting the slipper once more upon her small white foot. This Joram did, under the severe and watchful gaze of Lord Samuels, and the family proceeded on its way. But Saryon saw the look Joram gave Gwendolyn; he saw the color come to Gwen's cheeks and the breasts beneath her filmy gown rise and fall faster. The two were obviously plunging headfirst into love with all the speed and direction of two boulders plummeting down the side of a cliff.

Saryon was considering this unforeseen occurrence, feeling its weight increase the burden he bore, when a shadow fell across the catalyst. His head jerking up in alarm, Saryon breathed a sign of relief when he saw it was Joram.

"Forgive me, Catalyst, if I am disturbing your prayers . . ." the young man began in the cold tones he was accustomed to using when speaking to Saryon. Then he fell silent abruptly, staring moodily at the door, his dark eyes unreadable.

"You are not disturbing me," Saryon said, rising slowly to his feet, his hand on the back of the ornately shaped wooden pew. "I am glad you have come, in fact. I want very much to talk with you."

"The truth is, Ca—" Joram swallowed, his eyes shifted to the catalyst's face — "Saryon," he said haltingly, "is that I came here to . . . to thank you."

Saryon sat down rather suddenly upon the velvet pew cushions.

Seeing the astonished expression on the catalyst's face, Joram smiled ruefully — a smile that twisted his lip and brought a deeply buried glimmer of light to the dark eyes. "I've been a thankless bastard, haven't I," he said, a statement, not a question. "Prince Garald told me, but I didn't believe him. It wasn't until last night— I didn't sleep much last night," he added, a slow flush spreading over his tan face, "as you might guess.

"Last night"—he spoke the words reverently, with a lingering softness, sounding like a young, dedicated novitiate praising the Almin—"I changed last night, Cata— Saryon. I thought about everything Garald said to me and—suddenly—it made sense! I saw what I had been, and I hated myself!" He spoke rapidly, without thinking, purging his soul. "I realized what you did for us yesterday, how your quick thinking saved us . . . You have saved us—saved *me*—more than once and I've never—"

"Hush," whispered Saryon, glancing fearfully at the chapel door that stood partially open.

Following his gaze and understanding, Joram lowered his voice. "—never said a word of thanks. For that . . . and for everything else you've done for me." His hand motioned to the Darksword that he wore strapped in its sheath on his back, hidden beneath his clothes. "The Almin knows why you did it," he added bitterly. Sitting down on the pew beside Saryon, Joram looked up at the window, his dark eyes reflecting the beautiful colors of the glass.

"I used to tell myself that you were like me, only you wouldn't admit it," Joram continued, speaking softly. "I liked to believe that you were using me to help yourself. I used to think that about everyone, only most were too hypocritical to admit the truth.

"But that's changed." The reflected light gleamed brightly in Joram's black eyes, reminding the catalyst of a rainbow against a storm-darkened sky. "I know now what it is to care about someone," he said, raising his hand to prevent Saryon from interrupting him, "and I know that you did what went against your conscience because you cared for others, not because you were afraid for yourself. Oh, maybe not me!" Joram gave a brief, bitter laugh. "I'm not stupid enough to think that. I know how I've treated you. You helped me create the sword and you helped me kill Blachloch for the sake of Andon and the people in that village."

"Joram—" Saryon began brokenly, but he could not continue. Before Saryon could stop him, the young man moved out of the pew and knelt on the floor at the catalyst's feet. The dark eyes turned away from the sunlit window and Saryon saw them glowing with an intensity that recalled the forge fires, the coals burning brighter and brighter as the breath of the bellows gave them life; a life that would reduce them — in the end — to ashes.

"Father," Joram said earnestly, "I need your counsel, your help. I love her, Saryon! All night, I couldn't sleep — I didn't want to sleep, for that would have meant losing her image in my heart and I couldn't bear it, not even for an instant. Not even for the chance that I might dream of her. I love her and"— the young man's voice changed subtly, becoming darker, cooler, "— and I want her, Father."

"Joram!" The pain in Saryon's heart was like a physical obstruction. He wanted to say so much, but the only words that burst forth through the terrible ache were, "Joram, you are Dead!"

"Damn that!" Joram cried in anger.

Saryon glanced fearfully at the door again and Joram, springing to his feet, strode across the small room and slammed it shut. Turning, he pointed at the catalyst. "Don't ever say that to me again. I know what I am! I've fooled people this long. I can go on fooling them!" He made a furious gesture, pointing upstairs. "Ask Mosiah! He's known me all my life! Ask him, and he'll tell you, he'll swear by his mother's eyes, that I have magic!"

"But you don't, Joram," Saryon said in a low voice that was firm despite his obvious reluctance in saying the words. "You are Dead, completely Dead!" He rubbed his hand along the arm of the pew. "This wood has more Life than you, Joram! I can feel its magic! The magic that lives in everything in this world pulses beneath my fingers. Yet in you there is nothing! Nothing! Don't you understand!"

"And I'm saying it doesn't matter!" The dark eyes flared, their heat intense and burning. Leaning down over the pew, Joram gripped Saryon's arm. "Look at me! When I claim my rights, when I am a noble, it won't matter! No one will care! All they'll see is my title and my money—"

"But what about her?" Saryon asked sorrowfully. "What will *she* see? A Dead man who will give her Dead children?"

The flame from Joram's eyes seared Saryon's soul. The young man's grip tightened on the catalyst's arm until Saryon winced in pain, but he said nothing. He couldn't have spoken had he wanted to, his heart was too full. He sat quite still, his compassionate gaze never leaving Joram.

And slowly, the fire in the dark eyes died. Slowly the coals burned themselves out. The light glimmered and was gone, the color drained from the face, leaving the skin pale, the lips ashen. Cold darkness returned. Joram's grip loosened and he straightened up. His face was, once more, severe, set rock-hard with purpose and resolve. "Thank you once again, Catalyst," he said evenly, his voice as hard as his face.

"Joram, I'm sorry," Saryon said, his heart aching.

"No!" Joram held up his hand. For an instant color came back to his skin, his breathing quickened. "You told me the truth, Saryon. And I needed to hear it. It's something . . . I'll have to think about . . . to deal with." Drawing a deep breath, he shook his head. "I'm the one who is sorry. I lost control. It won't happen again. You will help me, won't you, Father?"

"Joram," Saryon said gently, rising to his feet to face the young man, "if you truly care about this young girl, you will walk out of her life right now. The only groom's gift you can bring her is grief."

Joram stared at Saryon in silence. The catalyst saw his words had touched the young man. There was a struggle going on inside. Maybe what Joram had said was true, maybe he *had* changed in the long night, or maybe this change had just come about gradually, naturally, under the long influence of patient friendship, patient caring.

How the struggle in Joram's soul might have resolved itself, what better decision Joram might have made at that moment when he was hurt and vulnerable, Saryon was never to know. For at the moment, chaos erupted. The family had just returned home from the Cathedral when the Emperor's carriage was seen approaching, falling from the heavens like a star.

"So, Simkin," said the Emperor languidly, "what have you gotten youself into this time?"

The confusion into which the Samuelses' household was thrown upon receiving this august personage into their midst was not to be described. The Emperor had actually descended from his carriage and floated into the front court garden before anyone could do anything other than stare. Fortunately Simkin had, at that moment, flung himself out the front door and into the Emperor's arms, wailing about "shame" and "degrading" and "thumbscrews!"

The Emperor took Simkin in hand; Lady Rosamund came to her senses and — like the excellent general that she was — assembled her troops and rode forth upon the domestic field. Graciously welcoming the Emperor into her home, she led him into the parlor, enthroned him in the best chair in the house, and deployed her family and guests around him.

"Really, Bunkie, I couldn't say," Simkin replied in hurt tones. "It's dashed humiliating, don't you know, to have hands laid upon one at the Gate as though one were a murderer. . . ."

Saryon, standing humbly in a corner, stiffened at this comment and he saw Joram's eyes flash in swift alarm. Simkin, noticing nothing, rattled on.

"The deuce of it," he continued gloomily, "is that now I'm forced to lurk about inside this . . . establishment . . . and while the house is very fine and Lady Rosamund has been hospitality itself" — he kissed his hand to her negligently, as she curtsied to the floor — "'tisn't what I'm accustomed to, of course." He dabbed a corner of one eye with the orange silk.

"Actually, Simkin, we think you should count yourself fortunate," the Emperor replied, with a smile and a lazy wave of a hand. "A charming residence, my lord," he said to Lord Samuels, who bowed low. "Your lady wife is a jewel and we see her counterpart in your lovely daughter. We will do what we can for you, Simkin" — the Emperor rose to take his leave, sending another ripple of confusion through the household — "but we think you should stay here, in the meantime, if Lord Samuels will put up with you, that is."

Milord bowed — several times. He was effusive, expansive. He would be only too proud, too pleased. The honor of entertaining a friend of His Majesty's was overwhelming. . . .

"Yes," said the Emperor in fatigued tones. "Quite. Thank you, Lord Samuels. Meanwhile, Simkin, we shall endeavor to find out what the charge is, who's brought it, and do what we can about it. May take a day or two, so don't go paradin' about the streets. We can only do so much with the *Duuk-tsarith*, you know."

"Ah, yes. Dogs!" Simkin glowered, then sighed deeply. "Very good of you, I'm sure, Your Majesty. If I might have a word" — he drew the Emperor to one side, whispering in his ear. The words "Contessa," "chafing dish," and "unfortunately discovered naked" were audible, and once the Emperor laughed out loud in a truly light-hearted manner that Saryon, who had been at court many times, had never heard. His Majesty clapped Simkin on the back.

"We understand—'nd now, must be going. Affairs of state and all that. We never rest on the Almin's Day," remarked the Emperor to the assembled family, who were waiting in line to bid their august guest farewell. The Emperor proceeded to the front door. "Lord Samuels, Lady Rosamund"—the Emperor gave his hand to be kissed—"thank you once again for extending your hospitality to this young scalawag. We have a holiday coming upon us soon. A grand ball at the Palace. Come along, won't you, Simkin, and bring Lord Samuels and his family with you. Eh?" The Emperor's gaze touched on Gwendolyn. "Would you like that, young lady?" he said, dropping the affected tone and manner and regarding the young woman with a fatherly smile in which Saryon saw a hint of wistfulness and pain.

"Oh, Your Majesty!" Gwen whispered, clasping her hands together, so overwhelmed with pleasure at the idea that she completely forgot to curtsy.

"That's all right, my lady," the Emperor said kindly, when Lady Rosamund rebuked her daughter for her lack of manners. "We remember what it was to be young." Again, the wistfulness, tinged with regret.

The Emperor was standing inside the door and Saryon was congratulating himself on having survived this latest crisis without incident when he saw Simkin glance about mischievously. Saryon's heart jolted. He knew what the young man had in mind and, catching Simkin's eye, he shook his head emphatically, trying desperately to lose himself in the woodwork.

But Simkin, with an ingenuous smile, said casually, "Egad, the shock of this frightful incident has unnerved me. I've neglected to present my friends to Your Highness. Your Majesty, this is Father Dungstable . . ."

"Dunstable," murmured the wretched catalyst, bowing low.

"Father," said the Emperor with a graceful gesture and a slight dip of the perfumed and powdered head.

"And two friends of mine—actors," said Simkin easily. "Stage names, Mosiah and Joram. We could present a charade at the ball . . ."

Saryon didn't hear what else Simkin said—and neither did the Emperor.

The man, with an air of amused and patronizing tolerance, extended his hand to Mosiah, who kissed it, his face nearly as red as the rubies on the Emperor's fingers. Joram came forward to do the same.

The young man had been standing somewhat behind Saryon, in the shadow of an alcove, when he was introduced. Moving forward, he touched the hand and bowed over it — though he did not kiss it — then straightened. As he did so, he stepped into a pool of sunlight, shining through a window directly opposite. The sun brought out the finely shaped lines of Joram's face, the high cheekbones, the strong, proud chin. It glistened in Joram's hair; his mother's hair; hair renowned in story and song for its beauty; hair that, like the hair of a corpse, seemed possessed of its own life . . .

The Emperor stopped in his empty, meaningless gesture and stared. The blood drained from the man's face, the eyes widened, the lips moved soundlessly.

Saryon caught his breath. *He knows! The Almin help us! He knows.*

What will he do? the catalyst wondered, panic-stricken. *Call the* Duuk-tsarirth? *Surely not! Surely he couldn't betray his own son. . . .*

Saryon looked around wildly. Surely everyone must notice! But no one was watching seemingly, no one but him.

Hurriedly, he looked back and blinked in astonishment.

The Emperor's face was calm. The shock of recognition had been as a ripple on the surface of placid water, nothing more. He gave the young man a smile in exactly the same empty manner that he had given him his hand. Joram stepped back into the shadow — he had noticed nothing, his eyes dazzled from staring directly into the sun. The Emperor turned away negligently, resuming conversation with Simkin as though nothing had happened.

"Consummate actors, my friends," Simkin was saying, dabbing at his lips with the orange silk. "They're included in the invitation to the Palace, of course, Highness."

"Friends?" The Emperor appeared to have forgotten them already. "Oh, yes, of course," he said magnanimously.

"Odd time of year for a holiday, isn't it, Your High and Mightyship?" continued the irrepressible Simkin, accompanying the Emperor out the door amidst a flurry of bows and flutterings by the household of Lord Samuels. The Emperor's carriage floated above the street. Made entirely of faceted crystal, it had been shaped to catch and reflect the sunlight, and it accomplished this so well that few could look at it without being blinded by the glare. "I can't recall, offhand, what it is we're celebrating?"

The Emperor's reply to this question was lost, the entire neighborhood having turned out to cheer and wave. Lord Samuels's reputation and status were fixed in that instant. Certain of his neighbors who had entertained hopes of rising to the Guildmaster's level were in that instant uprooted and cast aside as neatly and quickly as the Druids uprooted dead trees. Ascending into his carriage, the Emperor extended his blessing to one and all, and then the star lifted back into the heavens, leaving the earthbound mortals below to bask in the waning light of glory.

Inside the house of the Samuels, joy was unbounded. Lady Rosamund glowed with pride, her gaze going with satisfaction to the aforementioned neighbors. Gwen was in raptures over the invitation to the ball, until she realized she had nothing to wear and burst into tears. Mosiah stood staring after the Emperor and the marvelous coach in a dazed state from which he was rescued by cousin Lilian's bumping into him — quite by accident, the blushing girl assured him. Upon receiving his apology, she wondered if he would be interested in seeing the inner garden, and led him outdoors, cooing with delight at his "quaint" way of talking.

And Joram discovered that he had routed his enemy — horse, foot, and artillery.

Coming over to the young man, Lord Samuels laid a hand affectionately on Joram's shoulder. "Simkin tells me you believe yourself to have some claim upon estates here in Merilon," the lord said gravely.

"My lord," said Joram, eyeing him warily, "the story about the wicked uncle isn't true . . ."

Lord Samuels smiled. "No, I never believed that for a moment. Wormed the truth out of Simkin last night. It's much more interesting, as a matter of fact. Perhaps I can be of help. I have access to certain records . . ." So saying, he drew the young man away into his private study and shut the door behind them.

No one noticed the catalyst, for which Saryon was grateful. He returned to the family chapel, where he was certain of being alone, and sank down upon the cushions of the pews. The sun no longer shone through the stained-glass window, the room was left in cool shadows. Saryon began to shiver uncontrollably, not from cold, but from a vast, overwhelming fear.

Having witnessed the treachery of man, he had lost his faith in his god. The universe was to him nothing more than one of those gigantic machines he had read about in the ancient texts of the Sorcerers of the Dark Arts: a machine that — once started — ran by itself, operating by physical laws. Man was a cog in the wheels, driven by his own physical laws, his life dependent upon the motion of the other lives around him. When a cog broke, it was replaced. The great machine kept going and would do so, on and on, perhaps forever.

It was a bleak glimpse of the universe, and Saryon found no comfort in it. Yet, it was better than the view that the universe was run by some petty god who doted on power and dabbled in politics, who allowed his name to be mouthed sanctimoniously by his Bishop, who herded his "flock" like so many sheep.

But now, for the first time, Saryon began to consider another possibility, and his soul shrank from the thought in awe. Suppose the Almin *was* out there and He was vast and mighty in His power. Suppose He knew the number of the grains of sand that lay upon the shores of Beyond. Suppose He knew the hearts and minds of men. Suppose He had a plan as vast as dreams, a plan no mere mortal could begin to see or comprehend.

"And suppose," whispered Saryon to himself, staring at the stained-glass window where the symbol of the Almin was represented in the nine-pointed star, "that we are a part of this plan and that we are being rushed toward our destiny, swept to our doom like a man caught in the river rapids. We might cling to rocks, we might strive to reach the shore, but our strength is unequal to the task. Our arms are torn from their safe hold, our feet touch the bank, and then the current catches us once more. And soon the dark waters will close over our heads. . . ."

Letting his head sink into his hand, Saryon closed his eyes, a tight feeling in his chest as though he were truly drowning, his lungs burning for air.

Why had this terrifying notion come to him? Because he knew the holiday they would be celebrating within two weeks of this day. Joram would be entering the palace of Merilon eighteen years after he had left it — eighteen years to the day.

Joram would be celebrating the anniversary of his own death.

5

Threads of the Web

F ar below the Palace of Merilon, far below City Above and
City Below, far below the Gardens and the tomb of the great wizard who led his people here from a world seeking to destroy them,
there is a chamber whose existence is known only to members of
that Order which — in reality — rules Thimhallan. In that secret
chamber one night, eight people came together. Dressed in black
robes, their hands clasped before them, they stood in a circle
around a nine-pointed star that had been drawn upon the floor.
Each hooded head faced in the same direction, toward the ninth
point of the star, despite the fact that the place on the floor was
currently empty. All waited patiently; patience was their watch-
word. Patience, they knew, was generally rewarded.

The air shivered and the ninth point of the star upon the
floor was covered by the hem of black robes. Glancing around
the circle to see that all were present, the ninth member nodded
her hooded head and, with a clap of her hands, caused a huge
leather-bound book with blank pages of brittle parchment to
appear in the center of the circle, hovering, suspended in the air.

"You may proceed," she said to the member standing on the
first point of the star.

The *Duuk-tsarith* began his report. As he spoke, his words
were recorded, traced by lines of flame upon the parchment in
the huge book.

"A child was lost in the marketplace this day, madam," he said. "She has since been found and returned to her parents."

The witch nodded. The next spoke.

"We have solved the murder of Lucien the alchemist, madam. Only one person could have possibly known enough to substitute a chemical which, when combined with another, would produce a violent explosion, rather than the elixir of youth for which the alchemist was said to be searching."

"The alchemist's apprentice," said the witch.

"Precisely."

"Motive?"

"The apprentice and Lucien's wife were lovers. Under 'questioning,' the apprentice confessed both to his crime and to hers. Both are being held for sentencing."

"Satisfactory." The witch nodded once more, her eyes going to yet another point on the star.

"The search for the Dead man, Joram, continues, madam. A record of those who were or might have been Field Magi entering Merilon has been compiled. Eleven have been reported thus far and these have all been checked. All have legitimate reasons for being in the city and seven have been positively eliminated. In addition, the catalysts have supplied us with a list of all new brethren of their Order who have entered the city. Comparing the two lists, we have come up with an interesting match."

He paused, looking questioningly at his leader, mentally asking if this was a matter for the entire conclave or for her alone. The witch considered and, after a moment, dismissed the others and closed the great book.

"Proceed," she said when they were alone.

"The catalyst's name is Father Dunstable. A House Catalyst, he left Merilon several years ago. He has returned to Merilon, he says, upon the death of his Master and the breaking up of the household."

"A story that can be verified."

"We are doing so, of course, madam. He does not match the description of this Father Saryon, but a disguise could have been easily effected. The interesting point is that he entered town with one of the young men we know to have been at one time a Field Magus."

"Any other companions?"

The warlock hesitated. "We know of one, madam, and there may have been others. The Gate was crowded that day and an incident occurred which involved considerable confusion."

"This was?"

"The attempted arrest of one of the catalyst's companions, madam. Simkin."

The witch frowned. "This complicates matters. The Emperor himself has seen fit to intervene on Simkin's behalf. Not that Simkin is of any consequence." The witch made a deprecating motion with her hand. "That matter was trivial and easily smoothed over. But we must not make it appear that we are harassing the young man. The Emperor would be displeased, and matters are too delicate in that area to allow him any excuse to strike out against us — or Prince Xavier. Therefore, proceed with caution. Isolate the Field Magus, if you can, and bring him in for questioning. Or perhaps . . ." She hesitated, her lips pursed in thought.

"Madam?" queried the warlock respectfully. "You were saying?"

"Simkin has worked for us before, has he not?"

"Yes, madam, but . . ." It was now the warlock's turn to hesitate.

"But?"

"He is erratic, madam."

"Nevertheless" — the witch made her decision — "see what you can accomplish there. He could be of inestimable help. Be discreet, of course. You know how to handle him, I presume?"

The warlock bowed. "And the catalyst?"

"The Church will deal with their own, as always. I will inform Bishop Vanya, but I daresay he won't want to move without proof. Continue your investigation."

"Yes, madam."

The witch fell silent, her white teeth biting her lower lip. The warlock remained standing unmoving before her, knowing he was not dismissed either from her thoughts or from her presence. Her eyes, gleaming in the shadows of her hood, sought him out at last.

"There was no other companion? No other person present with these three?"

The warlock had been waiting for that question. "Madam," he said in a low voice, aware that she did not tolerate excuses, yet knowing that she must accept her own limitations, "there was a large crowd at the Gate, and a great deal of confusion. The young man, Joram, after all, *is* Dead. Not only that, but if he truly does have the power of the darkstone, he could remain invisible to our eyes."

"Yes," the witch muttered. "You have the household under surveillance?"

"As best we can, considering the Emperor has taken them under his protection. I have hesitated to question the staff. . . ."

"You do right. Servants gossip, and we must be careful not to alarm these young men. Remember that when you deal with Simkin. If it *is* them, the least hint of trouble and they will flee. Our only hope is to keep them in the city. Once in the Outland, we have lost them. Give them time, lull them into complacency, and they will make a mistake. When they do, we will be ready."

"Yes, madam." The warlock bowed and, sensing himself dismissed, vanished.

The single word "Patience," whispered in the air, followed after him like a benediction.

6

The Garden

The people of Merilon know that the inner garden, or House Garden as it is known, is the heart of every home. Every dwelling — no matter how humble — has its garden, even if it is nothing but a bed of flowers in the center of a cobblestone walk. From its green serenity springs the joy and solace necessary for a household's well-being. Legend holds that the amount of Life with which a family is blessed grows in the House Garden.

Of course, the wealthy in Merilon own gardens of rare and remarkable beauty. An inner garden that was well tended and properly cultivated could bless a house in other ways, as Lord Samuels well knew. Status took root and flourished in a House Garden. Thus, as with so many other things in his life, Lord Samuels's gardens were not only beautiful . . . they were good business as well.

A House Garden is not easy to maintain. Lord Samuels could have afforded a gardener, but that would have appeared to be rising too far above his station. He kept the garden himself, therefore, going out each morning before work to make certain that all was in order. The dragonlilies, for example, had a most disconcerting tendency to flute blue flame at certain hours of the day. Decorative and useful as a timepiece, the plants could be harmful unless carefully watched. He had to prune the choral bamboo daily; some stalks grew faster than others, and it was forever falling out of tune. The wind palms had to be adjusted each morning to the weather. Their swaying fronds generated a constant and pleasant breeze that was welcome on warm days, but uncomfortable on cool ones. In that instance, the palms had to be magically subdued.

These were minor problems, however. Lord Samuels's garden was, in general, well planned, well ordered, and much admired. Admittedly it was small compared to the gardens of the upper class. But Lord Samuels had cleverly compensated for this deficiency. The garden paths that wound among the thick, lush plantings, trees, and flowers were a maze of twists and turns. Once in the garden, the visitor not only lost sight of the house but his sense of direction as well. Walking among the hedges that Lord Samuels caused to shift about in their positions daily, a person could "lose" himself quite pleasantly in the garden for hours.

This was, next to flirting, Gwendolyn's favorite pastime.

Gwen was relatively well-educated, it being currently in vogue for the *Albanara* to educate their daughters. Every morning she spent studying her lessons with Marie, supposedly learning advanced theories and philosophies of magic and religion. It pleased Lord Samuels to look in daily on his daughter at her studies, her golden head bent solemnly over a book. When he left for work, that pleasant sight lingered in his memory. What he did not know was that the book either disappeared promptly after his departure or was replaced with one that dealt with more interesting matters — such as bold Sir Hugo, the highwayman.

Occasionally Lady Rosamund took over morning lessons, instructing her daughter on the management of the household, dealing with servants, and the raising of children. These lessons Gwendolyn enjoyed almost as much as Lady Rosamund, both spending a great deal of time building and furnishing splendid castles in the air. But, no matter how much she delighted in being with her mother or in reading about Sir Hugo, Gwen looked forward each day to the end of lessons when she and Marie went for their daily stroll in the garden.

Lady Rosamund always said, laughingly, that Gwen had the blood of a Druid in her veins, for the girl had a way with plants quite remarkable for one not born to that mystery. She could coax blossoms from the most sulky rosebush by her voice alone. Saplings that had lost the will to live lifted their spindly limbs at her gentle touch, while choking weeds cowered at her approach and attempted to hide from her sight.

Gwen was never happier than when wandering through the garden in the mornings. And it was undoubtedly chance that brought Joram into the garden this time of day as well. At least he *said* it was chance — he had simply wanted a breath of fresh air. Certainly he appeared surprised to see her floating above him amid the rose trees, her golden hair — elaborately coiled and braided about her head — shining in the sunlight, her pink gown with its fluttering ribbons, making her seem not unlike a rose itself.

"I bid you sun arise, sir," said Gwendolyn, the colors of the roses in her cheeks.

"Sun arise, my lady," said Joram gravely, looking up at her from where he stood upon the ground.

"Won't you join me, please?" Gwen asked, motioning upward.

To Gwen's astonishment, Joram's face darkened, his black brows coming together in a thick, hard line above his eyes. "No, thank you, my lady," he said in a measured voice. "I do not have sufficient Life —"

"Oh," cried Gwen eagerly, "Marie will grant you Life, if your own catalyst is not about yet this morning. Marie? Where are you?"

Looking around for the catalyst, Gwen missed seeing the swift spasm of pain that briefly contorted Joram's face. Marie, coming up behind her mistress, was looking directly at the young man and saw it quite clearly. Though she could not guess what it meant, she was sensitive enough to understand that — for some reason — he could not or would not use his magic. Like any good servant, she provided him with an excuse — her own failing.

"If my lady and the gentleman will both forgive me," she said, "I feel somewhat too fatigued. I was up during the night with the little ones."

"And I've been a selfish beast, draining your energy all morning. Forgive me," Gwen said, instantly contrite. "I'll come down. Don't move." Her filmy gown swirling about her, enveloping her in a cloud of pink, Gwen drifted down to the ground, hovering just above the path so that she would not bruise her bare feet on the rocks.

Marie glanced at Joram, and received a look of gratitude. But there was another look in the dark eyes — a piercing scrutiny, as if he was trying to guess how much she knew — that the catalyst found unsettling.

"I will show you through the garden, if you like, sir," Gwen said timidly.

"Thank you, I would like that very much," Joram replied, but his dark eyes remained on Marie, increasing her discomfort. "My father was a catalyst," he added, seeming to feel the need for explanation. "I am *Albanara*, but I have a very low level of Life."

"Indeed, sir?" Marie returned politely, feeling confused and — if it hadn't seemed too absurd — threatened by the intensity of the young man's gaze.

"A catalyst?" Gwen asked innocently. "And you're not a catalyst yourself? Isn't that unusual?"

"My life has been unusual," Joram said gravely, turning from Marie to Gwen, politely giving her his hand to support her as she moved slowly through the air at his side.

"I would like to hear about your life very much," Gwen said. "You've been out in the world, haven't you?" Sighing, she glanced about the garden. "I've spent all my life here. I've never been outside of Merilon. Tell me about the world. What is it like?"

"Sometimes, very harsh," said Joram in low tones, the dark eyes now wistful and shadowed. Glancing down, he saw the white hand resting in his calloused palm — her skin smooth and soft, his skin scarred from the forge fires.

"I will tell you my story, if you want to hear it," he said, abruptly shifting his gaze to a magnificent stand of tigerstripe lilies. "I told it to your father, last night. My mother, like you, was born and raised in Merilon. Her name was Anja. She was *Albanara* . . ."

He continued talking, telling Anja's tragic tale (as much as he considered safe for the young woman to know), his voice sometimes faltering or dropping so low that Gwen was forced to drift nearer to him to hear.

Marie, following at a discreet distance behind, watched without seeming to look, listened without seeming to hear.

"Your mother died, and so you came here, to seek your fame and fortune?" Gwen said, her eyes shining with tears when the story had come to an end.

"Yes," answered Joram steadily.

"I think it's a splendid thing you're doing," said Gwen, "and I hope you find your mother's family and make them feel absolutely wretched about the terrible way they treated her. I can't think of anything more cruel! To be made to watch the man you love perish like that!" Gwen shook her head, a tear glistened on her cheek. "No wonder she went mad, poor thing. She must have loved your father very much."

"And he loved her," Joram said, turning on the path and reaching out to take hold of Gwendolyn's other hand. "He suffered living death, for her sake."

Gwen flushed up to the roots of her golden hair; the bodice of the pink gown rose and fell very fast. She saw the unmistakable message in Joram's eyes, she felt it surge from his hands to hers. A delightful pain shot through her heart, marred by a stab of fear. Holding hands like this suddenly seemed very wrong. With a conscious glance at Marie, Gwen drew her hands away from the young man's grasp; he did not try to stop her.

Placing her hands behind her back — out of harm's way — Gwen turned from the disturbing look in the dark eyes and began to talk of the first thing that came to her mind. "One thing I don't understand, though," she said, her brow creased in thought. "If the Church forbade your mother and father to marry, how was it that you were conceived? Did the catalysts —"

At this moment, Marie came hurrying to her mistress's side. "Gwendolyn, my pet, you are shivering. I believe the *Sif-Hanar* have made a mistake this morning. Do you not find it cold for spring?" she asked Joram hastily.

"No, Sister," he answered. "But then, I am accustomed to being out in all types of weather."

"I'm not at all cold, Marie," Gwen started to say irritably when a sudden thought struck her. "You are right, as always, Marie," she said, rubbing her arms. "I *am* a bit chilled. Be a dear and go inside to fetch my shawl."

Too late, the catalyst saw her mistake. "My lady can summon the shawl to her," Marie said, somewhat sternly.

"No, no." Gwendolyn shook her head, smiling mischievously. "I am drained of Life, and you are too fatigued to grant me more. Please bring it to me, Marie. You know how upset Mama gets when I catch cold. We will wait here for you to return. This gentleman will have no objection, I suppose, to keeping me company?"

The gentleman had no objection whatsoever, and Marie had no choice but to return to the house in search of the shawl, which Gwen prayed was well-hidden.

Still keeping her hands safely behind her back, yet feeling a perverse longing to experience that strange, delightful pain again, Gwendolyn turned to face Joram. Raising her head, she looked into the dark eyes and the pain returned, although not quite as pleasant. Once again, she had the sensation that the warmth and joy of her soul was being absorbed by this young man, that it was feeding some deep hunger inside him, and that he was giving nothing back in return.

The look in the dark eyes was frightening, more frightening than his touch, and Gwen averted her gaze. "It . . . it is cold," she faltered, drifting backward slightly. "Perhaps I should go inside. . . ."

"Don't go, Gwendolyn," he said in a tone that sent a thrill through her being, as though she had reached into a storm cloud and touched lightning. "You know how I feel about you . . ."

"I don't know how you feel, not in the slightest," Gwen returned coolly, her fear replaced by the sudden enjoyment of the game. Now they were playing by rules she understood. "What's more," she said loftily, turning away from him, her hand reaching out to caress a lily, "I don't care to know."

It was the same flirtatious speech she had used to the elegant son of the Duke of Manchua, and that ardent youth had thrown himself at her feet — literally — declaring his undying devotion and countless other agreeable absurdities that she and her cousins had giggled over during the night. Her hand on the lily, she waited for Joram to say and do the same.

There was only silence.

Glancing at him from beneath her long eyelashes, Gwen was appalled by what she saw.

Joram looked like a man sentenced to death. His face was pale beneath the tan, his lips ashen and pressed together to keep from trembling or perhaps from uttering the words that burned in his eyes. His jaw muscles clenched. When he spoke, it was with visible effort. "Forgive me," he said. "I have made a fool of myself. I was mistaken in your kindness, it appears. I will take my leave—"

Gwen gasped. What was he saying? What was he doing? He was leaving! Actually turning and starting to walk away, his boots crunching on the marble pebbles of the path that sparkled in the sun! But this wasn't part of the game.

And suddenly she realized that—to him—this *was* no game. The story of his life came back to her and she heard it, this time, with a woman's heart. She felt the bleakness, the harshness. She remembered the hunger in his eyes, and some part of her saw the darkness there, too.

For a moment Gwen hesitated, trembling. Part of her wanted to hang back and let him go, remain a little girl, playing the game still. But another part whispered that if she did, she would lose something dear, something precious, never to find it again her entire life. Joram continued walking away. The pain inside Gwen was no longer pleasurable, it was cold and hollow and empty.

Magic drained from her body, she sank to the ground. Joram was moving farther and farther away. Ignoring the sting of the sharp rocks cutting into the flesh of her delicate feet, Gwendolyn ran down the path.

"Stop, oh, stop!" she cried in anguish.

Startled, Joram turned at the sound of her voice.

"Please, don't go!" Gwen pleaded, reaching out to him. Tripping over her long, fluttering skirts, she stumbled and nearly fell. He caught her in his arms.

"Don't leave me, Joram," she whispered, looking into his eyes as he held her close, his hands gentle and tender, yet trembling even as she trembled. "I do care! I do! I don't know why I said those things! It was wrong and cruel of me—" Hiding her face in her hands, she began to cry.

Joram clasped the young woman in his arms, smoothing the silken hair beneath his fingers. Blood pounded in his ears. The fragrance of her perfume, the softness of the body pressed close to his, intoxicated him. "Gwendolyn," he said in a shaking voice, "may I ask your father for permission to marry you?"

She did not look at him or she might have seen the darkness inside him, crouching like a savage beast in a corner of his soul; a darkness he himself believed was chained and manageable. Had she seen it, girl that she was still, she would have run, for it was a darkness only a woman who has wrestled similar darkness within her own soul can face unafraid. But Gwendolyn kept her eyes hidden and only nodded, in answer.

Joram smiled and — seeing Marie coming in the distance, the shawl in her hand — whispered a hasty warning to Gwen to compose herself, adding that he would talk to her father without delay. Then he was gone, leaving Gwen standing on the path, hurriedly blinking back her tears and trying as best she could to wipe the blood from the cuts on her feet, concealing the wounds from the loving eyes of her governess.

The third evening following the momentous occasion of the Emperor's visit, another couple walked in the garden, milord having brought milady here for the express purpose of having a private talk with her.

"So the story of the wicked uncle is not true?" Lady Rosamund asked her husband in disappointment.

"No, my dear," said Lord Samuels indulgently. "Did you really think it would be? A child's tale. . . ." He dismissed it with a wave of his hand.

"I suppose not," Lady Rosamund said with a sigh.

"Do not be downcast," said milord in a low voice as he drifted through the evening air at her side. "The truth, while not as romantic, is far more interesting."

"Truly?" Milady brightened, looking up fondly at her husband's face in the moonlight, thinking how handsome he was. The conservative blue robes of the Guildmaster became Lord Samuels well. Just over forty years old, milord kept himself in good physical condition. Since he was not a nobleman, he was not tempted to indulge in the dissipations of the upper class. He had not grown fat from too much food or red-faced from too much wine. His hair, though graying, was thick and plentiful. Lady Rosamund felt a good deal of pride in him, as he felt in her.

Their marriage, arranged by their families as were so many in Merilon, had not been one of love. Their children were conceived — as was right and proper — through the intercession of the catalysts, who transferred the man's seed to the woman in a solemn religious rite. The physical joining of two people was considered a sin — being barbaric and animalistic. But Lord Samuels and Lady Rosamund were more fortunate than most. Affection for each other had grown through the years, springing from mutual respect and suitability of minds and purpose.

"Yes, truly," Lord Samuels continued, glancing at the roses with a critical eye and reminding himself to check for aphids on the morrow. "Do you recall a scandal, some years ago—"

"Scandal!" Milady looked alarmed.

"Be easy, my dear," Lord Samuels said soothingly. "It was seventeen—almost eighteen—years ago. A young woman of high birth . . ." milord paused, "I may say *very* high birth," he added meaningfully, obviously enjoying keeping milady in suspense, "had the misfortune to fall in love with the family catalyst. The Church disallowed their marriage and the two ran away. They were later discovered in very shocking and dreadful circumstances."

"I recall something of the sort," Lady Rosamund said. "But I don't think I ever knew any details. We were not yet married, if you remember, and my mama was very protective."

Leaning down, Lord Samuels whispered something in milady's ear.

"How frightful!" Lady Rosamund drew back from him in disgust.

"Yes." Milord appeared grave. "A child was conceived in this unholy fashion. The father was sentenced to the Turning. The Church took the young woman in, gave her shelter and a place to stay while she was with child. There is every reason to believe that had she returned to her family, all would have been forgiven. She was, after all, an only child, and they were wealthy enough to hush matters up. But the terrible experience drove the young woman mad. She took her baby and fled the city, living as a Field Magus. Her family searched for her, but without success. Both parents of this unfortunate woman are now dead—as she is herself, according to the young man. The lands and property reverted to the Church with the stipulation that if the child lived, he should have his inheritance. If this young man can prove his claim . . ."

Lady Rosamund turned to face her husband, her gaze fixed searchingly upon his face. "You know the name of this family, don't you?"

"I do, my dear," he said gravely, taking her hand in his. "And so do you. At least, you will recognize it when you hear it. The young man says his mother's name was Anja."

"Anja," milady repeated, frowning. "Anja. . . ." Her eyes widened, her lips parted, and she placed her hand over her mouth. "Merciful Almin!" she murmured.

"Anja, only daughter of the late Baron Fitzgerald—"

"—cousin to the Emperor—"

"—related in one way or another to half the Noble Houses, my dear—"

"—and one of the wealthiest men in Merilon," both said together.

"Are you certain?" Lady Rosamund asked. Her face was pale, she laid her hand upon her bosom to calm her beating heart. "This Joram could be an imposter."

"He could be," Lord Samuels conceded, "but the matter is so easily checked, an imposter would know he couldn't hope to succeed. The young man's story has the ring of truth. He knows enough, but not too much. There are gaps, for example, that he doesn't attempt to fill, whereas an imposter would, I believe, try to have all the answers. He was completely confounded when I told him who his mother really was and what the estate might be worth. He had no idea. The young man was genuinely dazed. What's more, he said Father Dunstable could verify his story."

"You spoke to the catalyst?" Lady Rosamund asked eagerly.

"Yes, my dear. Just this afternoon. The man was reluctant to talk of it—you know how these catalysts hang together. Ashamed, no doubt, to admit that one of his Order could fall so low. But he admitted to me that Bishop Vanya himself had sent him to search for the young man. What could be the reason except that they want someone to take over the estate?" Lord Samuels was triumphant.

"Bishop Vanya! Himself!" Lady Rosamund breathed.

"You see? And"—Lord Samuels leaned closer to speak to milady confidentially once more"—the young man has asked my permission to pay court to Gwendolyn!"

"Ah!" Lady Rosamund gave a little gasp. "And what did you say?"

"I said—sternly, mind you—that I would consider it," Lord Samuels replied, clasping the collar of his robes in a highly dignified manner. "The young man's identity will have to be verified, naturally. Joram is reluctant to go to the Church with what little evidence he has now, and I don't blame him. Might weaken his case further down the road. I promised I would make a few more inquiries, see what additional proof we can uncover. He'll need a record of his birth, for example. Shouldn't be too difficult to obtain."

"What about Gwen?" Lady Rosamund persisted, brushing aside such masculine issues.

Lord Samuels smiled indulgently. "Well, you should talk to her at once, my dear. Discover her feelings in the matter—"

"I think those are obvious!" Lady Rosamund said, somewhat bitterly. It was a bitterness that soon passed, however, having its roots only in the very natural sorrow at the prospect of losing her beloved daughter.

"But, in the meantime," Lord Samuels continued more gently, "I think we might allow the two of them to go around together, provided we keep our eyes upon them."

"I don't really see how we could do otherwise," said Lady Rosamund with some spirit. At a gesture, she caused a lily to snap off its stem and glide into her hand. "I have never seen Gwen so infatuated with anyone as this Joram. As for them going around together, they've been nowhere else but with each other the past few days! Marie is always with them, but . . ." Milady shook her head. The lily slipped from her hand. She dropped down slightly in the air, nearly touching the ground. Her husband caught hold of her.

"You are tired, my dear," said Lord Samuels solicitously, supporting his wife with his own magic. "I have kept you up too long. We will discuss this further tomorrow."

"It has been a wearing few days, you must admit," Lady Rosamund replied, leaning on his arm for comfort. "First Simkin, then the Emperor. Now this."

"Indeed it has. Our little girl is growing up."

"Baroness Gwendolyn," Lady Rosamund said to herself, with a sigh that was part maternal pride, part motherly regret.

One evening three or four or maybe five days later, Joram entered the garden in search of the catalyst. He wasn't certain himself how long it had been since he had asked Gwendolyn to marry him and she had agreed. Time meant nothing to Joram anymore. Nothing meant anything to him except her. Every breath he took was scented with her fragrance. His eyes saw no one but her. The only words he heard were spoken by her voice. He was jealous of anyone else who claimed her attention. He was jealous of the night that forced them to part. He was jealous of sleep itself.

But he soon discovered that sleep brought its own sweetness, though it was a sweetness mingled with aching pain. In his sleep, he could do what he dared not do during the day — give in to his dreams of passion and desire, fulfillment and possession. The dreams took their toll — Joram would wake in the morning, his blood on fire, his heart burning. Yet the first sight of Gwendolyn walking in the garden fell like a cooling rain upon his tormented soul. So pure, so innocent, so childlike! His dreams sickened him, he felt ashamed, monstrous; his passions seemed bestial and corrupt.

And yet his hunger was there. When he looked at the tender lips speaking to him of azaleas or dahlias or honeysuckle, he remembered their warm, soft touch in his dreams and his body ached. When he watched her walking beside him, her lithe, graceful body clothed in some pink cloud of a gown, he remembered clasping that body in his dreams, holding her close to his breast with no flimsy barrier of cloth between them, remembered making her his own. At such times, he would fall silent and avert his eyes from her gaze, fearful she would see the fire raging there, fearful this fair and fragile flower would wilt and die in its heat.

It was in the throes of this bittersweet torture that Joram entered the garden late one night, searching for the catalyst, who — so the servants said — often walked here when he could not sleep.

The rest of the household had gone to their beds. The *Sif-Hanar* had decreed that there be no wind tonight, and the garden, therefore, was hushed and quiet. Rounding a corner, Joram affected to be surprised when he found Saryon sitting alone upon a bench.

"I am sorry, Father," Joram said, standing in the shadows of a eucalyptus. "I did not mean to interrupt you." Half turning, he started — very slowly — to withdraw.

Saryon turned at the sound of the voice, raising his head. The moonlight shone full upon his face. It was a strange face, this facade of Father Dunstable, and Joram always found it startling and somewhat disquieting. But the eyes were those of the scholar he had known in the Sorcerers' village — wise, mild, gentle. Only now, in addition, Joram saw a haunted expression in the eyes when the catalyst looked at him, a shadow of pain that he could not understand.

"No, Joram, don't go," Saryon said. "You do not disturb me. You were in my thoughts, in fact."

"In your prayers, too?" Joram asked as a joke.

The Priest's sorrowful face grew so pale that the words fell flat. Joram heard Saryon sigh heavily. The catalyst passed his hand over his eyes. "Come, sit by me, Joram," he said, making room on the bench.

Joram did so. Sitting down beside the catalyst, he relaxed and listened — for the first time — to the silence of the garden at night. Its peace and tranquility drifted down upon him like a gentle snowfall, its cool shadows easing his burning mind.

"Do you know, Saryon," Joram said hesitantly, unaccustomed to speaking his thoughts, yet feeling somehow that he owed this man something and longed to pay the debt, "the other day — when we were together in the chapel — was the first time I had ever been inside a . . . a holy place. Oh" — he shrugged — "there was a church of sorts in Walren, a crude building where the Field Magi went once a week to get their daily dose of guilt from Father Tolban. My mother never darkened the door, as I suppose you can guess."

"Yes," murmured Saryon, looking at Joram with a puzzled expression, astonished at this unusual outpouring of words.

"Anja talked about god, about the Almin," Joram continued, his gaze fixed upon the moonlit roses, "but only to give thanks to him that I was better than the others. I never bothered to pray. Why should I? What did I have to be thankful for?" the young man said, the old bitterness creeping into his voice. He grew quiet, his gaze going from the delicate white flowers on the vine to his hands — so skilled and supple, so deadly. Clasping his hands together, he continued to stare at them, unseeing, as he spoke.

"My mother hated catalysts — for what they had done to my father — and she fed me on hatred. You told me once — Do you remember?" he glanced at Saryon, " — that it is easier to hate than to love? You were right! Oh, how right you were, Father!" Joram's hands parted, clenched into fists. "All my life, I have hated," the young man said in a low, passionate voice. "I'm beginning to wonder if I *can* love! It's so hard, it hurts . . . so much. . . ."

"Joram," Saryon began, his heart full.

"Wait, just let me finish, Father," Joram said, the words almost exploding out of him with pent-up frustration. "Coming in here, tonight, I suddenly thought of my father." The dark brows came together. "I've never thought of him, much," he said, staring at his hands once more. "When I did, it was to see him standing there on the Borderland, his stone face frozen and un-moving, the tears dropping from eyes that stare eternally into a death he'll never know. But now, in here"—lifting his head, glancing around the garden, Joram's face softened—"I think of him as he must have been—a man like myself. With . . . passions like mine, passions *he* could not control. I see my mother as she must have been then, a young girl, graceful and beautiful and . . ." He hesitated, swallowing.

"Innocent, trusting," Saryon said gently.

"Yes," Joram answered inaudibly. Looking at the catalyst, he was astounded at the sight of the anguish he saw in the man's face.

Saryon caught hold of the young man's hands, gripping them with an intensity as painful as his words.

"Leave! Now, Joram!" the catalyst said urgently. "There is nothing for you here! Nothing for her but bitter unhappiness—as there was for your poor mother!"

Stubbornly, Joram shook his head, the curling black hair falling down over his face. He broke free of the catalyst's grip.

"My boy, my son!" Saryon said, clasping his own hands together. "It pleases me more than anything that you feel you can confide in me. I would be but a poor recipient of your confidence if I did not advise you to the best of my ability. If only you knew— If only I could—"

"Knew what?" Joram asked, looking up swiftly at the catalyst.

Saryon blinked and bit off his words, swallowing them hastily. "If only I could make you understand," he finished lamely, sweat beading on hs lips. "I know you plan to marry this girl," he said slowly, his brows knotted.

"Yes," Joram answered coolly. "When my inheritance is settled, of course."

"Of course," repeated Saryon in hollow tones. "Have you given any thought to what we discussed the other day?"

"You mean about me being Dead?" Joram asked evenly.

The catalyst could only nod.

Joram was silent another moment. His hand going absently to his hair, he began to rake through it, combing it with his fingers as had Anja, so long ago. "Father," he said finally, in a tight voice, "don't I have a right to love, to be loved?"

"Joram—" Saryon began helplessly, fumbling for words. "That isn't the point. Of course you have that right! All humans have it. Love is the gift from the Almin—"

"Except to those who are Dead!" Joram sneered.

"My son," Saryon said compassionately, "what is love if it does not speak the truth? Can love grow and flourish if it is planted in a garden of lies?" His voice broke before he could finish, the word "lies" seeming to shine in the darkness brighter than the moon itself.

"You are right, Saryon," said Joram in a firm voice. "My mother was destroyed by lies — lies she and my father told each other, lies she told herself. It was the lies that drove her mad. I've thought about what you said to me, and I have decided —" He paused, and Saryon looked at him hopefully.

"— to tell Gwendolyn the truth," Joram finished.

The catalyst sighed, shivering in the cool night air. That hadn't been the answer he hoped to hear. Drawing his robes closer about him, he pondered his next words carefully. "I am glad, glad beyond measure, that you realize you cannot deceive this girl," he said finally. "But I still think it would be better to drop out of her life — at least right now. Perhaps, someday, you can return. To tell her the truth will put your own life at risk, Joram! The girl is so young! She may not understand, and you will only endanger yourself."

"My life means nothing to me without her," Joram responded. "I know she is young, but there is a core of strength within her, a strength born of goodness and her love for me. There is an old saying of your Almin's, Catalyst." Looking at Saryon, Joram smiled, a true smile, one that brought a soft light to the dark eyes. "'The truth shall make you free.' I understand that now and I believe it. Good night, Saryon," he added, rising to his feet.

Hesitantly, he laid his hand on the catalyst's shoulder. "Thank you," he said awkwardly. "I sometimes think . . . if my father had been more like you — if he had been wise and caring — then the tragedy of his life and mine might never have happened."

Joram turned away abruptly and walked with rapid strides down the winding, twisting garden path. Embarrassed and ashamed over having bared his soul, he did not look back at Saryon as he left.

It was well that Joram did not see the catalyst. Saryon's head sank to his hands, tears crept from beneath his eyelids. "The truth shall make you free," he whispered, weeping. "Oh, my god! You force me to eat my own words and they are poison to me!"

7

The Killing Frost

everal more days passed after the meetings in the garden — days of idyllic bliss for the lovers, days of torture for the catalyst, slowly sinking beneath the burden of his secret. Lord Samuels and Lady Rosamund smiled upon the "children" with delight. Nothing in the house was too good for the future Baron and his friends, and Lady Rosamund began to consider how many people could be fit into the dining room for the wedding breakfast and if it would be proper to invite the Emperor or not.

Then one morning Lord Samuels went out to his garden as usual, only to return almost immediately to the house, using language that shocked the servants and caused his wife — seated at breakfast — to raise her eyebrows in reproof.

"Damn the *Sif-Hanar*!" Lord Samuels thundered. "Where's Marie?"

"With the little ones. My dear, whatever is the matter?" Lady Rosamund asked, rising from the table in concern.

"A frost! That's what's the matter! You should see the garden!"

The family rushed outside. The garden was truly in a pitiable state. One look at her beloved roses, hanging black and withered on their stems, caused Gwendolyn to cover her eyes in despair. The trees were rimed with white; dead blossoms fell like snow; brown leaves littered the ground. With Marie to grant him Life, Lord Samuels did what he could to repair the worst of the damage, but he predicted it would be many days before their garden recovered.

This damage was not confined to Lord Samuels's garden alone. All of Merilon was in an uproar and, for a few quaking moments that morning, several of the *Sif-Hanar* envisioned themselves languishing in the dungeons of the *Duuk-tsarith*. It finally came out that the fault lay with two of them, each of whom had assumed the other was going to regulate the temperature of the dome in the night. Neither did. The wintry weather outside caused the weather inside to turn from spring to fall in an instant, and all of Merilon was drooping, wilting, brown and dying.

Lord Samuels went to work in a foul temper. The day passed in gloom, and evening did nothing to improve anyone's spirits, for Lord Samuels returned home in a darker mood than before. Saying little to anyone, he went out to the garden to survey the damage. On his return, he sat down to dinner with his guests and family as usual, but he was silent and thoughtful during the meal, his gaze resting on Joram, much to that young man's consternation.

Gwendolyn, noticing her father's subdued spirits, immediately lost her appetite. To ask what was bothering him would be an unpardonable breach of etiquette — the only conversations considered suitable for the dinner table were lighthearted recounts of the day's activities.

Lady Rosamund, too, noticed her husband's dark mood and wondered fearfully what had happened. It was obvious that this was more than worry over the garden. There was nothing she could do, however, but try to cover for it as best she could and entertain their guests. Lady Rosamund chatted about this and that, therefore, with a semblance of cheerfulness that only made the meal more gloomy.

Young Master Samuels had learned to fly up out of his crib that morning, she reported, but, scaring himself by this feat, he had apparently lost his sense of magic and tumbled down to the floor, frightening everyone for a few moments until the lump on his head was examined by Marie and pronounced not serious.

No word had been received from Simkin, who had that morning — unaccountably and without saying anything to anyone — disappeared. But a high-placed friend of a high-placed friend of a lower-placed friend of milady's informed her that he had been seen at court, in company with the Empress. This same friend of a friend of a friend reported that the Empress was in low spirits, but that this was only natural, considering the anniversary that was coming up.

"What a dreadful time that was," recalled Lady Rosamund, shuddering delicately, nibbling at an iced strawberry. "That day when the Prince was declared Dead. We had the most splendid party planned, to celebrate his birth, and we had to cancel it. Do you remember, Marie? All the food we conjured up . . ." She sighed. "I believe we sent it down to the cousins, so that it wouldn't go to waste."

"I remember," Marie said gravely, trying to keep the conversation going. "We — Why, Father Dunstable, are you all right?"

"He's swallowed something the wrong way," said Lady Rosamund solicitously. "Bring him a glass of water." She motioned to a servant.

"Thank you," murmured Saryon. Choking, he thankfully hid his face in the goblet of water one of the House Magi sent floating his direction. So shaken was the catalyst that he was forced to clasp it in his trembling hand and drink it in this awkward fashion instead of using his magic to keep the goblet suspended near his lips.

Shortly after this, Lord Samuels rose abruptly from his chair.

"Joram, Father Dunstable, will you take your brandy in my library?" he said.

"But — dessert?" said Lady Rosamund.

"None for me, thank you," Lord Samuels replied coldly, and left the room after casting Joram a meaningful glance. No one else said a word. Gwen sat huddled in her chair, looking very much like one of her frost-blighted roses. Joram and Saryon excused themselves to Lady Rosamund, and Lord Samuels led his guests into his library, the servant following.

A figure started up out of a chair.

"Mosiah!" said Lord Samuels in astonishment.

"I beg your pardon, my lord," Mosiah stammered, flushing.

"We missed you at dinner, young man," Lord Samuels said coldly. This was a polite fiction. In the prevailing gloom of the dining room, no one had noticed the young man's absence at all.

"I guess I forgot about the time. I was so involved in reading—" Mosiah held up a book.

"Go ask the servants to get you something to eat," Lord Samuels cut him off, opening the door wide in a gesture of dismissal.

"Tha—thank you, my lord," stuttered Mosiah, his eyes going from the lord's grim face to Joram's worried one. He looked to Saryon for an explanation, but the catalyst only shook his head. Bowing, Mosiah left the room and Lord Samuels motioned to the servant to pour the brandy.

The library was a cozy chamber. Obviously designed by and for the man of the house, it was filled with numerous pieces of finely shaped wood—a large oaken desk, several comfortable chairs, and a great many lovingly shaped bookcases. The books and scrolls contained therein were suitable to Lord Samuels's rank and position in society. He was an educated man, as was necessary to rise to the rank of Guildmaster, but he was not *too* educated. That would have been viewed as an attempt to rise above his station, and Lord Samuels—like his wife—was careful to keep a respectful distance between himself and his betters. For this, he was widely admired, particularly by his betters, who were frequently heard to observe that Lord Samuels "knew" his place.

Joram glanced at the books as he entered. Drawn to knowledge as a starving man to food, he was already familiar with every title in the library. When he was forced—of necessity—to be parted from Gwen, he spent most of his time in here with Mosiah. True to his promise, Joram had taught his friend to read. Mosiah was an apt pupil, quick and intelligent. The lessons went well, and now, in his enforced confinement, Mosiah found the library a blessing.

He had begun his studies in earnest, working his way painstakingly through the texts, often without help; Joram being somewhat preoccupied. In particular, Mosiah was entranced by the books on the theories and uses of magic, having never been exposed to anything like this before. Joram considered these books boring and useless, but Mosiah devoted most of his leisure hours—and there were many—to the study of his magic.

Saryon, in his turn, did not notice the books at all. The catalyst barely noticed anything in the room, including the chair which milord drew up for him with a gesture and then had to

reposition quickly as the catalyst — absorbed in his thoughts —
started to sit down in midair.

"I beg your pardon, Father Dunstable," Lord Samuels apologized as the catalyst literally collapsed into the chair that scooted
up beneath him.

"My fault, my lord," Saryon mumbled. "I wasn't watching
. . ." His voice died.

"Perhaps you should get out more, Father," Lord Samuels
suggested as the servant was causing the brandy to flow from a
crystal decanter into fragile goblets of glass. "You and that
young man, Mosiah. I can understand why this young man pre-
fers my garden to the fabulous gardens of City Below" — he gave
Joram a meaningful look, a slight frown marring his forehead —
"but I do think you and Mosiah should see the wonders of our
beautiful city *before you leave.*" There was an unconscious emphasis on the words.

Alarmed, Joram glanced at Saryon, but the catalyst could
only return his look with a shrug of the shoulders. There was
nothing either could do or say; Lord Samuels was obviously
keeping the conversation carefully innocuous until the servant
had been dismissed. Joram stiffened, his hands curled over the
arms of his chair.

"I understand that you once lived here, Father Dunstable?"
continued Lord Samuels.

Saryon could trust himself only to nod.

"You are familiar with our city, then. But this is the young
man — Mosiah's — first visit. Yet my lady tells me he spends his
hours in here, reading!"

"He likes to read, my lord," Joram said shortly.

Saryon tensed. A week with Prince Garald had given Joram
a thin coating of courtesy and court manners. The young man
believed fondly that this had changed his life. But Saryon knew
it was only temporary, like the cooled top crust of a lava flow.
The fire and rage were there still, bubbling just below the surface. Let the crust crack, and they would spew forth.

"Will there be anything more you require, my lord?" the
servant asked.

"No, thank you," Lord Samuels replied. Bowing, the servant
left the room, shutting the door behind him. With a spoken
word, Lord Samuels cast a spell of sealing on it, and the three
were alone in the library that smelled faintly of musty parchment and old leather.

"We have a matter of some unpleasantness to discuss," Lord Samuels said in a cool, grave tone. "I find it never helps to put these things off, and so I will get right to the point. A difficulty has arisen concerning the records of your birth, Joram."

Lord Samuels paused, apparently expecting some response — perhaps even a confused admission from the young man that he was, after all, an imposter. But Joram said nothing. His dark eyes maintained their fixed, steady gaze, staring so intently into Lord Samuels's eyes that it was His Lordship who eventually lowered his head, clearing his throat in some embarrassment.

"I am not saying that you have deliberately lied to me, young man," Lord Samuels continued, his brandy hovering untasted in the air beside him. "And I admit that perhaps I compounded the problem by becoming too . . . enthusiastic. I believe I may have raised false hopes in you —"

"What is the problem with the records?" asked Joram, his voice so brittle that Saryon shuddered, seeing the rock start to crack.

"To put it simply — they do not exist," replied Lord Samuels, spreading his hands out wide, the palms empty. "My friend has found the record of this woman's, Anja's, admittance to the Font's lying-in chambers. But there is no record at all of her baby's birth. Father Dunstable" — milord interrupted himself — "are you feeling quite well? Should I send for the servant?"

"N-no, my lord. Please . . ." Saryon murmured in an inaudible voice. He took a gulp of brandy, gasping slightly as the fiery liquid bit into his throat. "A slight indisposition. It will pass."

Joram opened his mouth to speak again, but Lord Samuels raised his hand and, with an obvious effort of self-control, the young man remained silent.

"Now, there are undoubtedly reasons why this could be. From what you have told me about your mother's tragic past, it would be consistent with her distraught state of mind at this period of her life to think she might have taken the records of your birth with her. Particularly if she thought she could come back and use them to claim what was rightfully her inheritance. Did she ever mention to you that she had such records in her possession?"

"No," Joram answered. "My lord," he added stiffly.

"Joram" — Lord Samuels's voice grew stern, annoyed at the young man's tone — "I want very much to believe you. I have gone to a great deal of trouble to investigate your claims. I did this not only for you, but for my daughter, as well. My child's happiness means everything to me. I can see quite clearly that she is . . . shall we say . . . infatuated with you. And you with her. Therefore, until this matter can be resolved, I think it is in both your best interests if you leave my house—"

"Infatuated? I *love* her, my lord!" Joram interrupted.

"If you do truly love my daughter as you claim," Lord Samuels continued coolly, "then you will agree with me that it is in her best interests that you leave this house immediately. If this claim of yours can be proven, of course, I will give my consent to—"

"It is true, I tell you!" Joram cried passionately, half rising from his chair.

The young man's dark eyes burned, his face flushed in anger. Frowning, Lord Samuels made a slight movement toward the small silver bell that would summon the servants.

Seeing this, Saryon reached out his hand and laid it restrainingly upon Joram's arm, causing the young man to sink slowly back into his chair.

"I'll get proof! What proof do you want?" Joram demanded, breathing heavily. His hands clutched the armrests of the chair in his effort to control his temper.

Lord Samuels sighed. "According to my friend, the midwife he spoke to in the Font is of the opinion that the former midwife—the one who was there at the time of your birth—remembered that occasion, due to the . . . um . . . unusual circumstances surrounding it. If you had a birthmark"—milord shrugged—"anything that she might recall, the Church would undoubtedly accept her testimony. She is now a high-ranking *Theldara* attending the Empress," Lord Samuels added by way of explanation to Saryon, who wasn't listening.

The catalyst's head was bursting with intense pain; blood beat in his ears. He knew what Joram was going to say, he could see the light of hope dawning upon the young man's face, he could see the lips moving, his hands going to the fabric of the shirt that covered his chest.

I must stop him! the catalyst thought desperately, but a paralyzing fear gripped him. Saryon's lips were rigid, he could not speak. He could not draw breath. He might have been turned to stone. He could hear Joram talking, but the words came to him with a muffled sound as if spoken out of a thick mist.

"I do have a birthmark!" The young man's hands tore his shirt open. "One she's certain to remember! Look! These scars . . . on my chest! Anja said they were caused by the clumsy midwife who delivered me! Her nails dug into my flesh as she drew me from my mother's womb! These will prove my true identity!"

No! No! Saryon screamed silently. Not the nails of a clumsy midwife! He remembered it all with vivid, aching clarity. Those scars — the tears of your mother! Your real mother, the Empress, weeping over you in the magnificent Cathedral of Merilon; her crystal tears falling upon her Dead baby, shattering, cutting; the blood running red down the baby's white skin; Bishop Vanya's look of annoyance, for now the tiny baby would have to be purified all over again . . .

The books were caving in on Saryon . . . The books . . . forbidden books . . . forbidden knowledge . . . The *Duuk-tsarith* surrounding him . . . Their black robes, smothering him . . . He was suffocating . . . He couldn't breathe . . .

These . . . will prove my true identity. . . .

Darkness.

8

In the Night

"**W**ill he live?"

"Yes," said the *Theldara*, coming out of the room to which they had carried the inert, and to all appearances lifeless, catalyst. She studied the young man standing before her intently. In the stern face and thick black hair, she saw little resemblance to the features of the sick man. Yet the pain and anguish and even fear visible in the dark eyes made the Druidess doubt.

"Are you his son?" she asked.

"No . . . no," responded the young man, shaking his head. "I am a . . . friend." He said this almost wistfully. "We have traveled far together."

The *Theldara* frowned. "Yes. I can tell from the body's impulses that this man has long been separated from his home. He is a man accustomed to peace and quiet pursuits, his colors are grays and soft blues. Yet I see auras of fiery red emanating from his skin. If it were not impossible in these days of peace," the *Theldara* continued, "I would say this catalyst had been involved in a battle! But there is no war . . ."

Stopping, the Druidess eyed Joram questioningly.

"No," he replied.

"Therefore," the *Theldara* continued, "I must judge the turmoil to be internal. This is affecting his fluids; indeed, it is affecting the total harmony of his body! And there is something else, some dread secret he bears . . ."

"We all bear secrets," Joram said impatiently. Looking beyond the *Theldara*, he tried to see into the darkened room. "Can I visit him?"

"Just a moment, young man," said the *Theldara* sternly, catching hold of Joram's arm in her hand.

The *Theldara* was a large woman of middle age. Considered one of the best Healers in the city of Merilon, she had, in her time, wrestled with the insane until her healing powers brought order to their troubled minds. She cradled the living in her arms when they came into the world, she cradled the dying as they left it. Possessed of a strong grip and a stronger will, she was not the least bit intimidated by Joram's scowl at her touch, and held onto him firmly.

"Listen to me," she said in a low voice, so as not to disturb the catalyst lying within the room near them. "If you are his friend, you will draw this secret out of him. As a thorn in the flesh poisons the blood, so this secret is poisoning his soul and has very nearly led to his death. That and the fact that he hasn't been eating well, nor sleeping regularly. I don't suppose you noticed that, did you?"

Joram could do nothing but stare at the woman grimly.

"I thought not!" The Druidess sniffed. "You young people, wrapped up in your own concerns!"

"What happened to him?" Joram asked, his gaze going to the darkened room. Soothing music, prescribed by the *Theldara*, was emanating from a harp she had placed in the corner, unseen hands plucking the strings in a rhythm calculated to restore harmony to the discordant vibrations she could sense within her patient.

"It is known among laymen as Almin's Hand. The peasants believe that the hand of god strikes the victims down. We know, of course," the *Theldara* answered crisply, "that it is a drastic upset of the body's natural flow of fluids, causing the brain to starve. In some cases, this brings on paralysis, an inability to talk, blindness . . ."

Joram turned to look at the Druidess in alarm. "This hasn't happened to—" He couldn't go on.

"To him? Your friend?" The *Theldara* was noted for her biting tongue. "No. You can thank the Almin and myself for that. He is a strong man, your friend, or he would have succumbed long ago to the strain of this terrible burden beneath which he labors. His healing energies are good and I was able, with the help of the House Catalyst"—Joram caught a glimpse of Marie, standing in the room near the bed—"to restore him to health. He will be weak for a few days, but he will be fine. As fine as he can be," the *Theldara* said, letting loose her hold on Joram, "until that secret is purged from his body, its poisons drained. See to it that he eats and sleeps—"

"Will it happen again?"

"Undoubtedly, if he doesn't take care of himself. And next time . . . Well, if there *is* a next time, there probably won't be any more times after that. Bring me my cloak," the *Theldara* instructed one of the servants, who vanished instantly in search of it.

"I know this secret," said Joram, his dark brows coming together.

"You do?" The *Theldara* looked at him in some astonishment.

"Yes," said Joram. "Why does that surprise you?"

She pondered a moment, considering, then shook her head. "No," she said firmly, "you may think you know his secret, but you do not. I felt its presence with these hands"—she held them up—"and it is buried deep inside him, so far down that my probing of his thoughts could not touch it."

Looking at Joram shrewdly, the *Theldara*'s eyes narrowed. "You mean the secret he keeps that is yours, don't you? The fact that you are Dead. He may keep that knowledge hidden to the world, but it floats at the top of his thoughts and is easily read to those of us who know how. Oh, don't be alarmed! We *Theldara* take an ancient oath to respect our patients' confidences. It comes from the old world, one of the greatest of our kind named Hippocrates. We must take an oath this binding, who can see so far into the heart and the soul."

Holding out her arms, she allowed the House Magi to slip the cloak over her shoulders. "Now, go to your friend. Talk to him. He has shared your secret for a long time. Let him know you are prepared to share his."

"I will," said Joram gravely. "But I—" He shrugged helplessly. "I can't imagine what it could be. I know this man very well, or at least I thought I did. Isn't there a clue?"

The *Theldara* prepared to leave.

"Just one," she said, checking to see that her herbal potions and concoctions were each in their respective places in the large wooden tray that accompanied her. Finding all in order, she raised her head to look once more at Joram. "Often, this type of attack is brought about by a shock to the system. Think back to what you were discussing at the time the attack came on him. That might give you some clue. Again"—she shrugged—"it might not. The Almin alone knows the answer to this one, I am afraid."

"Thank you for helping him," Joram said.

"Humph! I wish I could say the same for you!" The *Theldara* gave a final, bitter nod, then, bidding her tray follow, she floated down the corridor to take her farewell of Lord Samuels and Lady Rosamund.

Joram stared after her unseeing, his mind's eye going back to the scene in the library. He and Lord Samuels had been discussing how to prove Joram's claim to the Barony. The young man couldn't remember Saryon saying anything, but then, Joram admitted to himself unhappily, he hadn't been paying any attention to the catalyst. His thoughts had been centered on his own concerns. What had been said right before the catalyst collapsed? Joram sought back in his mind.

"Yes." His hand went to his chest. "We had been talking about these scars. . . ."

Gwendolyn sat in her room, alone in the darkness. Her eyes burned from the tears she had cried and now, having no more tears left and fearful that her face would be red and swollen in the morning, she was bathing it in rose water.

"Even if I cannot talk to Joram, he will see me," she said to herself, sitting at her dressing table.

The moon, its cold light enhanced by the magic of the *Sif-Hanar*, shed a pearlized glow over Merilon. The moon's light touched Gwen, but she could not see its beauty and, in fact, it chilled her. The moon's cold eye seemed to stare at her tears without caring or compassion; its white rays on her skin made the warm flesh appear corpselike in its pallor.

Gwen preferred the company of the darkness and, rising to her feet, she drew the curtain shut with her hand—a task she ordinarily would have performed by a gesture and the use of magic. But she was physically drained, and there was no magic left in her.

Lord Samuels, following the assurances of the *Theldara* that Father Dunstable would be quite well in the morning, had informed his daughter that she was not to speak to Joram or allow him to address her until this matter of the young man's inheritance could be firmly established.

"I do not accuse him of being an imposter," Lord Samuels had said to his daughter, who was weeping bitterly in her mother's arms. "I believe his story. But if it cannot be proven, then he is a nobody. A man without wealth, without family background. He is"—milord had shrugged helplessly—"a Field Magus! That is what he was and, until he can rightfully claim better, that is what he must remain! Worse than that, he must live in the shadow of disgrace—"

"It wasn't his fault!" Gwen had cried passionately. "Why should he pay for his father's sin?"

"I know that, my dear," said Lord Samuels. "And I am certain that, if he achieves his Barony, everyone else will feel the same way. I am sorry this had to happen, Gwendolyn," milord had said, stroking his daughter's hair with a kind hand, for he truly doted on his girl and it broke his heart to see her in such grief. "It is my fault," he had added, sighing, "for encouraging this connection before I knew the facts. But it seemed such . . . such a good investment in your future at the time. . . ."

"And things may come out right yet, my pet!" Lady Rosamund had brushed her daughter's hair back from the tear-laden eyes. "Day after tomorrow is the Emperor's ball. The midwife now attends Her Majesty. Your father will arrange to meet her and we will find out then if she recognizes Joram. If she does, why, what a wonderful time we will have! If not, think of the young noblemen who will be in attendance and who will be very happy to help you put this young man out of your life."

Put this young man out of your life. Alone in her room, Gwen clasped her hands over her aching heart and bowed her head in sorrow. *Investment in your future.*

"Am I that heartless?" she asked herself. "Is there nothing more to me than a desire for wealth, for an easy, happy, fun-loving life?" Surely, she thought guiltily, looking around her in the moonlight that the filmy curtains could not shut out, surely that is how I must appear or my parents would not have said such things.

Recalling her words and her dreams over the past few days, her guilt increased tenfold.

"When I've dreamed of Joram," she murmured, "I've dreamed of him in fine clothes, not the plain clothes he wears now. I've pictured him floating over his estate, his servants around him, or riding his horses at a gallop in a game of King's Ransom, or taking me with him as he visits the farms once a year, all the peasants bowing to us in respect. . . ." She closed her burning eyes. "But *he* was a Field Magus! A peasant — one of those who bowed! And if he fails to prove his claim, that's likely what he'll go back to being. Could I stand beside him, my feet in the dirt, bowing? . . ."

For a moment, she doubted. Fear overcame her. She had never been to a Field Magi village before, but she had heard about them from Joram. She pictured her white skin burned and blistered by the sun, her fair hair tangled by wind, her body worn and weary and hurting by day's end. She saw herself plodding back home through the fields, walking because she lacked the energy to fly. But there was Joram beside her, walking with her to their hut. He had his arm around her, supporting her tired footsteps. They would return home together. She would cook their simple meal ("I suppose I could learn to cook" she whispered.) while he watched their children playing. . . .

Gwendolyn flushed, a warmth flowing through her body. Children. The catalysts would perform the ceremony, transferring his seed to her body. She wondered how they did it, for it was a subject about which her mother never spoke. No well-bred woman did, for that matter. Still, Gwen couldn't help but feel curious, and it was odd that this curiosity should come over her now, when she was picturing Joram eating his meal, looking at her, his dark eyes shining in the firelight . . .

The warmth of that fire spread through Gwen, enveloping her in a sweet golden aura that seemed in her mind to outshine the pale, cold light of the moon. Laying her head down on her arms, she began to cry again, but these tears sprang from a different well, one deeper and purer than she had ever imagined existed. They were tears of joy, for she knew that she loved Joram unselfishly. She had loved him as Baronet, she could love him as peasant. No matter what happened or where he went, her place was with him, even if it was in a field. . . .

If Gwendolyn had known the true rigors of the life she so innocently planned sharing with Joram, the heart that was beginning for the first time to feel the strong pulsing of a woman's love might have faltered. The simple hut she conjured up in her mind was at least five times the size of a real Field Magus's crude dwelling. The simple meal she pictured cooking would have fed a real peasant family for a month and, in her fond dream, all her children were born healthy, and thrived in their environment. No tiny graves dotted the landscape of her imagination.

But, in her present mood, that might not have mattered. Indeed, the harder the life, the more she embraced it, for that would prove her love! She raised her head, tears glistening on her cheeks. She hoped that Joram would *not* be able to claim the Barony! She pictured him crushed, dejected. She pictured her father grabbing her and starting to drag her away.

"But I will break free!" she said to herself in a fervor that was almost holy. "I will run to Joram and he will take me in his arms and we will be together forever and ever. . . ."

"Forever and ever," she repeated, falling to her knees and folding her hands. "Please, Heavenly Almin," she whispered, "please let me find a way to tell him! Please."

A feeling of peace and contentment stole over her and she smiled. Her prayer had been answered. Somehow, she would find a way to meet Joram in secret tomorrow and tell him. Leaning her head against her bed, she closed her eyes. The moonlight, penetrating the filmy curtain, touched the lips and froze their sweet smile. The tears upon her cheeks dried in its cold radiance, and Marie, coming in to check on her darling, shivered as she put the girl to bed and muttered a prayer to the Almin herself.

It was well known that those who slept too long in lunar light were subject to its curse. . . .

Joram spent the night at the catalyst's bedside. No moonlight shone upon his thoughts, for the *Theldara* had made certain its unsettling influence did not disturb her patient. The harp in the corner of the room continued to play its soothing airs — the music of a shepherd playing his flute, greeting the dawn that eases his night's watchfulness and relaxes his cares. A crystal globe hovered over the catalyst, shedding a soft light upon his face to keep away the terrors that lurk in darkness. Near it, liquid bubbled in another globe, sending forth aromatic fumes that cleansed the lungs and purged the blood of impurities.

How much good this did for Saryon was open to question, since, as the *Theldara* said, the secret of Joram's true identity was more deadly to him than a cancerous growth. No herbs could draw out its poison, no healing gifts of the *Theldara* could call upon his body to use its own magic and fight the destroyer. Saryon lay sleeping under a sedating enchantment cast by the *Theldara*, apparently oblivious to all around him. That was probably the only treatment that could benefit him now, and it was only temporary, for the enchantment would soon wear off and he would be left to struggle along beneath his burden once more.

But if the soothing music and the aromatic herbs did little for the catalyst, they were a blessing to Joram. Sitting at the bedside of the man who had done so much for him — had done so much and received such small thanks — Joram remembered vividly the lost and lonely feeling he had experienced when he thought the catalyst might have died.

"You understand me, Father," he said, holding onto the wasted hand that lay upon the coverlet. "None of the others do. Not Mosiah, not Simkin. They have magic, they have Life. You know, Saryon, what it is to yearn for the magic! Do you recall? You told me that once. You told me that as a child you were bitter at the Almin for making you a catalyst, for denying you the magic.

"Forgive me! I've been blind, so blind!" Joram laid his head down upon the catalyst's hand. "Blessed Almin!" he cried in stifled agony. "I look at my soul and I see a dark and loathsome monster! Prince Garald was right. I was beginning to enjoy killing. I enjoyed the feeling of power it gave me! Now I see it wasn't power at all. It was a weakness, a cowardice. I couldn't face myself, I couldn't face my enemy. I had to catch him unaware, strike from behind, strike while he was helpless! But for Garald and you, Father, I might have become that dark and loathsome monster within. But for you — and for Gwendolyn. Her love brings light to my soul."

Raising his head, Joram stared down at his hands in disgust. "But how can I touch her with these hands, stained with blood? You are right, Saryon!" He stood up feverishly. "We must leave! But no!" He stopped, half turning. "How can I? She is my light! Without her, I am plunged into darkness once more. The truth. I must tell her the truth. Everything! That I'm Dead. That I'm a murderer. . . . After all, it doesn't really sound that badly when I explain. . . . The overseer killed my mother. I was in danger. It was self-defense." Joram sat down beside Saryon once more. "Blachloch was an evil man who deserved death not once but ten times over to pay for the suffering he inflicted on others. I will make her see that. I will make her understand. And she will forgive me, as you have forgiven me, Father. Between her love and forgiveness and your own, I will be cleansed. . . ."

Joram fell silent, listening to the playing of the harp that was now the soft singing of a mother's lullaby to the infant sleeping in her arms. It brought no soothing reminiscences to the young man. Anja's lullabies had been of an uglier tone, telling him night after night the bitter story of his father's terrible punishment.

And though the *Theldara* had no way of knowing it, the lullaby brought dread dreams to Saryon. In his enchanted sleep, he saw himself—a young Deacon—carrying a child wrapped in a royal blanket through a deserted, silent corridor. He heard himself singing that lullaby—the last the baby would ever hear—in a voice that was thick and choked by tears.

On the bed, the catalyst twitched and moaned, his head moving feebly on the pillow in refusal . . . or denial. . . .

Joram, not understanding, looked at him in anguish. "You do forgive me, don't you, Father?" he whispered. "I need your forgiveness. . . ."

9

In the Morning

"**K**nock, knock. Hullo? I say, is anybody home? I — Almin's teeth and toenails, dear boy!" Simkin gasped, falling backward into the wall and clutching at his heart. "Mosiah!"

"Simkin!" cried the other young man, almost as startled as his companion.

Rounding a corner of a hallway, the two had nearly collided.

"Ye gads!" Dressed from head to toe in bright green satin, Simkin yanked the perennial orange silk from the air and began wiping at his brow with a shaking hand. "You've very nearly scared me out of my pants, dear boy, as happened to the Duke of Cherburg. Dressing up as the *Duuk-tsarith* was just the Marquis's little joke. Anyone could tell those black robes he was wearing weren't real. But the Baron is a nervous man. Thought he'd been nabbed by the warlocks, lost his magic, and there he was — his breeches down around his ankles, all his secrets exposed. It caused quite a sensation at court, though I thought it rather a large fuss over something so little. I expressed my condolences to the Duchess. . . ."

"I scared *you*?" Mosiah said when he could get a word in sideways. "What do you think you're doing, just popping out of thin air like that? And where have you been?"

"Oh, here and there, hither and yon, round and about," Simkin said cheerily, glancing vaguely into the living room of Lord Samuels's house. "I say, where is everyone? In particular, the Dark and Gloomy Lover. Still mooning about the girl, or has he had his fun with her and gotten over it?"

"Shut up!" snapped Mosiah furiously. Looking around, he caught hold of Simkin's arm and dragged him into the library. "You idiot! How dare you talk like that? We're in enough trouble as it is!" He slammed the door shut.

"Are we?" asked Simkin, looking enthused. "How positively jolly. I was getting frightfully bored. What have we done? Not got caught in a compromising position? Our hand up her skirt?"

"Will you quit it!" Mosiah said, shocked.

"Down her bodice?"

"Listen to me! Lord Samuels claims that Joram can't prove his identity and nearly threw him out of the house last night, but Saryon had some kind of fit or something and they had to call the *Theldara*—"

"The catalyst? A fit? How is the old boy?" asked Simkin coolly, helping himself to some of Lord Samuels's brandy. "Ah, still domestic," he muttered, frowning. "He could afford better. I wonder why he doesn't? However, I suppose we must make allowances." He drained the glass. "Not dead, is he?"

"No!" snarled Mosiah. Catching hold of Simkin's arm, he forcibly removed the brandy bottle. "No, he's all right. But he has to rest. Lord Samuels said we could stay, but only until the Emperor's party tomorrow night."

"What happens then?" Simkin asked, yawning. "Joram turn into a giant rat at the stroke of twelve?"

"He's supposed to meet someone there, some *Theldara* who saw him when he was a baby or something and can identify him as being Anja's son."

Simkin looked puzzled. "I say, this all sounds quite amusing, but has it occurred to anyone that Joram has changed slightly since then? I mean, what are we going to do to nudge the old girl's memory? Strip the dear boy and put him on a bearskin rug? I recall we did that with the— Oh, sorry. Swore on my mother's grave I'd never tell that story." He went extremely red. "Where was I? Oh, yes. Babies. It's been my experience, you know, that all babies look alike. The Emperor's mother and all that."

"What?" Pacing worriedly around the room, Mosiah was only half listening.

"All babies look like the Emperor's mother." Simkin nodded profoundly. "Large round head that she can't hold up, puffy cheeks, squinty eyes and this kind of befuddled expression—"

"Oh, will you get serious?" Mosiah said in exasperation. "Joram's got some kind of scars on him from when he was born. You know, you've seen them. Those little white marks on his chest?"

"I don't know that I've ever taken much interest in his chest," remarked Simkin, "except to note a distinct lack of hair. I suppose, though, it all went to his head."

"There used to be talk in our village about those scars," said Mosiah reflectively, ignoring Simkin. "I remembered Old Marm Hudspeth saying they were a curse; that Anja sank her teeth into him and sucked his blood. I never heard him say how he really got them. 'Course, it isn't the type of question one asks Joram, after all. Maybe I was afraid to ask." Mosiah gave a nervous laugh. "Maybe I was afraid he'd tell me. . . ."

"So now the curse becomes the blessing, just like in the House Magi's tale," said Simkin, a smile playing about his lips. He smoothed his mustache with one finger. "Our frog becomes a Prince. . . ."

"Not Prince," said Mosiah, exasperated. "Baron."

"Sorry, dear boy," said Simkin. "Forgot you grew up in the wilderness, illiterate and all that. Say," he continued hurriedly, seeing Mosiah growing angry again, "I came back to get you all to come with me. Merriment and jollification taking place in the Grove of Merlyn, down below. Artists practicing the performances they're going to present for His Boringness tomorrow night. Quite entertaining, really. One's allowed to throw things if they botch the job. Starts any minute, near noon. Where's Joram?"

"He won't come," said Mosiah. "Lord Samuels told him he couldn't see Gwendolyn anymore, not until this all was settled. But then Samuels left for the Guild, and Joram hopes to meet her anyhow. He's been out in the garden since breakfast. Saryon's too weak to go anywhere."

"Then it's you and me, dear boy," said Simkin, clapping Mosiah on the back. "I'll bet you've been entombed in this place for days, haven't you?"

"Well . . ." Mosiah glanced outside longingly.

"Relax! No need to worry about getting caught. You'll be with me," Simkin said easily. "I've the Emperor's protection. No one dares touch me. Besides, there'll be the most tremendous crowd. We'll lose ourselves amidst the throng."

"Hah!" Mosiah snorted, giving Simkin's glaring green finery a scathing glance. "I'd like to see you lose yourself . . ."

"What? Don't you like this?" the young man asked, wounded. "I call it *Shocking Green Grape.* Still, you are right. It does stand out a bit. I'll tell you what. Come with me and I'll tone it down. There"—he waved his hand—"how's this? I'll call it . . . let's see . . . *Rotting Plum.* Now I'm as drab as you. I say, old fellow, do come." Simkin yawned again, dabbing gloomily at his nose with the orange silk. "I've spent I don't know how many hours at court simply bored to pieces. That happened to the Earl of Montbank, you know. During one of the Emperor's stories. Most of us simply went to sleep, but when we awoke we found the Earl, scattered all about the parlor. . . . Anyway, I've had Dukes and Earls up to here! I thirst for the common touch."

"I'd like to give you a common touch!" Mosiah muttered, flexing his hands as Simkin wandered over to study the titles on Lord Samuels's bookshelves.

"What did you say, dear boy?" Simkin asked, half-turning.

"I'm thinking," said Mosiah.

Secretly, the young man was longing to see the Grove of Merlyn, said to be one of the wonders of Thimhallan. Touring these fabulously beautiful gardens, plus the chance to view the artistic delights of the illusionists, seemed a dream come true to the Field Magus. But he knew that Saryon wouldn't want him to go outside; the catalyst had emphasized over and over again how important it was that they remain hidden indoors.

We've been here almost two weeks, Mosiah told himself, and nothing's happened. The catalyst is well-meaning, but he's such a worrier! I'll be careful. Besides, Simkin's right. Strange as it may seem, he *does* have the Emperor's protection. . . .

"I say," said Simkin suddenly, "wouldn't it be fun to change this highly somnambulic volume on *The Diversity of Household Magics* to something more interesting? *Centaur Bondage,* for example . . ."

"No, it would not!" said Mosiah, making up his mind. "Come on, let's get out of this place before you destroy what little credibility we have left around here." Grasping hold of

Simkin firmly by his drab, plum-colored sleeve, Mosiah dragged him out the door.

Meekly allowing himself to be led along, Simkin cast a backward glance at the bookshelf, muttered a word, and winked. The orange silk fluttered through the air, wrapped itself around *The Diversity of Household Magics*, and then disappeared, leaving in its place another volume in a brown leather binding.

"Complete with detailed, colorful illuminations," said Simkin to himself, grinning in delight.

Joram went walking in the garden that morning, hoping to meet Gwendolyn, just as she had gone walking, hoping to find him. But when he did come upon her, sitting listlessly among the roses in the company of Marie, the young man bowed coldly, turned, and began to walk away.

He couldn't bring himself to talk to her. What if she refused to speak to him? What if she could not love him for the person he was, instead of the person he might become?

"And what if I don't become a Baron?" Joram asked himself. The sudden realization that his plans and hopes and dreams might come falling down around him nearly buried him in the rubble. "Why didn't I think of this last night? How could she love a man who doesn't know who he is!"

"Joram, please . . . Wait a moment . . ."

He stopped, his back turned, refusing to look at her. Gwen had called out to him, but, behind him, he heard Marie's voice remonstrating in low tones — "Gwendolyn, go inside. Your father has forbidden —" and he smiled in bitter satisfaction.

"I know what Papa said, Marie," returned Gwen's voice with a firmness born of sorrow and pain that sent a thrill through Joram's heart, "and I will respect his wishes. I only want" — her voice faltered here — "to inquire after Father Dunstable. I should think you would be concerned about the catalyst's health, as well," she added in rebuke.

Joram turned slightly as the voices drew nearer. He could see Gwen now, out of the corner of his eye. He saw the sleepless night in the shadows beneath the blue eyes. He saw the traces of the tears that not all the magic and rose water of Thimhallan could completely erase from the pale face. She had cried over losing him. His heart beat so he would not have been much surprised to see it leap out of his chest and fall at her feet.

"Please, Joram, stay for just a moment. How is Father Dunstable this morning?"

There was the touch of a soft hand upon his arm, and Joram looked into the blue eyes — eyes filled with such love, such unhappiness, that it was all he could do to keep himself from taking the young woman in his arms and, holding her close, shield her with his own body from the pain *he* was bound to inflict. For a moment his heart was too full for him to talk. He could only stare at her, the dark eyes burning with a fire warmer than any that ever melted iron.

And yet what would they say to each other? Marie was watching them sternly, disapprovingly. Once I answer the question about the catalyst, Marie will order her charge inside. If Gwen refuses, there will be a scene . . . the House Magi summoned, perhaps even Lord Samuels. . . .

Joram looked at Gwen, Gwen looked up at him.

Does the Almin hear the prayers of lovers?

Certainly it seemed so, for at that moment there came a wail from inside the house.

"Marie!" one of the House Magi shrieked. "Come quickly!"

Another House Magi hurried out into the garden in search of the catalyst. Master Samuels, playing at being a bird, had actually flown into the aviary. He was now being chased by an angry peahen for disturbing her nest and appeared to be in dire peril of his life. The catalyst must come!

Marie hesitated. The little boy might well be in danger of being pecked, but — wise woman that she was — she knew her darling in the garden was in worse danger still. Another wail, this one more frantic, sounded from Master Samuels. There was no help for it. Bidding Gwendolyn follow her immediately — a command Marie knew had about as much chance of being obeyed as if she had ordered the sun out of the sky — the catalyst sped off with the servant to rescue, soothe, and chastise Master Samuels.

"I . . . can . . . only stay . . . a moment," said Gwen. Blushing beneath the intense stare of the dark eyes and conscious that she was disobeying her father, she started to remove her hand from Joram's arm when Joram caught hold of it.

"Father Dunstable is resting comfortably this morning," he said.

"Please, don't," Gwen said, confused by the feelings his touch aroused in her. Gently pulling her hand away from him, she put both hands behind her back. "Papa wouldn't . . . That is, I mustn't . . . What were you saying about the kind Father?" she asked finally, desperately.

"The *Theldara* said it was a . . . um . . . mild attack," Joram continued, a prey to sudden longings and desires himself. "Something about the blood vessels constricting and preventing the blood from reaching the brain. I don't understand it, but it could have been very bad, paralyzing him permanently. As it is, she said Father Dunstable's own magic forces were able to completely heal the damage. I—I was going to thank Marie for her help," Joram added gruffly, being little used to thanking anyone, "before she left. If you would do so when you go into the house . . ." Once more, he bowed and started to leave, and again, the soft hand on his arm stopped him.

"I—I prayed to the Almin that he would be well again," Gwen murmured in such a low voice that Joram had to move closer to her in order to hear. Gwen accidentally left her hand upon his arm and Joram was quick to capture it.

"Is that all you prayed for?" he asked her softly, his lips brushing the golden hair.

Gwendolyn felt the touch of his lips, soft as it had been. Her entire body was sensitive to him suddenly; her very hair seemed to tingle at his nearness. Raising her head, Gwen found herself much closer to Joram than she had expected. The strange feelings of pleasurable pain that had stirred within her when he held her hand became stronger and more frightening. She was very much aware of him, of his physical body. The lips that had touched her hair were parted, as though they thirsted. His arms were strong and they crept around her, drawing her into a darkness and a mystery that made her heart both stand still with fear and race with wild excitement.

Alarmed, Gwen tried to pull away, but he held her fast.

"Please, let me go," she said faintly, averting her face, afraid to look up at him again, afraid of letting him see what she knew must be plain in her eyes.

Instead, he pressed her close. The blood surged through her body; she was warm inside yet shaking with chills. She could feel his warmth surround her; his strength comforted her and, at the same time, frightened her. She lifted her head to look into his eyes and tell him to let her go . . .

Somehow, the words were never spoken. They were on her lips but then his lips touched hers and the words were swallowed up, vanished in a thrill of sweet pain.

Perhaps the Almin doesn't hear the prayers of lovers, after all. If He did, He would have left them in that fragrant garden forever, clasped in each other's arms. But the wailing of Master Samuels ceased, a door banged, and Gwen, blushing deeply, hurriedly tore herself free of Joram's embrace.

"I — I must go," she cried, backing away, stumbling in panicked confusion.

"Wait, one word!" Joram said swiftly, taking a step after her. "If . . . if . . . something happens, and I don't receive the inheritance, will that matter to you, Gwendolyn?"

She looked up at him. Maidenly confusion, girlish vanities melted in the desperate longing and hunger she saw within him. Her own love flowed out to fill this blank emptiness as the magic flows from the world through a catalyst to its user.

"No! Oh, no!" she cried, and now it was she who reached out and clasped hold of him. "A week ago, I might have answered differently. Yesterday morning, even. Yesterday I was a girl playing at romance. But last night, when I knew I might lose you, I realized then it didn't matter. Papa says I'm young and that I will forget you as I've forgotten others. He's wrong. No matter what happens, Joram," she said earnestly, moving nearer to him, "you are in my heart and you will stay there, always."

Joram bowed his head; he could say nothing. This was precious, so precious he dreaded to lose it. If he did lose it, he would die. Yet . . . he had to tell her. He had promised Saryon, he had promised himself.

"I need you, Gwendolyn," he said gruffly, gently withdrawing from her embrace but keeping hold of her hand. "Your love means everything to me! More than life . . ." He paused, clearing his throat. "But you don't know anything about me, about my past," he continued earnestly.

"That doesn't matter!" Gwen began.

"Wait!" Joram said, gritting his teeth. "Listen to me, please. I've got to tell you. You must understand. You see, I'm D —"

"Gwendolyn! Come inside this moment!"

There was a rustling among the honeysuckle plants and Marie appeared. The catalyst's usually cheerful, pleasant face was pale and angry as she glanced from the flushed, disheveled young woman to the pale, fervent young man. At the sight of her, Joram dropped Gwen's hand, the words died on his lips. Catching hold of Gwendolyn, Marie led her away, scolding her angrily all the while.

"But you won't tell Papa, will you, Marie?" Joram heard Gwen say, her voice drifting back to him with the fragrance of the lilacs. "It was *you* who ran off and left me, after all. I wouldn't want Papa to be mad at *you* . . ."

Joram stood, staring after them, not knowing whether to curse the Almin or thank Him for His timely intervention.

10

The Grove of Merlyn

The Grove of Merlyn was the cultural heart of Merilon. Built to honor the wizard who had led his people from the Dark World of the Dead to this one of Life, it was now a repository for the arts. The wizard's tomb was the heart of the Grove. A ring of oak trees surrounded the tomb, patiently standing their guardian watch over the centuries. A carpet of lush, green grass spread out from the feet of the oaks, unrolling until it reached the tomb itself. The grass was soft and pleasant to walk on, the area around the tomb peaceful and quiet — which was probably the reason few people ever visited there.

Outside the oak ring lay the main part of the Grove. Hedges of brilliant picket rose, whose blossoms were every color of the rainbow and then some, formed a gigantic maze around the tomb. Within this maze were small amphitheaters where artists painted, actors acted, clowns capered, and music played day in and day out. The maze itself was simple to navigate — visitors could, if lost, simply fly over the hedge rows. But this was considered "cheating." Tall locust trees — standing higher than the hedges — were daily shaped by the Druids into fantastical "guides" through the maze, which itself shifted daily. Part of the fun of entering the Grove was to figure out the maze; the trees often offered "clues." The fact that the maze always led to the tomb was considered its weakest point. Many of the nobility had been to the Emperor protesting this — stating that the tomb was outdated, ugly, and depressing. The Emperor discussed the matter with the Druids, but they were obstinate, refusing to change. Knowledgeable visitors, therefore, never penetrated the maze. It was only the uninitiated or uninformed tourist — like Mosiah — who followed it to its heart.

The Field Magus had seen the ring of oaks from a distance and felt drawn to them; they reminded him of his home on the borders of the forest. Upon reaching the trees, he discovered the tomb, and entered the sacred ring with reverential awe. Coming to stand beside the ancient tomb of the wizard, Mosiah laid his hand upon the stone that had been shaped out of love and grief. It was a simple tomb, made of white marble magically enhanced so that no trace of another color marred the stone's purity. It stood four feet high and was six feet long and — at first glimpse — appeared plain and unadorned.

Solemnly, whispering a prayer to propitiate the spirits of the dead, the young man ran his hand along the tomb's surface. The marble felt warm to the touch in the Grove's humid air, and there was a sense of deep sadness lingering about the tomb that made Mosiah understand, suddenly, why the revelers avoided this place.

It was the sadness of homesickness, he realized, recognizing and identifying the feeling that was growing on him. Even though the old wizard had left his world willingly to bring his people to a world where they could live and thrive without persecution, he had never felt at home here.

"His mortal remains are buried in this ground. I wonder where his spirit lives?" Mosiah murmured.

Moving to stand at the tomb's head, still running his hand across the smooth marble, Mosiah felt ridges beneath his finger. There *was* something carved into the surface. Slowly he walked around the tomb to where he could see the shadows cast by the sun's light, and on the opposite side, he could barely make out what had been etched in the rock. The wizard's name in ancient letters and something beneath it he could not read. Then . . . something else below that . . .

Mosiah gasped.

Hearing a snicker, he looked around to find Simkin standing beside him, an amused smile upon his face. "I say, dear boy, you are a delight to take places. You gape and gawk to perfection, and over the oddest things, too. Can't imagine why you enjoy hanging about this moldy old ruin, though . . ." Simkin added with a disparaging glance at the tomb.

"I wasn't gawking," Mosiah muttered irritably. "And don't talk about this place like that! It seems sacrilegious somehow. Do you know anything about this?" He gestured at the tomb.

Simkin shrugged. "I know so much, one thing blends with another. Try me."

"Why is there a sword on it?" Mosiah asked, pointing to the figure carved below the wizard's name.

"Why not?" Simkin yawned.

"A weapon of the Dark Arts, on a wizard's tomb?" Mosiah said, shocked. "He wasn't a Sorcerer, was he?"

"Almin's blood, didn't they teach you anything except how to plant potatoes?" Simkin snorted. "Of course he wasn't a Sorcerer. *DKarn-Duuk*, a warlock of the highest ranking. According to legend, he asked that the sword be carved there. Something about a King and an enchanted realm where all the tables were round and they dressed in clothes made of iron to go on quests after cups and saucers."

"Oh, for the love of — Just forget it!" Mosiah said, exasperated.

"I'm telling the truth," Simkin said loftily. "The cups and saucers were of religious significance. They kept trying to get a complete set. And now, are you going to stand here all day moping or shall we have some fun? The illusionists and shapers are in the pavilion, practicing."

"I'll go," said Mosiah, glancing in the direction Simkin indicated. Beautiful, multicolored silk streamers hung suspended from midair, fluttering magically over the crowd. He could hear tantalizing sounds of laughter, gasps of wonder and awe, and applause coming from all directions, and his pulse beat faster at the thought of the marvels he was to soon witness. Yet, as he turned from the tomb, he felt a stab of pain and regret. It was so quiet here, so peaceful . . .

"I wonder what happened to the enchanted realm?" Mosiah murmured, running his hand for the last time over the warm marble as they started to leave.

"What always happens to enchanted realms. I suppose," Simkin said languidly, pulling the orange silk from the air and dabbing his nose with it. "Someone woke up and the dream ended."

Throngs of people floated and hovered and drifted beneath the gaily colored silks of the illusionist amphitheater. Mosiah had never imagined so many people could be in one place at one time, and he stopped at the entrance, daunted by the crowd. But Simkin, darting here and there like a bright-plumaged bird, put his hand on his friend's arm and guided him into the pavilion with surprising ease. Flitting into this person, dancing around that one, brushing up against another, Simkin kept up a steady flow of lively conversation as he moved ever nearer the front of the crowd.

"Beg pardon, old chap. Was that your foot? Mistook it for a cauliflower. You should really have the *Theldara* do something about those toes. . . . Just passing through, don't mind us. Do you like this ensemble? I call it *Rotting Plum*. Yes, I know it's not up to my usual standards, but my friend and I are supposed to be traveling incognito. Pray take no notice of us. Duke Richlow! Sink me! In town for the gala? Did I do that? Frightfully sorry, old boy. Must've jostled your elbow. Actually that wine stain rather helps your somewhat drab robe, if you don't mind my saying— Well . . . if you've no imagination, allow me." Simkin snatched the orange silk out of the air. "I'll have you as spotless, old chap, as your wife's reputation. Ah, is it my fault you drink this cheap brand that won't wash out? Try a lemon rinse. It does wonders for the Duchess's hair, doesn't it? Ah, Contessa! Charmed. And your privileged escort? I don't believe we've met. Simkin, at your service. Any relation to the Contessa? Cousin? Yes, of course, I should have known. You're about the eighth cousin I've met. Kissing cousin, too, I'll wager. I envy the Contessa her large family . . . and you are unaccountably large, aren't you, dear boy? I was just thinking, Contessa, it's such a coincidence that all your cousins are male, six feet tall, with such perfect teeth . . ."

Heads turned. People laughed and pointed, some floating higher or lower to get a better view, many moving nearer to hear the irreverent young man's barbed comments. Floundering along in Simkin's wake, Mosiah felt his skin alternately burn with embarrassment or go cold with fear. In vain he tugged on

Simkin's sleeve — which once came off in his hand to the delight of two Earls and a Marchioness — in vain he reminded him in a low voice that they were supposed to be "mingling with the throng." This only goaded Simkin to perpetrate greater outrages — such as changing his clothes five times in as many minutes "to throw off pursuit."

Glancing about uneasily, Mosiah expected any moment to see the black-robed figures of the *Duuk-tsarith* appear. But no black hoods shot up from among the flowered and plumed and bejeweled heads, no correctly folded hands cast a pall over the laughter and merriment. Gradually, Mosiah began to relax and even to enjoy himself, figuring that the dread watchers must not find much to watch in this gay throng.

Simkin could have told Mosiah — had the innocent Field Magus asked — that the *Duuk-tsarith* were here as they were everywhere, watching and listening, discreet and unobserved. Let the tiniest ripple mar the glittering surface of the festivities and they were present in an eyeblink to smooth it out. Three university students — having imbibed too much champagne — began singing songs considered to be in poor taste. A dark shadow appeared, like a cloud passing over the sun, and the students were gone, to sleep off their inebriation.

A troupe of players, presenting what they thought was a harmless little satire on the Emperor, were whisked away at intermission with such skill and dispatch that the audience never noticed and left, thinking the play had ended. A cutpurse was apprehended, punished, and released so swiftly and silently that the wretched fellow had the feeling it had all been some sort of horrible nightdream except that his hands — now magically deformed so that they were five times larger than normal — were a monstrous reality.

Mosiah knew nothing of this, he saw nothing. He was not intended to see or know. The pleasure of the crowd must not be disturbed. And so he forgot himself, forgot his plain clothing (Simkin had offered to change it but Mosiah — after seeing himself attired in rosebud-pink silk trousers — adamantly refused), and gave himself up to the beauty that surrounded him. He even managed, more or less, to forget about Simkin. No one seemed to take offense at the bearded young man's offhanded insults or scandalous remarks. He dragged so many skeletons out of closets that Mosiah expected to see them dancing along behind him. But though here and there a noble mustache quivered or a rouged cheek paled, the Dukes and Barons, Countesses and Princesses, mopped up their own blood and watched in delight as Simkin neatly knifed his next victim.

Knowing that he would soon get lost by himself, Mosiah stayed near the witty fool. But his attention left the finely dressed lords and ladies who obviously had no use for him either. They took in his simple clothes and sunburned skin, his calloused hands and work-thickened arms, and appeared to spit him out again immediately, their lips twisting as though he'd left behind a bad taste.

"Why does Joram want to be a part of this?" Mosiah asked himself as Simkin stopped to stab yet another merry party with his rapier wit. The feeling of homesickness that Mosiah had experienced beside the tomb of the wizard returned. He had never felt more alone than when surrounded by these people who cared nothing for him. Memories of his father and mother came back to him and tears stung his eyes. Blinking rapidly, he swallowed them, hoping no one noticed. Then, to wrench his mind free of its childish wallowings, he began to concentrate on the floating stage in front of him.

Mosiah's eyes widened, his breath left him in a sigh, and he was so enthralled that he slowly drifted down to stand on the soft green grass. He had been so confused by the crowd, so intent on watching for the *Duuk-tsarith*, and so flurried by Simkin that he had passed by several such stages without noticing what was going on. But this . . . this was remarkable! He had never dreamed of anything so wonderful.

Actually, it was nothing more than a Water Dancer. She was good, but not great, and Mosiah, a small group of children, an elderly catalyst who was half blind, and two moderately drunk university students were her only audience. The children soon flew off, bored. The catalyst took a short nap standing up and the university students wavered off in search of more wine. But Mosiah stayed, enraptured.

The stage — a platform of crystal — floated above one of the many sparkling streams that ran through the Grove; the Druids having altered the course of the great river that flowed through Merilon, bringing it into the Grove so that it could provide nourishment to the plants and trees and entertainment to the populace. Using her magical arts, the Water Dancer caused the waters of the stream below her stage to leap up and join her in her ballet.

The young girl was lovely, with hair the color of the water. She seemed clothed in water, too; her thin wet gown clinging to her lithe body as the water spiraled up and twisted about her in an intricate dance. By her magical arts, the water came to life. It caught her and held her in its foaming arms; the rippling of her own body made her one with her element.

Too soon the dance ended. Mosiah thought he might have watched until the river itself dried up. The girl on her crystal stage — water running from her body in sparkling rivulets — waited a moment, smiling down on Mosiah expectantly. Then, seeing that he had no money to throw to her, she tossed her wet blue hair and caused the stage to rise up in the air, drifting further downstream.

Mosiah followed her with his eyes and was just about to take the rest of his body along when he suddenly became aware of a crowd gathering around him. Startled, he discovered that Simkin had floated down out of the air to stand beside him on the grass. The bearded young man had changed his dress, too. He was now wearing the motley and cap and bells of a fool, and he was, Mosiah slowly realized in growing alarm, gesturing at *him.*

"Brought to you, lords and ladies, at great expense and tremendous personal risk from the darkest, deepest wilderness of the Outland! Here it is, lords and ladies, the genuine article, the only one in Merilon. I present for your enjoyment — a peasant!"

The crowd laughed appreciatively. Mosiah, blood pounding in his ears, caught hold of Simkin by a multicolored arm. "What are you doing?" he snarled.

"Go along with me, there's a good chap!" Simkin muttered in an undertone. "Look, over there! The *Kan-Hanar* who nearly caught us at the Gate! Told him we were actors, remember? Must appear legitimate, mustn't we?"

Suddenly he shoved Mosiah backward. "Ye gads! It's attacking!" he shouted. "Savage creatures, these peasants, lords and ladies. Back, I say! Back!" Taking off his belled cap, Simkin waved it furiously at Mosiah, to the enjoyment of the crowd.

Staring at Simkin in confusion, Mosiah was wondering fleetingly if he had enough Life within him to turn himself invisible, or at least enough to choke Simkin to death, when the bearded young man came dancing up to him and began stroking his nose!

"See here?" Simkin called to the audience. "Quite docile. At the close of the act, I'll put my head in his mouth. What *are* you doing, Mosiah?" Simkin hissed in his friend's ear. "Strolling troupe of players, what? Remember? The *Kan-Hanar* is watching! You're doing a remarkable impression of a flounder, dear boy, but I'm afraid someone's going to find it a bit fishy after a while. Come up with something more original. We don't want to draw attention to ourselves. . . ."

"You've already taken care of that! What the devil am I supposed to do?" Mosiah whispered back angrily.

"Bow, bow," said Simkin between clenched teeth. Smiling and bowing and waving his hat to the crowd, he put his hand on the back of Mosiah's neck. Digging his fingers into his skin, Simkin forced his "savage peasant" to duck his head awkwardly. "Let's see," he muttered, "are you lyrical? Can you sing, dance, tell the odd joke? Keep bowing. No? Mmmmm. I've got it! Swallowing fire! Perfectly simple. You don't suffer from gas, do you? Might be dangerous . . ."

"Just leave me alone!" Mosiah snapped, breaking away from Simkin with difficulty. Standing up, his face flushed and his palms sweating, he faced the crowd, who were staring at him expectantly. Mosiah's limbs were as cold as ice; he was frozen, unable to move or speak or even think. Looking out at the people hovering over him, staring down at him as he stood on the grass, Mosiah saw the *Kan-Hanar* — or at least it was a man in the robes of the *Kan-Hanar.* He couldn't be certain if it had been the one at the Gate or not. Still, he supposed they couldn't take chances. Now, if there was only something he could do! . . .

"Hey, Simkin! Your peasant's boring. Take him back to the Outland—"

"No, wait! Look! What's he doing?"

"Ah, that's more like it. He's painting! How original!"

"What is that?"

"It's . . . yes, my dear . . . it's a house. Made out of a tree! How marvelous and primitive. I've heard the Field Magi live in these quaint little hovels but I never thought I'd see one! Isn't this fun? This must be his village he's painting for us. . . . Bravo, peasant! Bravo!"

The comments continued, along with the applause. Simkin was saying something, but Mosiah couldn't hear. He couldn't hear anything anymore. He was listening to the voices from his past. He was painting a picture, a living picture, using the air for his canvas, his homesickness for his brush.

The crowd around the young man grew larger as the images created by Mosiah's magic shifted and changed in the air above his head. As the images became clearer and more detailed — the young man's memory giving them life — the laughter and the excited chatter of the crowd gave way to murmurs. Then awed silence. No one stirred or even spoke. All watched as Mosiah portrayed to the glittering, gay audience the lives of the Field Magi.

The people of Merilon saw the houses that had once been trees, their trunks magically transformed by the Druids into crude dwellings, the roofs made of branches woven and thatched together. Fierce winds of winter drove the snow through the cracks in the wood, while the magi expended their precious Life to surround their children with bubbles of warmth. They saw the magi eating their scant meals while outside, in the snow, wolves and other hunger-driven beasts prowled and nosed about, smelling warm blood. They saw a mother cradle a dead infant in her arms.

Winter eased his cruel grip, allowing the warmth of spring to seep through his fingers. The magi returned to the fields, breaking up ground that was still half-frozen or plodding in mud to their knees when the rains came. Then they took to the air, seeds falling from their fingers to the plowed earth, or they set the seedlings, nurtured through the dying days of winter, into the soil. Children worked beside their parents, rising at dawn and returning to their homes when the light of day failed.

Summer brought land to be cleared, homes repaired, and the never-ending weeding and tending of the young plants, the constant fight with bugs and animals for a share in the crops, the burning sun by day and the often violent thunderstorms by night. But there were simple pleasures, too. The catalyst and his young charges out during the noon hour, the children tumbling through the air, learning to use the Life that would eventually earn them their bread. There were the few, peaceful moments between dusk and nightfall when the Field Magi gathered together at day's end. There was Almin's Day. They spent the morning listening to the reedy voice of the catalyst describing a heaven of golden gates and marble halls that they did not recognize. In the afternoon, they worked twice as hard to make up for lost time.

Fall brought fiery colors to the trees and hours of back-breaking labor to the Field Magi as they harvested the fruits of their toil, only a part of which they would ever share in. The Ariels came flying to the village, bearing huge golden disks. The magi loaded the corn and potatoes, wheat and barley, vegetables and fruits, onto the disks and watched as the Ariels bore them away to the granaries and storage houses of the nobleman who owned the lands. When this was done, they took their own small share and planned how to make it last the winter, already breathing on them with his bitter breath. Their children gleaned in the fields, picking up every vestige and scrap, each grain as precious as a jewel.

And then it was winter again, the snow swirling about the small dwellings, the magi fighting boredom and cold and hunger, the Field Catalyst huddled in his dwelling, his hands wrapped in rags, reading to himself of the Almin's great love for his people. . . .

Mosiah's shoulders slumped, his head bowed. The images he had painted above the crowd dissolved as the Life drained out of the young man. The people regarded him in silence; and, fearfully, Mosiah raised his eyes, expecting to see faces bored, scornful, derisive. Instead he saw puzzlement, wonder, disbelief. These people might have been watching a portrayal of the lives of creatures living on a far distant world instead of humans, like themselves, living on their own.

Mosiah saw Merilon for the first time, truth illuminating the city in his eyes with far greater brilliance than the light of the meek spring sun. These people were locked in their own enchanted realm, willing prisoners in a crystal kingdom of their own manufacture and design. What would happen, Mosiah wondered — looking at them with their costly robes and soft bare feet — if someone *would* wake up?

Shaking his head, he glanced around in search of Simkin. He wanted to leave, get out of this place. But suddenly people were crowding around him, reaching for his hand, touching him.

"Marvelous, my dear, absolutely marvelous! Such a delightful, primitive style. Colors so natural. How do you achieve it?"

"I've been crying like a child! Such quaint ideas, living in trees! Strikingly original. You must come to my next gala . . ."

"The dead baby. A bit overstated. I prefer more subtle imagery myself. Now when you present that again, I believe I'd change that to . . . mmmm . . . a lamb. That's it! Woman holding dead lamb in her lap. Much more symbolic, don't you think? And if you altered the scene with the—"

Mosiah stared around, bewildered. Making incoherent replies, he was backing away when a firm hand gripped his arm.

"Simkin!" cried Mosiah thankfully. "I never thought I'd be grateful to see you, but—"

"Flattered, I'm sure, old chap, but you've put yourself in rather a bad situation and this is no time to share hugs and kisses," Simkin said in an urgent whisper.

Mosiah looked around in alarm.

"Over there." Simkin nodded his head. "No, don't turn! Two black-robed observers have decided they're art critics."

"Name of the Almin!" Mosiah swallowed. *"Duuk-tsarith."*

"Yes, and I believe they got a great deal more out of your little exhibition than the tea-and-crumpet set here. They know reality when they see it, and you've just proclaimed yourself a Field Magus as blatantly as if you'd sprouted corn out your ears. In fact, that might have been less damaging. I can't think what put it into your head to do something so inane!" Simkin raised his voice. "I'll take that under advisement, Countess Darymple. Dinner party a week from Tuesday? I'll have to look at his schedule. I'm his manager, you see. Now, if you'll just excuse us a moment— No, Baron, I really can't say where he conjures up these crude clothes. If you want some like them, try the stables. . . ."

"You were the one who got me into this!" Mosiah reminded him. "Not that it matters now. What are we going to do?" He glanced fearfully at the black hoods hovering on the outskirts of the crowd.

"They're waiting for the excitement to die down," Simkin muttered, pretending to fuss with Mosiah's shirt, yet all the while keeping his gaze fixed on the warlocks. "Then they'll move in. Do you have any magic left?"

"None." Mosiah shook his head. "I'm exhausted. I couldn't melt butter."

"We may be the ones melting," Simkin predicted grimly. "What was that, Duke? The dead baby? No, I don't agree. Shock value. Audible gasps. Women fainting. . . ."

"Simkin, look!" Mosiah felt faint himself with relief. "They've gone! Perhaps they weren't watching!"

"Gone!" Simkin glanced about in increased agitation. "Dear boy, I hate to burst your bubble — it's so frightfully messy — but that means that they are no doubt standing next to you, hands outstretched —"

"My god!" Mosiah clutched at Simkin's multicolored sleeve. "Do something!"

"I am," said Simkin coolly. "I'm going to give them what they want." He pointed. "You."

Mosiah's mouth dropped open. "You bastard," he began angrily, and stopped in amazement. It was his *own* sleeve he was hanging onto in a state of panic. It was his own arm beneath that sleeve, the arm was attached to his body. In fact, his own face looked back at him, grinning.

A hubbub of voices started all around him, laughing, exclaiming, crying out in wonder. Dazed, Mosiah turned and saw himself. He saw himself drifting in the air above himself. Everywhere Mosiah looked, in fact, he saw Mosiahs as far as the eye could see.

"Oh, Simkin, this is your best yet!" cried a Mosiah in a distinctly feminine voice. "Look, Geraldine — that is you, isn't it, Geraldine? We're dressed in these simply wonderful primitive clothes, and look at these trousers!"

"Play along!" said the Mosiah who Mosiah was holding, giving him a swift poke in the ribs. "This spell won't last long and it won't fool them forever! We've got to get out of here! I say, Duke! Absolutely brilliant of old Simkin this, what?" said Mosiah in a loud voice. "Play along!" he ordered in an undertone.

"Uh, right, B-baron," Mosiah stammered in a deep bass, hanging onto what used to be Simkin as his last link with reality.

"Start moving!" Simkin/Mosiah hissed at him, drawing him along toward the exit. "I must go and show this to the Emperor!" he called out. "His Highness simply will not believe what Simkin, that genius, that sheer master of magic, that king of comedy —"

"Don't overdo it!" Mosiah growled, shoving his way through the throngs of himself that surrounded him.

But he couldn't make himself heard.

"The Emperor! Let's go show the Emperor!"

Everyone picked up the cry. Laughing and pushing, Mosiahs began to call for the carriages. Mosiahs conjured up carriages. Some Mosiahs simply vanished. Corridors popped open in multitudes, large holes into nothingness, until the air in the Grove began to resemble rat-gnawed cheese. Mosiahs by the hundreds stepped into these, throwing the *Thon-Li*, the Corridor Masters, into vast confusion.

"You know," said Simkin/Mosiah in satisfaction, pulling a bit of orange silk from the air and dabbing at his nose with it, "I *am* a genius."

Stepping into a Corridor, he dragged another Mosiah after him. "I say, old chap," one of the befuddled *Thon-Li* heard him ask, "that *is* really you, isn't it?"

On the Run

"Mosiah, that fool!" Joram fumed, packing back and forth. "Why did he leave the house?"

"I think Mosiah's been remarkably patient. After all, you can't expect him to share your interests in gardening," Saryon said acidly. "He's been cooped up in this house for well over a week with nothing to do but read books while you have—"

"All right, all right!" Joram interrupted irritably. "Spare me the sermon."

Sighing, his brow furrowed in concern, Saryon lay back among his pillows, his hands plucking nervously at the sheets. It was evening. Mosiah had been gone all day, no one knew where. Not that anyone in their host's household was particularly worried. It was perfectly natural that the young man should get out and see the sights of Merilon.

Joram ate dinner with the family, and though Lord Samuels and Lady Rosamund were polite, they were cold and detached. (Had they known about the incident in the family garden, they might have been decidedly warmer, but Marie kept her young mistress's secret.) The talk at dinner centered around Simkin. He'd performed a marvelous illusion in Merlyn's Grove that afternoon. No one knew the details, but it had created a sensation in the city.

"I hope Simkin comes back tomorrow, to escort us to the ball, don't you, Joram?" Gwendolyn dared address this remark to the young man. Before he could answer, however, Lord Samuels intervened.

"I think you should go to your room now, Gwen," he said coolly. "Tomorrow will be a busy day. You need your sleep."

"Yes, Papa," Gwen replied, obediently rising from the table and retiring to her room; not, however, without a backward glance at her beloved.

Joram took the opportunity to leave the table as well, saying abruptly that he must return to the catalyst.

Weak but now conscious, Saryon was able to sit up in his bed, and even consume a small amount of broth. The *Theldara* had visited him in the morning and pronounced him recovered, though she had advised rest, the continuation of the soothing music, aromatic herbs, and the broth of a chicken. She had also hinted strongly that she would be willing to talk about anything the catalyst felt like discussing. Saryon had accepted the music, the herbs, and broth, but had said humbly that he had nothing to discuss. The *Theldara* had left, shaking her head.

Over and over, Saryon considered his dilemma. In a fevered dream, he saw Joram as the fool in the tarok deck — walking the edge of a cliff, his eyes on the sun above him, while a chasm yawned at his feet. More than once, Saryon started to tell him the truth, to stretch out the hand that would keep him from tumbling over the cliff. But just as he started to do so, he woke up.

"That would open his eyes to the chasm," the catalyst muttered to himself, "but would he meekly draw back from the edge? No! Prince of Merilon. It would be all he dreamed. And he wouldn't understand that they would destroy him. . . . No," the catalyst decided after endless reflection. "No. I will not tell him. I cannot. What is the worst that will happen to him now? He will meet this *Theldara* and be revealed as an imposter. Lord Samuels will not want to create a scene at the Palace. I will take Joram and we will leave the Palace quickly and quietly. We will go to Sharakan."

Saryon had it all figured out, all arranged. And then this . . . Mosiah disappearing. . . .

"Something's happened to him!" Joram muttered. "There was all that talk about Simkin at dinner. Some illusion he performed. You don't suppose Mosiah was with him?"

Saryon sighed. "Who knows. No one in the house saw Mosiah leave. No one's seen Simkin for days." He was silent a moment, then he said, "You should leave, Joram. Leave now. If something did happen to him —"

"No!" Joram said sharply, coming to a halt in his pacing and glaring at the catalyst. "I'm too close! Tomorrow night —"

"He's right, I'm afraid, Joram," said a voice.

"Mosiah!" Joram said in grim relief, watching as the Corridor opened and his friend stepped out. "Where have you —" his voice died in astonishment as another Mosiah materialized right behind him, this one wearing a bit of orange silk tied around his neck.

"Helps me to tell us apart," the orange-silk Mosiah said by way of explanation. "I was getting slightly muddled. 'Pon my honor," he continued languidly, "I'm beginning to find this life of a fugitive from justice quite entertaining."

"What is this?" Joram demanded, staring at the two in amazement.

"It's a long story. I'm sorry. I've put us all in terrible danger," Mosiah — the real Mosiah — looked at his friend earnestly. Once in the light, it was easy to tell him from Simkin, even without the orange silk around the neck. His face was pale and strained with fear; there were smudgy shadows beneath his eyes. "They haven't been here, have they?" he asked, glancing about. "Simkin said they wouldn't, not while they thought I was in fashion."

"Who hasn't been here?" Joram asked, exasperated. "What are you talking about — in fashion?"

"The *Duuk-tsarith*," Mosiah answered, barely above a whisper.

"You better tell us what happened, my son," Saryon said, his voice breaking, fear catching him in the throat.

Hurriedly and somewhat incoherently, his eyes darting around the room, Mosiah told them what had occurred in the Grove of Merlyn. "And there are copies of me everywhere," he said in conclusion, spreading his hands as though to encompass the world. "Even when Simkin's illusion began to fade, people started conjuring up the image on their own! I don't know what the *Duuk-tsarith* must be doing or thinking . . ."

"They may be confused for a while," Saryon said gravely, "but it won't take them long to recover. Of course, they will have connected you with Simkin. They will go to the Palace first, make discreet inquiries . . ." He shook his head. "It will be only a matter of time before they find out where you've been staying. He is right, Joram, you must leave!"

Seeing Joram's rebellious face, the catalyst raised a feeble hand. "Hear me out. I'm not saying you should leave the city, though that is what I would most strongly advise. If you are determined to attend the Emperor's party tomorrow—"

"I am."

"Then, stay in Merilon. But at least leave this house tonight. It would be a pity," Saryon added, asking the god he no longer believed in to forgive him his lie, "to come so close to gaining your inheritance, then to lose it through lack of caution. I think—"

"Very well! Perhaps you are right," Joram broke in impatiently. "But where could I hide? And what about you?"

"You could hide where we've been hiding all day—the Grove of Merlyn," said Simkin. "Bored to tears, too, I might add."

"I'll be all right here," Saryon said. "As Father Dunstable, I am the safest of any of you. My leaving, in fact, would look extremely suspicious. As it is, perhaps I can throw them off the trail."

"I don't know why you're all worried about our bald friend here," Simkin remarked, his very mustache drooping with gloom. "It's me who should be depressed! I've started a new fashion trend that I find personally disgusting! Everyone in court is dressed like he planned to go out wallowing with pigs or mucking about in the beans."

"We should be going," Mosiah said, fidgeting nervously. "I have the feeling I'm being watched by eyes I can't see, touched by hands I can't feel! It's getting on my nerves. But I don't think we should hide in the Grove. I think we should leave the city. Now. Tonight. We can travel safely tonight. There are still hundreds of me running around. Simkin can change us all into Mosiahs. We could slip out the Gate in the confusion."

"No!" Joram said impatiently, turning away.

But Mosiah moved to stand in front of his friend, so that Joram was forced to confront him.

"This place isn't for us," Mosiah said earnestly. "It's beautiful and it's wonderful but . . . it isn't any of it real! These people aren't real! I know I'm not explaining this very well . . ." he hesitated, thinking, "But when I created the images of our home, the illusions of our friends and families seemed more alive to me than the living people watching!"

"The people are like their seasons here in Merilon," Saryon said softly, his eyes staring at the ceiling. "It is always spring for them. Their hearts are as green and hard as the buds of a young tree. They have never blossomed in the summer, nor given fruit in the fall. They have never felt the touch of winter's chill winds to give them strength. . . ."

Joram glanced from Mosiah to Saryon, his gaze dark. "A Field Magus who's a catalyst and a catalyst who's a poet," he muttered.

"You always have me," said Simkin cheerfully. Going over to the harp, he proceeded to disrupt the spell surrounding it and began to play a gay dance tune that set the taut nerves of everyone in the room vibrating. "I'm the fixed point of insanity in any sane situation. Many people find this comforting."

"Stop that!" Angrily, Mosiah placed his hands over the harpstrings. "You'll wake the whole house!"

Joram shook his head. "It doesn't matter what you say. I'm not going. And neither are you," he added, his dark gaze turning to Mosiah. "Tomorrow night, my identity will be established. I will become Baron Fitzgerald, then no one can touch any of us!"

Flinging his arms wide in exasperation, Mosiah looked at Saryon pleadingly. "Isn't there anything you can say, Father, to convince him?"

"No, my son," the catalyst replied in quiet sorrow. "I'm afraid not. I've tried . . ."

Mosiah stood silently a moment, his head bowed in thought. Then he held out his hand to Joram. "Goody-bye, my friend. I'm leaving. I'm going back home. I miss it —"

"No, you're not!" snapped Joram tensely, ignoring the hand held out to him. "You can't go yet. It's too dangerous. Lay low, for one more day. I'll come with you to this Grove, if that will make you happy." He glanced at the catalyst. "And by tomorrow night, everything will be fine! I know it!" His fist clenched.

Mosiah drew a deep breath. "Joram," he said sadly, staring out the window into the moonlit garden. "I really want to go home —"

"And I want you to stay," Joram interrupted, catching hold of Mosiah's shoulder. "I'm not much better at saying things than you are," he said in a low voice. "You've been my friend ever since I can remember. You were my friend when I didn't want one. I did . . . I've done everything I could to drive you away." His hands tightened their grip on Mosiah, as though now fearful to let go. "But, somewhere deep inside me, I —"

A discordant twang came from the harp. "Beg pardon," said Simkin, shamefacedly grabbing the strings to silence them. "Must have nodded off."

Joram bit his lip, his face flushed. "Anyway," he continued, speakng now with an effort, "I want you to stay and see this through with me. Besides," he added with an attempt at lightness that failed completely in the tense atmosphere, "how can I get married, without you at my side? Where you've always been . . ." His voice died. Abruptly, Joram withdrew his hands and turned away. "But you do what you want," he said gruffly, staring out the window in his turn.

Mosiah was silent, staring at his friend in wonder. He cleared his throat. "I — I guess one more day . . . wouldn't matter so much," he said huskily.

Saryon saw tears glimmering in the young man's eyes; the catalyst felt tears of his own. There was no doubting Joram's sincerity or the obvious pain it cost him to reveal his heart to another. Yet a cynical voice inside Saryon whispered, "He is using him, using you, manipulating you all to work his will just as he has done and will ever do. And what is sad is that he doesn't even know he is doing it. Perhaps he can't help it. It was born with him. He is, after all, a Prince of Merilon."

"Simkin," said Joram, turning to the young man who had pulled the bit of orange silk from the air and was now blowing his nose loudly, "will the Grove be a safe place to hide?"

Simkin gave a wrenching sob, weeping into the silk.

"What's the matter?" Joram asked with a touch of impatience, though a smile played around his lips.

"This reminds me of the time my dear brother, Little Nat — you've heard me mention Little Nat — or was it Nate? Anyway, Little Nat lay dying, having consumed a quantity of stolen strawberry pies. He denied it, of course, but he was caught red-handed, or -lipped, as the case may be. Though we rather suspected it wasn't the pies killed him so much as the carriage that ran over him as he was floating home. His last words to me were, 'Simkin, the crust was underdone.' There's a moral there, somewhere," he said, applying the silk to his red-rimmed eyes. "But it eludes me."

"Simkin—" Joram's voice tightened.

"I've got it! Half-baked! This plan is half-baked. Still," he said after reflection, "we *should* be able to continue hiding in the Grove. There won't be a soul there tomorrow. Everyone will be watching the festivities at the palace. The *Duuk-tsarith* will be kept busy handling the crowd. Mosiah can remain when we leave for the Palace tomorrow night. . . ."

"Won't you be staying with me?" Mosiah asked in some anxiety.

"And miss the party?" Simkin appeared shocked. He waved his hand. "Our Dark and Uncouth Friend here isn't noted for his charm or his court manners. I must be at his side to guide him through the maze of civilities, the treacherous tangle of hand-kissing and ass-licking—"

"*I'll* be with him, you know," the catalyst said acerbically.

"And no one is more pleased about that than I," said Simkin solemnly. "Between ourselves, it will undoubtedly take both of us to carry this off," he predicted airily. "Besides, in case any of you have forgotten, it was because of me you received the invitation."

"You'll be all right while we're gone. And tomorrow night, after the party, we'll meet you in the Grove," Joram said to Mosiah. "We'll bring you back here to help celebrate my Barony and my engagement," he said firmly.

Tomorrow night, we'll meet Mosiah in the Grove and escape from there, said Saryon to himself. Perhaps this will work out after all.

"I'll wait for you," Mosiah agreed, though there was a trace of reluctance in his voice.

Joram smiled, actually a full smile. The dark eyes brightened with a rare warmth. "You'll see," he promised. "Everything will be fine. I'll—"

"Well, best be off." Simkin interrupted, springing into the air so suddenly that his foot caught in the harpstrings, causing a most ungodly twanging. After a violent struggle, he managed to free it. "Come, come." Bustling about Mosiah and Joram, he herded them along to the door like sheep. "Can't use the Corridor with our Dead friend, here. The streets should be safe enough, though I imagine Mosiahs are on the decrease."

"Wait! What will you tell Gwen— I mean, Lord Samuels," Joram asked the catalyst.

"He'll tell them that I've taken you to court to rehearse for our play tomorrow night," said Simkin easily, tugging at Joram's shirtsleeve. "I say, do come along, dear boy! Nights shadows are creeping through the streets and some of them are flesh and blood!"

"I'll talk to Gwen," Saryon said with a wan smile, understanding Joram's true concern.

To Saryon's astonishment, Joram came over to the bedside. Reaching down, he took the catalyst's wasted hand in his.

"I'll see you tomorrow night," he said firmly. We'll celebrate."

"As the Duchess d'Longeville said on the occasion of her wedding to her sixth husband," Simkin remarked, drawing Joram out the door.

Saryon heard them walking softly down the hallway, then Simkin's voice came drifting back through the silence in the house. "Was it her wedding? Or his funeral?"

The night deepened around Merilon—as deep as night was allowed to sink, that is. This was not very far, the darkness merely moistening the populace, never drowning it. Though Saryon was weak and exhausted, he drifted along on the top of sleep, restless and troubled, neither falling into peaceful oblivion nor quite bobbing to the surface.

The catalyst's room was dark and quiet; the harp—refusing to play—sat in sullen silence in a corner. The tapestries were drawn to blot out any harmful effects of either sun or moon. The aromatic herbs had been removed; Saryon said they choked him. The only sound in the room was the catalyst's rasping breathing.

Rising out of night's flood tide, silent as the night itself, two figures robed in black appeared in the catalyst's room. They floated over to the man's bed. Leaning down, a soft female voice called quietly, "Father Dunstable."

No response from the slumbering figure.

"Father Dunstable," said the voice again, this time more urgently.

The catalyst shifted uneasily at the sound, turning his head upon the pillow as though to blot it out, his hand starting to draw the bedclothes up around his neck.

Then, "Saryon!" called the black-robed woman.

"What?" The catalyst sat upright, staring about him in confusion. At first he could see nothing—the shapes hovering over his bed like dark angels were one with the night. When he did see them, his eyes opened wide, a strangled sound came from his throat.

"Act swiftly," ordered the woman. "He may suffer another attack."

Her companion was already casting his spell, however. Saryon's body went limp, his head sank back onto the pillow, his eyes shut in an enthralled sleep.

The witch and the warlock regarded each other with satisfaction over the inert body.

"I told you the Church would handle the matter," the witch said. She motioned to their victim. "He is to be taken immediately to the Font."

The warlock, hands folded in front of him, nodded.

"Have you searched the house?" she continued.

"The young men are gone."

"I expected they would be." The witch gave an almost-imperceptible shrug. The hood of her black robe turned ever so slightly in the direction of the catalyst. "It doesn't matter," she said softly. "It doesn't matter all all." She made a gesture with one slender hand. "Go."

Her companion bowed. With a word of command, he caused the catalyst's body to rise up into the air. Filaments finer than silk shot from the fingers of the warlock, winding themselves rapidly about Saryon until he was firmly encased in a cocoon of enchantment. The warlock spoke another word and a Corridor gaped open before him; the *Thon-Li* had been awaiting his signal. Another motion of the hand sent the bound catalyst floating through the night air and into the Corridor. The warlock followed. The Corridor shut swiftly and silently behind them.

The witch remained standing a moment longer in the quiet room, allowing herself a moment of well-earned congratulation. But there was still much to be done. Putting her hands together in a prayerlike attitude, the witch raised them to her forehead, then drew them down before her face, continuing downward.

As her hands moved, she murmured arcane words. Her appearance changed. Within moments, the image of the *Theldara* who had been treating Saryon stood in the room.

The witch spoke aloud now, testing her voice's pitch and modulation to make certain it was correct. "Lord Samuels, I regret to tell you that Father Dunstable was taken ill during the night. His young friend sent for me. I have removed the catalyst to the Houses of Healing. . . ."

Postlude

Hands of night gripped him, winding their enchantments around him. He traveled Corridors of darkness that took him to more darkness. There he lay and waited for the horror that he knew was coming. A voice called his name and he knew the voice and did not want to listen to it. Frantically he grabbed for the charm around his neck, knowing it would protect him, but it wasn't there! It was gone, and he knew then that the hands of night had taken it from him. Part of him fought against waking, but part of him longed to end this dark dream that seemed to have lasted his entire life. The voice was not angry with him, but gentle and filled with a quiet sorrow. It was his father's voice, punishing his disobedient son. . . .

"Saryon . . ."

"Obedire est vivere. Vivere est obedire," Saryon muttered feverishly.

"To obey is to live. To live is to obey." The voice was very sad. "Our most holy precept. And you have forgotten that, my son. Wake up now, Saryon. Let us help you through the darkness that surrounds you."

"Yes! Yes, help me!" Saryon reached forth his hand and felt it taken, gripped firmly. Opening his eyes, expecting confusedly to see his father—the gentle wizard barely remembered—the catalyst saw, instead, Bishop Vanya.

Saryon gasped, and struggled to sit up. He had some dim remembrance of being bound, and he thrashed against his bonds, only to find that they were nothing more than sweetly scented sheets. At a gesture from Bishop Vanya, a young Druid caught hold of the wild-eyed catalyst by the shoulders and pressed him gently back into the bed.

"Relax, Father Saryon," the Druid said kindly. "You have suffered much. But you are home now, and all will be well . . . if you let us help you."

"My—my name—It's not Saryon," said the shaken catalyst, glancing about him as the Druid arranged the cool pillows beneath his head.

He was not, as he had dreamed, being held prisoner in a dark and fearful dungeon surrounded by figures in black robes. He was lying in a sunlit room filled with blooming plants. He recognized this place . . . Home, the Druid said. Yes, thought Saryon, filled with a sense of peace and relief that brought tears to eyes. Yes, I am home! The Font. . . .

"My son," said Bishop Vanya, and the voice was tinged with such profound grief and disappointment that tears fell down Saryon's face, his strange face, the face that belonged to another man, "do not blacken your soul further with this lie. Its corruption has spread from your heart to your body. It is poisoning you. Look here. I want you meet someone."

Saryon turned his head as a figure stepped into his view.

"Saryon," said Bishop Vanya, "I want you to meet Father Dunstable, the *real* Father Dunstable."

Swallowing a bitter taste in his mouth, Saryon closed his eyes. It was all over. He was doomed. There was nothing he could do now, nothing but protect Joram. And he would do that, though it cost him his life. After all, what was that life worth anyway, he thought in despair. Nothing much . . . Even his god had abandoned him. . . .

He heard murmured voices and he had the impression that Bishop Vanya was dismissing both the Druid and the catalyst. Saryon didn't know and he didn't care. The Bishop will send for the *Duuk-tsarith* now, he thought. They have ways, they say, of seeing into a man's mind, of boring through the flesh and blood and bone, of penetrating the skull and dragging out the truth. The pain is excruciating, if you fight it, so they say. Likely I won't live through it. He felt lighthearted at the thought and suddenly impatient that nothing was happening. Get on with it, he ordered them silently, irritably.

"Deacon Saryon," began Bishop Vanya, and the catalyst was surprised at hearing his old title. He was surprised, too, at the continued tone of sadness in the Bishop's voice. "I want you to tell me where we can find the young man, Joram."

Ah! Saryon had been waiting for this. Firmly, he shook his head. Now they'll come, he thought.

Instead, however, there was only silence. He heard the rustle of Vanya's rich, silken robes as he shifted his bulk in the chair. He heard the Bishop's slow, labored breathing. It was the breathing of an elderly man, Saryon realized suddenly. He'd never thought of the Bishop as old. Yet he himself was in his mid-forties. Vanya had been middle-aged when Saryon was a youth. The Bishop must be, what, seventy, eighty? Still there was only silence, interrupted by the breathing. . . .

Cautiously, Saryon opened his eyes. The Bishop was staring at him, regarding him with a thoughtful air, as though undecided on a course of action. Now that the catalyst looked at his superior closely, he could see other signs of aging on the face. Odd, he'd only seen him, what, a year ago? Less than a year. Had it been just that long since Vanya had come to him in that wretched hovel in Walren? It seemed like centuries. . . . And it seemed that those centuries had marked his Bishop as well.

Saryon sat up, leaning against the bed's headrest, staring intently at Vanya. He had seen the Bishop shaken only once before in his life, and that had been at the Testing ceremony of the tiny Prince. Joram's Testing, when they had discovered that he was Dead. And now that Saryon looked at his superior closely, he saw the same expression on the man's face — one of worry, concern. . . . No, it was more than that. It was fear. . . .

"What is it? Why do you look at me like that?" Saryon demanded. "You have lied to me! I know that now, I've known it for months. Tell me the truth! I have a right to know! In the name of the Almin," the catalyst cried suddenly, sitting forward, stretching out a trembling hand, "I deserve the truth! This has come near costing me my sanity!"

"Calm yourself, Brother," said Bishop Vanya sternly. "I lied to you, yes. But it was not of my choice. I lied because I am forbidden by the strongest and most binding vow to the Almin to reveal this dread secret to anyone. But I am gong to tell it to you, in order that you will understand the gravity of the situation and help us to remedy it."

Puzzled, Saryon lay back on the pillows, his gaze never leaving Vanya's face. He did not trust the man. How could he? Yet, search as he might, he saw no sign of dissembling, no sign of slyness. There was only an old man, overweight, his face pale and flabby, one pudgy hand crawling nervously along the arm of the wooden chair.

Bishop Vanya drew a deep, shivering breath. "Long ago, at the end of the terrible Iron Wars, the land of Thimhallan was in chaos. You know, Saryon. You have read the histories. I need not go into detail. It was then that we catalysts realized that we had the chance, finally, to gain control of the fragmented world and use our power to bind the shattered pieces together. Each city-state would continue to govern itself ostensibly, but they would do so under our watchful guidance. The *Duuk-tsarith* would be our eyes and ears, our hands and feet.

"In this, we were successful. There has been lasting peace for hundreds of years. Peace until now." He heaved a sigh, shifting his great bulk uneasily in his chair. "Sharakan! Those fools! Renegade catalysts preaching freedom from the tryanny of their own Order! The King consorting with Sorcerers of the Dark Arts. . . ."

Saryon felt his skin burn with shame. Now it was he who shifted in his bed, but he kept his gaze fixed upon his Bishop.

"Ordinarily" — Vanya waved a pudgy hand — "this would not have been anything we could not handle. There have been disturbances in the past, not quite this serious, but we dealt with them, using the *Duuk-tsarith*, the *DKarn-Duuk*, the Field of Contest. But this . . . This is different. There is another factor involved. . . . Another factor."

Vanya fell silent again, the struggle in his mind clearly visible on his face, on his entire body in fact. He frowned; the hand curled over the arm of the chair; the knuckles turned white. "What I am about to tell you, Saryon, is not in the histories."

Saryon tensed.

"In order that they might rule better, the catalysts of the time of the Iron Wars sought to look into the future. There is neither the need nor the time to describe to you how that is done. It is a skill we have lost. Perhaps" — Vanya sighed again — "it is just as well. At any rate, the Bishop of that era along with one of the sole surviving Diviners undertook to use this powerful magic that involves direct contact with the Almin Himself. It worked, Saryon." Vanya's voice was hushed with awe. "The Bishop was allowed to look into the future. But it was not as he had foreseen, as anyone had foreseen. These were the words he spoke to the astounded members of the Order who were gathered around him.

"'There will be born to the Royal House one who is dead yet will live, who will die again and live again. And when he returns, he will hold in his hand the destruction of the world—'"

The words were meaningless to Saryon. It was as if he were hearing a tale told by one of the House Magi before bedtime. He stared at the Bishop, who said nothing more. He was regarding Saryon intently, letting the impact of the words come from within the man rather than without, knowing that this way it would have the most profound effect.

It did. Understanding hit Saryon like the thrust of a sword, sliding into his body, cutting through to his very soul.

"Born to the Royal House . . . one who is dead . . . live . . . die again . . . destruction of the world. . . ."

"Name of the Almin!" Saryon choked. The sword of his realization might have been made of steel, draining him of life. "What have I done? What have I done?" he cried in despair. A wild hope throbbed in his heart. He's lying! He's lied to me before. . . .

But there was no lie on Vanya's face. There was only fear— stark and real.

Saryon moaned. "What have I done?" he repeated in misery.

"Nothing that can't be undone!" Vanya said urgently, leaning forward to grasp the catalyst's hand. "Give us Joram! You must! Never mind how it happened, but the Prophecy is slowly being fulfilled! He was born Dead, he lived. Now he has darkstone— the weapon of the Dark Arts that came near destroying our world the last time!"

Saryon shook his head. "I don't know," he cried brokenly. "I can't think. . . ."

Bishop Vanya's face flushed an ugly red, the pudgy hand clenched in frustration and anger. "You fool!" he began furiously, his voice breaking.

This is it, Saryon thought fearfully. Now he will send for the warlocks. And what will I tell them? Can I betray him, even now?

But Vanya regained control of himself, though it was with an obvious effort. Sucking in several deep breaths through his nose, he forced his hand to relax and he even managed to look at the catalyst with a smile, though it was closer to the smile of a corpse than of living man.

"Saryon," he said in hollow tones, "I know why you are protecting this young man, and it is very commendable of you. To love and help one's fellow man is why the Almin places us in this world. And I promise you, Saryon—by all that is holy, by all I believe in—that this young man will not be killed." The Bishop's red face became mottled, splotched with white. "Indeed," he muttered, wiping sweat from his forehead with the sleeve of his robe, "how can we kill him? 'Die again.' That's what the Prophecy says. We must insure that he lives. That will be our care. . . ."

The tension on Saryon's face eased. "Yes!" he whispered to himself. "Yes, that is true. Joram must not die! He must live—"

"It was what I sought to do when he was a babe," Vanya said softly, his eyes on Saryon. "He would have been nurtured, protected, sheltered. But that wretched, insane woman . . ." He stopped talking, holding his breath.

Saryon's face was bathed in radiance, his eyes turned upward to heaven. "Blessed Almin!" the catalyst whispered, tears coursing down his cheeks. "Forgive me! Forgive me!"

Dropping his head into his hands, Saryon began to weep, feeling the darkness pour out of his soul, purging it as the *Theldara* purges a festering wound.

Bishop Vanya smiled. Standing up, he walked over to the bed and sat down beside the sobbing catalyst. He put his arm around Saryon and drew him close.

"You are forgiven, my son," said the Bishop smoothly. "You are forgiven. . . . Now, tell me . . ."

BOOK THREE

I

Among the Clouds

Carriages for hire stood in line on Conveyance Lane, waiting for customers. Beautiful, bizarre, ofttimes both, the equipages were fantastic beyond imagining. Winged squirrels drawing gilded nutshells, diamond-encrusted pumpkins pulled by teams of mice (these were quite popular with teenage girls), and the more staid and conservative assortment of griffin- and unicorn-pulled conveyances, designed for Guildmasters and others who preferred less ostentatious means of travel. Impatient to be gone, Joram would have chosen the first carriage at the stand—a giant lizard magically altered to resemble a dragon. But Simkin, pronouncing this to be in shocking bad taste (much to the ire of the carriage's owner), moved along the row of conveyances, examining each with a critical eye.

A black swan, mutated by the *Kan-Hanar* to gigantic proportions, was finally—after much thoughtful scrutiny on Simkin's part and much impatient fuming on Joram's—pronounced suitable.

"We'll have it," Simkin announced majestically to the driver.

"Where are you going?" asked the driver, a young woman clothed in white swan's down, her eyes magically touched to resemble the eyes of the bird.

"To the Palace, of course," said Simkin languidly, taking his place with calm aplomb on the swan's back. Nestling down amidst the shining black feathers, he sighed in contentment and motioned for Joram to join him. As Joram climbed up beside his friend, the driver scrutinized both young men and her black-rimmed eyes narrowed.

"I need to see the official invitation to get through the Border clouds," she said crisply, her gaze of disfavor going in particular to Joram, who had refused to allow Simkin to dress him up for the occasion.

"My dear boy," Simkin had said to Joram mournfully, "you'd be a sensation if you'd only put yourself in my hands! What I could do with you! With that beautiful hair and those muscular arms! Women would be dropping at your feet like poisoned pigeons!"

Joram had pointed out that this might be somewhat of an inconvenience, but Simkin was not to be so easily deterred.

"I have just the color for you — I call it *Coals of Fire!* A burnt orange, don't you know. I can make it hot to the touch, small flames licking about your ankles. Of course, you'd have to be careful who you danced with. The Emperor had a party once where a guest went up in flames. Heartburn got out of hand . . ."

Joram had refused the *Coals,* choosing instead to wear an almost exact copy of the style of clothes Prince Garald wore — a long, flowing robe devoid of decoration with a simple collar ("No neck ruff?" Simkin had cried in agony).

Joram had chosen green velvet for the robe's fabric, in memory of the green dress Anja had worn until the day she died. That tattered green dress was the only remnant of her happy life in Merilon, and it seemed most fitting that her son should wear this color the night he went to reclaim the place in his family. Joram felt very close to Anja tonight, running his hand over the smooth velvet. Perhaps this was because he had seen her standing before him last night in a dream, and he knew that her restless, wandering spirit would not find peace until her wrongs had been redressed. At least that is what he assumed the dream meant. She had been reaching out to him, her hands folded in supplication, begging . . .

"Well, if you're going to go to the Palace the walking person-ification of a wet blanket, then I'll do likewise," Simkin had announced gloomily, changing his flamboyant regalia that had included, among other things, a six-foot-high rooster's tail. With a wave of his hand, he had then clothed himself in a long robe of pure white.

"Name of the Almin!" Mosiah had said, staring at Simkin in disgust. "Change back! That last combination was ghastly but it was better than this! You look just like a pallbearer."

"Do I?" Simkin had appeared pleased, the notion taking his fancy. "Why, then, it's suitable to the occasion, don't you see? Anniversary of the Dead Prince and all that. I'm quite glad I thought it up."

Nothing they had said could talk him out of it after that, and it was only after long argument that Simkin had foregone adding a white hood to cover his head in the manner of those who escort the crystal coffins of the dead to their final resting place.

"I want my fee in advance, too," the driver continued. "It's a strange thing, people hiring carriages to take them to the Palace. Most of those who are *invited*"— she laid emphasis on the word—"own their own carriages and have no need to hire mine."

"Egad, m'dear! But I'm Simkin," the young man replied as if that quite settled the matter. Gathering his white robes comfortably about him, Simkin waved the orange silk at the driver. "Proceed," he ordered.

The young woman blinked her swanlike eyes in astonishment at this, staring at Simkin in either speechless wonder or speechless rage, neither of which made the slightest impression on the young man.

"Go along!" he said impatiently. "We'll be late."

After another moment's hesitation, the driver took her place at the great bird's neck and, grasping the reins, ordered the black swan to rise. "If we're stopped at the Border," she said ominously. "it's on your head. I'm not going to lose my permit over the likes of you two."

Nervously, Joram followed her gesture, looking up into the clouds.

"There are more eyes in those clouds than hailstones," said Simkin casually as the swan spread its wings and propelled itself upward, leaping off the ground with its taloned black feet. "Watch it, there," he added solicitously, catching hold of Joram who had nearly fallen overboard at the sudden jolt. "Forgot to warn you. Bit of a jarring takeoff, but—when you're airborne—there's nothing smoother than a good swan."

"*Duuk-tsarith?*" Joram asked, referring to clouds not birds. Despite their fluffy pink-and-white puffiness, the clouds appeared suddenly as threatening to Joram as the boiling black thunderheads that wreaked havoc yearly on the farming villages. "Will they stop us, do you think?"

"My dear boy," said Simkin, laughing and laying his slender hand upon Joram's arm, "relax. After all, you're with me."

Glancing at Simkin, Joram saw the young man's bearded face was calm and nonchalant, his manner so much at ease that Joram quit worrying. As for relaxing, that was quite out of the question. He burned with a fire of excitement and anticipation that would have made Simkin's proposed orange outfit seem pale by comparison. Joram knew that he would find his destiny tonight, knew it as surely as he knew his own name. Nothing would stop him, *could* stop him. His dreams and ambitions mounted with every beat of the swan's wings; he even ceased to worry about the *Duuk-tsarith* and stared with grim defiance into the pink clouds as the bird's black feathers cut through them, scattering them into wisps of trailing fog.

The clouds parted and Joram saw the Crystal Palace of the Emperor of Merilon. Gleaming above them with a white radiance, it shone against the reds and purples of dying day; more brilliant than the evening star.

The beauty of the sight caused Joram's heart to swell until it seemed too big for his chest and came near choking him. Tears stung his eyes, and he bowed his head, blinking rapidly. He did not hide his tears so much from shame. He bowed his head in humility. For the first time in his life, Joram felt the proud spirit that burned in his heart stamped out, trampled underfoot, as he himself had stamped out sparks from his forge.

Brushing his hand across his eyes, he closely examined his fingers. Long and slender and supple, they were the fingers of a nobleman, not a Field Magi. That was from his practice of sleight of hand. And, like the sleight of hand itself, those delicate fingers were a trick to fool the viewer's eyes. Seen closely, the palms of his hands were calloused from the use of hammer and tools, the skin scarred with burns. Black soot had been ground so deeply into his pores that he thought he might have to resort to Simkin's magic to disguise it.

"My soul is like that," he said to himself in sudden, bitter despair, "as the catalyst tried to tell me — calloused, scarred, and burned. And I aspire to those heights."

He lifted his gaze to the Palace and saw not only the beauties of Merilon glistening serenely in the sky but Gwendolyn, too, shining far above him. And the old black depression, the destructive melancholia that he had not known for so long and had thought was gone from his newfound life, returned, threatening to engulf him in darkness.

He stirred, some bleak idea of rising from his feathered seat and hurling himself into the perfumed evening air seething in his brain. At that moment, Simkin's hand closed over Joram's arm, its grip painfully strong. Startled, angry that he had revealed himself, Joram turned a smoldering glower upon Simkin, only to find the young man regarding him with mild annoyance.

"I say, old bean, do you mind not wiggling? I fear it is irritating our birdish transport. I've seen him looking back at me with a distinct glint of anger in the beady black eye. I don't know about you, of course, but being pecked to death by one's hired carriage is not my idea of an impressive — or even interesting — and entertaining end."

Nonchalantly, Simkin turned his head, gazing out at other carriages that were spiraling upward toward the Palace. "Nor is tumbling into the clouds," he said, keeping a firm grasp upon Joram's arm. "It might almost be worth it, to see the expression on the faces of the *Duuk-tsarith* as you went sailing gracefully by them, but that fleeting bit of pleasure wouldn't last long, I fancy."

Joram drew a deep breath and Simkin released him, the two happening almost simultaneously, so that Joram wasn't certain, even then, if Simkin had been aware of his intention or was just indulging in nonsense. Whatever the case, Simkin's words — as usual — brought a half smile to Joram's tight lips and allowed him to wrench control of himself back from the monster that lurked within his soul, ready to claim him in a moment's weakness.

Settling himself more comfortably among the feathers — risking another irritated glance from the swan — Joram viewed the Palace with growing equanimity. He could see it in more detail now and, as he beheld the walls and towers, turrets and minarets, he lost his awe of it. Seen from a distance, it was beautiful, mysterious, beyond the reach of his thought or hand. But now, close up, he saw it was a structure, shaped by the skills of men different from himself only in that they had Life, whereas he had none.

With that thought, his hand reached behind him to touch the Darksword, reassuring himself of its reality, as the carriage swept up with a flurry of black wings and deposited the young men on the crystal steps of the Palace of the Emperor of Merilon.

2

The Nine Levels
of Life

"**Y**ou said you were going to walk!" Joram said. Reaching up, he caught hold of Simkin by the sleeve of the long white robes just as the young man was sailing off into the air like a tall, thin feather.

"Oh, beg pardon. Forgot in the excitement of the moment," Simkin said, drifting back down on the crystal stairs of the Palace to walk beside his friend. Turning, he regarded Joram with an aggrieved expression. "Look, dear boy, I could give you enough magic to enable you to ride the wings of magic, as the poets put it —"

"No," said Joram. "No magic. I mean to be myself. They'll have to get used to seeing me walking around here," he added in grim tones.

"I suppose." Simkin appeared dubious, then he cheered up. "Undoubtedly they'll think it a new fad of mine. Speaking of which" — he grasped Joram's green-robed arm as they entered the golden front doors — "look there."

"Mosiah!" Joram gasped, stopping in alarm and scowling. "The idiot! I thought he agreed to stay behind in the Grove. . . ."

"He did! Don't have an apoplectic fit!" Simkin said, laughing. "That's one of the ones I created yesterday — a leftover.

Chap must have extraordinary abilities, to hold onto my illusion for so long. Perhaps he copied it! The cad! How dare he? I've a good notion to go over and turn him into a cow. Then we'd see how he likes it down on the farm—"

"Forget it," Joram caught hold of his friend once more. "We're here for more important things."

Together, they strolled past several powdered and jewel-encrusted footmen, who glared at Joram suspiciously until they saw Simkin. Laughing, one of the footmen winked, and waved them through with a gesture of a gloved hand. Entering the doors, Joram came to a halt, trying to look as if he belonged, trying to keep from staring.

"Where are we, and where do we go from here?" he asked Simkin in an undertone.

With a visible effort, Simkin wrenched an indignant glare from the fake Mosiah to examine his surroundings. "We're in the main entry hall. Up there"—he tilted his head back as far as it could go, nearly upsetting himself in the process—"is the Hall of Majesty."

Joram followed Simkin's gaze. The entryway in which he stood was a large cylindrical chamber. Rising hundreds of feet in the air, the chamber passed through nine separate levels of the Palace to culminate in a great dome at the top. Each level had its own balcony, looking down on the main entryway below and up into the dome above. And each level, Joram noticed, was a different color; the lowest being green.

"The levels represent the Nine Mysteries," said Simkin, pointing upward. "The level we stand on is Earth, therefore the flora-and-fauna motif. Above us is Fire, then Water, then Air. Above that is Life, since it takes those three elements to sustain life. Then there is Shadow, to represent our dreams. Finally there is Time, which rules all things. Then Death—Technology, then Spirit—the afterlife. And above all that," Simkin added, looking back at Joram with a mischievous grin, "is the Emperor."

Joram's lips twisted into a slight smile.

"Sink me," muttered Simkin, twisting his head, "I've given myself the most frightful crick in my neck. Anyway, dear boy," he continued on a more solemn note, leaning closer to Joram and speaking in an undertone, "you see why it is imperative that I give you magic! People are expected to ascend through the nine levels into the Emperor's presence."

He gestured to the glittering throng of magi around them. As the fanciful carriages pulled up in front of the shining crystal and golden-banded doors, they opened and released their occupants, who floated gracefully into the palace like milkweed seeds. The air rang with their voices, greeting friends, exchanging kisses and gossip and news. They were not loud or boisterous, and their clothes, though beautiful and varied as the colors of the sunset, were, in general, conservative. Even though this was a gala affair, it was, after all, the celebration of a tragic event. The revelry and merrymaking would be kept to a minimum, and all of the guests — when ushered into the presence of the royal couple — would be expected to murmur words of condolence on this, the eighteenth anniversary of the Prince's birth . . . Death . . . and death.

Watching in fascination — and also searching for Gwendolyn — Joram saw that all the magi upon entering the Palace continued to float up into the air, ascending upward through the nine levels into the dome where the Emperor and Empress received their guests. Joram also realized that Simkin was right — there appeared no other way to reach the upper levels except by magic.

"Where will the party be held?" he asked, glancing about the green level where they stood, which was decorated — as Simkin had said — with trees and flowers. "What level. This one?"

Made of gold and silver and crystal, encrusted with jewels, the trees and flowers resembled no trees or flowers that Joram had ever seen in his life. Light created by artificial suns gleamed brightly from the Fire level above, sparkling off the golden leaves and the jeweled fruit, dazzling the eyes. The unnatural forest, standing stiffly and silently, began to make Joram feel closed-in and trapped. The constantly shifting points of light, glancing off gilded branches and gleaming jewels, was dizzying.

"The party will be on all levels, of course," said Simkin, shrugging. "Why do you ask?"

A shadow crossed Joram's face. "How will I ever find Lord Samuels or Saryon or anyone in this . . . this crowd!" He gestured angrily, the darkness returning.

"If you'd only listen to Simkin!" said the bearded young man, heaving a sigh. "I've told you half a dozen times! Everyone is presented to the Emperor and Empress. Right now, everyone who is anyone is up there in the Hall of Majesty, standing around watching to see who has been invited and — what is more fun — who hasn't. They'll be there until the Emperor himself decrees it is time for the merriment to begin! Either you'll find Lord Samuels up there or he'll find you. Now, give me your arm. I'll use my magic and, *voilà*, up, up and away!"

"It won't work!" Joram whispered grimly. "Have you forgotten the Darksword?" He gestured behind him. "*It* will absorb your magic! *I* won't!"

"'Pon my honor, I did forget about that beastly sword," said Simkin. He glanced about him gloomily. "I say, this is incredibly dull and boring. No one even knows I'm here. I don't suppose you — Wait!" His face brightened. "The Stairs of the Catalysts!"

"What?" Joram asked impatiently, watching closely everyone that entered, especially young women with golden hair.

"The Stairs of the Catalysts, dear boy!" Simkin said, all joy and light once more. "*They* can't ride the wings of magic any more than you, old chap. *They* have to climb stairs to get into the Emperor's presence. Oh, not Bishop Vanya, of course. He has his own specially designed conveyance — a dove, it used to be, until His Tubbiness became too heavy for the poor bird. Squashed flat, I heard. Nothing but dove served at the Palace for days — roasted, broiled, stewed . . . Where was I?" Simkin asked, seeing Joram glower. "Oh, yes. Stairs. They begin right over here, t'other side of that solid gold oak. There" — he pointed — "you can see some of the holy brethren beginning the long trek now."

Their shoes slapping against the marble on which they walked, several catalysts were climbing the stairs that began on the bottom level and spiraled upward, round and round, finally ending in the Hall of Majesty at the top. Expressions of resignation and humility were visible on the faces of the holy brothers and sisters as they made the wearing climb, although here and there — particularly on the faces of the younger catalysts — Joram thought he saw darted glances of envy at the magi who floated by them with careless ease.

Joram's spirits began to rise. He felt almost as if he were buoyed up with magic. Hurriedly making his way through the forest of precious metal and jewels, he reached the staircase. Halting a moment at the lowest step to allow a catalyst to go in front of him, Joram glanced up at the hundreds of marble stairs that spiraled above him, each flight a different color to match its level, and he nodded to himself in satisfaction.

It is fitting that I climb these stairs, he said to himself. Just as it was fitting that I wear the green robes in memory of my mother. Joram thought with pain of the stone statue staring eternally into the realms of Beyond. My father must have climbed these stairs often. Saryon has climbed these stairs, maybe he's climbing them at this very moment!

Joram had a mental image of the catalyst, his face haggard and wan from his recent illness, struggling up the stairs, and he began to climb hastily, shoving past the slower catalysts. He'll need my help, Joram thought, bounding up the first flight with all the strength and energy of his youth and nearly bowling over an elderly Deacon in the process.

"What the devil are you doing on our stairs, Magus?" the Deacon growled, already huffing and puffing though he had eight more flights to go.

"It's a bet!" said Simkin hastily, rising up into the air next to Joram, who had — truth be told — momentarily forgotten his friend in his excitement. "Two skins of wine says he can't make it all the way to the top."

"Damn fool kids," muttered the Deacon, stopping to rest on a landing and glaring at Joram. "All I can say, young fop, is that you're going to win if your friend keeps going at that rate."

"Better slow down," Simkin suggested, hovering close to Joram. "Don't attract attention . . . I'll meet you at the top. *Don't* enter the Hall of Majesty without me!" he added in an uncommonly serious tone. "Promise?"

"I promise," said Joram.

It made sense, certainly, but he wondered why Simkin was so intense about it. There was no time to ask; the bearded young man had drifted into the arms of several laughing women. Continuing his climb, Joram took the stairs at a reasonable pace and, by the fifth level, was extremely glad he had done so. He paused a moment, leaning on the stair rail and breathing heavily, wondering if his legs were going to hold out. He still kept watch, but had seen no sign of Saryon or any of Lord Samuels's family, and began to realize that it would be the wildest fluke to find them in the crowd. Somewhere in the air above him, he could hear Simkin's voice, and then he caught a glimpse of the young man, whose white robes showed up remarkably well against the brightly colored clothes of the other magi.

"I call it *Death Warmed Over*," said Simkin, prattling away merrily to an admiring group. "Suitable for this jolly little gathering, what?"

Joram noticed, as he began climbing the stairs again, that Simkin didn't receive the usual laugh that generally accompanied his words. Indeed, some of the magi appeared rather shocked, and drifted away from him hurriedly. Simkin didn't appear to notice, but fluttered on to the next group to regale them with his tale of triumph in what he was now calling the Illusion of a Thousand Mosiahs. This time, he got his laugh and Joram forgot about him, concentrating on keeping his legs moving.

He had not been so intent on his climb as to fail to notice his surroundings. His pleasure in the beauty of the Palace increased as he reached each successive level. He could even look down now upon the gilded, bejeweled forest and wonder how he could have ever thought it stiff and unnatural. Seen from above, it was a realm of enchantment, as was each level he entered after that.

Flames licked the stairs of the Fire level. Heat radiated from walls made of molten lava, making Joram stop in alarm before he realized that it was illusion — all except for the heat, which left him sweating by the time he climbed through it and made him thankful to reach the Water level above.

Done entirely in blue crystal and made to look like the floor of the ocean, the Water level was populated with the illusions of sea creatures. Light from some unseen source seeping through the blue crystal walls gave one the impression of being beneath the water — an impression that was so real Joram actually caught himself holding his breath.

Gasping for air, he found an abundance of that element on the next level. Four giant heads, their cheeks puffed out, glared at each other from the four compass points, each seeming intent on blowing his neighbors into the next realm. Opposing winds gusted and whirled about, flattening Joram against the wall and making the stair-climbing even more difficult.

The Life level was peaceful and restful after this. It was dedicated to the catalysts — the giving of Life being their special province — and he joined many of them in sitting on the wooden pews, resting in the cathedral-like, holy silence. He studied his fellow stair-climbers intently, hoping to see Saryon — or rather, Father Dunstable — among them, but the catalyst wasn't there.

He's still weak, Joram remembered, wondering if they made special arrangements for sick brethren. Well, he wouldn't find him or anyone sitting around here. Rising to his feet, the young man continued his climb.

The Shadow level next was a disturbing place that Joram, the catalysts, and even the floating magi hurried through without pause. Representing dreams, it gave no impression of size or shape, being at once vast and tiny, round and square, dark and light. Objects hideous and lovely loomed out of the flitting shadows, bearing startling resemblances to people Joram knew but couldn't place, places he'd been but couldn't remember.

Hastening through it, ignoring the weariness in his legs, Joram arrived on the Time level. Overawed, he came to a complete stop and stared, forgetting why he had come or what he was doing here. This level presented — in the most stunningly realistic illusions — the vast sweep of the history of Thimhallan. But it moved so rapidly that it was nearly impossible to understand what was occurring until it was past. The Iron Wars came and went in the drawing of a breath. Joram saw swords flash in the air and he longed to study them, but they appeared and disappeared almost before he realized he had seen them.

He began to feel frantic, desperate, and it suddenly occurred to him that his own life was whisking away at the same, rapid pace. He could do nothing to halt it. Shaken, he continued on and came to the level of Death.

Joram stared around, puzzled. There was nothing on this level. It was a vast void — neither dark nor light. Just empty. The magi floated through it unseeing, uninterested. The catalysts climbed, heads bowed, their shoes slapping against the marble, their faces a little more cheerful since they realized they were nearing the top.

"This doesn't make sense," Joram muttered to himself. "Why is this empty? Death, the Ninth Mystery . . ." And then he understood. "Of course!" he murmured. "Technology! And that is why there is nothing here since it has — supposedly — been banished from the world. But there must have been something here, once," he said, looking around intently, peering into the void. "Perhaps the ancient inventions that I read about — the war machines that spewed forth fire, the powder that blew trees from the earth, the machines that printed words on paper. Now lost, perhaps forever. Unless I can bring it back!"

Gritting his teeth, Joram continued the climb. One more level to go.

This was the level of Spirit, the afterlife. Once, it must have been incredibly beautiful, impressing the viewer with the peace and tranquility experienced by those who have passed from this world to the next. But now it had a faded quality about it, as if the illusion were dwindling away. In truth, this was what was happening. The art of Necromancy — communicating with the spirits of the dead — had been lost in the Iron Wars, never to be recovered. No one quite remembered, therefore, what this level was supposed to look like.

Instead of feeling awed, Joram just felt tired and very glad the long climb was nearly at an end. He thought, briefly, of being forced to make this climb every time he came to visit the Emperor — after he was made a Baron, of course — and decided that he would find another means of conveyance. Perhaps a black swan. . . .

Emerging from the spirit world, he walked right into the sunset — or so it seemed to him — and he realized that he was, finally, standing in the Hall of Majesty.

3

The Hall of Majesty

His mind still dazzled by the visions of the wonders through which he had already passed, Joram stared around the Hall of Majesty, awestruck.

Floating above the top of the Palace like a bubble upon water, the hall was perfectly round and made entirely of crystal—as pure and clear as the air that surrounded it. Although now it was at rest over what was known as the Ascent of the Nine Mysteries, the crystal-bubble hall could be moved at a whim—a whim that took thirty-nine catalysts and an equivalent number of *Pron-alban* twelve hours to perform—to any other location beside, above, or below the Palace. Not only was the round bubble of a hall made of crystal—the walls so thin that one could tap on them with a fingernail and hear a tinkling, resonant chime—but so was the floor that cut through it about a quarter of the way up the side of the bubble. Joram, stepping hesitantly and dazedly off the Stairs of the Catalysts, had the distinct and unnerving feeling that if he walked forward he would be stepping into and onto nothing.

It was just past sunset. The Almin had spread his black cloak over most of the sky; the *Sif-Hanar* assisting that great Magician in the performance of his duty so that the revelers might enjoy the mysteries and beauties of the night. But, in the west, the Almin lifted the hem slightly to give a last glimpse of the dying day, its red and purple seeping beneath the blackness like a trickle of blood.

It was dark enough, however, that globes of light were beginning to wink on in the hall. Amidst them moved the Emperor's guests, walking the air of the crystal bubble — meeting, mingling, coming together, drifting apart. The lights, dimmed so as not to deter from the beauty of the falling night, gleamed on jewels and silk, sparkled in laughing eyes, glinted on soft waves of rippling hair.

Never had Joram felt the leaden weight of his own Lifeless body more so than at this time. He knew that if he stepped forward, walked out into this enchanted realm, the crystal floor must crack beneath his feet, the crystal walls shatter at his clumsy touch. And so he stood, irresolute, toying with the idea of descending, of retreating into his own darkness that had, at least, the advantage of being a familiar and comfortable refuge.

But another catalyst — a silent partner in his climb, toiling up a few steps behind Joram — pushed his way past with a muttered apology, moving around the young man to walk, seemingly, upon the night. The *slap slap* of the catalyst's sandals upon the solid crystal had a reassuring sound and gave Joram impetus to follow. Moving gingerly, the young man took several steps out onto the floor, then paused once again, overcome this time by the magnificence of the view.

Above him and around him, the stars took their accustomed places in the night sky like minor courtiers coming to pay their respects to the Emperor, keeping their distance as befitted their humble station. Below his feet, the city of Merilon outshone the poor stars. Their sparkle was cold and white and dead, while the city burned with color and life. The Guild Halls were ablaze with brilliance, the houses twinkled; here and there bright spirals of light left the city, snaking upward toward the Palace — more carriages joining the glittering throng of approaching guests.

And Joram stood above it all.

His heart swelling with the beauty of everything around him, Joram's soul swelled with the feeling of power. Tiny bubbles of excitement tingled through his blood; wine itself had never been more intoxicating. Though his body must remain earthbound, his spirit flew upward. He was *Albanara*, born to walk here, born to rule, and—within hours perhaps—these be-jeweled and glittering people who were so far above him now would crowd to prostrate themselves at his feet.

Well, perhaps that was a bit exaggerated, he told himself with a wry inner grin that did not relieve the gravity of his dark face but gave only a warm luster to the brown eyes. I suppose people don't prostrate themselves before a Baron. Still, I will decree that underlings walk when in my presence. I can't think it would be considered proper form to do otherwise. I shall have to ask Simkin, wherever the devil he is—

Thinking of Simkin caused Joram to remember that he had promised not to present himself to the Emperor without his friend, and he glanced about somewhat impatiently. Now that he was over his initial awe, he could hear names being called out at the farthest end of the crystal hall. The light shone most brightly there and, like leaves caught in a whirlpool, groups of magi were being swept in that direction. Trying to hear and see, looking for Gwen and Lord Samuels and Saryon, Joram moved closer, peering through the throng. Yet he could not move too far from the stairs. Simkin would undoubtedly look for him here. Where *was* that fool anyway! Never around—

"My dear boy, don't stand there gawping!" came an irritated voice. "Thank the Almin we left Mosiah behind. The sound of your chin hitting the floor must have been loud enough. Do try to look as bored by all this as everyone else is, there's a good chap."

Orange silk fluttering in the air, Simkin drifted slowly down from on high, his robes fluttering about his ankles.

"Where have you been?" Joram demanded.

Simkin shrugged. "The champagne fountains." He raised an eyebrow, seeing Joram frown. "Tut, tut! I know I have mentioned to you before, O Dark and Gloomy One, that your face will freeze in that alarming expression someday. I simply *had* to have something to do whilst you were toiling up through the nine levels of hell. Now you know why there are no fat catalysts in Merilon. Well, almost none." A rotund catalyst, sweat rolling off his tonsured head, glared at Simkin as he stumbled, panting, up the last of the stairs.

"Cheer up, Father," Simkin said, pulling the orange silk out of the air and offering it with a solicitous gesture. "Think of the lard you've lost! And you've contributed a remarkable shine to the floor. Mop your head?"

The priest, flushing even redder, shoved the young man's hand out of his way and, muttering something most unpriestlike, staggered across the floor to collapse in a nearby chair.

Placing his hands together in a prayerful attitude, Simkin bowed. "My blessing on you as well, Father." There was a flurry of orange silk and, suddenly, the catalyst disappeared.

Joram was staring at the empty chair where the man had been sitting when he felt a tug on the sleeve of his robe.

"And now, dear boy," Simkin said, "attend to me, please."

The voice was playful as usual but, turning, Joram saw an unusually hard glint in the pale blue eyes, a certain grimness in the negligent smile that caught his attention.

Simkin nodded slightly. "Yes, now the fun begins. You remember the cards said that you would be King, and I offered to be your fool? Well, up until now, you have been King, dear boy. We've followed your lead without question and without complaint though it has nearly got me arrested, the poor catalyst struck down by a curse from the Almin, and Mosiah on the run for his life." Simkin's voice was soft; it died away almost to a whisper at this point; his eyes studied Joram intently.

"Go on," Joram said. His tone was cool and even, but the expression on his face grew darker, and a faint flush beneath the skin seemed to indicate that somewhere, deep within, the arrow's barb had lodged.

Simkin's smile twisted sardonically. "And now, my king," he said, moving closer and speaking very softly, his eyes going to the crowd around them, "you must follow the lead of your fool. Because, in the hands of your fool rests your life and the lives of those who follow you. You must obey my instructions without question. Is that agreed upon, Your Majesty?"

"What do I have to do?" Joram's voice grated.

Moving closer still, Simkin placed his lips next to Joram's ear. His beard tickled against Joram's flesh; the heady fragrance of gardenia from Simkin's hair and the fumes of the champagne on his breath made Joram queasy. Involuntarily, he tried to pull back, but Simkin held him fast, whispering insistently, "When you are presented to their Majesties, *do not* — I repeat — *do not* stare at the Empress."

Standing back, Simkin smoothed his beard and glanced around at the crowd. Joram's frown relaxed to a half smile.

"You *are* a fool!" he muttered, twitching his green robes back into place. "You had me really scared there for a moment."

"Dear boy!" Simkin looked at him with such stern intensity that Joram was taken aback."I meant every word." He placed his hand on Joram's chest, over his heart. "Bow to her, speak to her — something flattering, inane. But keep your eyes down. Avert your gaze. Look at His Royal Boringness. Anything. Remember, you cannot see the *Duuk-tsarith*, but they are here, they are watching. . . . And now," Simkin said with a languid wave of the orange silk, "we really must take our places in line."

Drawing Joram's arm through his, he led him forward. "Fortunately for you, my earthbound friend, everyone is required to walk on foot when formally introduced into their Majesties' presence. Proper humility, show of respect and all that, plus it is devilishly hard to bow in midair. The Duchess of Blatherskill bowed from the waist, couldn't stop. Kept going. Head over heels. No undergarments. Quite shocking. Empress took to her bed for three weeks. Since then — we walk. . . ."

Moving across the crystal floor, joining other magi who were falling down around them like sparkling rain, Simkin and Joram walked toward the front of the hall. Joram glanced at Simkin, puzzled and disturbed at his words and his instructions. But the young man appeared not to notice his friend's discomfiture, prattling on about the unfortunate Duchess. Shaking his head, Joram passed the empty chair where the fat catalyst had been sitting. Joram saw Simkin looking at it with a most wicked grin.

"By the way," said Joram, glancing back at the chair as they passed it, "what did you do to him, anyhow?"

"Sent him back down to the bottom of the stairs," said Simkin languidly, dabbing at his nose with the orange silk.

Joram and Simkin joined the line of the wealthy and the beautiful of Merilon, all waiting to pay their respects to the royal couple before dispersing to the more interesting business of revelry and making merry. Some might think revelry would be difficult, considering the sorrowful nature of the anniversary they celebrated. And, indeed, those standing in the line that stretched across the crystal floor like a silk-clad bejeweled snake, were considerably more solemn and serious than they had been when first entering the Palace. Gone was the gay laughter, the lighthearted banter between friends, the gossip and the gushing over clothes or hair or daughters. Their eyes were downcast, their gown and robe colors subdued to a proper shade of *Sorrowful Mien*, as Simkin said in an undertone.

Conversations were carried on in low voices between couples now, instead of groups. Consequently, a hush settled over this part of the hall, broken only by the melodious voice of the heralds, announcing the names of those ushered into the Royal Presence.

So long was the line that Joram could not see the Emperor or Empress yet, but only the crystal alcove in which they sat. Gathered in a semicircle around that alcove stood those of the court who had already been presented and who were now watching to see what illustrious or amusing personages stood in line. The murmur of voices from the watching crowd was low, since they were in the Presence, but there was an almost continual flow of movement — heads turning, people pointing discreetly or not as the subject warranted. Joram, still searching for Lord Samuels and his family, saw many nods and smiles at Simkin. Arrayed in his white robes, the young man stood out against the myriad colors around him like an iceberg in a jungle, coolly affecting to take no notice of the attention.

Joram's eyes scanned the brilliant throng, stopping always at the glimpse of a blond head or even a tonsured one, hoping to find Saryon here as well. But there were so many people, and most of them were dressed so nearly alike (except for those few trend-setters who had come dressed as Field Magi, much to Simkin's amusement), that he deemed it nearly impossible to find those he sought.

"She is watching for me," he told himself, fondly picturing in his mind Gwendolyn standing on tiptoe, peeping up over the broad shoulders of her father, waiting with fast-beating heart for the announcement of each name and drooping in disappointment when it was not the name she longed to hear. The thought made him impatient and even fearful. Suppose they left! Suppose Lord Samuels grew tired of waiting. Suppose . . . Joram looked at the long line ahead of him impatiently, bitterly resenting each elderly Duke whose faltering steps had to be aided by his catalyst or the two gossiping dowagers who kept forgetting to move forward and had to be prodded by their neighbors. The line actually moved quite rapidly, all things considered, but it would have had to flash through the room like a thunderbolt to satisfy Joram.

"Quit fidgeting," muttered Simkin, treading on Joram's foot.

"I can't help it. Talk about something."

"Willingly. What?"

"I don't give a damn! Anything!" Joram snapped. "You said I'm supposed to say a few words to the Emperor. What? Nice night. Wonderful weather. I understand it's been spring for two years, any chance of summer showing up?"

"Shhh," hissed Simkin behind the orange silk. "Egads! I'm beginning to wish I'd brought Mosiah after all. This is an anniversary commemorating the Dead Prince. You offer your condolences, of course."

"That's right. I keep forgetting," Joram said moodily, his gaze flicking about the hall for the hundredth time. "All right. I'll offer my condolences. What did the kid die from, anyway?"

"My dear boy!" said Simkin in a scandalized whisper. "Even if you *were* raised in a pumpkin, you don't have to exhibit it to this extent! I was under the impression that your mother regaled you with stories of Merilon. This has to be the stellar story of all time. Didn't she tell you?"

"No," said Joram shortly, his dark brows coming together.

"Ah," remarked Simkin suddenly, glancing at Joram. "Mmmm, well, perhaps I understand . . . Yes, undoubtedly. You see"—he drew closer, keeping the orange silk in front of their faces as he talked—"the child didn't die. It was quite alive, very much alive, as I've heard the story told. Screamed its little head off during the formal ceremony and puked on the Bishop at the end." Simkin paused, looking at Joram expectantly.

Joram's face darkened, an almost perceptible shadow falling across it.

"Understand?" Simkin asked softly.

"The child was born Dead, like me," Joram said harshly. His gaze was on the floor now, his hands clasped firmly behind his back, their knuckles white. He noticed he could see his reflection on the crystal floor. The lights of Merilon far below shone through his ghostlike, transparent body; the image of himself stared darkly back at him.

"Shhh!" Simkin remonstrated. "Dead, yes. But like you, dear boy?" He shook his head. "He wasn't like anyone born in this world. From what rumors I've heard, Dead was an understatement. The kid didn't just fail one of the Tests. He failed all three! He had no magic in him whatsoever!"

Joram kept his gaze down. "Perhaps he wasn't as unlike some others as you might think," he muttered as the line inched its way nearer and nearer the front. His eyes still on the reflection at his feet, Joram did not see Simkin's swift, penetrating glance, nor did he remark the thoughtful way the young man stroked his smooth brown beard.

"What did you say?" Simkin asked carelessly, raising his head and affecting to blow his nose in the bit of orange silk.

"Nothing," Joram said, shaking himself as though seeking to wake from a nightdream. "Aren't we ever going to get there!"

"Patience," Simkin counseled. Floating off the floor an inch or so, he peered over the heads of the crowd, then settled back down. "Look, you can see the Royal Throne now and catch a glimpse of the Royal Head if you are lucky."

Craning his neck, Joram saw that they had really walked much nearer during their conversation. He could see the crystal throne and several times caught glimpses of the Emperor moving to converse with those in front of him and around him. He could barely see the Empress, seated to the Emperor's right since the royal line came down from her side of the family. But the Emperor was clearly within Joram's view and—glad to be able to fix his mind on something—the young man watched the scene before him with interest.

Seated in a crystal throne that stood on a crystal floor within a crystal alcove, it appeared very much as if His Majesty lounged among the stars. Dressed in the pure white satin of mourning, white light of the most remarkable brilliance beaming down on him, the Emperor was not only one with the stars but actually outshone the brightest among them. Having seen the opulence of the furnishings and trappings of the rest of the Palace, Joram was startled to note that both the crystal throne and the alcove itself were done in simple, elegant lines without decoration of any kind. The crystal flowed around the royal bodies like clear water, a flash of reflected light here and there giving the only evidence that there was anything real or solid about them.

Then Joram smiled. Glancing about the room, he realized that this was done intentionally! Even the chair in which the poor catalyst had collapsed—now several hundred feet behind them—was made of fabric magically spun so as to be transparent. Nothing, certainly no material object, should distract one's attention from the one reality as far as the Emperor's subjects were concerned—the reality of the Emperor and his Empress.

Close enough now to hear snatches of conversation when voices were lifted above the murmur of the crowd, Joram listened curiously. Accustomed to forming quick and often disparaging opinions about people, Joram had thought the Emperor — on first meeting — to be a man of colossal self-conceit and self-importance who could not see the world for his own nose, as the saying went. But, in listening to the Emperor's conversation, Joram was forced grudgingly to admit he had been wrong.

The man was shrewd and intelligent and — if cold and reserved, it was only to keep himself above the masses. He hardly needed the herald, it seemed, to tell him the names of those who came before him and, indeed, addressed many by familiar nicknames rather than by their more formal titles. Not only that, but he had something personal to say to each — inquiring of fond parents about a beloved child, questioning a catalyst concerning the priest's particular area of study, discussing the past with the old, the future with the young.

Intrigued by this phenomenal feat, considering the hundreds of people with whom the Emperor must come into contact daily, Joram watched in growing fascination. He recalled his meeting with the Emperor and the way the man's eyes had seemed to completely absorb him, had focused his complete and undivided attention on him for several seconds. Joram remembered feeling flattered, but also vaguely uncomfortable, and now he knew why. He had been committed to memory as Saryon committed a mathematical equation to memory and with about as much regard. Skilled to a certain extent in manipulating others, Joram could recognize and concede the touch of a master.

Yet, Joram knew — first from his mother and confirmed by Lord Samuels — that there was one person in this world the Emperor cared for very deeply. That was the Empress. The line moved nearer and Joram turned his gaze from the Emperor to his consort. All his life, he had heard of the woman's loveliness — a beauty remarkable even among the noted beauties of court; a beauty that was inborn, that needed no magical enhancement. Increasing his curiosity was the warning — for it could be called nothing else — given by Simkin:

Do not stare at the Empress.

The words echoing in Joram's mind, he took an unobtrusive step out of line in order to catch a glimpse of the woman seated on the crystal throne beside her husband. And then the line moved and she was clearly in his view.

Joram caught his breath. Simkin's words flew right out of his head, replaced by Anja's distantly remembered description. "Hair as black and as shining as the wing of a raven, skin smooth and white as a dove's breast. The eyes dark and lustrous, the face shaped to classic perfection, as though by the enchantments of a master. She moves with the grace of the willow in the wind—"

An elbow dug into Joram's midsection. "Stop it!" Simkin shot out of the corner of his mouth. "Look away."

Irritated, half-suspicious that he was the target of one of Simkin's elaborate jokes, Joram started to make a quick retort. But, once again, there was that strange expression on Simkin's usually devil-may-care face—serious, even fearful. Drawing closer—there were only ten or so people ahead of them now—Joram looked at the rest of those standing near him and saw that they, too, were each doing his or her best *not* to look directly or too long at the Empress. He saw them dart glances in her direction, even as he was doing himself, and then quickly look aside. And though each spoke to the Emperor in a loud, clear voice and seemed perfectly relaxed and at ease, the voice dropped when speaking to Her Majesty, the words spoken almost unintelligible.

Moving nearer, his eyes aching from the strain of darting glances at the Empress then looking quickly away again, Joram began to admit that there *did* seem to be something unusual about the woman. Certainly her celebrated beauty did not diminish as he drew closer, but he found himself oddly repulsed by it rather than attracted. The skin was pure and smooth, but faintly blue and translucent. The dark eyes were certainly lovely, but their luster was not the gleam of light from within. It was the reflection of light upon glass. Her lips moved when she spoke. Her hand and body moved, but it wasn't the willow's grace so much as the toyshaper's.

The toyshaper's . . .

Joram turned to Simkin, puzzled, but the bearded young man, playing with the orange silk in his hand, regarded his friend with a slight smile.

"Patience rewarded," he said. "We're next."

And then Joram did not have time to think about anything.

He heard, as if from a great distance, the herald strike the floor with his staff and call out in his melodious voice, "Presenting Simkin, guest of Lord Samuels . . ."

The rest of the introduction was lost in a ripple of laughter from the crowd. Simkin was performing some nonsense or other; Joram was too dazed and confused to be consciously aware of what. He saw Simkin move forward, white robes shining in the same bright light that spread a halo around the Emperor and the Empress.

The Empress. Joram felt his gaze drawn to her again, then the herald was saying, "Joram, guest of Lord Samuels and family."

Hearing his name, Joram knew he must take a step, but he was suddenly assailed with the consciousness of being the object of hundreds of pairs of eyes. Vividly, the memory of his mother's death rose to the surface of his mind. He could see the people, all staring at him. He wanted only to be alone. Why, why were they looking at him?

The Emperor and Simkin were talking, Joram saw, but he had no idea what was being said. He couldn't hear. There was a roaring in his ears like the rush of a storm wind. He wanted most desperately to flee, yet he couldn't move. He might have stood there forever except that the herald — always conscious of the necessity of keeping the line moving and accustomed to those who experienced this sublime awe in the presence of His Majesty — gave Joram a gentle prod. Stumbling, the young man lurched forward to stand before the Emperor.

Joram had just enough presence of mind to bow deeply, copying Simkin, and started to mumble something without any idea what he was saying. The Emperor cut in smoothly, recalling having met him at Lord Samuels's. Hoped his visit to Merilon was a pleasant one, and then the royal hand waved and Joram moved across the crystal floor to stand before the Empress. He was dimly aware of Simkin watching him and — if it would not be too unbelievable — Joram thought the young man's bearded lips were parted in a grin.

Joram bowed before the Empress self-consciously, wondering desperately what to say, longing to raise his gaze and look at this woman and yet feeling in another part of him the strongest urge to hurry away, his eyes averted as he had seen so many do before him.

Standing before her, he became conscious of a faint, cloying odor.

The most beautiful woman in the world — so it was told. He would see for himself.

Joram lifted his head . . .

. . . and stared into the lifeless eyes of a corpse.

4

The Champagne Fountain

"**N**ame of the Almin!" Joram murmured, shivering, cold sweat drying on his body. "Dead!"

"My dear boy, if you value your life and mine, do keep your voice low!" Simkin said in soft tones, a disarming smile on his face as he nodded to several acquaintances across the room. The two stood near the champagne fountain, this being the place Simkin said Gwen or Saryon would certainly come to meet them. This area — opposite from the alcove where the Emperor still held court — was becoming increasingly crowded as people drifted here in search of friends and merriment. The champagne fountain was, as Simkin said, a natural meeting place; shouts of greeting and boisterous laughter burst constantly around them.

Magically operated by a team of *Pron-alban* disguised as footmen, the champagne fountain stood over twenty feet tall. It was made entirely of ice — to keep the wine cool — and was done in fish motif. Champagne flowed from the mouths of icy sea-horses perched upon frozen waves. Wine shot from the pursed lips of glassy-eyed blowfish; frost-rimed sea nymphs offered guests sips of wine cupped in frigid fingers. Crystal goblets stood in rank upon rank in the air around the fountain, filling themselves at the beck and call of the revelers and hurrying to quench the thirst derived from standing in attendance upon the Emperor and his dead wife for two hours.

"It's treason to even think such a thing, let alone speak it in public," Simkin continued.

"How . . . how long?" Joram asked with a kind of morbid fascination, the same fascination that kept drawing his eyes in the direction of the crystal throne.

"Oh, a year, perhaps. No one knows for certain. She was in ill health for a long time and, I must admit, looks rather better now than she used to."

"But . . . why keep . . . ? I mean, I knew he loved her, but . . ." Joram lifted a glass of champagne to his lips, then set it down quickly, his hand shaking. "The Emperor must be mad!" he concluded hollowly.

"Far from it," Simkin said coolly. "You see the man in the red robes coming up to stand near the Emperor now?"

"A *DKarn-duuk*? Yes," Joram said, wrenching his gaze from the body of the woman in the throne to look at a man leaning down to say something to the Emperor. Though they were some distance away, Joram had the impression of a tall man, well-built, dressed in the red robes of the warlocks who were the War Masters of Thimhallan.

"Not *a DKarn-duuk*. *The* DKarn-duuk — Prince Xavier. He is *her* brother, which makes *him* the next Emperor of Merilon if her death were officially recognized." Simkin raised a glass of champagne to his lips in a mocking toast. "Farewell to His Boringness. Back to his estate in the rolling meadows of Drengassi or wherever he came from. If nothing worse happened to him. People who cross The DKarn-Duuk have a strange way of stepping into Corridors and never stepping out." Simkin swallowed the champagne in a gulp.

"If the man's so powerful, why doesn't he just take over?" Joram asked, eyeing him speculatively and thinking that this new world he was entering might be extremely interesting.

"The Emperor has a powerful counterforce — or should I say counterweight — on his side. Bishop Vanya. Which reminds me, I find it rather strange that His Fatness isn't in attendance, especially when there's free food. Oh, I forgot. He never comes to this anniversary party. Says it goes against Church policy or some such thing. Where was I?"

"The Emperor?"

"Yes, quite. Anyway, rumor has it that Vanya's sun rises and sets with the Emperor's. The DKarn-Duuk has his own man he would like to see fill Vanya's shoes — probably take three of them, come to think of it. The catalysts and the illusionists make certain the Empress is the life of the party, if you'll forgive the expression. And, it *is* a treasonable act to refer in any way to her health or lack of it. She holds court as usual, and the bright and the beautiful of Merilon and other city-states come to pay homage as usual, and no one looks directly at her or makes any but the most innocent reference to her. Sometimes even that doesn't work."

Simkin motioned for another glass of champagne to fill itself at the crystal fountain and come bobbing into his hand. An orchestra of enchanted instruments began playing waltzes in a corner, forcing Simkin to lean closer to Joram to continue his story. "I will never forget the night the old Marquis of Dunsworthy was talking to the Emperor over a game of tarok and the Emperor said, 'Don't you think Her Highness looks particularly well tonight, Dunsworthy?' And old Dunsworthy looks over at the corpse seated in a chair and stammers, 'I — I don't know. I find Her Highness seems a bit grave to me.' Well, of course, the *Duuk-tsarith* were on the wretched chap in an instant and that was the last we saw of him." Simkin sipped the champagne and wiped his lips with the orange silk. "I finished playing out his hand and won a silver off His Majesty."

Joram was about to reply, when he heard his name called. Turning, he looked into blue eyes alight with love and instantly forgot there was such a thing as death or politics in the world.

"Joram!" said Gwendolyn shyly. Holding out her white hand, she was conscious of the admiring stares of several other young men in the crowd, but she truly had eyes only for the man she loved.

Gwendolyn had spent hours — almost the entire day — working with Marie and Lady Rosamund on her gown. She changed the color so often that the room might have passed for the dwelling place of the *Sif-Hanar* who conjure rainbows. Flowers sprouted on the sleeves to be replaced by the feathers of small birds, then the small birds themselves made an appearance but were instantly banished by Lady Rosamund. At last, after many tears and miles of ribbon and a last-moment panic in the carriage that she "wasn't fit to be seen!" Gwendolyn was carried off to the ball, every dream of her young heart seeming to come true at this moment.

And what was the result of the effort and tears spent on the gown, tears spent with only Joram in mind? It was, unfortunately, largely wasted. Joram had only a confused impression of golden hair crowned with tiny white flowers known as baby's breath, and white neck and white shoulders, and only the most tantalizing hint of soft, white breast curving into something as blue and frothy as sea foam. Her beauty tonight enchanted him, but it was *her* beauty, not the gown's. Gwendolyn could have been wearing sackcloth and her enraptured admirer would never have noticed.

"My lady." Joram took the small, white hand in his own, holding it for just a moment longer than was considered proper before he kissed it lingeringly and then reluctantly released it.

"I— That is we—" Gwendolyn amended, blushing, "were afraid that you might not be able to come. How is Father Dunstable? We have all been terribly concerned."

"Father Dunstable?" Joram stared at Gwen, mystified. "What do you mean? Isn't he—"

"Forgive him, sweet child," Simkin interrupted smoothly, interposing himself between Joram and Gwen. Turning his back on Joram, he captured Gwen's hand in his own. He seemed about to kiss it, then apparently decided the effort was too great and lethargically held onto it instead. "Your beauty has completely overthrown his mind. I've seen more intelligent expressions on a catalyst. Not often, but occasionally. Speaking of catalysts, it would appear from your inquiry that our bald friend is none too well. Zounds, this astounds me."

"But, didn't Joram tell you?" Gwendolyn attempted to look at Joram, who had been cut off by Simkin on one side and the fountain on the other.

"Egad, m'dear," said Simkin loudly, blocking the couple's view of each other once more. "Champagne? No? Well, I'll drink yours then, if you don't mind." Two glasses floated over. "What were we discussing? I can't recall— Ah, Father Dunstable. Yes, you see, I've been cooped up in this stifling palace all day, listening to The DKarn-Duuk yammering about the war with Somebody-or-Other and the Emperor yammering about taxes and I've been quite bored out of my skull. Then I found

Joram here and, well, my pet, you can hardly blame me if the last thing I wanted to discuss was the health of a priest?"

"No, I suppose not . . ." began Gwen, her face rosy with embarrassment and confusion. Simkin's conversation was attracting a crowd; people gathered near to hear what scandalous thing he might say next, and the young girl was acutely conscious of the many eyes focused on herself and her companion.

Endeavoring to get near Gwen, Joram found himself elbowed out of the way and, remembering just in time that he must not call attention to himself, was forced to take a step or two backward. Simkin, meanwhile, was the center of attention.

"Well, what did happen to our Bald Friend?" he asked languidly. "Egad!" A look of horror caused the young man's eyebrows to ascend into his hair. "Bishop Vanya didn't mistake him for a pew cushion, did he?" Smothered laughter from the audience and much nudging. "That happened once to a catalyst known before the accident as Sister Suzzane. Quite flattened the poor thing. Now known as Brother Fred . . ."

The laughter grew louder.

"No, really!" Gwendolyn tried to withdraw her hand from Simkin's grasp.

But he smoothly held her fast, though without appearing to do so, regarding her with a bored expectancy that sent the audience into muffled giggles.

Gwendolyn had to say something. "I — We were awakened in the night by the . . . the *Theldara*, who had been in attendance on Father Dunstable. She said he had taken a turn for the worse and that she was transferring him to the Houses of Healing in the Druids' Grove."

"Turn for the worse, eh? I'm quite devastated. Prostrate with grief, truly. More champagne here!" Simkin called. The audience roared.

"Simkin, let me —" began Joram, pushing his way around once more. But Simkin cut Joram off casually, reached out a hand, and caught hold of another young man — one of the general crowd standing nearby.

"Marquis d'Ettue. Charmed."

The young Marquis was charmed as well.

"Here's this young woman, pining to dance with you. It's that shrimp-color jacket you're wearing. Quite bowls women over. My dear, the Marquis." And, before she could utter a protest,

Gwendolyn found her hand passed from Simkin into the hand of an equally astonished Marquis.

"But I—" Gwen protested weakly, looking at Joram over her shoulder.

"Simkin, damn you—" Joram again attempted to intercede, his face dark with impatience and frustration and the glimmerings of anger.

"Pleasure of this dance—" the Marquis stammered.

"Charming couple. Off you go!" said Simkin gaily, literally propelling the startled Gwendolyn into the Marquis's shrimp-colored arms. "Oh, there you are," he said, glancing around at the glowering Joram in affected surprise. "Where have you been, dear boy? There's your sweetheart, gone off to dance with another man."

More laughter.

Joram glared at him furiously. "Will you—"

"—comfort you in your afflicted state? Certainly. Give us a few moments alone, will you?" Simkin asked the assembled multitude, who obligingly—and with many smiles at Joram's expense—wandered off in search of new amusement. "Champagne, follow me!" Gesturing to several glasses perched on the rim of the flowing fountain, Simkin put his arm through Joram's and drew him over near the crystal wall, three bubbling champagne glasses dutifully bobbing along in his wake.

"What have you done?" Joram demanded angrily. "I've been searching for Gwendolyn for hours and now you—"

"Dear fellow, keep your voice down," Simkin said, the merriment and gaiety snuffed out of his face. "It was necessary to speak to you privately and immediately about the catalyst."

"Poor Saryon," Joram said, his face darkening, the black brows coming together. "I shouldn't have left him last night, but the *Theldara* assured me he was healing—"

"And so he is, dear boy," Simkin interrupted.

Joram tensed. "What do you mean?"

"I mean *They* have got him, old chap." Simkin smiled, but it was a smile for the crowd alone. Moistening his lips with champagne, he glanced nervously about the hall. "And we could be next."

Joram suddenly found it difficult to breathe. The air in this room had been in the lungs of too many others already. His heart pounded painfully, as though trying to squeeze the last bit of oxygen from his chest. There was a buzzing in his ears and, once again, he couldn't hear anything.

"I say, steady. Have a sip. People watching. Fun and merriment, remember?"

Joram saw Simkin's lips move and felt a glass thrust into his hand. His mouth was dry, he lifted it to his lips, and the bubbles of the wine burst on his tongue, cooling his throat. "Are you sure?" he managed to ask, taking a breath and struggling to regain his composure. "What if he really were taken ill . . ."

"Bah! The catalyst was perfectly well when we left. Apart from that, I've never known a *Theldara* to get a sudden urge to examine a patient in the middle of the night. But the *Duuktsarith*? . . ." Simkin's voice trailed off ominously.

"He won't betray me," Joram said in a low tone.

Simkin shrugged. "He may not have any choice."

Joram's lips tightened, his hands clenched. "I'm not leaving!" he said flatly. "Not until I've talked to this Druidess Lord Samuels promised to bring! And besides" — his brow cleared, he raised his head — "it won't matter. Soon I'll be a Baron. Then everything will be all right."

"Of course. Very well, if you're satisfied. Just thought I'd explain matters," Simkin said lightly, suddenly complacent once more. "As you say, what is it? A few bad hours for the catalyst. Nothing more. They welcome this sort of thing, so I've heard. Martyrdom. Makes them righteous. Ah, the fair one returns — I presume, to take you off to see Daddy from the look in her eye, which is, I note, now fixed on me with a decidedly unfriendly gaze. Say no more, I'm gone. Let me know when to start the celebration, kill the fatted calf and all that. We might use Bishop Vanya for the occasion. Remember, my dear boy, you have spent a most exhausting evening sitting up with a sick catalyst. Ta-ta!"

Leaving Joram alone — for which the young man was grateful — Simkin rose into the air and was immediately absorbed into the crowd. "Do you like it?" His voice floated back to Joram. "I call it *Death Warmed Over* . . ."

The hall was growing increasingly hot, the noise level rising. The presentations to the Emperor having ended, the people standing around the throne began to disperse, changing their raiment from mourning to more suitable colors of revelry. Joram leaned against the crystal wall, staring out into the night, wishing desperately he was out in the cool darkness that looked so inviting compared to the glaring light and heat within. He felt a momentary stab of conscience over the catalyst. Simkin's use of the word "martyrdom" chilled him. The thought of what Saryon might well be suffering because of him made him close his eyes, guilt sliding its thin blade into his soul.

But, after a moment, Joram was able to ignore the pain, covering the wound with bitter salve as he had covered so many in his life, never noticing the ugly scars they left behind. He would make it right for Saryon someday. He would take care of the catalyst for the rest of his life. . . .

"Joram?"

And here was Gwendolyn, looking up at him with the blue eyes that saw the wounds and longed to heal them. Reaching out, he caught hold of both her hands in his and pressed them against his feverish skin, finding another balm in her cool touch.

"Joram, what's wrong?" she asked, alarmed by the grim, haunted expression on his face.

"Nothing," he said gently, kissing the hands. "Nothing, now that you are with me."

Gwendolyn blushed prettily and retrieved her hands, conscious of Lady Rosamund hovering somewhere near. "Joram, Father sent me with a message which I was going to deliver, only Simkin—"

"Yes, yes!" Joram said fiercely. A dark flush stained his face, his eyes devoured her. "What message?"

"He . . . he wants you to meet him in one of the private rooms," Gwendolyn faltered, taken aback at the change in the young man. But the next moment, the excitement of her news swept all caution away. "Oh, Joram!" she cried, catching hold of his hands in her own. "The Druidess is with him! The *Theldara* who attended your mother when you were born!"

Child of Stone

Joram walked majestically through the crowd. In his mind, he was a Baron already; the beautiful woman at his side, his wife. Few people paid him any attention, except to wonder perhaps why he and the dainty young girl were walking on the floor like catalysts. But that would change, change soon! Maybe even in an hour or so, Lord Samuels would be walking—yes, walking—at Joram's side, introducing him as Baron Fitzgerald, hinting to his friends that the Baron was about to become a permanent member of the Samuels family. Then they will take notice of me, Joram thought with grim amusement. There won't be enough they can do for me.

I'll find Saryon, he planned, and I'll make that fat Priest who has used the catalyst to hound me apologize to both of us. Maybe I'll even see what I can do to have him removed from his office. And then I'll—

"Joram," said Gwendolyn, speaking somewhat timidly. The expression on his face was so strange—elated, eager, yet with a grim darkness she could not understand. "We cannot possibly go any farther walking."

"Why, where are your father and the Druidess?" Joram asked, suddenly realizing he'd lost track of his surroundings.

"On the Water level," said Gwen, pointing below.

The two stood on the balcony, looking down through the nine levels to the golden forest on the floor. It was a breathtaking view, each level glowing with its own color — with the exception of the level of Death, which remained nothing but a gray void. Magi were floating both up and down now, the revelries having extended to all the levels. Glancing at the stairs, Joram saw the catalysts toiling up them, their shoes making shuffling sounds, their breathing labored.

And that gave him the excuse he needed.

"You go on down, my lady," he told Gwendolyn, releasing her slowly and reluctantly. Preoccupied as he was, he had still been very much aware of the warmth and fragrance and the occasional touch of smooth skin and soft flesh moving so near him. "Tell your father I am coming. I will walk."

Gwendolyn looked so astonished at this and regarded the catalysts making their way up and down the stairs with such a pitying gaze that Joram could not help smiling. Taking her hand in his, he said to her inwardly, Soon, my dear, you will be proud to walk these stairs with your husband. Aloud he said, "Surely, you can understand that I could not ask Father Dunstable to grant me Life today, no matter how important the occasion. . . ."

Gwendolyn's face flushed. "Oh, no!" she murmured, ashamed. She had, in truth, forgotten about the poor catalyst. Of course, Joram might have gained Life through another catalyst, but there were many magi who were so fond of and loyal to their catalysts that to use another — a stranger at that — would have been tantamount to committing adultery. "Of course not. How foolish of me to forget and" — she raised her lovely eyes to Joram's — "how very noble of you to make this sacrifice for him."

Now it was Joram's turn to flush, seeing the love and admiration in the blue eyes and thinking how he had earned it with a lie. Never mind, he told himself swiftly. Soon she will know the truth, soon they will all know the truth. . . .

"Go ahead, your father is waiting," Joram said somewhat gruffly. He escorted her to the opening in the ornamental balcony used by the magi entering and leaving the Hall of Majesty and handed her off it with a bow. His heart lurched as he watched her step gracefully into nothing, and it was all he could do to remain standing and keep from reaching wildly to save her from what — in his case — would have been a deadly plunge to the golden forest nine levels below. But, smiling up at him, Gwendolyn drifted downward as gracefully as a lily riding the water, the layers of her gown floating out about her like petals, the bottom layers clinging to her legs, keeping her body covered modestly.

"Water level," Joram muttered, and, turning, ran to the stairs and hastened down them, nearly knocking over a puffing, irate catalyst — the same catalyst, he noticed in passing, that Simkin had taken such delight in tormenting.

Going down the stairs was certainly much easier than coming up. Joram might have been flying himself, he moved so rapidly, and it seemed no time at all before he was standing on the Water level, trying to catch his breath — whether from the descent or his mounting excitement he couldn't tell.

Gwendolyn was nowhere to be seen, and he was just about to go off searching for her impatiently when a voice called, "Joram, over here."

Turning, he saw her gesture to him from an open door he had not noticed amidst the waterlike surroundings. Hurrying past illusions of mermaids swimming with vividly colored fish, Joram reached the door, devoutly hoping that the private meeting chamber wasn't going to be a dark grotto filled with oyster shells.

It wasn't. Apparently, the illusions were confined to the area around the balcony, for Gwendolyn introduced Joram into a room that — except for the extreme opulence and luxury of the furniture — might have come from Lord Samuels's dwelling. It was a sitting room, designed to accommodate those magi who wished to relax and avoid the expenditure of magical energy. Several couches covered with silken brocade in fanciful designs were arranged in formal groupings around the cozy room, their tables standing attention at their sides.

On one of these stiff couches, looking extraordinarily like a small bird perched on the cushions, sat a tiny, dried-up woman. Joram recognized her, by the brown color and fine quality of her robes, as a Druidess of extremely high ranking. She was old — so old, Joram thought, she must have seemed elderly to his mother eighteen years ago. Despite the springtime weather and the closeness of the room, she crowded near a fire Lord Samuels had caused to burn in the fireplace. Her brown robes seemed to puff out from her frail body like the plumage of a shivering bird, and she further enhanced the image by constantly preening and plucking at the velvet fabric with a clawlike hand.

Lord Samuels stood on the floor — a mark of the solemnity of the occasion — to one side of the couch, his hands clasped behind his back. He was dressed in the subdued colors worn by the rest of the magi on this sad anniversary; his robes, though fine, were not nearly so fine as those worn by his betters — a fact duly noted and applauded by his betters. He bowed stiffly as Joram entered, Joram bowing stiffly in return. The Druidess stared at Joram curiously with bright, beady eyes.

"Thank you, Daughter," said Lord Samuels, his gaze turning to Gwendolyn with a fondness and pride even the seriousness of the forthcoming conversation could not diminish. "I think it would be best if you left us."

"Oh, but, Father!" Gwendolyn cried, then, seeing the tiniest hint of a frown on his face, she sighed. With a final glance at Joram — a glance that carried with it her heart and soul — she made a pretty curtsy to the Druidess, who chirped and fluttered in return, then withdrew from the room, shutting the door softly behind her.

Lord Samuels cast a spell upon the door, so that they would not be disturbed.

"Joram," he said coolly, stepping forward and gesturing with his hand, "allow me to present *Theldara* Menni. The *Theldara* was, for many years, the Druidess presiding over the Birthing Rooms of the Font. She now has the honor," he added in guarded tones, "of attending our beloved Empress, whose continued good health we pray for daily."

Joram noted that Lord Samuels carefully did not look at him as he said this; he had noticed that everyone who spoke of the Empress did so in measured words and without meeting the eye.

Joram himself found it difficult to meet the eyes of the Druidess and he bowed, thankfully avoiding the necessity. He was overwhelmed with disgust at the thought of this woman attending a corpse. His skin crawled and he fancied he could smell death and decay in the stuffy, overheated room. Yet he found himself wondering, with a terrible, morbid fascination, what magic they performed to keep the body in its suspended state. Did elixirs run through the silent heart instead of blood? Did potions pulse in the veins, herbs keep the skin from rotting? What magic words made the stiff hand move with that awful grace, what alchemy caused the dull eyes to shine?

He was conscious of the Darksword strapped to his back, feeling its presence reassuring. I have given Life to that which is lifeless, and for that I am labeled a Sorcerer of the Dark Arts, he said to himself. And yet what greater sin is this, to keep that which belongs to the gods — if one believes in such things — from finding its true destiny among the stars, keeping it chained in its prison house of flesh?

Straightening, he feared he could not bring himself to look at this woman without openly betraying his loathing. Then he sternly reminded himself that none of this was his concern. What did this Empress matter to him? It was his life that was important, not another's death.

Raising his gaze, shaking back the black hair that hung about his face, Joram stared at the Druidess with equanimity and even a slight smile. She made a kind of caw, as though aware of his thoughts and taking pleasure in them. Raising the clawlike hand, she held it out for Joram to kiss, and this he did, stepping forward and bowing low over it, though he could not — for the life of him — bring his lips to touch the withered flesh.

Lord Samuels indicated for Joram to be seated, and though he would have much preferred to continue standing, the young man forced himself to obey.

"I have not yet broached the matter with *Theldara* Menni, Joram, preferring as a point of honor to first enter into such a delicate subject in your presence."

"Thank you, my lord," Joram said, and meant it.

Lord Samuels bowed slightly and continued. "The *Theldara* has been kind enough to meet with us as a favor to my friend, Father Richar. I leave it to you, young man, to explain the situation."

The *Theldara* stared at Joram with eager eyes, her thin lips pursed in a beak-like manner.

This was unexpected. Somehow, Joram had not expected to have to explain matters himself, although he was grateful to Lord Samuels for not prejudicing his case one way or the other by discussing it without him. He wished Saryon was here. The catalyst had a way of reducing things to simple terms that were easy to understand. Joram felt vague about where to begin. He was also frightened, realizing just how much was at stake here.

"My name is Joram," he stated lamely, trying to think, trying to pull the pieces together. "My mother's name was Anja. Does — does that mean anything to you?"

The Druidess pecked at the word like a bread crumb, bobbing her small head, but otherwise keeping silent.

Not knowing whether that was a positive or negative response, Joram floundered on. "I was raised in a Field Magi village and . . . spent all my life there. But . . . my mother always told me I was of"—he felt his skin burn—"noble blood and that my family came from Merilon. She . . . my mother . . . said that my father was a . . . a catalyst. They had committed a criminal act—joining together bodily—and so created me. They were caught"—Joram could not keep the bitterness from tinging his voice—"and my father was sentenced to the Turning. He stands today, on the Border. . . ."

He fell silent, recalling the stone statue, feeling the warmth of the tear splashing on his body. Would he want me here? Joram wondered suddenly, then, angrily shaking his head, continued talking.

"My mother gave birth to me at the Font, so she told me. Then, taking me with her, she ran away. I don't know why she left. Maybe she was afraid. Or maybe, then, she was already a little mad. . . ." The word was hard to say and made him choke. He hadn't realized this would be so painful. He couldn't look at Lord Samuels now or even at the *Theldara*, but sat staring grimly at his hands that clenched and unclenched before him.

"She told me that one day we would return to Merilon and claim what was rightfully ours, but"—he drew a deep breath—"she died before she saw that day. For one reason or another, I fled the village where I had been raised and have been living since in the Outland. But then, I found a way to return to Merilon and claim my birthright."

"The problem, *Theldara* Menni," struck in Lord Samuels, aware that Joram had apparently said all he could, "is that there exist no records of this young man's birth. That is not unusual, I understand." He made a deprecating gesture with his hands. "The number of indigent and . . . shall we say . . . fallen women who come to the Font to bear their children is large and, in the confusion, records are known to be misplaced. Or—as is probable in Joram's circumstance—the mother left the Font in secret and, fearing she might be pursued, either destroyed the records or took them with her. What we are hoping is that you can identify him as—"

"There was a Birthing Moon that night, too," cawed the *Theldara* suddenly and shrilly.

"I beg your pardon?" Lord Samuels blinked. Joram, catching his breath, raised his head.

"A Birthing Moon," the old woman repeated irritably. "Full moon. We knew when we saw it in the sky that the nursery would be full as well, and we weren't wrong."

"Then, you do remember?" Joram breathed, sitting forward in his seat, his body trembling.

"Remember?" The Druidess laughed raucously, then coughed and wiped at her beaky mouth with the claw of a hand. "I remember Anja. I was there at the Turning," she said with some pride. "I went along to take care of her. She was poorly, and I knew it would be the death of the unborn babe — if not the death of the mother — to make her watch. But such was what they wanted. Such was the law." The old woman huddled into her robes, fluffing them around her.

"Yes, go on!" Joram wanted to grab her up and cradle her in his hands, so precious did she seem to him.

The Druidess stared into the fire, clucking and chirping to herself, jabbing at her beak with her claw until — suddenly, raising her head — she looked straight at Joram.

"I was right," she said shrilly, her voice ringing through the room. "I was right."

"Right? What do you mean?"

"Born dead, of course!" The Druidess clucked. "The babe was born dead. Strange it was, too." The old woman's eyes took on an eerie glint; her shrill voice softened to a whisper of pleasurable horror. "The babe had turned to stone inside the mother! Turned to stone — just like the father! I never saw the like before," she said, twisting her head up to peer at Lord Samuels and see the reaction she made. "Never saw the like! It was a judgment."

Joram's body stiffened. He might have been the babe — or the father.

"I don't understand." His voice cracked. Lord Samuels, in the background, made a motion, but Joram did not look up or take his eyes from the old *Theldara's* face. He had ceased to tremble; nothing moved within him, not even his heart.

The *Theldara* made a gesture with the clawed hands as of pulling an object forth. "Most of 'em limp as cats, poor things, when they're stillborn. Not this one, not Anja's child." The Druidess scratched at each word with her hand. "Eyes staring into nothing. Cold and hard as rock. It was a judgment on them both, I said."

"That can't be true!" Joram didn't recognize the sound of his voice.

The Druidess stuck her head out, her beady eyes squinting, her claw shaking at him. "I don't know whose mother's son you are, young man, but you're not Anja's! Oh, she was mad. There was no doubt." The birdish head bobbed. "And I see now that she did what we always suspected — stole some poor child from the nursery for the unwanted and pretended it was her own. That's what the *Duuk-tsarith* told us when they questioned us, and I see now it was true."

Joram could not respond. The woman's words came to him as in a dream. He could neither speak nor react. From the same dream, he heard Lord Samuels ask in a stern voice.

"The *Duuk-tsarith*? This, then, was investigated?"

"Investigated?" The old woman crowed. "I should say so! It took *them* to force the dead babe from Anja's arms. She had wrapped it in a blanket and was trying to make it nurse, warming its feet. When we tried to come near, she shrieked at us. Long talons grew from her fingers, her teeth turned to fangs. *Albanara*, she was," the Druidess said, shivering. "Powerful. No, we wouldn't get close. So we called the *Duuk-tsarith*. They came and took the dead babe and cast a spell over her to make her sleep. We left her, and it was that night she escaped."

"But, then, why aren't there any records of this?" Lord Samuels pursued, his face grave. Joram stared at the Druidess, but his eyes held no more life in them than the stone child's.

"Ah, there were records!" The Druidess clucked indignantly. "There were records." Her clawed hand made a fist the size of a teaspoon. "We kept very good records when I was there. Very good indeed. The *Duuk-tsarith* took them next morning, after we discovered that Anja was gone. Ask them for your precious records. Not that they'll matter much to you, poor lad," she added, looking at Joram pityingly, her head cocked to one side.

"And so you are certain that this young man" — Lord Samuels nodded at Joram, his gaze one now of sorrow and concern more than of anger — "was stolen from the nursery?"

"Certain? Yes, we were certain." The Druidess grinned, and she had no more teeth in her mouth than a bird has in its bill.

"The *Duuk-tsarith* said that was what had happened, and that made us certain. Very certain indeed, my lord."

"But did you count? Were there any babies missing?"

"The *Duuk-tsarith* said there was," the old woman repeated, frowning. "The *Duuk-tsarith* said there was."

"But did you check yourself to see!" Lord Samuels tried again.

"Poor lad," was all the *Theldara* said. Looking at Joram, her beady eyes glittered. "Poor lad."

"Shut up!" Joram rose unsteadily to his feet. His face was dark, blood glistened from a cut on his mouth where he had bitten through his lip. "Shut up," he snarled again, glaring at the *Theldara* in such fury that she crumbled back into the couch and Lord Samuels hurriedly stepped between the two.

"Joram, please," he began, "calm yourself! Think! There is much here that does not make sense . . ."

But Joram could neither see nor hear the man. His head throbbed, he thought it might burst. Reeling, half-blind, he clutched at his head, tearing at his hair in a frenzy.

Seeing the hair come out dripping blood from the roots, and seeing as well the madness in the young man's wild gaze, Lord Samuels attempted to lay soothing hands on Joram. With a bitter cry, Joram shoved the man away from him, nearly knocking him down.

"Pity!" Joram gasped. He couldn't breathe. "Yes, pity me! I am"—he struggled for breath—"nobody!" Again he clutched at his head, pulling his hair. "Lies! All lies! Dead . . . death . . ."

Turning, he stumbled from the room, groping blindly for the door.

"It will not open, young man. I have strengthend the spell. You must stay and listen to me! All is not lost! Why did the *Duuk-tsarith* take an interest in this? Let us look further . . ." Lord Samuels took a step forward with some thought, perhaps, of casting a spell upon Joram himself.

Joram ignored him. Reaching the door, he sought to open it, but—as Lord Samuels said—the spell stopped him. He couldn't even get his hands past the invisible, impenetrable barrier, and he beat at it in impotent rage. Without conscious thought, knowing only that he must escape this room in which he was slowly suffocating, Joram drew the Darksword from the scabbard on his back and slashed at the door with the weapon.

The Darksword felt itself wielded; the heat of its master's life pulsed in its metal body and it began to absorb the magic. The spell on the door shattered just as the wood shattered when the blade crashed into it. The *Theldara* began to scream—a high-pitched, shrill wail—and Lord Samuels stared in wonder and awe until he began to feel weak, Life draining from his body. The Darksword was nonselective, its forger not yet fully acquainted with its potential or how to use it. It sucked the magic from everything and everyone around it, enhancing its own power. The metal began to glow with a strange white-blue light that illuminated the room as the sword caused the fire to die and the magical globes of light on the mantelpiece to glimmer faintly and then vanish altogether.

Lord Samuels could not move. His body felt heavy and foreign to him, as though he had suddenly stepped inside the shell of another man and had no idea how to make anything operate. He stared in a dreamlike terror, unable to comprehend what was happening, unable to react.

The door fell in shards at Joram's feet. On the other side, reflected in the blue-white radiance of the fiercely blazing sword, stood Gwendolyn.

She had been listening, ear pressed against the door, her heart dancing with sweet, airy fantasies, her mind racing with plans to feign surprise when Joram should burst out and tell her the good news. One by one those airy fantasies had sprouted the wings of demons; their dance turned macabre. Babies of stone; the poor, mad mother nursing the cold, rigid body; the dark specters of the *Duuk-tsarith*; Anja fleeing into the night with a stolen child . . .

Gwendolyn had shrunk backward, away from the closed and magically sealed door, her hand pressed over her mouth so that she might not cry out and give herself away. The horror of what she had heard crept up over her soul like the foul waters of a fast-rising flood. Sheltered and protected all her life, the girlish part of her only dimly understood—such things as child-birthing were never discussed. But the woman deep inside reacted. Instincts bred thousands of years before caused her to share the pain and the agony; to feel the loneliness, the grief, the sorrow; and to even understand that madness—like a tiny star shining in the vast darkness of the night sky—brought consolation.

Gwendolyn had heard Joram's anguished cry, she had heard his rage and his anger, and the girl longed to run away. But the woman stayed, and it was the woman Joram faced when he slashed through the door. He stared at her grimly, sword in hand. Blazing fiercely and brightly, its glow was reflected in the blue eyes that looked at him from the ashen face.

He knew she had heard it all and he felt suddenly a vast and overwhelming sense of relief. He could see the horror in her eyes. Next would come the pity and then the loathing. He wouldn't avoid it. He would hurry it, in fact. It would be so much easier to leave hating her. He could sink thankfully into the darkness, knowing that he would never rise again.

"So, lady"—he spoke in low tones, as fierce as the sword's bright light—"you know. You know that I am no one, nobody." His face grim, Joram raised the Darksword, watching its white-blue blaze burn in the wide, staring eyes of the woman in the hall. "You once said that whatever I was would not matter to you, Gwendolyn. That you would love me and come with me." Slowly, switching the Darksword to his left hand, Joram held out his right. "Come with me, then." He sneered. "Or were your words lies like the words of all the rest?"

What could she do? He spoke arrogantly, goading her to refusal. Yet Gwen saw behind that; she saw the pain and anguish in his eyes. She knew that if she rebuffed him, if she turned from him, he would walk into the arid desert of his despair and sink beneath the sand. He needed her. As his sword drank up the magic of the world, so did his thirst for love drink up all she had to offer.

"No, not a lie," she said in a calm, steady voice.

Reaching out her hand, she caught hold of his. Joram stared at her in astonishment, struggling with himself. It seemed for a moment that he might hurl her away from him. But she held onto him tightly, gazing at him with steadfast love and resolve.

Joram lowered the Darksword. Still holding Gwen's hand, he hung his head and began to cry—bitter, anguished sobs that tore at his body so that it seemed they might rend him in half. Gently, Gwen put her arms around him and gathered him close, soothing him as she would a child.

"Come, we must go," she whispered. "This place is dangerous for you now."

Joram clung to her. Lost and wandering in his inner darkness, he had no thought of where he was, no care for his own safety. He would have sunk to the floor were it not for her arms around him.

"Come!" she whispered urgently.

Dully, he nodded. His stumbling feet followed her lead.

"Gwendolyn! No! My child!" Lord Samuels called out to her, pleading. He tried desperately to move, but the Darksword had drained his Life. He could only stand, helplessly, watching.

Without a backward glance at her father, Gwendolyn led the man she had chosen to love away.

6

Here's to Folly

Uncertain what to do or where to go, Gwen led Joram to the Fire level. Here, in a dark alcove made even darker and more shadowy by the fiery illusions around them, the couple hid, starting at every sound, scarcely willing to draw a breath.

"We must get away, before the *Duuk-tsarith* start searching for us, if they haven't already," Gwen whispered. "How long will my father be under that spell?"

Joram had regained a measure of control, though he held onto Gwen as a dying man clings to life. His arm around her, he pressed her close, his dark head resting on her golden one, his tears drying in her soft hair.

"I don't know," Joram admitted bitterly, glancing at the Darksword in his left hand. "But not long, I should imagine. I don't really know how this sword functions yet."

Looking at the ugly, misshapen weapon, Gwen shuddered. Joram drew her closer, protectively, ignoring the realization that it was himself from which he sought to protect her.

She did not understand, but she nodded anyway. Frightened and confused, already half regretting her decision, her own heart torn with sorrow for what she knew would be a devastating blow to her family, Gwendolyn was further confused by the stirrings of a painful pleasure she felt at being held fast in Joram's embrace. She longed to stay here, held close to his fast-beating heart. She wanted, in fact, to get closer, somehow, to feel the pleasure and the pain expand within her. But the thought of that made her quail with a fear that was cold in the pit of her stomach. And all-encompassing was the more real and pressing fear of capture.

"If we can get away from the Palace," she asked, "where will we go?"

"To the Grove of Merlyn," Joram said immediately, suddenly seeing everything clearly in his mind. "Mosiah is waiting for us there. We'll slip out of the Gate . . ." He paused, frowning. "Simkin. We need Simkin! He can get us out. Then, once we're away from this cursed city, we'll travel to Sharakan."

"Sharakan!" Gwen gasped, her eyes widening in alarm.

Joram smiled at her briefly, reassuringly. "I know the Prince there," he said. "He's a friend of mine." He fell silent, staring off into the distance. Perhaps Garald wasn't his friend. Not anymore, now that he was nobody. No. He shook his head. After all, he had the Darksword. He knew of darkstone and how to forge it. That made him someone. His expression grew grim, fierce. "And I'll forge darkstone," he muttered. "We'll raise an army. I'll return to Merilon," he said softly, his grip tightening on the sword. "And whatever I want I will take! That, too, will make me somebody!"

Feeling Gwendolyn shiver in his grasp, Joram looked down into the blue eyes. "Don't be frightened," he murmured, relaxing. "It will all be all right. You will see. I love you. I would never do anything to hurt you." Bending down, he kissed her gently on the forehead. "We will be married in Sharakan," he added, feeling her trembling lessen. "Perhaps the Prince himself will come to our wedding. . . ."

"Egad!" came a voice from out of the fiery, illusionary inferno that surrounded them. "Here's the Black Death searching high and low, nook and cranny, hither and yon for you two and I find you playing at slap and tickle in a corner!"

Joram whirled about, sword raised. "Simkin!", he gasped, when he could breathe normally again. "Don't creep up on me like that!" Lowering the sword, Joram wiped sweat from his face with the back of his swordhand. Gwen crept out from behind him, half-smothered from being pressed back against the wall.

"My dear turtledoves," said Simkin casually, "I can assure you that something much nastier and uglier than myself is likely to be creeping up on you at any moment. The alarm has been sounded."

Joram listened. "I don't hear anything."

"You won't, old bean." Simkin smoothed his beard with his hand. "This is the Palace, remember? Wouldn't do to upset His Majesty or to startle the Empress in her fragile state of health. But rest assured that there are eyes seeking and ears pricking and noses twitching. The Corridors are alive."

"It's hopeless," whispered Gwen, slumping back against Joram, tears sliding down her cheeks.

"No, no. Quite the contrary," Simkin remarked. "Your fool is here to save you from your folly. Rather a nice ring to that. I must remember it." Tilting his head back affectedly, Simkin peered at Gwen down his long nose. "You will make a charming Mosiah, my dear. One of my better ones." Wafting the orange silk that appeared suddenly in his hand, Simkin laid it solemnly over Gwen's head before she could protest, spoke a word or two, then, "Abracadabra!" he cried, whipping the silk away.

Mosiah leaned against Joram now, brushing tears from his face. Looking down at himself, he gave a cry of dismay and stared wildly back at Simkin.

"Charming," said Simkin, eyeing him complacently and with a glint of mischievous fun. "It's all the rage, you know."

Flushing, Joram started to remove his arm from the shoulders of what was now a virile, handsome young man. But the virile, handsome young man was in truth a frightened young girl. It was Gwen who had been strong at the outset, guiding the despairing Joram away from the room where her father stood, a helpless statue of flesh. It was she who had found this hiding place, she who had laid Joram's head upon her breast, comforting and holding him until he could fight back the darkness that was always there, ready to enslave him.

But now her strength was ebbing. The image of the *Duuk-tsarith*, those nightdream figures who laid chill, unseen hands upon their victims, dragging them to unknown places, had unnerved her. Now she found herself in a strange body. The virile young man began to weep uncontrollably, shoulders heaving, his face hidden in his hands.

"Damn it, Simkin!" Joram muttered, putting his arms awkwardly around Mosiah's broad shoulders, having the strangest feeling that he was comforting his friend.

"I say, this won't do," Simkin said sternly, glaring at Mosiah. "Pull yourself together, old chap!" he ordered, clapping the young man on the back soundly.

"Simkin!" Joram began angrily, then stopped.

"He's right," said Mosiah with a gulp, pulling himself away from Joram. There was even a hint of laughter in the blue eyes, shining through the tears. "I'm fine. Really I am."

"Thatta boy!" said Simkin approvingly. "Now, my Dark and Gloomy Friend, we must do the same for you— Oops, can't." The silk fluttered in the air in momentary confusion. "That confounded sword, you know. Put it away."

Reluctantly, frowning, Joram did as he was told, placing the sword in the sheath on his back, then drawing his robes around it. "What are you going to do?" he asked Simkin grimly. "You can't change *me* into Mosiah, not while I'm wearing the sword. And I won't take it off," he added, seeing Simkin's eyes brighten.

"Oh, well." Simkin appeared crestfallen for a moment, then he shrugged. "We'll do the best we can then, I suppose, dear boy. Change of clothing will have to suffice. No, don't argue."

With a flutter of orange silk, Joram was dressed in a pallbearer's costume identical to Simkin's—white robes and white hood.

"Keep the hood drawn over your face," said Simkin crisply, following his own instructions. "And do relax, both of you. You're attending a party at the Royal Palace of Merilon. You're supposed to look bored out of your skulls, not fightened out of your wits. Yes, that's better," he remarked, watching critically as Mosiah patted at his face with the orange silk, removing all traces of tears, and Joram unclenched his fists.

"If all goes well," Simkin continued coolly, "there'll be only one really bad moment—that's going out the front door—"

"The front!" Joram scowled. "But surely there are back ways . . ."

"My poor naïve boy." Simkin sighed. "What would you do without your fool? Everyone will be expecting you to go sneaking out the back, don't you see? *Duuk-tsarith* will be sprouting up around the back exits like fungus after a rain. On the other hand, there'll probably only be a couple dozen or so at the front. And we're not going to sneak! No, we are going to stagger out proudly! Three drunks, heading for a night on the town."

Seeing Mosiah's pale face, Simkin added cheerfully, "Don't worry. We'll make it! They'll never suspect a thing. After all, they're looking for a lovely young woman and a gloomy young man — not two pallbearers and a peasant."

Mosiah managed a wan smile; Joram shook his head. He didn't like this, any of it, but he supposed there was no help for it. He couldn't think of anything better, his brain was moving sluggishly; he had to goad it to take a step. Reality was rapidly slipping from him and he was suddenly quite content to let it go.

"I say," said Simkin after a moment, looking over at Joram. "I suppose this means the Barony fell through?"

"Yes," answered Joram briefly. The sharp pain of his discovery had subsided into a dull, throbbing ache that would be with him forever. "Anja's child died at birth," he said, his voice expressionless. "She stole a baby from the nursery for unwanted, abandoned wretches. . . ."

"Ah," said Simkin lightly. "Call me Nemo, what? And so, are we ready?" He reviewed his troops. "Set? Ah, almost forgot! Champagne!" he called.

A musical tinkling of glass sounded in response and an entire battalion of glasses filled with bubbling wine came floating through the air to fall in behind their leader.

"One each," said Simkin, thrusting a full glass into Mosiah's limp hand and another into Joram's. "Remember, gaiety, merriment, time of your lives!"

Raising his glass to his lips, he drained it at a swallow. "Drink up, drink up!" he ordered. "Now! For'ard! March!" Tossing the orange silk in the air, he sent it forth as a banner to wave proudly in front of them. Then, taking hold of Mosiah's arm in his, he motioned for Joram to do the same on the opposite side.

"Here's to folly!" Simkin announced, and together they tottered forward into the fiery illusions, the champagne glasses clinking merrily along behind.

7

The Latest in Fashion Trends

osiah — the real one — crouched in the shadows of the trees in the Grove of Merlyn, staring nervously into the darkness. He was alone in the Grove, he knew — a fact he had been repeating reassuringly to himself at least once every five minutes since night had fallen. Unfortunately, it had done little good. He was far from reassured. Simkin had been right when he said no one came here after dark. Mosiah understood why. The Grove took on an entirely different aspect at night. It returned to itself.

With the dawning of the sun, the Grove put on all the flowers and garlands and jewels that it owned. Flinging its arms wide, it welcomed its admirers, entertaining them in lavish style. Letting them pluck the fragile blossoms and toss them carelessly away to wither and die under foot. Watching with a smile as they tossed garbage into the crystal pools and trampled the grass. Listening to their empty words of praise and gushes of rapture that sprang from their mouths in puffs of dust. But at night — the fee collected — the Grove drew the blanket of darkness over its head, curled around its tomb, and lay awake, nursing its wounds.

A Field Magus, as sensitive to the thoughts and feelings of plants as a Druid — perhaps even more sensitive then some

Druids, whose lives had never depended on the crops they grew — Mosiah could hear the anger whispering around him, the anger and the sorrow.

The anger emanated from the living things in the Grove. The sorrow, so it seemed to Mosiah, came from the dead. The young man found the tomb of Merlyn strangely comforting, therefore, and lingered near it, resting his hand upon the marble that was warm even in the coolness of the night. From this vantage point, he warily watched and listened and repeatedly told himself that he was alone.

But Mosiah's uneasiness grew. Ordinary noises of a wilderness — even a tamed wilderness such as this — caused his skin to prickle and sweat to chill in the night air. Trees creaking, leaves whispering, branches rubbing — all had an ominous sound, a malicious intent. He was an intruder here, disturbing the Grove's fitful rest, and he was not welcome. So he paced back and forth beside the tomb, keeping a wary eye upon the forest, and wondering irritably just how long it took to become a Baron, anyway.

To keep his mind off his fear, Mosiah imagined Joram living in wealth, master of an estate with his pretty wife at his side and a bevy of servants to act upon his slightest wish. Mosiah smiled, but it was a smile that faded to a sigh.

Living a lie. All his life, Joram had lived a lie, and now he would continue to do so forever — *must* continue to do so, in fact. Though Joram might talk grandly of how wealth would free him, Mosiah had common sense enough to know that it would simply add its own chains to the ones already binding Joram. That the chains would be made of gold instead of iron would make little difference. Joram would never admit to being Dead, Mosiah knew. He would never admit to having murdered the overseer. (Unlike Saryon, Mosiah did not view the death of Blachloch as murder and never would.)

And then — what about children? Mosiah shook his head, running his hand over the tomb's shaped marble, absently tracing the lines of the sword with his fingers. Would they be born Dead, like their father? Would he hide them, as so many of the Dead were hidden? Was the lie to be perpetuated through generation after generation?

Mosiah could see a darkness spreading over the family, casting its shadow first over Gwendolyn, who would bear Dead children and never know why. Then the children, living a lie —

Joram's lie. Perhaps he would teach them the Dark Arts. Perhaps, by then, there would be war with Sharakan. Technology would come back into the world and bring with it death and destruction. Mosiah shuddered. He didn't like Merilon, he didn't like the people or the way they lived. The beauty and wonder that had first enchanted him now glittered too brightly in his eyes. But he supposed this to be his fault, not the fault of the people of Merilon. They didn't deserve —

A hand touched his shoulder from behind.

He turned instantly but it was too late.

A voice spoke, the spell was cast.

Life flowed from Mosiah and was greedily absorbed by the Grove as the young man tumbled, helpless, to the ground, his magic nulled by the hand of the black-robed figures that stood around him. But Mosiah had lived among the Sorcerers of the Dark Arts. He had been forced to live without the magic for months during that time and, what's more, he had been a victim of this spell before. Its shock value was lessened and therefore the Nullmagic spell — though its first effect was devastating — did not paralyze him completely.

Mosiah was shrewd enough not to let his enemies know that, however. Lying on the ground, his cheek pressed into the damp, cold grass, he tried to calm his terror and regain his strength, drawing on it from within himself rather than from the magic in the world around him. As he felt his muscles respond to his commands, his body come under his control, he had to fight a panicked desire to leap up and run. It would serve no purpose. He would never escape. They would simply cast a more powerful spell on him, one that he could not fight.

And so he lay on the ground, watching his attackers, letting his strength build up within, holding his fear at bay, and trying desperately to think what to do.

It was the *Duuk-tsarith*, of course. Almost invisible in the darkness of the Grove, the black-robed figures stood out against the white marble of the tomb near where Mosiah lay. There were two of them and they were talking together, so close to Mosiah that he might have reached out and plucked at the hems of the black robes. Both casually ignored the young man, having no reason to doubt the effectiveness of their spell.

"So they have left the Palace?" It was the voice of a woman, cool and throaty, and it sent a shudder of fear through Mosiah.

"Yes, madam," replied a warlock. "They were allowed to leave, as you commanded."

"And there was no disturbance?" The witch appeared anxious.

"No, madam."

"Lord Samuels, the father of the girl?"

"He has been taken in hand, madam. He persisted in asking questions, but was eventually made to see that this would not be conducive to his daughter's welfare."

"Questions silenced on the tongue fly to the heart and there take root and grow," muttered the witch, speaking an ancient proverb. "Well, we will deal with that when the time comes. It seems to me, however, that we must uproot these questions and replant them with the truth which, in time, will conveniently wither and die. That will be up to Bishop Vanya, of course, but until I have a chance to talk to His Holiness, take the girl into custody as well."

There was no answer, merely a shivering of the robe near Mosiah which indicated that the warlock had bowed in response.

Mosiah listened closely, his fear lost in his desperate need to know what had happened. How could they have discovered Joram? The Darksword protected him. And how could they have discovered me? Mosiah asked himself suddenly. Not only that, but connect the two of us apparently. No one knew we were meeting here except—

"They are on their way to the Grove?" the witch asked with a touch of impatience.

"So the betrayer said," the warlock responded, "and we have no reason to doubt him."

Betrayer! Sickness swept over Mosiah, wrenching his bowels, bringing a hot, bitter bile to his throat. So that was the answer. They had been betrayed, and now Joram was walking into a carefully laid trap. But who had turned them in? A vision of a bearded young man in white robes, wafting a bit of orange silk in the air, came vividly to Mosiah.

Simkin! He choked. Tears of rage stung his eyes. If it's the last thing I do, I'll kill you!

Calm, calm, his mind commanded. There's a chance. You must find Joram, warn him . . .

Mosiah forced himself to forget, to concentrate on one thing—escape. Cautiously, he moved a hand, holding his breath for fear the *Duuk-tsarith* would notice. But they were absorbed in their conversation, confident that their spell held the young man captive. Mosiah let his hand crawl silently over the ground and his heart leaped when his fingers touched the rough surface of a stick. Never mind that it was a tool, that he would be giving Life to that which was Lifeless.

His hand closed over the weapon. Raising his head ever so slightly, he peered upward. Elation flooded his body. The warlock stood with his back to him. A swift blow to the head, keep the limp body between himself and the witch, use it to block her spell. Mosiah's grip tightened on the stick. His muscles bunched. He sprang to his feet—

Cords of Kij vine sprouting sharp thorns leaped from the ground and wrapped themselves around the young man's upper arms and thighs. With an agonized cry, Mosiah dropped the stick as the thorns pierced his flesh and the vines bound him tight. Toppling over, he lay writhing in the grass at the feet of the warlock, who turned to look at him in some astonishment, then glanced apprehensively at the witch.

"Yes, you erred," she said to the warlock, who bowed his head, chagrined. "I will deal with your punishment later. Now, our time is short. I know his face. I must now hear his voice."

Kneeling beside the struggling Mosiah, the witch laid her hand upon him and the thorns suddenly vanished. With a gurgling sigh, Mosiah rolled over on the grass, moaning. Blood oozed from a hundred small puncture wounds, sliding down his arms, staining his clothes.

"What is your name?" the witch asked coolly, turning the young man's sweaty, pain-twisted face toward her, studying it intently.

Mosiah shook his head, or at least tried to; it was more of a spasmodic jerk.

Her face expressionless, the witch spoke a word and Mosiah caught his breath in fear as the thorns began to grow on the vines again, this time merely pricking his flesh but not digging into it.

"Not yet," said the witch, reading his thoughts on his pale face, seeing the eyes widen. "But they will grow and keep on growing until they pierce right through skin and muscle and organs, tearing out your life with them. Now, I ask you again. What is your name?"

"Why? What can it matter?" Mosiah groaned. "You know it!"

"Humor me," the witch said, and spoke another word. The thorns grew another fraction of an inch.

"Mosiah!" He tossed his head in agony. "Mosiah! Damn it! Mosiah, Mosiah, Mosiah. . . ."

Then their plan penetrated the haze of pain. Mosiah choked, trying to swallow his words. Watching in horror, he saw the witch become Mosiah. Her face — his face. Her clothes — his clothes. Her voice — his voice.

"What do we do with him?" the warlock asked in subdued tones, his mistake obviously rankling him.

"Throw him in the Corridor and send him to the Outland," the witch — now Mosiah — said, rising to her feet.

"No!"

Mosiah tried to fight the warlock's strong hands that dragged him to his feet, but the tiniest movement drove the thorns into his body and he slumped over with an anguished cry. "Joram!" he yelled desperately as he saw the dark void of the Corridor open within the foliage. "Joram!" he shouted, hoping his friend would hear, yet knowing in his heart that it was hopeless. "Run! It's a trap! Run!"

The warlock thrust him into the Corridor. It began to squeeze shut, pressing in on him. The thorns stabbed his flesh; his blood flowed warm over his skin. Staring out, he had a final glimpse of the witch — now himself — watching him, her face — his face — expressionless.

Then, she spread her hands.

"It's all the rage," he saw himself say.

8

The Illusion of a
Thousand Mosiahs

"I don't want to go in there," Gwendolyn faltered, gazing into the whispering blackness of the Grove.

"You . . . you and me . . . both," slurred Simkin, staggering into Joram and nearly knocking him over.

Irritably, Joram caught hold of the young man as Simkin's knees gave way and he sagged to the ground. Throwing his arms around Joram's neck, Simkin whispered confidentially. "B-boring as hell in there thish time of night."

"I don't want you to go in there, either," Gwendolyn added, shivering in the night air. Though the *Sif-Hanar* may have kept the balmy breezes of spring blowing in the city above, the thickness of the foliage in the Garden kept it much cooler than the city. Or perhaps there was a chill within the Grove at night that not even the magic of the *Sif-Hanar* could warm.

"Why couldn't your friend have met us outside?"

"He's on the run, remember," Joram answered, supporting Simkin, who was peering around with drunken solemnity, "like we are. Life will be different from now on, my lady."

He didn't mean to be harsh, but his anger and disappointment—submerged in the fear-laced excitement of escaping the Palace—had returned with the ride through Merilon on the wings of the black swan. It was further enhanced by the gloomy, forbidding atmosphere of the Grove and his irritation with Simkin, who had thoughtfully drunk all the glasses of champagne.

"*Duck-shrith* won't be able . . . track ush . . . by trail of bubbles," he declared.

Gwendolyn hung her head. She was back to her own form now, and to see the golden head drooping, the delicate body slump — hurt by his words — made Joram realize he would have to watch more carefully than ever to keep the dark beast chained up inside him.

"Stand up!" he snapped at Simkin, shoving him to an upright position.

"Aye, aye, cap'n." Simkin saluted, did a graceful pirouette, and sat down flat on the grass.

Ignoring him, Joram took Gwendolyn in his arms. "I'm sorry," he murmured. "Forgive me."

"No, I'm the one who should apologize," Gwen said, making a small attempt at a smile. "You are right. I must begin to consider things like that." Thrusting Joram from her, she stood tall, her lips firm, her head thrown back. "I'll go in there with you," she said.

"No, there's no need," Joram said, smiling the half smile that was lost in the darkness of the night. "You stay here with Simkin—"

"'Stay with me and be my love,'" recited Simkin drunkenly from where he sat in the grass, "'And we will cauliflowers grow' . . ."

"On second thought," said Joram, "perhaps you had better come with me."

"I will. I'd rather! I won't be frightened. Not any more. I want you to be proud of me," Gwen added wistfully.

"I am. And I love you!" Joram said, leaning down to brush his lips against hers, spreading balm over the wound festering in his soul. "Come with me, then. It isn't far. Mosiah will be by the tomb. We'll fetch him, and pick up this drunken sot on the way back. Then it's out the Gate as easily as we escaped the Palace and we're on our way to Sharakan!"

"What drunken sot?" asked Simkin, glaring around indignantly. "One thing, can't abide. Man . . . doesn't know . . . when to quit . . ."

* * *

Holding fast to each other's hands, a prey to the same feelings and unreasoning fears Mosiah had experienced in the angry Grove, Joram and Gwendolyn walked at a rapid pace, eager to meet their friend and leave this place. They did not talk. There was a hush over the Grove. Not a hush of peaceful repose, but a hush of in-held breath, the hush of the waiting hunter. A whisper would seem like a shout in the silence. Their heartbeats thudded loudly and, though Joram crept through the grass and Gwendolyn did not walk at all but drifted in the air by his side, the noise they made in passing sounded louder than the thunder of armies in their ears.

Following the stream that babbled merrily during the day but now ran through its banks as silently and malevolently as a snake slipping through the grass, Gwen and Joram made their way easily through the maze and came at last to the heart of the Grove.

The tomb of Merlyn stood alone in the center of the ring of oaks, its white marble glowing more cold and pale than the moon. The lovers' clasp tightened, they moved closer together. Joram was suddenly conscious of his white robes, gleaming in the eerie light reflected from the tomb. Once he stepped out into the open, he would be an easy target.

Not that there was anything to fear, he reminded himself. How could there be? They had escaped the Palace. . . .

"Wait!" he cautioned Gwen, and held back in the shadows of the trees which — though they were not friendly shadows — covered them both with a mantle of darkness. The two waited, watching, barely breathing. The glade appeared empty. There was no one by the tomb. Or was there? Was that a figure moving near it? It was too far to distinguish. . . .

Joram's hand itched to draw the Darksword, but he dared not. The sword would begin to suck up magic, draining both Gwen's strength and Mosiah's. They might need all the strength and all the magic these two possessed to get past the Gate; Joram bitterly counting Simkin as less than useless at this point.

"I think that's your friend!" whispered Gwen, squeezing Joram's hand.

"Yes." Joram stared into the darkness, seeing the figure walk around to the side of the tomb near them. "Yes, you're right! That's Mosiah. No, you wait here for us." He released her hand and started forward.

"Joram!" Gwen caught hold of the sleeve of his white robe.

"What, my dear?" His voice was gentle. He turned to face her, forcing his expression to one of patience. But he must not have fooled her, because her hand dropped from his sleeve limply.

"Nothing," she said with a fleeting smile barely seen in the tomb's ghostly light. "Only my foolish fears again. Please hurry, though," she said through lips so stiff she could barely move them.

"I will," he promised, and with a reassuring smile, he turned and walked out into the glade.

"Mosiah!" he risked calling softly into the night.

The figure turned, startled, peering into the darkness. Joram raised a hand. Then, as he saw the figure hestitate, it occurred to him that Mosiah wouldn't be expecting him in white robes. He was near enough now to see his friend's features, and he threw back the hood so that Mosiah could see his face.

"It's me, Joram!" he said more loudly, his confidence growing at the sight of his friend's familiar features.

At this, Mosiah grinned and let out a sigh of relief that echoed through the Glade. Arms outstretched, he hurried forward, and before Joram quite knew what was happening, his friend had clasped him in a thankful embrace.

"Name of the Almin, it's good to see you!" Mosiah said, hugging his friend close. "Where is everyone?"

"Gwen's waiting up by those trees," Joram began, awkwardly returning his friend's embrace, then instinctively endeavoring to free himself from Mosiah's arms. "Simkin's drunk as a lord. We have to leave Merilon," he added, wondering why Mosiah wouldn't let him loose. "Look," he said finally, irritably, trying to push his friend away, "we've got to get going! We're in danger. Now quit—"

He couldn't move his arms. Mosiah had him pinned tightly and was staring into his face with a cold smile, the tomb's light glittering in his blue eyes. "Mosiah!" Joram said angrily, fear rising in him, making him grow as cold as stone. "Let go!" He twisted suddenly, to break the young man's hold, but it was useless. The arms tightened around him, squeezing him with a clasp he knew now—the fear growing within him—was magic. He was caught in a spell! Joram squirmed, trying to reach the Darksword, but his body was fast losing all strength as the grip of the arms continued to tighten.

And then it became a struggle, not for the sword, but for life—a struggle to breathe. Joram gasped for air, staring into Mosiah's face, not understanding. Somewhere he heard a scream, a woman's scream that was cut off swiftly and skillfully. He tried to speak, but he had no breath. The darkness of the Grove was rapidly creeping over his eyes. Death was very near, and he ceased to fight, welcoming an end to the pain.

Skilled in such matters, the arms relaxed their hold. The face of Mosiah smiled and spoke a word, and then Mosiah's face was gone and Joram—in his last moments before consciousness fled—looked up and saw the white skin and expressionless face of a black-robed woman, who caught him in her arms as he fell.

Gently, she lowered him to the ground. As his senses slowly slipped from him, he heard her issue a warning to a dimly seen companion.

"Don't touch the sword."

9

Adjudication

Deacon Dulchase woke from a sound sleep with an irritated snort, rolling over in an effort to escape the hand that was shaking his shoulder.

"So I'm late for Morning Prayers," he grumbled, burrowing deeper into his mattress and burying his face in the pillow. "Tell the Almin to start without me."

"Deacon!" said a commanding voice urgently, continuing to harrass the priest. "Wake up. Bishop Vanya summons you."

"Vanya!" Dulchase repeated incredulously. The elderly, perennial Deacon struggled up from the depths of his comfortable repose, blinking in the globe of light that hovered near a black-robed figure standing above him *"Duuk-tsarith!"* he muttered beneath his breath, trying to nudge his sleep-soaked brain into functioning.

The sudden surge of fear at the sight of the warlock helped admirably, although by the time Dulchase had drawn his legs out from under the bedclothes and had his feet on the floor, the fear had been replaced by a cynical amusement. "They have me this time," he reflected, groping about with one hand to find the robe he had tossed at the end of the bed. "Wonder what it was? Undoubtedly that remark about the Empress at the party last night. Ah, Dulchase. You'd think at your age you would learn!"

With a sigh, he began to struggle into the robe, only to be stopped by the cold hand of the warlock who stood above him, faceless in his black hood.

"What's the matter now?" Dulchase snapped, figuring he had nothing to lose. "It isn't enough His Holiness decides to exact punishment in the middle of the night? Am I to go before him naked as well?"

"You are to dress in formal robes of ceremony," intoned the *Duuk-tsarith.* "I have them here."

Sure enough, now that Dulchase looked, he could see the warlock holding his best ceremonial robes folded over his arms in the manner of the most efficient of House Magi. Dulchase stared, first at the robes, then at the warlock.

"There has been no mention of punishment," the *Duuk-tsarith* continued in his cool voice. "The Bishop requests you hurry. The matter is urgent." The warlock shook out the robes carefully. "I will assist if I may."

Numbly, Dulchase stood up and — within the speaking of a word of magic — was attired in the formal robes of ceremony he had not worn since . . . when? The ceremony marking the Death of the young Prince? "What . . . what color?" the befuddled Deacon asked, running his hand over his head that had once been tonsured but was now as bald as the rocks of the Font in which he lived.

"What color, Father?" the *Duuk-tsarith* repeated. "I fail to understand —"

"What color shall I make the robes?" Dulchase asked irascibly, gesturing. "They're *Weeping Blue,* as you can see? Is it official mourning? I'll leave them the same. A wedding, perhaps? If so, I'll have to change them to —"

"Judgment," said the *Duuk-tsarith* succinctly.

"Judgment," repeated Dulchase, pondering. Taking his time, he made use of the chamber pot in the corner of his small room, noting — as he did so — that even the disciplined warlock was growing edgy over the delay. The fingers of the hands, supposed to be folded quietly in front of the man, were twisting round each other. "Mmpf," the Deacon snorted, making a great show of rearranging his robes around him again and turning them to the proper shade of neutral gray required for a trial. All the while, his brain — now wide awake — was trying to guess at what was happening.

A summons to Bishop Vanyas's in the dead of night. A *Duuk-tsarith* sent to escort him — not a novitiate as was customary. He was not being punished but told he was to sit in judgment. He was wearing robes of state that he had not worn in eighteen years — eighteen years almost to the very day, he realized — the anniversary of the Prince's death having been held last night. Deacon Dulchase could make nothing of it, however. Immensely curious, he turned back to the waiting *Duuk-tsarith*, who actually started to breathe a sigh of relief before he caught himself in time.

A young one, that, Dulchase noted, grinning inwardly.

"Well, let's get on with it," the Deacon muttered, taking a step toward the door. To his astonishment, he felt the cold hand on his arm again.

"The Corridors, Father," said the *Duuk-tsarith*.

"To His Holiness's chambers?" Dulchase glowered at the warlock. "You may be new around here, young man, but surely you know that this is forbidden —"

"Follow me, if you please, Father." The *Duuk-tsarith*, perhaps nettled by the Deacon's remark about his age, was obviously out of patience. A Corridor gaped in Dulchase's room; the cold hand propelled the old Deacon into it. An instant's sensation of being squeezed and compressed, then Dulchase stood in a huge, cavernous hall carved from the heart of the mountain fastness by — legend had it — the hand of the powerful wizard who had led them here.

This was the Hall of Life. (Its name from ancient times had been originally the Hall of Life and Death, in order to represent both sides of the world. This had become frowned upon in modern times and — with the banishment of the Sorcerers — it had been officially renamed.) Legend being true or not, the Hall did look very much as though it had been scooped out of the granite like the fruit from the rind of a melon. Located in the very center of the Font, built around the Well of Life from which the magic in the world gushed forth like unseen water, it was dome-shaped, extending hundreds of feet into the air, its rock ceiling ornamented by carved arches of polished stone. Four gigantic grooves gashed out of the rock wall at the front of the Hall were known as the Fingers of Merlyn and formed four alcoves where sat the four Cardinals of the Realm during occasions of state. Another large gouge in the rock wall, on the opposite side of the vast Hall, was known somewhat irreverently and unofficially as

Merlyn's Thumb. Here sat the Bishop of the Realm, across from his ministers. Spanning the length of the stone floor between them were row after row of stone pews. Cold and uncomfortable to sit upon, these stone pews had an even more irreverent name that was whispered and sniggered over by new novitiates.

The Hall's vast expanse was usually illuminated by the magical lights sent dancing upward by the magi who served the catalysts. Yet on this occasion the lights had not been brought to Life. Dulchase stared around in the cold darkness.

"Name of the Almin!" breathed the Deacon, nearly staggering in complete and total amazement as he realized where he was. "The Hall of Life! I haven't been here since . . . since . . ."

The memory of eighteen years ago came quickly, though Dulchase often found he had trouble recalling incidents that occurred only yesterday. That was a hallmark of growing old, so he'd been told. One tended to live in the past. Well, and why not? It was a hell of a lot more interesting than the present. Although that seemed likely to change, he thought, glancing about the dark Hall with a frown.

"Where is everyone?" he snapped at the young *Duuk-tsarith*, who — hand on his arm — was guiding him through the maze of pews toward Merlyn's Thumb.

At least that was where the old Deacon guessed they were headed, judging from what he could remember of the lay of the room. The warlock walked in a path of light cast by his hand held before him, Dulchase stumbling along in his wake. He could see practically nothing. The Well of Life was in the exact center of the Hall, he recalled, searching around for it. Yes, there it was, glowing with a faint, phosphorescent radiance, but, beyond that, the Hall was almost pitch-dark. Then, suddenly, a single light flared ahead of them. Squinting into it, Dulchase tried to see its source, but it was so bright that all he could see were several figures passing before it, eclipsing it momentarily.

The last time Dulchase had been here was to witness the trial of a male catalyst accused of joining with a young noble woman — Tanja or Anja or some such name. Ah! Dulchase shook his head in fond remembrance. The Hall had been crowded with members of his Order. All catalysts residing in the Font and in the home city of the accused — Merilon — had been required to attend. The details of the couple's crime had been described graphically by the Bishop in order to impress upon his flock the enormity of such a sin. Whether or not any were deterred from temptation because of it was never established. It was known that not one catalyst fell asleep during the three-day trial, and there had been such a state of fevered excitement among the novitiates at night that Evening Prayers had been lengthened from one hour to two for a month following.

Undoubtedly the punishment of the Turning — which all were called upon to witness — had a more profound effect. Dulchase still had nightdreams over that tragic scene. He kept seeing, over and over, the one hand of the man — as the stone slowly crept over his living body — clenching in a final gesture of hatred and defiance.

Angry at having dredged up these disturbing memories, Dulchase came to a halt. "Look here," he said stubbornly, "I insist on knowing what's going on. Where are you taking me?" He glanced around the darkened Hall. "Where is everyone else? What's happened to the lights?"

"Please come forward, Deacon Dulchase." A pleasant, if stern, voice echoed in the vastness. Dulchase saw now that the light and the voice came from the same place — Merlyn's Thumb. "All will be explained."

"Vanya," Dulchase muttered. He shivered, and thought with longing of his warm bed.

Years unopened, the Hall was chill and smelled of wet rock and mildewed tapestries. Sneezing, the Deacon wiped his nose on the sleeve of his robe and allowed himself to be led forward again until he came to stand, blinking like an owl in the light, before His Holiness, Bishop of the Realm.

"My dear Deacon, we apologize for disturbing your rest."

Bishop Vanya stood up — an unheard-of phenomenon in the presence of a lowly Deacon; moreover, a Deacon who had been a Deacon for forty years and would probably die a Deacon due to his sharp tongue and unfortunate habit of speaking his mind. There were those who said Dulchase himself would have long ago been slated for a place among the Stone Guardians had it not been for the protection of a certain powerful family in court. This show of respect from his Bishop was unprecedented, yet was followed by still more. Dulchase was bowing and endeavoring to recover from the shock when Vanya actually extended his hand, not for Dulchase to kiss the ring, but to give the Deacon the pleasure of touching the pudgy fingers.

I suppose if I died now, I'd ascend directly to the Almin, the old Deacon said to himself sarcastically. But he brought the Bishop's hand to press against his forehead with as much show of reverent ecstasy as he could muster at his age, and thought he must look very much as though he were suffering from gas. The touch of the fingers was unpleasant, as cold as a fresh-caught fish, and they trembled slightly in his grasp. Perhaps realizing this, Vanya snatched them away with unseemly haste and moved to sit back down, lowering his great red-robed bulk into the plainly shaped stone throne that sat in the alcove. The light shone from behind Vanya, Dulchase noted shrewdly, coming from some magical source in the wall. It left the Bishop's face in shadow, while illuminating all those who faced him.

Glancing around, his own eyes now accustomed to the bright light and wondering what he was supposed to do next, Dulchase noted that the *Duuk-tsarith* who had led him here was gone; either disappeared or had become one with the shadows. But he had the feeling that there were other members of that dark Order around, watching and listening, though he could not see them. There was only one other person present in the Hall that Dulchase could see. This was an aging catalyst clad in shabby red robes who huddled in a stone chair that appeared to have been hastily conjured up next to the Bishop's throne. The man's head was bowed. All Dulchase could see of him was thinning gray hair unkempt and tousled over an unhealthy-looking gray scalp. This man had not moved during Dulchase's welcome by the Bishop, but sat, staring down at his shoes, in a manner that was somehow familiar to the Deacon.

Dulchase tried to get a glimpse of the man's face, but it was impossible from where he stood, and the Deacon dared do nothing to attract the man's attention until he had been dismissed from the Bishop's presence. Glancing back at Vanya, the Deacon saw that His Holiness was no longer looking at him but was motioning — so it seemed — to the darkness.

Dulchase was not surprised to see the darkness respond, coalescing into the shape of the young warlock who had brought him here. The black-hooded head bowed to hear Vanya's whispered words and Dulchase took advantage of the moment to take a step near his fellow catalyst.

"Brother," said Dulchase softly and kindly — his sharp tongue could be both when he chose — "I fear you are not well. Is there anything —"

At these words, the catalyst raised his head. A haggard face regarded him, tears shimmering in the eyes at the sound of a kind voice.

Dulchase's voice died. He not only swallowed his words in his astonishment, he nearly swallowed his tongue as well.

"Saryon!"

Lost in wonder, his mind literally reeling beneath the load of shock, curiosity, and growing fear, Dulchase sank thankfully into another stone chair that appeared — at a command from another *Duuk-tsarith* lurking about in the shadows — at Bishop Vanya's right hand, opposite Saryon, who sat at his left. The curiosity and shock Dulchase could account for — he had no idea what was transpiring. The fear was subtle, less easily defined, and it arose, he realized finally, from the anguished expression on Saryon's face — an expression that had so marked the man that Dulchase wondered now, looking at him, how he had recognized him.

Though only in his forties, Saryon appeared older to Dulchase than Dulchase himself. His face was a sallow color, ashen in the bright light illuminating them from Merlyn's Thumb. The eyes that had been the kindly, slightly preoccupied eyes of the single-minded mathematician had now become the eyes of a man caught in a trap. He watched Saryon searching as if for escape, the eyes sometimes darting here and there frantically, but more often focused on Bishop Vanya with a look of despairing hopefulness that wrung the Deacon's heart with pity.

This was what engendered the Deacon's fear. Older than Saryon and more worldly wise than the sheltered scholar, Dulchase saw no hope for the wretched catalyst in the Bishop's smooth, composed face or His Holiness's cold, glittering gaze. Worse still had been the touch of those fishlike fingers. Dulchase had the sudden terrible feeling that he had lived too long. . . .

He fidgeted in the cold stone chair that the heat from his body appeared incapable of warming. It had been a half-hour since his arrival and no one had spoken a word, other than the *Duuk-tsarith* with their whispered spell-casting and conjuring of furniture. Dulchase stared at Saryon, Saryon stared at Vanya, and the Bishop stared, scowling, into the darkness of the vast Hall.

If this doesn't end soon, I'll say something I'll regret, Dulchase remarked to himself. I know I will. What the devil is the matter with Saryon? The man looks like he's been living with demons! I —

"Deacon Dulchase," said Bishop Vanya suddenly in a pleasant voice that immediately set Dulchase on his guard.

"Your Eminence," Dulchase responded with an attempt at equal urbanity.

"There is a position open for a House Master in the Royal House of the city-state of Zith-el," Vanya said. "Would this be of interest to you, my son?"

My son, my ass. Dulchase snorted, eyeing Vanya. You may be old enough to have fathered me, but I doubt any issue ever came from those fat loins . . . His thought trailed off, the Bishop's words having finally sunk into the Deacon's head. He stared at Vanya, blinking again as the bright light — by some trick of magic — shone full upon his face.

"A . . . a House Master," Dulchase stammered. "But . . . that requires a Cardinal, Your Eminence. Surely you can't —"

"Ah, but I can!" Vanya assured him expansively, waving the pudgy hand. "The Almin has made his will known to me in this. You have served Him faithfully many years, my son, without reward. Now in the golden time of your life, it is fitting that you be given this assignment. The papers have been drawn up, and as soon as we conclude this trifling matter before us, we will sign them and you can be on your way to the palace.

"Zith-el is a charming city," the Bishop continued conversationally. He did not once glance at Saryon — who was continuing to watch him, his soul in his eyes — but talked to Dulchase as though they were the only two in the vast Hall. "A remarkable zoo. They even have several centaur on exhibit there — well-guarded, of course."

House Master! A Lord Cardinal! This to a man who had been constantly reminded that were it not for his patronage, he might be slogging through rows of beans, a lowly Field Catalyst. Dulchase could smell a rat; he believed now he had sniffed it upon entering. *This trifling matter before us*, Vanya had said. *We will sign the papers. . . .*

Dulchase sought some clue from Saryon, but the man's gaze was once more intent upon his shoes, though his lowered face looked — if it were possible — more agonized than before. "I — I don't know, Holiness," Dulchase faltered, hoping to buy time until he found out what it was he was selling. "This is so sudden, and to come upon me like this, when I have just been asleep —"

"Yes, we are sorry, but this matter is one of urgency. You will be able to catch up on your rest in the Palace. But there is no need to make a decision now. In fact, it might be best to wait until this small matter is concluded." Vanya paused, his full, fat face turned toward the Deacon, who, however, could not see its expression for the light behind it. " — Concluded satisfactorily, we pray the Almin."

Dulchase smiled bitterly, Vanya having piously raised his eyes heavenward. So, the Bishop assumed this old Deacon could be bought and sold. Well, I could be, Dulchase admitted. Every man had his price. Dulchase's glance went to Saryon's stricken face. In this case, it just might be too high.

Apparently considering matters concluded, Vanya made a gesture with his hand. "Bring the prisoner." The darkness behind him moved. "And now we will explain the reason you have been dragged from your warm bed, Cardinal . . . I mean . . . Deacon Dulchase," said the Bishop, clasping his hands together across his rotund middle. This might have been a meaningless gesture, but Dulchase saw the fingers laced tightly, the knuckles turning white with the strain of appearing to remain perfectly calm.

Dulchase ceased watching Vanya, however, to look at Saryon in alarm. At the word "prisoner," the catalyst had shrunk into himself so that it seemed he would willingly become part of the stone chair upon which he sat. He appeared so ill that Dulchase nearly sprang up to demand that a Druid be summoned when he was halted by a burst of yellow light.

Three flaring, hissing rings of energy appeared before Bishop Vanya. The young *Duuk-tsarith* materialized beside them, and, seconds later, a young man took shape within the rings. They circled the young man's muscular arms and his legs, coming near but not touching the flesh. Dulchase could feel the rings' warmth from where he sat some distance away, and he cringed as he vividly imagined what would happen should the young man try to escape his magical bonds.

The prisoner did not seem likely to try to escape, however. He appeared stupified, standing with his head bowed; long, lank black hair curled over his shoulders and hung down around his face. He must be about eighteen, Dulchase guessed, looking at the well-formed muscular body with envy and regret. We're here to sit in judgment on this young man, Dulchase reasoned. But why? Why not let the *Duuk-tsarith* handle it? Unless he's a catalyst? . . . No, impossible. No catalyst ever had muscles like that. . . . And why only the three of us? And why us three?

"You are wondering, Deacon Dulchase, what is going on," Bishop Vanya said. "Again, we apologize. You, alone, I fear, are the only one in the dark. Deacon Saryon—"

At the sound of this name, the young man's head snapped up. Tossing back the black hair, he squinted in the bright light and, as his eyes became accustomed to it, looked around.

"Father!" he cried thickly. Forgetting his bonds, the young man took a swift step forward. There was a sizzle and a smell of burning flesh. The young man sucked in his breath in pain, but beyond that made no outcry.

Amazed that the prisoner should know Saryon, Dulchase was equally amazed at Saryon's response. Averting his eyes, the catalyst held up a hand involuntarily—not as a man warding off an attack, but as one who feels himself unworthy of being touched.

"Deacon Saryon," Bishop Vanya was continuing imperturbably, "is aware of what is transpiring, and I will now explain it to you, Brother Dulchase. As you know, the law of Thimhallan demands that a jury of catalysts be convened to sit in judgment upon any case which involves either a catalyst or a threat to the realm. All other cases are handled by the *Duuk-tsarith.*"

Dulchase was only half listening to Vanya. He knew the law and he had already guessed that this must be a case involving a threat to the realm—though how this one young man threatened the realm was beyond him. Instead, Dulchase was studying the prisoner. As he did so, he began to believe this young man *could* be a threat.

The dark black eyes—those eyes looked familiar, where had he seen them?—staring at Saryon actually burned with an inner intensity. The brows, thick and black and drawn in a line across the bridge of the nose, bespoke a passionate inner nature; the firm jaw; the handsome, brooding face; the luxuriant black hair falling in rampant curls over the shoulders; the proud stance, the unfearing gaze. . . . This was truly a formidable personality, one who could conceivably shift the stars if he chose.

And where have I seen him? Dulchase asked himself again with that gnawing anger that comes from knowing something in the subconscious but without being able to drag it to the surface. I've seen that regal tilt of the head, that shining hair, that imperious gaze. . . . But where?

"The young man's name is Joram."

Catching the name, Dulchase's attention turned immediately back to Vanya. No, he thought in disappointment, that name doesn't mean anything. Yet I know —

"He is brought here on several charges, not the least of which is threatening the safety of the realm. That is why we are sitting in judgment. Perhaps you are wondering why there are only three of us, Deacon Dulchase." Bishop Vanya's voice took on a grim note. "You will learn that, I imagine, as I go on to present the startling and frightening facts of the case against this young man.

"Joram!" The Bishop spoke in a sharp, cold voice, apparently hoping to draw the prisoner's gaze to himself. But he might have been a squawking parrot for all the young man cared. His gaze was on Saryon and it had never once shifted. The catalyst's hands rested limply in his lap, his head bowed. Of the two, Dulchase fancied, the catalyst appeared more the prisoner. . . .

"Joram, son of Anja," spoke Vanya again, angrily this time. The warlock, with a word, caused the rings to shrink, drawing in upon their captive. Feeling their heat, the young man reluctantly and defiantly shifted his dark eyes to the Bishop. "You are charged with the crime of concealing the fact that you are Dead. What do you plead to this charge?"

Joram — that was the young man's name apparently — refused to answer, lifting his chin in the air. The movement sent a thrill of recognition through Dulchase — a thrill, yet frustration, too. He knew this kid! Yet he didn't. It was like an itching in the small of the back that one could never quite scratch.

The warlock spoke another word. The rings flashed, there was that horrible sizzle and smell and a quick, agonized gasp from the young man.

"I plead guilty," Joram said, but he said it proudly in a rich, deep voice. "I was born Dead. It was the Almin's will, as I was taught by one I respect and honor." He glanced again at Saryon, who appeared so crushed by this that he might never rise again.

"Joram, son of Anja, you are charged with the murder of the overseer of the village of Walren. You are charged with the murder of a warlock of the *Duuk-tsarith*," Vanya continued severely. "How do you plead to these?"

"Guilty," Joram said again, though there was less pride. The dark face became unreadable. "They deserved death," he muttered in low tones. "One killed my mother. The other was a man of evil."

"Your mother attacked the overseer. The man of evil — as you call him — was acting in the interests of the realm," Bishop Vanya said coldly. The young man did not reply, but simply stared back at him defiantly, the dark eyes steady and unwavering.

"These are serious charges, Joram. The taking of a life for any reason is most strongly forbidden by the Almin. For that alone you could be sentenced to Beyond. . . ."

At last, something touched Saryon, lifting the man from his stupor of despair. The catalyst raised his head, looking swiftly and meaningfully at Bishop Vanya. Dulchase saw a glint of spirit — fear and anger brought life to the haunted eyes. The Bishop, however, appeared oblivious to the catalyst's stare.

"But these charges pale before the crimes against the state that have brought you here to be sentenced. . . ."

So that's why there's only three of us, Dulchase realized. Secrets of the realm and all that. And, of course, that's why I'm being made a Cardinal — to keep my mouth shut.

"Joram, son of Anja, you are charged with consorting with Sorcerers of the Dark Arts. You are charged with having read forbidden books . . ."

Dulchase saw Joram's dark eyes shift to gaze upon Saryon once more, this time in shock. He saw Saryon, his brief flicker of spirit quenched, curl in upon himself, writhing in guilt. Dulchase saw the young man's splendid shoulders slump, he heard Joram sigh. It was a small sigh, but a sigh of such exquisite pain that it wrenched Dulchase's cynical heart. The proud head turned away from the catalyst, the black hair falling over the face as though the young man would hide willingly within that darkness forever.

"Joram! Forgive me!" Saryon burst out, stretching forth his hands beseechingly. "I had to tell them! If you only knew —"

"Deacon!" Vanya said in a taut, almost shrill voice. "You forget yourself!"

"I beg your pardon, Holiness," Saryon murmured, shrinking back into his chair. "It won't happen again."

"Joram, son of Anja," the Bishop continued, breathing heavily, his hands crawling on the arms of the stone chair. He leaned forward. "You are charged with the heinous crime of bringing darkstone — the cursed product of the Prince of Demons — back into a world that had banished it long ago. You are charged with the forging of a weapon out of this demonic ore! Joram, son of Anja, how do you plead? How do you plead?"

There was silence — a noisy silence, but silence nonetheless. Vanya's labored breathing, Saryon's ragged breaths, the hissing of the glowing rings, all beat at the silence but could not penetrate it. Dulchase knew that the young man would not answer. He saw the fiery rings draw nearer and nearer, and he quickly averted his gaze. Joram would suffer himself to be burned clear through before they would wring a word from him. Realizing this as well, Saryon leaped to his feet with a hollow cry. The *Duuk-tsarith* looked at Vanya questioningly, obviously wondering how far to go.

The Bishop glared at Joram in cold fury. He opened his mouth, but another voice — a voice that slid across the tense surface like oil — broke the silence at last.

"Your Eminence," said the voice from the darkness, "I do not blame the young man for refusing to answer. You are not, after all, using his correct name. 'Joram, son of Anja.' Pah! Who is that? A peasant? You must call him by his real name, Bishop Vanya, then perhaps he will deign to answer your charges."

The voice might have been a thunderbolt hurled from the skies for the dread impact it had on the Bishop. Though Dulchase could not see Vanya's face with the light behind it, he saw the head beneath the heavy miter bathed in sweat and heard the breath rattle in the man's lungs. The pudgy hands went limp; twitching feebly, the fingers closed up in a ball like the legs of a frightened spider.

"Call him by his real name," continued the smooth, calm voice. "Joram, son of Evenue, Empress of Merilon. Or, shall we say, *late* Empress of Merilon. . . ."

10

The Prince of Merilon

"**N**ephew," said Prince Xavier, bowing his red-hooded head slightly in ironic greeting to Joram as he glided past the prisoner and came to a halt before the Bishop's throne. The Hall was well-lit now. At a command from the powerful warlock, globes of light appeared in the air, shedding a warm, yellow glow down upon those assembled in the Hall. No longer did Bishop Vanya have the ability to hide his face within shadows. His face was visible for all to see and everyone saw the truth.

Dulchase pressed his hand over his heart. Another shock like this will kill me, he told himself. In fact, it might kill a number of us.

Bishop Vanya had attempted a blustered denial, but his words dried up and blew away beneath The DKarn-Duuk's withering gaze. Unlike poor Saryon, who had shrunk within himself to the point of shrinking from sight altogether, the Bishop became bloated. Blotches of red mottled his white skin, sweat rolled off his forehead. He lay back in his chair, gasping slightly for breath, his rotund stomach heaving up and down, his hands plucking nervelessly at the red robes. He said nothing, but stared intently at the warlock. Prince Xavier stared back at Vanya, hands folded before his robes, his demeanor calm and assured. But there was mental war being waged between the two; the air fairly crackled with unspoken moves and counter-moves, each trying to gauge how much the other knew and what use he could make of it.

Standing within the fiery rings, the gamepiece over which the two fought, Joram was in a state of bewilderment that came near causing Dulchase to break out into fits of laughter. Indeed, the old Deacon did actually emit a nervous chuckle before he could suppress it. Realizing he was becoming hysterical from the strain, he managed to convert the chuckle into an odd-sounding cough that caused the young *Duuk-tsarith* guarding the prisoner to glance at him sharply.

Dulchase knew now where he had seen those eyes, that regal tilt to the head, that imperious look. The boy was his mother all over again. Joram saw the truth plainly on Vanya's face, as did everyone else in the Hall, but — slowly — he shifted his gaze to Saryon as if for confirmation. The catalyst had been sitting huddled in his chair, his head in his hands ever since The DKarn-Duuk's obviously unexpected and unwanted arrival. Sensing the young man's thoughts turned toward him, Saryon raised his haggard face and looked directly into the dark, questioning eyes.

"It is true, Joram," the catalyst said in a soft voice, speaking as though he and the young man were the only two people in the room. "I've known it . . . so long! So long!" He broke down, shaking his head, his hands trembling.

"I don't understand!" Joram's voice was thick, choked. "How? Why didn't you tell me the truth? By the Almin!" He swore softly, bitterly. "I trusted you!"

Saryon moaned, rocking back and forth in the cold stone chair. "I did it for the best, Joram! You must believe me! I . . . I was wrong," he faltered, with a glance at Vanya. "But I did it for the best. You can't understand," he finished somewhat wildly. "There's more to it —"

"Indeed there is, Nephew," said Prince Xavier suddenly, whipping around with such speed that his robes shimmered about him like living flame. Throwing back his red hood with his thin hands, the warlock faced Joram, studying the young man's face with interest. "You favor our side of the family — your mother's and mine — which is why you have fallen into this predicament. Had the weak blood of that fool your father run in your veins, you would have dropped into obscurity and been happy tending carrots in that village where you were raised."

With a gesture, The DKarn-Duuk caused the flaming rings around the young man to vanish. Weak from the strain, exhaustion, and shock, Joram staggered and nearly fell. He caught himself, however, pulling himself upright. He's existing on nothing but pride alone, Dulchase thought in admiration. The same admiration was reflected on the face of Prince Xavier, who glanced at Bishop Vanya.

"The young man is weary. He has been, I assume, kept in prison since his capture last night?"

Bishop Vanya nodded, but did not reply.

"Have you eaten, drunk?" The DKarn-Duuk turned back to Joram.

"I need nothing," the young man said.

Prince Xavier smiled. "Of course not, but you should sit down. We are going to be here some time." Once more, his eyes glanced at the Bishop. "Explanations are, I believe, in order."

Bishop Vanya sat forward, his mottled face regaining some of its color. "I want to know how you found out!" he cried hoarsely, his pudgy hands grasping the arms of the chair. "I want to know what you know!"

"Patience," said The DKarn-Duuk. Making a motion with his hand, he caused two more stone chairs to spring up from the floor, and with a graceful gesture, he invited Joram to sit. The young man glanced at the chair suspiciously, transferring the same suspicious glance to his uncle. Prince Xavier absorbed the suspicion with his thin-lipped smile, neither denying it nor accepting it. Once again, he gestured, and Joram sat down suddenly, as though his weakened body had made the decision for him.

The DKarn-Duuk took a seat beside the young man, his own body drifting gracefully into the chair. Assuming a seated position, he kept himself floating above the seat about an inch, however — whether for comfort's sake or flaunting his magical power, Dulchase wasn't certain. But the old Deacon knew he'd had enough.

Rising, bones creaking, to his feet, Dulchase faced his Bishop, his hand placed humbly over his heart.

"Eminence," said the catalyst, and was secretly pleased to note Prince Xavier's start at hearing him speak, "I am an old man. I have lived sixty years of my life in peace, finding consolation for what some might consider a boring life in the observation of the never-ending follies of my fellow humans. My tongue has been my curse. I admit that freely. I could not forebear on many occasions to comment on these follies. Thus I have remained a Deacon, and will be content to die a Deacon, I assure you. I just don't want to die a Deacon too soon, if you understand."

The DKarn-Duuk appeared to enjoy this, glancing at Dulchase out of the corner of his eye, the smile playing about his thin lips. Bishop Vanya was glowering at him, but Dulchase was in the comfortable position of knowing that his superior was apparently in worse trouble than he could ever possibly be, and so continued.

"I am subject to nightdreams, Eminence," Dulchase said simply. "But my nature is such that I forget about them immediately come morning. I am experiencing one of these dreams now, Holiness. It is extremely bad and I foresee that it will only get worse." He bowed most humbly, hand over his heart. "If you will excuse me, I will return to my bed and wake myself up before that happens. I have no doubt that no remembrance of any of this will linger in my old brain. You are illusions and, as such, I bid you good-night. Eminence." He bowed to the Bishop. "Your Highness." He bowed to The DKarn-Duuk. "Your Royal Highness." He bowed more deeply to Joram, who was watching him with, Dulchase noted, a half smile of his own, a smile that did not touch the lips but warmed the dark eyes.

Dulchase shivered. Yes, I must leave, he told himself heavily, and, turning, he took a step toward the stairs at the end of the Hall. Winding up into the mountain, they would take him, eventually, back to his cozy cell.

But Prince Xavier's voice stopped him. "I sympathize, Deacon. I really do," said the warlock coolly. "But it is too late to end this dream, I fear. Besides, you are still sitting in judgment. Your verdict is needed. And"—though his back was turned, Dulchase knew The DKarn-Duuk was glancing at Vanya—"I need witnesses. You will please, therefore, wake up and attend."

Dulchase considered making one final attempt to escape. He opened his mouth and saw the eyes of the warlock narrow ever so slightly.

"Yes, my lord." Dulchase acquiesced without enthusiasm, relapsing gloomily back into his chair.

"Now, where to start?" Prince Xavier placed the tips of his fingers together delicately, tapping them against the thin lips. "There are several questions on the floor. You, Holiness"—a fine irony—"demand to know how much I know and how I found out. You, Nephew"—again, the irony—"have asked very simply, 'How?' meaning, I assume, 'how' you are here when the world and *most* of those dwelling within fondly believe you to be dead. With all due respect, Holiness"—Bishop Vanya gnawed his lip, the sarcasm of The DKarn-Duuk making him livid with rage that he dared not express—"I will answer my nephew's question first. He is, after all, my sovereign."

Prince Xavier made a bow to Joram, lowering his eyes respectfully, then lifting them to see Joram scowl at him darkly. "No," answered the warlock, "I am not making sport of you, young man. Far from it. I am in earnest, *deadly* earnest, I assure you." The thin lips no longer smiled. "You see, Joram, the right of succession to the throne of Merilon passes through the Empress's side of the family. Lamentably, your mother has left us to go Beyond, into the realm of *death*." The DKarn-Duuk spoke the word with emphasis, watching those around him cringe involuntarily. "A grievous tragedy that will *soon* become a matter of public knowledge." He glanced at Vanya, who was sucking in air through his nose, glaring at him in impotent fury. "You, Joram, are now Emperor of Merilon." He sighed, smiling. "Enjoy your rule while you may. It will not last long. For, you see, as Her Late Majesty's brother, *I* am next in line after you."

Joram's expression smoothed, the dark eyes cleared.

He understands, Dulchase thought, lowering his head to his hand and resting his elbow on the arm of the chair in despair. Name of the Almin, it's murder, then. . . .

A muffled groan from Saryon indicated that he, too, understood. "No," he began wretchedly, "you can't! You don't—"

"Shut up!" Prince Xavier said coldly. "You are broken, old puppet. You have played your role foolishly, but that was, in many respects, not your fault. The one who pulled your strings bungled his script.

"And now, Nephew, I will answer your questions both for your own benefit and for the benefit of those who sit in judgment and who will decide your fate."

Dulchase heaved a sigh and wished himself at the bottom of the Well.

"What knowledge I reveal," The DKarn-Duuk continued, "I have gained from questioning many people this night. The Bishop will, I trust, correct me in anything I say that is in error.

"Eighteen years ago, His Holiness, Bishop of the Realm, made a mistake. It was only a small mistake." The warlock waved his hand deprecatingly. "He misplaced a child. But it would prove to be a disastrous mistake for him. The child he misplaced was no ordinary child. The child was the Dead Prince of Merilon. Three of you— my mistake"— Prince Xavier smiled unpleasantly at Joram—"four of you were present during the ceremony wherein the baby—you, young man—were declared officially Dead. Your father, the Emperor, turned his back upon you, but your mother, my sister, refused to give you up. She knelt beside your crib, weeping tears of crystal. These tears shattered when they struck you, cutting your flesh."

Joram, now very pale, placed his hand upon his bare chest. Dulchase saw the white scars there and closed his eyes, remembering.

"Through the intervention of the Emperor, the Empress was finally convinced to release her child into the custody of Bishop Vanya, who was to take the baby back to the Font and perform the Death Watch. Word came to the Palace some days later that the child's physical body had died. Everyone mourned, except myself, of course. Nothing personal." He nodded to Joram, who—with a look of grim amusement—nodded back.

"I like you, Nephew," Prince Xavier said approvingly. "A pity. Now, where was I? Ah, yes. Vanya's mistake."

The Bishop made a hissing sound, much like overheated air escaping a magical bubble.

Ignoring him, Xavier continued. "His Holiness took the baby to the Font. The Head of the Palace Guard accompanied him, so that there would be a witness. Vanya carried the child to the Chamber of the Dead and laid the baby upon a stone slab. That was before the time when more and more Dead were born among the families of Merilon. The Prince was the only baby present in the Chamber. It was then Vanya did a foolish thing, Nephew. He left the child there without placing a guard. Why? That will be explained in a moment. Patience. 'All things come to he who waits,' as the old saying goes."

With a gesture, Prince Xavier brought forth a globe of water from the air and sipped at it as it hovered obligingly near his mouth. The silence lay so heavily over the room that every swallow could be plainly heard. "A drink, my sovereign?"

Joram shook his head, never taking his eyes from the warlock's face. The DKarn-Duuk did not offer the water to the catalysts, but sent the globe back into the air with a word of command. "The baby was left alone, unguarded. Oh, certainly it was understandable. There had never been a guard upon those Chambers, so deep within the confines of the sacred mountain. And what was there to guard, after all? A child left to die? Ah, no!" Prince Xavier's cool voice changed subtly, growing warm and sinister, sending a thrill through his hearers.

"A child left to live!"

II

The Truth Shall Make You Free

A strangled sound came from Merlyn's Thumb.

"Yes, Vanya," Prince Xavier continued, "I know about the Prophecy. The *Duuk-tsarith* are loyal—loyal to the state. When it became clear to the Head of their Order that *I* was now the state, the witch revealed everything to me. Yes, you are confused, Nephew. Up until now, all was easily understood. Listen carefully, for I will speak the Prophecy known previously only to Bishop Vanya and the *Duuk-tsarith.*"

In a soft voice, The DKarn-Duuk spoke the words that would whisper in Dulchase's ear every night from that moment on.

"There will be born to the Royal House one who is dead yet will live, who will die again and live again. And when he returns, he will hold in his hand the destruction of the world—"

Prince Xavier fell silent, his gaze intent upon Joram. The young man was pale, the full lips bloodless. But the expression on the dark face did not change, he did not speak.

"That is why I betrayed you, my son!"

The pent-up words burst from Saryon's throat as blood spurting from a torn heart. "I had no choice! His Holiness made me see! The fate of the world was in my hands!" Wringing those hands, Saryon gazed pleadingly at Joram.

What does Saryon hope for, Dulchase thought pityingly. Forgiveness? Understanding? Dulchase looked into Joram's stern face. No, the old Deacon said to himself, he won't find it in those dark depths.

But, for a moment, it seemed he might. Joram's eyelids flickered, the tight lips trembled; he turned his head ever so slightly toward the catalyst, who was watching with pathetic eagerness. But the pride bred in him by birth and fostered in him by madness froze the tears and checked the impulse. He averted his face even farther from Saryon, who sighed and slumped back into his chair. Joram's attention remained on The DKarn-Duuk.

"I will go on," said the warlock with a touch of impatience, "if there are no more interruptions. You understand now why the Prince could not be allowed to die. He had to live — or the Prophecy would be fulfilled. Yet everyone must think him dead, it being inconceivable that a Dead Emperor one day occupy the throne of Merilon."

"You see Vanya's quandary, Nephew?" Prince Xavier spread his hands, his sarcasm soft and lethal. "I don't know what he intended to do with you, Joram. What did you plan, Bishop? Will you tell us?"

There was no answer, other than the Bishop's labored breathing.

The DKarn-Duuk shrugged. "It is not important. Probably, he had plans for keeping you locked in some secret cell within the Font where you would have lived a prisoner until he could hit upon a solution. Ah, I see that I am not far wrong in my guessing."

Dulchase, glancing at Vanya, saw a nerve begin to twitch in the man's jaw.

"His plan, whatever it was, went awry. He had purposefully left no guard, intending to slip back down into the Chamber that night and remove the Prince to a safer area. Imagine his horror, Nephew, when he returned to the Chamber and found the baby gone!"

Dulchase could imagine. The skin of his bald head crawled, his feet were icy.

"Our Bishop — ever thinking — did not panic. He was able, after quiet investigation, to gain some clue as to what had occurred. A woman named Anja had given birth to a stillborn child. When the *Theldara* told the mother this and showed her the dead child, Anja went mad. She refused to give up the body. The *Theldara* sent for the *Duuk-tsarith* to take the baby away from her. Through their magical arts, they did so, and left Anja supposedly sedated. But she fooled them. I have heard, Nephew, that you are skilled in the art of sleight of hand and illusion and that these were taught you by this woman you knew as your mother. That does not surprise me. She was skilled in that art, as we know from her having fooled the *Duuk-tsarith*, people not easily deceived.

"Bishop Vanya could discover nothing for certain, of course, but he deduced — and I agree with him — that the woman fled her room and wandered about the Font, searching for the way out. She happened upon the Chamber of the Dead. Here she found a baby, a living baby! Snatching up the child, Anja escaped the Font in the night. By the time Vanya discovered what had happened, the skilled wizardess had covered her tracks well.

"Thus, Nephew, for years Bishop Vanya has lived with the knowledge that somewhere in this world, you, the Prince, were alive. Yet, try as he might, he could not find you. The only ones allowed in on this secret were the highest ranking of the *Duuk-tsarith*, who, of course, assisted in the search. Any reports of living Dead were checked out carefully, they tell me. The first to come close to matching was you, Joram, who revealed yourself to them when you killed the overseer. The description of your mother fit Anja; you were the right age.

"But Vanya couldn't be certain. Fortunately, you made matters easy for the Bishop by fleeing into the Outland. A warlock — one of the *Duuk-tsarith's* best, known as Blachloch — was there already, performing a covert operation with the Sorcerers. This man was alerted to watch for you. His men found you easily and he kept you under his surveillance.

"Once more, however, the Bishop was in a quandary. He did not now dare try to keep you in the Font, where, so the saying goes, 'the walls have ears and tongues.' He had too many enemies who were prepared to step into his place. Vanya decided that it would be just as safe, keeping you in the Outlands under the watchful eyes of not only the warlock but a catalyst as well." The DKarn-Duuk gestured at the huddled figure of Saryon. "But Vanya had not counted upon you discovering darkstone. Slowly, inexorably, Nephew, it seemed that the Prophecy was being fulfilled. You were — or shall we say *are* — becoming too dangerous."

Prince Xavier fell silent, seemingly lost in his own thoughts. No one else spoke. Vanya sat in his chair, his fingers crawling up and down the arm, staring at The DKarn-Duuk as a losing card player stares at his opponent, trying to calculate his next move. Joram, the stern mask of pride beginning to slip, appeared almost stupid from weariness and shock. He looked at nothing with dull, glazed eyes. Saryon was drowning in his own misery. Dulchase felt sorry for the man, but there was little it seemed he could do.

The old Deacon's head ached; he was shivering from cold and nerves so that he had to keep his teeth firmly clamped together to stop them from rattling in his head. He was angry, too. Angry at having been dragged into this absurd, dangerous situation. He didn't know who to believe. Didn't, in fact, believe any of them. Oh, some of it he must concede was true. The kid was obviously the Empress's son — that hair and those eyes couldn't lie.

But — a Prophecy to destroy the world? Every generation of mankind had been told by one prophet or another that it was doomed. How this Prophecy came about, the Deacon didn't know. But he could guess. Some old man living on bugs and honey for a year has a vision and sees the end of the world. Probably all due to constipation. But now, hundreds of years later, it was going to cost this kid his life.

Forgetting himself, Dulchase snorted in disgust. The sound split the tense atmosphere like thunder. Everyone in the room started, and all eyes — even the cold, flat eyes of The DKarn-Duuk — turned on the old Deacon.

"Head cold," Dulchase muttered, making a show of wiping his nose on the sleeve of his robe.

To his relief, Bishop Vanya took advantage of the break in the charged atmosphere to stir his great bulk. "How did you find out?" he asked Prince Xavier once more.

The warlock smiled. "Still trying to save your skin, aren't you, Eminence? I don't blame you. It covers a large quantity of blubber that would undoubtedly be an extremely disgusting sight if it leaked out for all to see. Who else knows? you're wondering. Are they in a position to take your place? Am *I* in a position to put them there?"

Vanya's complexion went sallow. He started to make some reply, but Prince Xavier raised a thin hand. "No more blustering. You may relax, in fact, Bishop. I could replace you, but I find it suits me not to — provided, of course, that you and I reach agreement on a final solution to *our* problems. But we will discuss those further. Now, to answer your question. A gentlemen of the upper middle class came to me last night, distraught over the disappearance of his daughter."

Joram raised his head, the dark eyes flashing.

Prince Xavier turned immediately from the seemingly mollified Bishop to the young man seated at his side. "Yes, Nephew, I thought that might stir your blood."

"Gwendolyn!" Joram said, his voice cracking. "Where is she. What have you done to her! By the Almin!" His fist clenched. "If you've hurt her —"

"Hurt her?" The DKarn-Duuk was cool, his tone rebuking. "Give us some credit for common sense, Joram. What would it benefit us to harm this girl whose only crime has been the misfortune of falling deeply in love with you?"

Prince Xavier turned back to the Bishop.

"Lord Samuels came to me in the Palace last night at my request. I was aware, of course, that the *Duuk-tsarith* were searching for the young man with what I thought unusual zeal. I was naturally curious to know why, and Lord Samuels was eager to answer my questions. He told me all he knew of Joram and of the strange testimony of the *Theldara*. There were many unanswered questions that piqued my curiosity. Why had the records on Anja disappeared? Why insist that a child had been stolen from among the waifs and orphans when it was obvious that one had not?

"I immediately sent for the Head of the *Duuk-tsarith*. At first, she was reluctant to talk. Upon my exhibiting how much I already knew, and upon emphasizing the advantages of speaking versus the disadvantages of remaining silent and loyal to one *who did not deserve her loyalty*" — Prince Xavier emphasized this, to the renewed fury of the Bishop — "she decided to cooperate, and told me all I wanted to know. You need not worry, Nephew. Your young lover is back in the bosom of her family, no doubt shedding copious tears over your capture. She has one more trial to undergo, which — though painful — is necessary. They tell that, in the ancient world, it was customary to cut off a diseased limb to save the life of the body as a whole. She is young. She will recover from the wound, especially when she discovers that the man she loved is a Dead man being convicted for the murder of two citizens of the realm and for dabbling in the Dark Arts."

Color was returning to Bishop Vanya's bloated face. He cleared his throat, coughing.

"Yes, Eminence," Prince Xavier continued, a sneer curling the thin lip, "I will keep your secret. It is in the best interests of the people to do so. There is, of course, a condition."

"The Empress," Vanya said.

"Precisely."

"Her death will be made known tomorrow," the Bishop said, swallowing. "We have long counseled this course of action"— Vanya's eyes went to the two catalysts present — "as being only fitting to give the poor soil the eternal rests it seeks. But the Emperor opposed our will. There is no doubt"— the Bishop glanced at Prince Xavier nervously — "that the Emperor is insane?"

"None," responded the warlock dryly.

The Bishop nodded in relief, licking his lips.

"There is just one other small matter," Prince Xavier said.

Vanya's face darkened. "What is that?" he asked suspiciously.

"The Darksword —" began the warlock.

"None shall touch that weapon of abomination!" Vanya roared, his face flushing red. Veins popped out in his forehead; his eyes were nearly engulfed by swelling flesh. "Not even you, DKarn-Duuk! It will be present at the Judgment as evidence of this young man's guilt. Then it will return to the Font, where it will be locked away forever!"

There was no doubting, from the Bishop's tone, that Prince Xavier, in cultivating the soil of a newly plowed field, had suddenly struck a gigantic boulder. He might move it, but that would take time and patience. Much better, for the moment, to go around. Shrugging, he bowed in acquiescence.

"You have my sword, but what is to become of me?" Joram demanded in low, proud tones. A bitter smile twisted his face. "It seems you have a true dilemma on your hands. You cannot kill me, without fulfilling the Prophecy. Yet you can't afford to let me live. There have been too many 'mistakes' made already. Lock me up in the deepest dungeon — there wouldn't be one night you slept easily without wondering if I haven't, somehow, managed to escape."

"I grow fonder of you by the minute, Nephew," Prince Xavier said with a sigh, rising to his feet. "Your fate is, I fear, in the hands of the catalysts, since you are a threat to the realm. And, I have no doubt, Bishop Vanya has — at last — found a solution to this thorny problem. My work here is concluded. Eminence." The DKarn-Duuk bowed slightly. "Revered Brethren." He nodded to Saryon, who was staring at Vanya with wide, terror-stricken eyes, and to Dulchase, who shifted uneasily in his chair and refused to meet the man's flat gaze.

Casting the red hood of his luxuriant robe over his head, The DKarn-Duuk turned last to Joram.

"Rise and bid me farewell, Nephew," said the warlock.

Reluctantly, with the defiant toss of his black hair, the young man obeyed. He stood up, but he made no movement beyond that. Clasping his hands behind him, he stared straight ahead, into the darkness of the empty Hall.

Stepping forward, Prince Xavier took hold of the young man by the shoulders with his thin hands. Flinching, Joram instinctively tried to free himself from the warlock's grasp, but he checked himself, too proud to struggle.

Smiling, The DKarn-Duuk leaned near the young man. Placing his hooded head next to Joram's cheek, he kissed him, first on the left side, then on the right. Now the young man faltered, cringing visibly, his flesh shrinking from the touch of the cold lips. Jerking spasmodically, he pulled himself from the man's grasp, rubbing the flesh of his bare arms as though to rid himself of the touch.

A corridor opened behind Prince Xavier. Stepping into it, he vanished. The light he had brought with him disappeared as well. Most of the Hall was plunged into darkness, except for the faint, ghastly radiance emanating from the Well of Life in the center and the harsh, bright light streaming out from behind the Bishop's throne.

Though still obviously shaken, Vanya appeared to be regaining his composure. At a gesture from the Bishop, the young *Duuk-tsarith* came forward from the shadows. He spoke a word and, once more, Joram was surrounded by three fiery rings, their flaming light casting an eerie glow in the deep gloom of the Hall. The Bishop stared in silence at the young man, sucking air in loudly through his nose.

"Holiness," began Saryon, rising slowly and haltingly to his feet, "you promised he would not be killed." The catalyst clasped his trembling hands before him. "You swore to me by the blood of the Almin. . . ."

"Get down on your knees, Brother Saryon," said Bishop Vanya sternly, "and beg Him for your own redemption!"

"No!" Saryon cried, throwing himself forward.

Struggling to his feet, Vanya heaved his great bulk from the throne and, thrusting the catalyst out of his way, walked over to stand before the young man. Joram watched him without speaking, the bitter half smile on his lips.

"Joram, son of —" Vanya began, then stopped, confused. The half smile on the young man's face widened into a proud smile of triumph. The Bishop's face grew livid with anger. "You are correct, young man!" he said, his voice quivering. "We dare not let you live. We dare not let you die. As you have been Dead among the Living, so now you will find a living Death."

Dulchase sprang up, his throat constricting. No! he wanted to shout. I won't be a party to this! He tried to speak, but nothing came out. For once, his tongue failed him. They had trapped him neatly. He knew too much. He would go to Zith-el, where they had a remarkable zoo . . .

Saryon gave an anguished cry, falling on his knees to the floor before Vanya's throne.

The Bishop paid no attention to either of his catalysts. Joram's gaze went once to the wretched Saryon, but it was cool and unforgiving and almost immediately returned to the Bishop.

"Joram. Having been found guilty as charged of all counts presented against you by three catalysts as prescribed by the laws of Thimhallan, I hereby sentence you to the Turning. This dawn, you will be taken to the Border where your flesh shall be turned to stone, your soul left to live within your body to contemplate your crimes. Forever more, you will stand Guard at the Border, dead but alive, staring eternally into Beyond."

12

Obedire Est Vivere

There came a soft knock upon the closed door.

"Father Saryon?" called a gentle voice.

"Is it time?"

There were no windows in the small chapel. The harsh, bright dawn of a new day might come to the world outside, but it would never penetrate the cool darkness of this sanctuary.

"Yes, Father," said the voice in hushed tones.

Slowly, Saryon raised his head. He had spent the remainder of the night kneeling on the stone floor of one of the private chapels in the Font, seeking solace in prayer. Now his body was stiff, his knees bruised. His legs had long ago lost any feeling.

How he wished the same might be said of his heart!

Reaching out a hand, Saryon grasped the prayer rail before him and struggled to stand. A stifled groan escaped his lips, returning circulation sending sharp needles of pain through his limbs. He tried to move his legs and discovered he was too weak. Leaning his weary head upon his hand, he blinked back the tears.

"You who have denied me everything else, grant me strength to walk," he prayed bitterly. "I will not fail him in this, at least. I will be with him at the end."

Placing both hands on the prayer rail, gritting his teeth, Saryon struggled to his feet. He stood still for several moments, breathing heavily, until he was certain he could move.

"Father Saryon?" came the voice again, a tinge of worry. There was a scratching on the chapel door.

"Yes, I'm coming," Saryon snapped. "What is your hurry? Impatient to see the show?"

Shuffling forward, his shoes dragging the ground as he forced his hurting muscles to move, the catalyst crossed the small room in a few steps and fell against the door, his strength giving way.

Pausing to wipe the chill sweat from his brow with a shaking hand, Saryon at last found the energy to remove the magical seal he had placed last night upon the door. It was not a powerful spell; the catalyst had cast it himself using the small amount of Life within his body. But he wondered if he had the ability to break it. After a moment's hesitation, the door opened, swinging inward silently.

The pale face of a novitiate looked in at him. The woman's eyes were wide and frightened; she bit her lip at the sight of his ashen face, and lowered her gaze.

"I — I was concerned about you, Father," she said in a quivering voice. "That is all." Passing a slender hand over her eyes, she added brokenly, "I do not want to see this, but it is required —" Her words failed.

"I am sorry, Sister," Saryon said wearily. "Forgive me. It has been . . . a long night."

"Yes, Father," she said more strongly, lifting her gaze to meet his. "I understand. I have asked the Almin for courage to undergo this trial. He will not fail me."

"How fortunate for you," Saryon sneered.

The priest's tone of sudden, bitter anger startled the novitiate, who stared at him, half-frightened. Saryon sighed and started to ask her forgiveness again, then gave it up. What did her forgiveness matter? What did anyone's matter except for one person's. . . . And that he would never have, did not deserve.

"Is . . . is that . . . the sword?" The novitiate's frightened eyes — as bright and soft as a rabbit's, Saryon thought — went to a shapeless mass of darkness lying on the rosewood altar, barely visible in the light cast from the small globe she held in her hand.

"Yes, Sister," Saryon said briefly.

That was the reason for the magical seal upon the door. Only one person had been considered fit to handle the weapon of darkness.

"This will be part of your penance, Father Saryon," Bishop Vanya had decreed. "Since you assisted in creating this foul tool of the Sorcerers of the Ninth Mystery, you will spend the rest of your life guarding it. Of course," the Bishop had added in a softer, more pleasant voice, "there will be those of our Order required to study it that we may learn more about its evil nature. You will grant those elected to undertake this task all the benefit of your knowledge of the Dark Arts."

Humbly, Saryon had bowed his head, accepting his penance gratefully, firm in his belief that this would cleanse his soul and grant him the peace he sought so desperately. But the promised peace had not come. He thought it had — until last night, when he had looked into Joram's dark eyes. The young man's bitter words, "I trusted you!" seemed to the Priest to have been scribed in flame upon his soul. Forever they would burn within him; he would never be free of the agony.

It was that flame, he supposed dully, burning up his prayers of supplication to the Almin — prayers begging for mercy, for forgiveness of his sins. The words drifted like ashes from his mouth and scattered in the wind, leaving his heart a charred and blackened lump in his chest.

The novitiate glanced at a window in the corridor where the light of the night stars was slowly beginning to fade.

"Father, we must go."

"Yes." Saryon turned, and with slow and faltering steps walked over to the altar.

The Darksword lay like a dead thing. The light the novitiate held in her hand gleamed softly in the highly polished rosewood of the intricately shaped altar; it did not gleam in the black metal of the sword. His heart heavy with grief and sorrow, Saryon lifted the weapon awkwardly, his flesh shrinking from the touch. Clumsily, he slid it back into the scabbard — nearly dropping it. Bowing his head, he gripped the sword in clenched hands and raised it heavenward, crying out the most earnest prayer he had ever uttered in his life.

"Blessed Almin, I care no longer for myself. I am lost. Be with Joram! Somehow, help him to find the light he struggles to attain!"

The only sound in the chapel was a muffled, pitying "amen" from the young novitiate.

Cradling the heavy sword in his arms, Saryon walked from the chapel.

13

The Borderland

The Borderland.

The edge of the world. Snowcapped peaks and pine forests and sparkling rivers in the center of the land flow into rolling meadowlands and populated cities and vast forests that in turn give way to tall stands of waving prairie grass. The grass dies out, and then there is nothing but empty, windswept dunes of shifting sand. Beyond the sands hang the mists of Beyond. Staring eternally into the mist, with their unseeing stone eyes, are the Watchers.

Condemned humans, transformed magically into statues of stone that nevertheless retain life within their frozen bodies, the Watchers stand thirty feet tall. Male and female, each is spaced about twenty feet from its fellow. Almost all are catalysts. Magi are punished by being sent Beyond; it being considered too dangerous to allow the powerful magi to remain in the world, even in a frozen form. But the humble catalyst is a different matter, and when it was determined that Guards were needed upon the Borderlands, this seemed a fitting and suitable way to provide for them.

What do they watch for, these silent beings, some of whom have withstood the stinging of the blowing sand for centuries? What would they do if they saw something materialize within the drifting mists? None know, the answers having been long forgotten. There is nothing out there except Beyond — the Realm of Death. And from that Realm none have ever returned.

Located to the east of Thimhallan, the Borders are the first part of the land touched by the rays of the rising sun. Upon rising, the sun's light is a pearly gray, shining through curtains of mist so thick that even heaven's ball of fire cannot burn them away. Then, gleaming pale and cold — a ghost of itself — the sun can be seen shimmering faintly above the horizon where the mists give way to the blue, clear sky. When the sun is finally free of the Realm of Death, its light bursts forth, pouring down upon the land below in thankfulness, bringing the living of Thimhallan a new day.

It was at this time, when the sun's first full rays struck the earth, that Joram's flesh would be changed to stone.

Thus it was in the gray of early dawn that the participants and witnesses of the solemn rite began to gather on the sand dunes. Twenty-five catalysts are needed to grant Life to the Executioner for the Turning, and these men and women were the first to arrive. Although generally summoned from all parts of Thimhallan to represent the entire population, so hurried was this trial that these catalysts were taken entirely from the Font. Many of the younger had never seen the ceremony, most of the elder had forgotten it. Those catalysts chosen to take part in the ritual could be seen stumbling sleepily from the Corridors onto the sand, many with books in their hands, hastily studying the rite.

Next to arrive was the Executioner. A powerful magus — one of the top-ranking members of the *Duuk-tsarith* — this man was the catalysts' own warlock. He worked for them alone, and was in charge not only of security within the Font, but also attending to duties such as this. His black robes changed to the gray of judgment for this occasion, the Executioner stepped silently from the Corridor. He was alone, his face covered by his hood. The catalysts, glancing at him askance, shunned him, moving hastily from his path. He paid them no heed. Hands folded within the cavernous sleeves of his robes, he stood as still as stone himself in the sand, perhaps rehearsing the complicated spell in his mind, perhaps concentrating the massive mental and physical energies that would be needed for its casting.

Next came from the Corridor two *Duuk-tsarith*, escorting a man of lordly, if weary, bearing, and a young woman, who appeared to be on the verge of collapse. Cringing away from the touch of the warlocks, the girl clung to her father. At the sight of the stone Watchers, she gave a heartbroken cry. Her father supported her in his arms, or it seemed she would have fallen where she stood and never risen again.

Several of the catalysts shook their heads and a few of the older ones stepped forward to offer the Almin's consolation and blessing. But the girl turned from them as she turned from the *Duuk-tsarith*, burying her head in her father's breast and refusing to look at them.

The warlocks who accompanied the two led them near a place in the sand that was empty except for a mark that had been hastily drawn upon it. When she saw the mark — a wheel with nine spokes — the young woman collapsed and a *Theldara* was hastily summoned.

The Cardinal came next, remembering just as he stepped from the Corridor to change his silver-trimmed white robes of his office to the gray, silver-trimmed robes of judgment. Joining several of the older catalysts, who bowed reverently, the Cardinal glanced at the slowly brightening mists and frowned. He was overheard to mention irritably that they were running behind schedule. Gathering the twenty-five of his Order together, he arranged them in a circle around the mark of the spoked wheel. When the catalysts were placed to his satisfaction and each had turned his or her robe to gray, the Cardinal bowed to the Executioner, who slowly and solemnly took his place in the center of the circle.

All was in readiness. The Cardinal sent word via the Corridor back to the Font, and, after a moment's breathless anticipation, the void gaped open. Expecting the Bishop's entourage, everyone twisted his head and strained to see. But it was only the *Theldara*, coming to tend to the young woman. This provided a small amount of diversion. Restorative potions were administered, and within moments the girl was on her feet, some semblance of color coming and going in her pallid face.

There was a moment's restless movement around the circle of catalysts — the Cardinal frowned terribly and made a mental note of the most flagrant transgressors. But their patience was rewarded. The Corridor gaped again, a hole of nothing.

The crowd gasped. A most unexpected phenomenon occurred.

Stepping out of the Corridor was the Emperor. As everyone watched in shock, another flurry of movement within the void brought forth the Empress as well, seated in a white-winged chair. Her eyes stared straight ahead into the Realm of Beyond; many would whisper afterward (when her death had been officially announced) that there was an expression of wistful longing in them, as though yearning for the rest being denied her. The two were alone, no attendants accompanied them, and the Emperor hovered above the sand, looking about him expectantly.

Stunned, the Cardinal stared, openmouthed; the catalysts glanced at each other in amazement and consternation. It even caught the attention of the girl; she raised her head and glanced at the royal couple — particularly the dead Empress — then hurriedly diverted her gaze with a shudder. Only the Executioner remained unmoved, his hooded head faced forward, the shadowed eyes fixed upon the circle.

Finally, the Cardinal left the circle of catalysts and took a hesitant step toward the Emperor, though he hadn't any idea what to do with the man. Fortunately, at that moment, the Corridor gaped once more, producing Bishop Vanya and The DKarn-Duuk, the red and crimson of their robes like splashes of blood against the background of white sand.

Both appeared considerably taken aback at the sight of the Emperor and his wife.

"What is he doing here?" Bishop Vanya said in an undertone, glancing at Prince Xavier with a scowl.

"I have no idea," the warlock replied coldly, glancing at Bishop Vanya in turn. "Perhaps he is in need of a little light entertainment."

"The walls of the Font have eyes and ears and mouths as well," the Bishop remarked testily, his face flushing at the suspicion he saw clearly in the dark eyes of The DKarn-Duuk. "He has learned the truth."

It seemed for an instant that Xavier lost his famous composure, much to the Bishop's satisfaction.

Leaning close, he hissed. "If the young man talks, if he makes this public in the Emperor's presence —"

"He won't," Vanya interrupted. Lips pursed in smug satisfaction, his squinting eyes went to Lord Samuels and his daughter, standing forlornly in the sand behind the circle of catalysts.

Understanding the Bishop's meaning, Xavier relaxed. "Has the young man been told she will be here?"

"No. We hope the shock of the sight of her will keep him silent. If he tries to speak, the catalyst — Father Saryon — has instructions to warn him that the girl will suffer."

"Mmmmm," was all the warlock replied. But the sound had an ominous quality. The Bishop was reminded forcibly of the buzzing snake, which is said to emit a warning to its victims before it strikes. There was no time for further conversation, however, it being incumbent upon the two to attend their liege lord and his dead lady with a show of homage and respect.

A royal gallery was necessary now, of course, to provide seats for the Emperor and Empress. Bishop Vanya and the DKarn-Duuk would sit here as well, along with the Cardinal, these gentlemen having previously intended to simply stand on the outskirts of the circle in their haste to have this done quickly.

That was impossible now. Several *Duuk-tsarith* were summoned from the Corridor to conjure up the gallery with the assistance of the Cardinal himself, since none of the catalysts in the circle could spare the energy. The Cardinal granted the warlocks Life with an ill-humored air and was seen to fret over the delay, glancing continually into the mists that were growing brighter with every passing second.

But the warlocks did their job efficiently and the gallery took shape within the speaking of a word and the gesture of a hand. The air coalesced into hundreds of soft cushions, a silken canopy fell from the sky like a wayward cloud, and Their Majesties, the Bishop. The DKarn-Duuk, and the rest were soon settled. Sitting at the head of the circle of catalysts, they had an excellent view of the Executioner and the wheeled circle drawn in the sand. Beyond that, the mists of the Boundary of the World roiled and seethed in the morning light.

Heaving a sigh of relief, the Cardinal hastily signaled for the prisoner.

14

The Doom of
the Darksword

The Corridor opened again, this time in the very center of the circle of catalysts.

Saryon stepped forth, bearing the Darksword in his arms, carrying it awkwardly and gingerly, as a father carries his new-born babe. The Cardinal appeared shocked at this — bringing a weapon of evil into the solemn rite — and he looked to his Bishop for instruction.

Rising from his seat, Bishop Vanya spoke sternly. "It has been decreed that Deacon Saryon is to stand at the side of the Executioner, the Darksword raised, so that the last sight this young man's eyes see will be the thing of evil he has created."

The Cardinal bowed. There were mutterings among the catalysts, a breach of discipline that was instantly hushed by a shocked hiss from the priest. All was silent once more, so silent that the whisper of the wind sliding along the sand spoke clearly to each present, though only Saryon understood its words, having heard the wind mourn long ago.

"The Prince is Dead. . . ."

The Corridor opened, a final time. Flanked by two *Duuk-tsarith*, the prisoner stepped out onto the sand. Joram's head was bowed, the black hair falling, disheveled, over his face. He was forced to move slowly and deliberately—the same fiery rings encircling his arms and upper body. Ugly, red, blistering weals were visible on his flesh, and rumor whispered quickly among the guests in the gallery that the young man had made a last foolish, furious struggle to avoid his fate.

It seemed he had learned his lesson, for now he stood as though struck senseless by despair, unseeing, uncaring. The *Duuk-tsarith* led his stumbling footsteps to the spoked wheel in the sand and positioned him in its center. He moved mechanically, no will of his own remaining in the body. The Bishop found his gaze drawn irresistibly from the young man to the corpse of his mother. The resemblance was uncanny and Vanya hastily shifted his gaze, a shudder making the rolls of fat at the back of his head quiver.

The prisoner was now the responsibility of the Executioner. The gray-robed warlock made a subtle gesture with his hand. The *Duuk-tsarith* guarding the young man prepared to leave.

"Joram!" cried a broken voice from outside the circle. "Joram! I—"

The words were cut off in a choked sob.

Joram raised his head, saw who it was that cried his name, and turned his gaze on the Executioner. "Take her away. Make them take her away!" he said in low, fierce tones. His eyes burned with a dull, sullen, dying glow. The muscles in the arms bunched spasmodically, the hands clenched, and the *Duuk-tsarith* remained standing near.

"Let me speak to him," Saryon said.

"I want no words of yours, catalyst!" Joram snarled. "I want nothing for myself!" He lifted his voice; it was tinged with darkness, madness, and the *Duuk-tsarith* drew closer. "Take the girl away! She is innocent! Take her away or I swear by the Almin I'll scream the truth until my mouth is stone—*Ahhh!*"

The young man cried out in pain, the fiery rings closing around him, burning his flesh.

"Please!" Saryon pleaded desperately.

The Executioner's hooded head moved slightly. He made a gesture with his hand and the *Duuk-tsarith* backed away. Dropping the Darksword in the sand at the Executioner's feet, Saryon turned and floundered through the sand toward Joram. The young man watched him, bitter hatred in his eyes. When Saryon drew close, Joram spit on the catalyst's shoes. Saryon cringed, as though he had been struck across the face.

"With my next breath, I call the Emperor 'Father,'" Joram said through clenched teeth. "Tell them that, traitor! Unless she is freed—"

"Joram, don't you understand?" Saryon said softly. "That is why she is here! To insure your silence. I have been told to tell you that—if you speak—she will meet the same fate as your moth— as Anja. She will be cast out of her family and out of the city."

Saryon saw the flame in Joram's soul burning violently and, for a moment, he thought the fire might consume whatever was good and noble in the young man.

What can I say? the catalyst thought frantically. No platitudes will save him now. Only the truth. Yet it may drive him over the edge and he will drag her down with him.

"I warned you, my son," Saryon said, looking into the smoldering eyes. "I warned you of the grief that you would bring upon her, upon us all. You would not listen. Your life has been so centered on your own pain that you have never felt the pain of others. Feel it now, Joram. Feel it and cherish it, because it will be the last thing upon this earth that you will ever feel. That pain will be your salvation. I would to God"—the catalyst bowed his head—"that it were mine."

For a moment, there was silence, broken only by the whisper of the wind through the sand and by Joram's harsh breathing. Then Saryon heard a catch in the breath and looked up quickly. The flame in the eyes flickered, then—drowned by tears—it died. A sob wrenched the body, the shoulders heaved. Joram sank to his knees in the sand.

"Help me, Father!" He gagged on his tears. "I am afraid! So afraid!"

"Get rid of these!" Saryon ordered the *Duuk-tsarith*, making a furious gesture at the fiery rings. Hesitating, the warlocks looked to the Executioner, who nodded peremptorily. Time was running out.

The fiery rings vanished.

Kneeling beside Joram, Saryon clasped his arms around the young man. The muscular body stiffened, then relaxed. Burying his head in the catalyst's shoulder, Joram shut his eyes, shut out the sight of the Executioner in his gray robes, shut out the sight of the Watchers lined up in the sand, shut out the sight of the corpse of his mother watching—unknowing—her Dead son forced into eternal life. He could not bear it. The fear that had haunted him in the long darkness of the night overwhelmed him.

To stand, forever, year after year, gnawed at by the passage of time, always waking, always dreaming, never to find rest . . .

"Help me!"

"My son!" Saryon cradled the burned, anguished body, smoothing the long black hair. "For you are my son! It was I who gave you life," he muttered. "And now I will give you life again!"

The catalyst's arms tightened their grip on the young man. "Be ready!" Saryon whispered with sudden intensity into Joram's ear.

Hands took hold of Saryon; the *Duuk-tsarith* pulled him back and shoved him aside. Grabbing hold of Joram, they dragged the young man to his feet and positioned him once more in the center of what had once been a spoked wheel drawn in the sand but was now a confused muddle. Taking a position on either side of him, the *Duuk-tsarith* grasped Joram's arms firmly and held him in readiness for the Turning.

Blinking back his tears, Joram ignored the warlocks. He stared at the catalyst in wonder and saw unusual firmness and resolve on Saryon's haggard face as he slowly, and with seeming disgust and reluctance, lifted the Darksword in its scabbard from the sand. He held it up before him, one hand just below the hilt.

Joram, watching intently, saw Saryon — with a quick jerk of his hand — loosen the sword in the scabbard. The young man glanced around swiftly to make certain no one had noticed. No one did. All eyes were fixed upon the Executioner. Joram tensed, ready, though he had no idea what Saryon's plan might be.

The young man heard Gwendolyn sobbing; he heard the catalysts begin their prayers, drawing the Life from the world. Clasping hands, they began to focus their energies upon the Executioner. Joram heard the Executioner begin to chant, but he shut the sound from his mind. He shut out all the sounds as he had shut out the sight of the world from his eyes moments before. He concentrated on Saryon with his entire soul, his entire being. He knew that if he let it, fear would take hold of him again and claim him for its own.

Bishop Vanya rose ponderously, once again, to his feet. In a loud, sonorous voice that carried above the sound of the chanting and praying and blowing wind, he read the charges.

"Joram. (Dispensing with parenting to the puzzlement of some, he cast a sidelong, uncomfortable glance at the Emperor, who was seen to smile slightly.) You are a Dead man who walks among the Living. You are charged with the taking of the lives of two citizens of Thimhallan. Further, and most heinous, you are charged with having consorted with Sorcerers of the Dark Arts and with having created, while living among them, a weapon of evil that is an abomination in this world. You have been found guilty of these charges by a tribunal of catalysts.

"Their judgment is that you be Turned to Stone, set to stand here upon the Borders of our land, an eternal warning to those who might be tempted to walk the same dark paths you trod. The last light of your eyes will fall upon the tool of demons you forged. When all is ended, the symbol of the foul arts that ensnared you will be carven upon your chest. May the Almin grant that in the long years to come, you repent of your crimes and that you find forgiveness in His sight.

"May He have mercy upon your soul. Executioner, do your duty."

Joram heard the words and there was an instant when he struggled with himself, anger welling up within him so that it seemed the truth must burst out. He longed to wipe the sanctimonious expressions from the faces of those around him, longed to see them sweating and pale. His gaze went to the Emperor, his father, and a wild hope sprang up in Joram's breast. He will support me! the young man thought. He knows who I am, that's why he is here. He has come to save me!

Joram's gaze shifted abruptly, as though drawn by some word meant for his ears alone. He stared, once again, into the dead eyes of his mother. The corpse sat motionless, eyes fixed in the translucent face. Joram understood then, and he sighed. His glance flicked back to the Emperor. His father stared not at the young man but through him, giving no sign of recognition. There was only that strange, sad smile on the lips that had appeared when Vanya left out the customary name of family from the pronouncement.

You are my son, echoed the catalyst's words. *I gave you life.*

The chanting of the Executioner grew louder. The warlock raised his hands.

Saryon stepped to the warlock's side, standing on the man's left as catalysts are taught to do when entering battle with their wizards. Slowly, Saryon raised the Darksword, holding it with both hands just beneath the hilt.

Joram, his eyes on the catalyst, saw that Saryon held not the sword itself, but the scabbard. His pulse quickened, his muscles twitched. It was all he could do to hold himself stiffly in the center of the wheel that had been trampled almost to oblivion in the sand beneath his feet. He kept his gaze upon Saryon and the sword. The *Duuk-tsarith* moved away from him, retreating to the edges of the circle of catalysts.

Joram stood alone upon the sand.

With a loud cry, muffled by his hood, the Executioner called for Life. Head bowed, each catalyst concentrated all his energy upon the warlock, drawing magic from the world. Opening their conduits, they sent Life flowing into the wizard's body. So powerful were the focused energies of all the catalysts that the magic was visible — blue flame swirled about the bodies and clasped hands of the priests. Flaring like blue lightning, it leaped from them into the body of the Executioner.

Suffused with power, the man pointed both hands at Joram. When he spoke next, the spell would be cast, the Turning would begin.

The Executioner drew a breath. The gray hood quivered. He uttered the first syllable of the first word and, at that moment, Saryon hurled himself forward, the catalyst's body interposing itself between the Executioner and Joram. The blue light, darting from the warlock's hand, struck Saryon. Gasping in pain, he tried to take a step, but he could not move.

His feet and ankles were white, solid stone.

"My son!" Saryon cried, his gaze never shifting from Joram, "the sword!" With his last strength, even as the terrible, cold numbness was spreading up into his knees, Saryon flung the weapon from him.

The Darksword fell at Joram's feet. But the young man might have been changed to stone as well. He could only stare at Saryon, dazed and horror-stricken.

"Joram, escape!" Saryon cried in an anguished voice, writhing in excruciating pain, his feet frozen to the sand.

Black shadows seen out of the corner of his eye brought Joram to his senses. Anger and grief propelled him to action. Reaching down, he drew the sword from its scabbard in one swift stroke and turned to meet his enemies.

Garald's teaching came to him. Joram swung the sword in front of him, meaning at first only to keep the *Duuk-tsarith* at bay until he could fall back and assess his position. But he had not counted upon the sword's own power.

The Darksword came forth into air that was charged with magic as Life flowed from the catalysts into the Executioner. Thirsting for that Life, the Darksword began to suck the magic into itself. The arc of blue light jumped, flaming, from the Executioner to the sword. The catalysts cried out in fear, many trying to close the conduits. But it was too late. The Darksword gained in power every second and it kept the conduits open forcibly, draining the Life from everything and everyone around it.

Running forward to stop Joram, spells crackling at their fingertips, the warlocks saw a radiant blue light flare from within deep darkness. A ball of pure energy hit them with the force of an exploding star and the black-robed bodies disintegrated in a blinding flash.

The Darksword hummed triumphantly in Joram's hands. Blue light twined from its blade around the young man's body like a fiery vine. Dazed by the shattering explosion and the sudden disappearance of his enemies, Joram stared at the sword in disbelief and uncertainty. Then the knowledge of the tremendous power he held swept over the young man. With this, he could conquer the world! With this, he was invincible!

Shouting in exultation, Joram whirled around to face the Executioner —

— and saw Saryon.

The spell had been cast. The power of the Darksword could neither alter it, change it, nor stop it.

Saryon's feet, limbs, and lower body were white stone, solid, unmoving. The bitter-cold numbness was rising; Joram could see it freeze the catalyst's flesh as he watched, advancing upward from the groin to the waist.

"No!" Joram cried in a hollow voice, lowering the sword.

The DKarn-Duuk was shouting something. Bishop Vanya roared like a wounded animal. Joram had a vague impression of Corridors opening, black-robed figures streaming from them like ants. But that's all they were to him — insects, nothing more.

Springing forward, Joram grasped Saryon's arms. With a wrenching effort, the catalyst raised his hands in supplication.

"Run!" Saryon managed to utter the single word before his diaphragm froze, choking off his voice. "Run" pleaded the man's eyes through a shadow of pain.

Rage filled Joram. Floundering through the sand, he came to stand before the Executioner. The Darksword burned blue, continuing to suck Life from the world, and the Executioner had fallen to one knee. The casting of the spell had cost him much of his energy and the Darksword was draining even more. But he managed to lift his hooded head, staring at Joram with cool detachment.

"Reverse the spell!" Joram demanded, raising the sword, "or by the Almin I swear I will strike your head from your body!"

"Do what you like!" the warlock said weakly. "The spell, once cast, cannot be called back. Not even the power of that weapon of darkness can change that!"

Blinded by tears, Joram lifted the sword to carry out his threat. The warlock waited, too drained of enrgy to move, facing his killer with grim courage.

Joram paused, raising his eyes from his enemy to look around him. Most of the catalysts had fallen to their knees in exhaustion; some had lost consciousness and lay unmoving in the sand. The *Duuk-tsarith* hovered on the fringes of the broken circle of fallen priests, uncertain what to do. The warlocks had felt their Life being sucked from them the moment they stepped from the Corridor. None dared approach Joram while the sword still retained its awesome power.

Their fear was reflected in the mottled skin of Bishop Vanya and the fearful eyes of Prince Xavier. Joram saw it clearly, and he smiled the bitter half smile that darkened his face. No one could stop him now and they knew it. The Darksword could blast open the Corridors, carry him anywhere in this world, and he would be lost to them once again.

A sound came from behind him, barely heard even in the deathly silence that surrounded him. It was a sigh, the last breath escaping from lungs solidified to rock.

Joram abruptly lowered the sword. Ignoring the Executioner, in whose eyes he saw swift, if puzzled relief; ignoring the *Duuk-tsarith*, waiting tensely to make their move; Joram turned his back upon them all and slowly made his way through the shifting sands. Coming to stand before the catalyst, he saw the entire body changed to stone; the only living flesh being the head and neck. Reaching up, Joram touched the warm cheek with his hand, stroking it gently, feeling it cool beneath his touch even as he did so.

"I understand now what I must do, Father," Joram said softly, picking up the scabbard lying in the sand at the catalyst's stone feet.

Lifting the Darksword, he slid it back into its scabbard and laid it gently and reverently in the catalyst's outstretched arms.

A single tear trickled down Saryon's face and then the eyes turned white and fixed. The spell was complete. From the feet to the head, the warm, living flesh was cold, solid rock. But the expression frozen forever on the stone face was one of sublime peace, the lips slightly parted in a last prayer of thankfulness uttered by the soul.

Comforted by that look, Joram laid his head for a moment upon the stone breast. "Grant me a measure of your strength, Father," he prayed.

Then he stepped back from the living statue, staring defiantly at the pale and fearful faces watching him.

"You call me Dead!" he shouted. His gaze went to the Empress. Bereft of the magic that gave the corpse a semblance of life, the body of the woman lay in a crumpled heap at the feet of her husband, who had not once looked down. He might have been a corpse as well, for the lifeless expression on his face.

Joram looked away, up into the blue sky. The sun had freed itself from the mists of death and was shining down upon the world in serene, uncaring bliss. The young man sighed, it might have been an echo of Saryon's last breath.

"But it is you who have died," he said softly, sorrowfully. "It is this world that is dead. You have nothing to fear from me."

Turning on his heel, he walked away from the stone statue, moving slowly and resolutely across the sand. He heard the sudden commotion behind him as the warlocks surged into action, no longer afraid of the sword that lay dark and lifeless in the catalyst's frozen grasp. But Joram did not quicken his pace. He walked with the Almin, no mortal could touch him.

"Stop him!" Bishop Vanya's voice was hoarse with terror, for suddenly he saw Joram's intent. The DKarn-Duuk leaped from the gallery, his face contorted with fury.

"Stop him at all costs!" the warlock shrieked, his red robes swirling about him like blood-tinged water.

The black-robed *Duuk-tsarith* cast their spells, but many had been weakened already by the power of the Darksword. Or perhaps some trace of that power lingered still about its master, for no magic touched or halted Joram. He did not even glance behind him, but continued walking, his dark, black hair blown back from his face by a chill wind. Shreds of mist reached out to him, curling about his feet. Still he kept walking.

One sound made him hesitate, however. It was a woman's voice, and it cried to him not in pleading or in regret but in love. "Joram," she called. "Wait!"

Gwendolyn's father, a look of horror on his face tried to clasp his arms around his daughter. They closed on nothing but air. She had vanished. Some watching say that — at this moment — they caught a glimpse of a white gown and saw the sunlight glinting upon golden hair before it was swallowed in the mists.

Joram kept walking. The mists of Beyond gathered thickly about him, then he was completely lost from sight. The fog boiled, frothing and rolling like a pearl-gray wave to crash in utter silence upon the sandy shore at the edge of the world.

There was vast confusion among those left standing upon the beach. Bishop Vanya gave a strangled cry, clutched his throat, and pitched forward, senseless.

The DKarn-Duuk, seeing his prey escape, ran to the stone statue and tried to grab the Darksword. But the stone catalyst held it fast, some property of the metal, perhaps, fusing it to the man's arms. Or maybe it was the scabbard, for the runes upon it glowed with a holy silver light. Whatever the case, Prince Xavier could not budge it.

Lord Samuels ran distractedly along the shoreline, crying out for his daughter. Accosting the *Duuk-tsarith*, he begged for their help. The black-robed figures only looked at him in cool pity and, disengaging themselves from his clutching hands, stepped into the Corridors, returning to their duties within the world.

The catalysts helped each other to stand, the stronger assisting the weaker. Staggering through the sand, they made their way to the Corridors that would take them home again to the Font. Any who looked at the stone statue of Saryon hastily averted their eyes.

Slowly, the Executioner rose to his feet and limped haltingly over to the DKarn-Duuk. The warlock was still staring longingly at the Darksword held fast in the statue's grip.

"Shall I make the man the same size as the rest, my lord?" the Executioner asked, his gaze going to the other Watchers that stood thirty feet tall.

"No!" snarled Prince Xavier, his eyes glittering. "There must be some way to retrieve that damn sword!" His hands reached out to touch it. "Some way . . ." he muttered.

Corridors opened and cleared rapidly. *Theldara* carried the stricken Bishop back to the Font. The body of the Empress, wrapped in white linen, was taken to the Palace. The DKarn-Duuk, surrounded by *Duuk-tsarith* and accompanied by the Executioner, returned to whatever dark and hidden place his Order inhabited, there to begin frantic studies into the properties of darkstone. Lord Samuels, stricken nearly mad with grief, returned to his home to break the news of their dreadful loss to his wife.

Soon, the only one standing on the beach was the Emperor. No one had spoken a word to him. They had removed the body of his wife from where it lay at his feet and he had never even looked down. He stood as still as stone himself, staring fixedly into the mists — that strange, sad smile upon his lips.

Joram had passed Beyond, and the wind blowing among the sand dunes whispered, "The Prince is Dead. . . . The Prince is Dead."

Coda

Twilight came to the Border, touching the mists with whorls of red and pink, purple and orange.

The beach was empty, except for the stone statue that stood there, staring out into the Realm of Death. Even the Emperor had gone at last, though no one knew where. He had not returned to the Palace and they were searching for him, needing him to begin the ceremonies for his dead wife.

A palm tree — a rather tall, thin, and sleek palm tree — located on the fringes of the grass near the beach shook itself, stretched, and gave a cavernous yawn.

"Egad," stated the palm irritably. "I'm stiff. Should know better than to fall asleep standing up like that. And I've been out in the sun all day. I've probably ruined my complexion!"

With a shiver of leaves, the palm changed form — turning into a bearded young man of indistinguishable age, dressed in a flamboyant costume consisting of skintight trousers over silken hose and a velvet coat that came to his knees. Trimmed in ostrich feathers, the coat parted in front to reveal a matching vest — likewise trimmed in ostrich feathers. Lace spilled from the feather-decorated cuffs and bubbled up around his neck. The entire ensemble was done in wide stripes of brownish orange and dark red.

"Perfect for the funeral. I'll call it *Rust in Puce*," Simkin said, conjuring up a mirror and examining himself in it critically. He stared intently at his nose. "Ah, I did get sunburned. Now I'll freckle." He sent the mirror away with an irritated gesture.

Thrusting his hands into pockets that appeared when he put his hands into them, Simkin flitted moodily along the beach.

"Perhaps I'll cover my skin all over with spots," he remarked to the empty sand. Drifting across the beach, he came to a halt before the statue of the catalyst and slowly lowered himself to stand in front of it.

"Sink me!" Simkin said after a moment, profoundly moved. "I *am* impressed! A remarkable likeness! Bald pate and all."

Turning from the statue, Simkin looked into the mists of Beyond. The mists took on night's blackness, their bright colors fading as twilight's dying grasp slipped from the world. Creeping and curling in upon the shore, they seemed, like the incoming tide, to advance a little farther each time. Simkin watched, smiling to himself, and smoothing his beard.

"Now the game begins in earnest," he murmured.

Drawing forth the bit of orange silk from the air, he tied the silk around Saryon's stone neck. Then, humming to himself, Simkin disappeared into the evening, leaving the statue to stand in awful solitude on the silent shore, the orange banner fluttering from its neck; a tiny flicker of flame in the gathering gloom.

FORGING THE DARKSWORD

BY MARGARET WEIS & TRACY HICKMAN

In the enchanted realm of Merlion, magic is life.

Born without magical abilities and denied his birthright, Joram is left for dead. Yet he grows to manhood in a remote country village, hiding his lack of powers only through constant vigilance and ever more skilful sleight-of-hand, until he can keep his secret no longer. Fleeing to the Outlands, Joram joins the outlawed Technologists, who practice the long forbidden arts of science.

Here he meets the scholarly catalyst Saryon, in the midst of a battle of wits and power with a renegade warlock of the dark Duuk-tsarith caste. Together, Joram and Saryon begin their quest toward a greater destiny – and the forging of the powerful, magic-absorbing Darksword.

0 553 17586 6

Coming Soon

TRIUMPH OF THE DARKSWORD

BY MARGARET WEIS & TRACY HICKMAN

From the bestselling authors of THE DRAGONLANCE LEGENDS

In a realm where magic *is* life, Joram was one of the Dead. Born without power, he was denied his royal birthright and sentenced to the *turning* – his mind to be imprisoned inside a husk of living stone.

Yet at the last moment, Saryon took his place, suffering the eternal torment for his young master. And Joram and his wife Gwendolyn vanished into the mists that marked the Border of the World . . .

Now, ten years later, Joram and Gwendolyn have returned to reclaim their rightful place in Merilon.

Rejoined by Saryon, the mage Mosiah and Simkin, Joram will fulfill the ancient prophecy of the Darksword – the prophecy that puts in his hands the power to destroy the world . . . or save it.

0 553 17536 X

THE GREY HORSE

BY R. A. MACAVOY

From a time when Ireland strained against the reins of English rule, comes a saga lush with enchantment. It begins on an afternoon when the wind blows wet from Galway Bay and a magnificent grey stallion appears in the Irish town of Carraroe. With the horse comes magic, for in its noble shape stands Ruarí MacEibhir, who has come in a time of great peril to win the heart of the woman he loves.

'I have been a MacAvoy fan since TEA WITH THE BLACK DRAGON. No fantasy writer working today has a defter touch with Irish magic, and I have rarely encountered a more beguiling character than Ruarí MacEibhir. Not only is the story exciting, but the characters are memorable . . . To read THE GREY HORSE is to spend time in several magical worlds at once – that of the horse, of Ireland, and of MacAvoy's dazzling imagination'

Morgan Llywelyn, author of LION OF IRELAND

0 553 17559 9